Miller's View

A Trilogy

Marlene W. Potts

Library of Congress Control Number: 2014907836
ISBN: 979-8-89465-047-0 (sc)
ISBN: 979-8-89465-048-7 (e)

This is a work of fiction. Characters, names, places, businesses, incidents, and events are either the products of the author's imagination or used in a fictitious manner. Any resemblance to actual persons, living or dead, or actual events is purely coincidental.

Printed in the United States of America.

Integrity Publishing
39343 Harbor Hills Blvd Lady Lake,
FL 32159

www.integrity-publishing.com

Miller's View

BOOK #1

DETECTIVE JONATHAN MILLER grabs his phone, rubs his eyes, and tries to focus on the clock by the bed. The voice at the other end of the line makes no sense to him.

The dispatcher tries again. "A motorist has spotted a man's body in the wooded area near exit 36 off Route 55 in Hammond. I will tell them you're on your way."

Jonathan stretches and tries to undo some of the knots the last twenty-four hours have tied in his muscles. The tips of his fingers are just a whisper away from the ceiling. He dresses in khakis, a navy-blue polo shirt—slightly stained from last night's dinner— and his comfortable Frye slip-ons. He runs his fingers through his thick, curly hair and is on the scene within twenty minutes.

He steps out of the car and looks toward the spot where the body was found. His green eyes narrow down to a slit as they follow the bright yellow crime scene tape down an embankment and about fifty feet into the thick brush.

"No ID. No wallet. Nothing in his pockets," the officer on scene informs him.

Detective Miller is now thankful for Louisiana's recent dry spell. The field he is trudging through is typically four to six inches deep in water and mud. He holds the flashlight at eye level and searches the area as he nears the victim. The grass and bushes are only slightly damaged. *The body had to have been carried.* Miller visually checks the victim and notices that he is clean and well-dressed. *There is no blood or anything else to tell me what happened to this man. There is nothing on this road for miles, so where did he come from and where was he going?* One set of tire tracks is discovered leaving the area, so Miller takes pictures of the marks for comparison, but there isn't a car in sight. "Just dumped here, I guess. This is not our crime scene." His thoughts escape his lips.

Where was he killed? The young detective looks around for clues and realizes he can't see his car from where he is standing. He cannot see any of the cars. If it weren't for the flashing red and blues, he would not be able to locate them.

The bushes are so thick, and the sun is just now peeking over the horizon. At the time of the call, it would have still been very dark. How could someone drive by doing a minimum of forty-five miles per hour — and no one does forty-five on this stretch of blacktop — see a body from the road?

After the emergency responders lift and load the body into the ambulance, they head for the coroner's office, and Detective Miller heads to his office. As he drives, his head spins with questions; *this is going to be a long day.* Headquarters is quiet this time of the morning. Only a few scattered desk lamps illuminate the files of working officers. Miller plops his fatigued body into a worn but comfortable leather swivel chair and yanks the chain that wakes up his lamp. He needs to find a name for the victim discarded on the side of the road.

Hammond only has a population of about 17,700 people in the Parrish of Tangipahoa and more than half are women. *If this guy's a local, it shouldn't take long to ID him.* Miller fingers his well-used Rolodex and calls on longtime friend Jason Harper, his contact at the local television station.

He explains the situation and finds that Harper is all too willing to help him. Deciding it would be in poor taste to show the dead man's photo on the news, Miller has a sketch artist draw a likeness of his victim. He faxes the face to Jason, who puts it into the hands of the broadcaster. It's just in time to make the early morning news.

"Breaking news. Hammond local police need your help in identifying this person. Black male. Twenty-five to thirty-five years old. Short brown hair and hazel eyes. About 6' 1" and 170 pounds. If you have any information regarding this man, please contact Detective Jonathan Miller at Police Headquarters."

It doesn't take long before the calls come in. The locals don't mind making phone calls; just don't come knocking at the front door. That's when they tend to play the "hear no, see no, and speak no evil" game. People have seen this guy all around town, and they didn't mind letting Miller know. He learns that he has been hanging around some of the local diners, antique, and hardware shops over the past couple of months, asking questions about a girl. But the call Miller is holding his breath for comes days later.

"Hammond Police headquarters. Homicide division. Detective Miller speaking."

"I know that guy you're looking for," the croaky voice says.

This gets Miller's attention, and he straightens up in his chair.

"How do you know him?"

"He rents an apartment from me."

"Where is this apartment?"

The voice on the other end gives Miller the address. The loud click comes before he can get a name.

"Great. Now, I have a face and an address. Officer Branson, you're with me on this one." Miller grabs his sport coat and heads for the Treasure Cove Apartments about ten miles away from the 55.

Officer Branson checks to make sure he has all his gear and then double-times it to catch up to Miller. Ted Branson is even newer to the department than the fast-rising Detective Miller and he has his eyes set on a gold detective badge of his very own.

Miller, on the other hand, hit the fast track to detective right out of the academy. Being a fourth-generation family member on the force only added to his gilded position. His quick assessment of crime scenes is unmatched in the department.

At the end of the winding road, a long, two-story building holding no more than twelve small apartments stands before them. The thick vines cover most of the upper-level balcony and the bushes out front are unkempt and under-watered. A few worn, wicker chairs wait patiently, yearning to be used on the long verandah.

A middle-aged man—barely chest-high to Jonathan—steps out of the side door and meets them as they approach. His thick legs and pot belly are not complemented by his partially balding head and thick glasses.

"You the landlord of this building?"

"Yeah."

"What's your name?"

"Tom Bradley"

When he speaks, Miller recognizes the voice from the phone call. He catches the tell-tale rasp of a habitual smoker in his voice and stains on his fingers.

"Follow me."

The landlord leads Miller and Branson into the apartment. Much to his dismay, he discovers nothing of value. A few pieces of furniture—remnants of a flea market—scatter the one-bedroom unit. The red plaid sofa and orange chair scream "teenage girl" against the lime green shag rug on the floor. The dark brown curtains hang on just enough hooks to keep them off the floor.

Nothing matches. This man would've made Martha Stewart cry.

"The man was here long enough to make his bed. He left clothes in the closet and drawers. He didn't pack his suitcase. Everything's still here, so he must have been coming back." Branson moves throughout the room, careful not to disturb the surroundings.

Miller turns to Bradley, still nervously lurking in the doorway as he watches the detective move about the apartment. "Does this guy have a name?"

"Yeah, of course. Edwards. Donald or David. No… Daniel. Yeah, that's right. Daniel Edwards."

A search of the apartment yields no clues as to Edwards' activities. No pictures of his life are found in any of the small rooms; it's as if he's just passing through. There's no sign of a struggle in the apartment. It's sparse but clean. No dirty dishes have been left in the sink. The refrigerator is not only empty but clean. There's not even trash in the trash can. *He didn't have coffee or breakfast here. Maybe he ate at a local diner for breakfast.*

Miller wanders into the bathroom and rifles through the cabinets and drawers for any clues. It, too, is spotless, as if the man never used it. He catches a faint whiff of bleach. It's not fresh— maybe days old—but he can smell it. He looked into the cabinets. No bleach container. "Branson! Check the kitchen cabinets for bleach." *Weird. There's toothpaste, but no toothbrush; soap, but no towel or washcloth; shaving gel, but no razor.* He carefully lifts the can and holds it up to check for any sign of fingerprints. Nothing. "What's wrong with this picture?"

Branson just shrugs in response. "It rules out DNA testing, that's for sure. I found no bleach in the kitchen."

"Hey!" Miller turns toward Tom. "When was the last time you saw Mr. Edwards?"

"Maybe two or three days ago. Could've been a week. I don't pay attention to when my tenants come and go, ya know?"

"Has anyone been in this apartment since the last time you saw Daniel Edwards?"

"Um… I don't think so."

"Do you use a cleaning service?"

"Nope."

"Have you ever seen anyone come into this place *with* Mr. Edwards?"

"Um… I don't think so."

The young officer tries not to laugh at either the dumb answer or the croaky voice.

As Miller and the officer are about to leave, he notices a pair of round, gold-rimmed glasses on the floor, just at the foot of the orange chair. The rose-tinted lenses seem a little odd for a man. Maybe they belong to someone who visited. Miller reaches for the glasses. "What does the world look like through rose-colored lenses, Mr. Edwards?" He places the glasses on his face.

"Whoooooaaa! What was that?"

He snatches the glasses from his face, startling Branson and Bradley. When he slowly puts the glasses back on, the room changes before his eyes. Images of Daniel Edwards move about in front of him. He quickly takes them off again and hands them to Branson. "Here, look in these. What do you see?"

"They're in need of a good cleaning, sir." Branson takes them off and rubs them clean with his shirt tail.

"But what do you see?"

Officer Branson puts them back on. "You and a very, ugly, plastic Tiffany-style lamp." He returns the glasses to Miller.

Miller cautiously puts the glasses on again, slowly trailing his glance around the room above the rim of the glasses. As his eyes move back to the lenses, he watches as a scene unfolds before him. He looks over the rims at the officer then back at the scene in the glasses. He reaches out to touch the images, but nothing is there. "How is this possible?" He hands the glasses back to the officer. "Look again. Go on and look again!"

The young man, after seeing Miller's reaction, is reluctant, but slowly puts the glasses on again. "Sir, I don't see anything unusual. What did you see?" Branson hands the glasses back.

"Never mind." He shakes his head, hoping to clear the cobwebs. "Must not have gotten enough sleep last night or not enough coffee this morning." He decides to keep his mouth shut about the glasses. He places the glasses in a plastic bag as he and Branson leave the apartment and return to headquarters. *What the hell was that?* Miller's head whirls with the images from the glasses.

The scene in the glasses showed Edwards going through his morning routine. He made coffee, shaved, brushed his teeth, and combed his hair. He was preparing to make breakfast when he stopped and looked in the direction of his front door. Edwards appeared to have had a normal morning up to the point where he looked at the door, yet everything he used that morning was clean or missing.

What kind of glasses are these? Miller holds up the plastic bag. They appear to be just glasses—small, round, gold rims, rose tint on the lenses, but nothing unusual at all. He scratches his fingers through his thick, curly hair. Curious, Miller removes the glasses from the bag again. Running his fingers over the rims and examining the lenses and earpieces, he searches for anything out of the ordinary. They are a puzzle to solve on their own, but that will have to wait. Daniel Edwards needs his help to find a killer.

Miller's pocket vibrates as his phone quietly informs him that someone needs his attention. He reaches in and pulls it from his pocket just far enough to read the ID screen—Ted Branson. He lets him wait.

He doesn't yet have a cause of death. The initial toxicology screen shows no alcohol or illegal drugs in his system. His phone vibrates again. This time it's the coroner.

"I have finished my preliminary report. The young man has been dead for at least six days. He must have been someplace pretty darned cold to slow decomposition, but he wasn't in the elements that long. There would be more signs of animal activity on the body. If not the insects, the gators would have gotten him. His heart looks a little inflamed. If something happened, it was quite sudden. There is no scar tissue from a prolonged heart problem. His brain, liver, and lungs are normal, so natural causes are unlikely. Other than that, the young man was healthy.

A heart attack is one possibility, but I can't say with one-hundred percent certainty what killed this man."

With no other leads, Detective Miller turns again to the rose-colored glasses in the plastic bag. He pulls them out and examines again them from earpiece to earpiece. They look like ordinary reading glasses, but they may hold more information about what happened to the man now lying in the morgue than he might ever find anywhere else. He slowly puts them on and watches as the scene comes into focus.

Edwards walks up behind a young woman. She's dressed in a lavender sundress with a subtle ruffle at the hem. Her sandals have the tiniest of a heel and she only stands about five-foot-nothing. This makes Edwards a good head and shoulder taller, so it is easy to see over her. The two are reading the menu on the outside of a small café window. It is written in French. When the young woman turns, Miller is taken aback by her beauty. She is about to walk away—either not able to read the language or simply not interested in the selections—when Daniel steps in front of her, playfully blocking her way. He engages her in conversation. She is surprised, but she responds with a smile. She examines his face and demeanor; she seems to like that he's older and very handsome.

Daniel says just the right thing and she turns around to stay and have lunch. He talks to her with a southern boy kind of charm and smile. His hazel eyes complement his fair skin, but his smile is what seems to win her over.

They pick up their lunches and take them to a small café-style table outdoors. The opaque clouds float overhead in a sea of bright blue; it's pleasant and very warm, but the striped umbrella above them provides some respite from the afternoon sun. The light breeze plays with the ruffles of the umbrella above their heads, as well as the hem of her dress.

He's captivated by the woman. She moves with the ease and grace of a dancer. Her skin is the color of milk chocolate with a glisten of honey. Her dark hair falls into a bazillion ringlets past her shoulder, and the wide, colorful, beaded headband is the only thing keeping them under control.

They seem to enjoy each other's company and conversation. Miller watches her face. Her laughter appears light, easy, and genuine. Her smile is bright yet coquettish and says she's comfortable with her life, but her eyes tell him there's another story—much more than she's saying over lunch.

Detective Miller watches the scene but frequently keeps his focus on the young woman as the two complete their lunch and stand to leave. Edwards reaches into his pocket and pulls out a small notepad and pen, jots down something, and hands it to her. She smiles and turns to leave. He watches her go then sits down, pulls his reading glasses from his pocket, and writes what Miller assumes is a note about their encounter as the images in the glasses begin to fade.

MILLER SITS AT his desk and takes a deep breath as he removes the glasses and thinks of how he's going to find this woman. She may be able to give some insight as to who Edwards was and why he was here, but even if the department had the high-tech facial recognition software he'd heard so much about, he wouldn't be able to use it on the glasses.

He is not going to let that stop him. He is confident he can recreate a characterization of the woman in the glasses. Perhaps he can solve one small piece of his puzzle. He reaches for his phone and calls up the headquarters' sketch artist. When he arrives, Miller describes the young woman, giving as much detail as he can remember from the glasses. The artist captures everything from the sparkle in her eyes to the warmth in her smile.

"How's this?" The artist turns the sketch pad around to Miller.

She seems to leap from the page into Miller's head.

"It's very, very good."

"She's pretty. Who is she?"

"I don't know. I'm hoping your sketch will help me figure that out."

"How did you get this much detail?"

It's almost like a memory, just not my memory. "That's a long story for another time. Thanks for your help."

He turns to his computer and types in French café and gets a short list of restaurants in the downtown area. Grabbing the paper likeness and list off his desk, he and officer Branson head to the main part of the city. He now needs to find the café where the two had lunch.

After hours of driving through the city, they spot the table and chairs outside the le Café on Main Street. It's exactly as he saw it in the glasses; even the fluttering umbrellas are there. He can almost visualize the couple still sitting and chatting as if nothing has happened, but something has gone *terribly* wrong and now this man is dead. The beautiful woman might very well be the last person to have seen him alive. They get out of the car, and Miller tries to locate the owner while Branson scours the surrounding building.

The store owner tries to take the paper from him, but he grips the paper as if afraid to let her go. The man examines the face. "Well, it kinda looks like Callie St. Claire. Yeah, that could be her. She was just here about a month ago with that guy from the news this morning."

"Do you know where I can find this Callie St. Claire?"

"I'm not sure, but I think she lives with those folks in Laplace along the river's edge."

It could take a while to find her down there. The detective's mind is spinning. He's coming up with more questions than answers. *Who is this woman? Where is she and how is she connected to Edwards? Did she kill him? Is she connected to whoever did? Why? There's always a why.*

Reaching a dead-end at the restaurant, Miller and Branson head to the community of homes along the banks of the Mississippi where a whole sub-culture of people live in the wooded area that runs along the river. They've created their own language—a combination of French and broken-southern country English—and lifestyle that keeps them separated. It always amazes Miller how they're so different from the rest of the town's people just a few miles away, but the young Branson is not excited about knocking door to door to look for this girl. He's heard rumors and stories about the people there and they make him uneasy.

Miller shows the sketch of the young woman to several residents who seem particularly nervous about his presence. "Have you seen this girl?" He asks an elderly gentleman.

The man stands chest high to Miller. His eyes are bright and sparkle with a youth that is long gone from the rest of his face and body. "Naw, suh. I neva did see her 'round here," he answers through missing front teeth. "Her a purty lil thing, though." He laughs and almost whistles through the missing teeth.

"Thanks." Miller sighs as he heads for the next little shack in the area. He gets the same answer from the next ten houses. "Naw, suh," is the only thing he hears. The next stop is a small, tattered cottage about fifty yards into the brush.

Miller and Branson approach the small cabin. Miller carefully navigates the dilapidated stairs of the screened porch as he moves toward the front door. The wood creaks beneath his weight, and he prays with every step that he won't go straight through.

Branson steps up behind him and to the left to peer up the wooden stairs leading to the upper level. It's too dark to see anything. A woman looks through the screen door.

"Excuse me, Ma'am. Have you seen this young woman?" Miller asks the small frame of a woman as he hands her the sketch. He towers over her, so looking beyond her into the small, dark cabin isn't difficult.

The only thing Miller can make out is a light shining through the crack close to the floor of one room. There's nothing about the place that makes him want to look around. He looks the woman up and down and notices some similarities to the drawing. Her facial structures are close enough to make her a possible relative; her hair and skin are almost the same colorings as Callie. He envisions her twenty or thirty years earlier and decides she was probably a very attractive woman in her prime, but time has not been kind. The wrinkles on her face are so deep the sweat flows through them down her face.

She scans the picture in silence for what seems like a lifetime then looks up at Detective Miller with a big grin. "Her look kinda familiar, suh, but not sure. I see her in town sometime." Her voice has a dark undercurrent to it that is contradictory to the big smile on her face.

"Do you know her name?"

"I think I hear 'em call her Callie, but she don' live 'round these parts. Why you lookin' for her, suh?"

"I need to ask her some questions about a case I'm working on.

Do you know where she lives?"

"Naw, suh."

"Do you live here alone?"

"Naw, suh. It's me and my sweet girl."

"Would you mind if I show her the picture?"

"I think she sleepin'. Maybe 'nother time."

Miller notices the smile is gone and the undercurrent has dropped a fathom. He feels a chill run down his back, despite the eighty-degree temperature of the late afternoon.

"Another time. Thanks."

Detective Miller leaves with little more than he started with. He couldn't know that a piece to his puzzle sits quietly on the other side of one of those doors. He heads back to the office, no closer to finding this woman.

He decides to pull the strange glasses from the plastic bag that holds them. He's never had such an odd source to help him with a case, but he somehow needs to find another clue to this puzzle. He slowly puts the glasses on, and the images begin to flow.

Daniel Edwards watches as Callie window-shops across the street. He notices that her blue jeans are slightly tattered and she's in a faded black tank top, unlike the chic attire he's used to seeing her in. Her flip-flops are also faded and worn. Edwards calls out her name, but apparently, his voice is drowned out by the traffic noise, so he makes a mad dash across the street before he loses sight of her.

He cups his hands to his mouth and calls out again. She doesn't turn his way. He calls out yet again. She still doesn't answer. He approaches, taps her on the shoulder, and speaks to her. The touch startles the young woman out of her daydream over the cute sky-blue handbag and she turns to face him.

Daniel Edwards is excited and animated in his conversation. The look of confusion visibly clouds her face, but Daniel doesn't seem to notice. Miller watches intently as this scene plays out in the glasses.

Daniel seems to be doing most of the talking and after the exchange goes on for a few minutes, Miller notices a change in Callie's behavior; her posture seems uneasy as she begins to shift like a cat poised to run. She looks from side to side as if searching for the best direction in which to make her exit.

The images begin to slowly fade. "No! Not yet!"

The first images from the glasses were much different. The young woman's behavior had been more relaxed and friendly. Miller didn't see Daniel do anything that would cause Callie to act so differently. *Another piece to the puzzle.* He has to find this woman. He has to find her connection to Edwards.

Miller's thoughts are interrupted by a call from a dispatch operator.

"Detective Miller, this is dispatch. The missing vehicle in the Edwards' case has been located about three miles east of the area where the victim was found."

"I'm on my way. ETA is fifteen minutes." The face of Callie St. Claire smiles up at him from his desk. He grabs his jacket and makes his way to where the car is located.

~~**~~

Branson watches Miller leave the building. He waits just long enough to make sure he won't wander back up the stairs. Pretending to place a note on Miller's desk he finally catches a glimpse of the sketch Miller has been carrying around. *Cora? Why is he looking for Cora?* Branson leaves the building and makes a call.

"Hello, who is this?

"It's me, Ted. Where are you?"

"I'm at the marketplace, why?"

"Detective Miller is looking for you. He already knows where your mom lives. He is connecting the two of you to Daniel Edwards."

"I don't know a Daniel Edwards."

~~**~~

When Miller arrives, he's directed off the road approximately 500 feet into the trees. Someone had tried to hide the abandoned car with the nearby dead brush. The small two-seat sports car doesn't appear to be damaged.

Miller checks out the inside of the car and realizes the steering wheel is too close to the seat. Edwards was pretty tall, so it seems very unlikely he was the last driver. Someone shorter had to have driven the car after Daniel and, strangely, the car is just like the apartment—too clean.

He scans the scene for first impressions. He doesn't see any signs of trouble. His gaze sweeps to the tires and he's able to make a visual match to the pictures he took at the original scene. He also catches sight of footprints not far away. Someone with small feet walked through the brush and grass—away from the car—for about fifty feet before stepping toward the road.

Miller takes photos of the prints. *Another vehicle was probably waiting for them.*

"The car has been checked for prints and blood. Nothing," says the officer on scene. "The VIN tracks back to Daniel Edwards, a P.I. out of Georgia."

"Well, PIs usually travel with cameras, note pads, and other such items. Where's his stuff?"

"Nothing like that was found in the car, sir. The car appears to have been wiped down. No fingerprints, not even his. I wish my car was this clean."

"Anybody finds that odd other than me?" His fingers find their way to his hair.

"Yes, Sir."

"Okay, call Eddy's tow truck and have it picked up and taken to town. Have our people go over it again with a fine-tooth comb."

"Yes, sir. Right away."

Miller turns to leave when his phone vibrates in his pocket. He looks back as the forensic team completes their sweep of the area and bags whatever they deem important for analysis. *Someone has cleaned Edwards' apartment and his car. Murderer? Accomplice?* Miller breathes deeply to steady his nerves and mentally prepare for what's ahead. Before he sits down in the car he glances at his phone. *Two missed calls?* His screen read missed calls from Ted Branson and private number.

MILLER NEEDS TO piece together his clues from the rose-colored glasses. Nothing is making any sense and he has to find a way to fit these pieces into a logical order. Reluctantly, he sits back as the glasses release another secret from their hiding place.

The room is dark and hazy from the cigarette smoke. Edwards is sitting at a table, but the corner is dark. Miller knows ugly things take place in dark corners—schemes are hashed out, secrets that should never come out are revealed, and the worst of human nature is unleashed. It seems this is one such instance.

There is an envelope bulging to the point the seal is coming undone. It slides across the table with the help of the second person. The hand is large—too large to be female. It's dark and severely scarred, but the figure remains in the shadows so as not to be seen by most in the place. Moments after taking the envelope, Edwards gets up and leaves. The scarred hand picks up its drink and retreats into the shadows.

As the images fade, Miller takes notes of the new piece to his puzzle. He gives the rose-tinted informant a short reprieve then tries again. He needs to keep pushing. His little informant does not disappoint.

Miller watches as Edwards drinks iced tea at the New Orleans train station. He fingers a small key as he watches the slow, sauntering crowd. The tiny gold key catches light and flickers with each turn. There's something engraved on the key, but it's moving too fast to determine what it is. Something catches Edwards' attention and the key stops turning long enough for Miller to see a number eight. The subject of Edwards' attention walks toward him. Her thin-strapped dress is the color of a warm summer sky and her curly hair is pulled up off her shoulders. Her gait is a little slower than the rest of the crowd as if her flats are hurting her feet. She has no interest in the masses around her as she clutches her matching shoulder bag tight to her body perhaps protecting it or its contents. She has no luggage of any kind. She doesn't appear to be waiting for or retrieving another passenger.

She keeps vigil as she walks, maintaining her distance from everyone around her. Edwards watches attentively but is careful not to get caught staring. He never approaches—never speaks. As the young woman gets closer, he looks a shade of confused Detective Miller has never seen.

He feels a sense of frustration welling up as the images begin to fade. He turns to look at officer Branson.

"We're headed to New Orleans."

"Sir?"

"I need to check out something at the N.O. Train Station."

The station is bustling with activity—pickups, drop-offs, or people waiting for their departure time. Not many people are just strolling through without a reason. Miller scouts out the crowd.

"Detective, what are we looking for here?" Confusion fills Branson's eyes.

"Something that might take a small gold key imprinted with numbers that include an eight."

"You mean like the storage lockers?"

"Where are they?"

"I believe they're on the lower level."

"Show me."

"This way."

As they head in the direction of the lockers, Miller takes in all of the faces he passes along the way, hoping against hope to get a glimpse of the young woman from the glasses. They finally locate the lockers. Miller stops in his tracks and stares at the rows and rows of lockers.

"What now, Sir?"

"We need a number eight."

"Sir? Uh… just eight or eight in combination with something else like eighty-one, one-eighty-one, or eight-one-one?"

Miller's shoulders drop hard and a shadow creeps across his face. He is feeling the strain of these vague clues and he fights back the doubt that is aggressively making its way into his head. "I don't know. Maybe someone has a master key to all of these lockers."

"I'm not sure there is one. People put their money in and take the key. I will check with management." Branson could tell from Miller's expression that he should find another answer.

"You do that."

"Yes, Sir. Right away."

From his perch against the wall, Miller has a great vantage point for watching people. The face he needs isn't coming his way. After what seems like hours later, Branson and an elderly gentleman in a grey, ill-fitted uniform finally approach.

"I'm not sure how I can help you," he says to Miller.

"I'm looking for a locker used by a young man from Atlanta. The only clue I have is that the key has the number eight on it. It could have another number, but I can't see it."

"Great! So, where's the key?"

"We have no idea."

"We have over 300 lockers here. It will take hours to go through them. How will you know if you have the right one, even if we go through all of them?"

"I think we have an idea of what we're looking for and we don't need to go through all of them, just the ones with an eight in the number."

"Okay."

The gentleman and Branson head off to begin the massive locker search while Miller ponders the case. *Why is nothing fitting? Callie St. Claire, where are you?* He now carries the rose-tinted glasses in his inside jacket pocket. They are the only thing pointing him in the right direction. He puts the glasses on again, but before the images become clear, Branson comes around the corner, screaming.

"Detective! I think we found it! It wasn't eight, but thirty-eight! Thank God it wasn't 208, huh?"

Detective Miller tucks the tinted glasses back into his pocket and follows the excited Branson around the corner. The elderly station worker has the locker sitting wide open and the look of total satisfaction on his face. Miller pulls a pair of rubber gloves from his pant pocket and slips them on with the ease of a surgeon. He carefully moves things around to see what's there.

"Let's bag it all and take it back to headquarters."

"This is personal property. You can't take this." The elderly man puffs out his chest and tries to look important.

"I could get a warrant for it, but the owner of this stuff was found on the side of the road four days ago. I don't think he's gonna need it anymore." Miller turns to leave.

"Oh, sorry. Then I guess it's okay." Officer Branson empties the contents of the locker into a large brown bag and closes the door. He thanks the station worker and hustles to catch up to Miller.

Miller is excited about their find. *Finally, something useful!* Once they get everything back to headquarters, Branson takes a magnifying glass to every item in the brown paper bag while

Miller takes the glasses from his pocket and faces them with steely eyes. *Why am I the only one who sees the images?* He shakes his head.

What he does know is that when he puts them on, he gets another small piece to this puzzle. Once again, he slips them on his nose.

As the images clear, Miller sees Daniel and Callie. Miller can see why Daniel is interested. Callie is probably one of the most beautiful women he's ever seen in New Orleans. She is dressed in a flawless butter yellow dress that shows the tiny curves of her waistline. Her ringlets are held up in the back with a bedazzled barrette. They are relaxed and seem to have a lot to talk about. Miller watches them walk to a table. Callie's walk is borderline runway model—easy and graceful. It's not the awkward, painful gait from the train station. They are having dinner together. The exchange appears to be open and relaxed; the laughter seems sincere. The nervous Callie he noticed outside the store front is gone and she again is enjoying his company.

Miller wonders if the girl is bipolar. Her comfort level shifts with each vision.

Miller glances at his watch. It's late. He turns to Branson. "Maybe another run through the homes along the river will turn up something tomorrow. Go home and get some rest. We'll start fresh in the morning."

He needs to go back to his apartment. He hasn't spent much time there since this case started. A hot shower and change of clothes sound pretty good about now. Sleep sounds even better. Maybe fresh eyes will also help.

His apartment is clean and comfortable. He had help decorating the place to make it look like a reasonably intelligent single man lived here, but even he has a few family photos sprinkled about. The Sherlock Holmes series by Doyle and top crime writers like Baldacci and Cornwell line his bookshelves, feeding his passion like sweet fruit. On his coffee table rests a small photo album of all of the victims he's been able to help; it serves as a reminder of why he does what he does. It isn't a penthouse suite in Vegas, but it is one of the nicest Hammond has to offer.

He makes a 360-degree spin and makes a mental comparison to Edwards' place. Edwards must not have been there very long, and it didn't seem as though he's planning on making Hammond, Louisiana his home. He made no effort to make the apartment his personal space, even for a little while.

But someone had cleaned. Someone wanted no trace of Daniel in that apartment.

SLEEP ISN'T GOING to be easy. Miller's mind is racing at a fierce pace. He reaches for his rose-tinted informant then decides the morning will be soon enough for his next clue. He needs to sleep, but he also needs to find that girl. He can see her face very clearly as he stares up from his bed. The sketch of her face is incredibly accurate. He couldn't have done any better had he handed the artist a photo. Miller sinks his head into his down-filled pillow and drifts into a coma-like sleep with Callie St. Claire's image right in front of him. The image of Callie creeps from his ceiling into his dreams.

The bright morning sun through Miller's window shouts its wake-up call. Miller throws the blanket over his head, stalling the inevitable. He is clearly not ready to get up. He realizes he shared his whole night with her but can't quite remember what happened. He shuffles to the bathroom as if his kid brother is holding onto his ankles. *Hot shower. Yeah, that will do it. Wash that kid away.* He smiles at his silliness.

Feeling refreshed and a little lighter in his step, he dresses and heads for headquarters. He tries to decide his next step in finding this girl. He pats his jacket pocket to be sure he has not forgotten the glasses. He knows they will provide the next clue.

The phones are ringing off their hooks at headquarters when he arrives.

Another officer screams across the room. "Detective Miller, call on two."

"Detective Jonathan Miller. How can I help you?"

"Callie St. Claire doesn't live along the river. She and her mom, Ilysa, live on the west side of Hammond, close to Route 12. And Detective, hold your sketch up to a mirror."

"Who is this?" Click.

Why do people just hang up on me? West Hammond? Then why do people keep sending me to the river? And why would I hold the sketch up to a mirror?

Miller pushes back in his chair, kicks his feet up on the edge of his desk, and closes his eyes. He runs through the crazy cast of characters.

There's the nervous Tom Bradley, Callie St. Claire, Ilysa, the man with the scarred hand, and, of course, Daniel Edwards. I think I need to go back to the beginning.

Miller calls dispatch. "Yeah, this is Detective Jonathan Miller. I need a copy of the 911 call for the Edwards' case."

"I can have it for you in a couple of hours."

"Thanks. Call me when you have it."

Miller and Branson spread the evidence from the train station locker on the table in front of them, wondering where to start. Branson eyes the contents with the excitement of a child at Christmas. He notices the camera bag and decides to start there. Edwards had taken pictures of the beautiful Callie St. Claire all over town. Sometimes, she was very well dressed and groomed while at others, her clothing appeared to be tattered and worn. She often walked like a model, but it seemed at other times, she just didn't care. Edwards had been watching her for over a year. He also had pictures of Tom talking to the man with scarred hand. Although his back is to the camera in the photos, Miller can see the same hand that had crept from the shadows in the bar.

While Branson sifts through the camera's contents, Miller pulls out a small notebook and begins flipping through the pages. He stops longer on one page, smiling. "Hey, Branson. Edwards was working for the man with the scarred hand. He called his client P.S. in his notes. P.S. had Edwards looking for a woman named Ilysa James and possibly a child. Edwards tracked her from Atlanta, Georgia, across Alabama and Mississippi, to Hammond, Louisiana. He finally found the so-called child, aka Callie, who is now about twenty years old. The client has been looking for several years."

Branson's eyes glaze over as he listens. *Callie, not Cora!*

He knows most of the story. He is unaware of the connection between Edwards and the hunt for Callie and Ilysa; Cora had told him almost everything. He can be sure that if he tells Miller he knows a girl who looks like the one in the picture, his career is going to be very short. He knows how that conversation will go. The time just isn't right. He decides to stay quiet, but he doesn't know how long he has before Miller puts two and two together.

Miller pulls the glasses out of his pocket. Co-workers look strangely in his direction as he mumbles to himself, speaking his observations aloud. He knows they can't possibly know what he's experiencing but is quite content to let them think he's talking to himself. "So, what can you tell me about this woman?" He asks, just before he puts on the glasses.

The images dance in front of him as if Edwards is pointing the way to his killer.

Ilysa's belly is full of activity. She knows the time is soon and calls her sister, Elyse, to help. Elyse feels the firm abdomen, nods her head quickly, and hurries out of the house to gather the things she'll need for the birthing.

Just days later, Ilysa feels the first pain of labor. She wouldn't be in pain for long. Her babies are impatient. Within just a few hours, Ilysa screams and pushes as she delivers her first baby girl. She's born with a full head of hair and spirit to take on the world. Callie comes into the world with a full-blown yell and gasping for air as if she knows something is wrong.

Elyse cuts the cord and wraps Callie in a blanket. She looks up and over the sheet and says something to comfort and quiet her sister as she quickly hands Ilysa her beautiful baby, Callie.

Ilysa lets out another horrible scream and begins pushing once again. The second baby comes with no noise, no movement, no breath… nothing. Ilysa holds her baby tight as she cries for her second child and softly whispers a name as their faces fade away.

Detective Miller has a new clue he couldn't have anticipated. He remembers one of the faces from the glasses. He had met her in the little house near the river's edge. She also mentioned having a baby girl. *I guess I'm going back to the river.*

It doesn't take Miller long to find his way back to Elyse's cottage. "Ma'am, do you remember helping a woman give birth to twin girls about twenty years ago?"

"Yes, suh. I help lots of women in these parts. Twins is common here, girls 'specially."

"I think one twin didn't survive. Do you remember what happened to them?"

"Them, suh?"

"Yeah, them. As in the woman, Ilysa James, and the baby girl she gave birth to."

"No, suh. That was a long time ago."

"If I find that you're lying to me, I'll have you arrested for interfering with this investigation."

"If I 'member sumpthin, I'll tell ya."

"I *will* find them."

"Be careful 'bout what you tryin' to find in these parts, suh." The undercurrent in her voice is even deeper than before. "Unburyin' the past sometimes wake up ugly things." The smile fades to a look that matches her voice.

Miller turns to leave with an uneasy feeling in the pit of his stomach. He has solved over thirty homicide cases in his three years as a detective on the force. This case is giving a new meaning to bizarre.

His phone buzzes. It's dispatch. "Detective Miller? The recording you were waiting for is ready."

"Great. Be right there."

Miller finds the 911 call recording on his desk when he walks into his office. He pops the tape into a small player on his desk and puts on the headphones.

"911. What's your emergency?"

"I'm on Route 55 just before exit 36 and I think I see a man lying in the woods." The voice is low, almost inaudible.

"Is he is moving?"

"I don't think so."

"Is he hurt?"

"I don't know."

This time, Miller catches enough of the voice to determine it's female.

"Is there any way you could go and check to see if he needs assistance?"

"I've already passed the area, but you might want to hurry. This is almost feeding time for the gators."

"Can you give me your name for the detective handling the case?" Click.

The caller disconnects.

Miller replays the tape. Which female? Callie, Ilysa, or the little woman from the river? Someone wanted Edwards found. He replays the tape; a woman. Must be someone who cares. She not only calls with a location, but she also specifies it is a man. She knows who he is, but she must also know how he died. *What else does she know?*

Miller is typically the last one to leave the office and tonight is no different. Over and over, he listens to the taped recording of the call. He is more intrigued by what he doesn't hear than what he does. There are no sounds from the car—no sounds from outside, traffic, or any other background noises. It's deathly quiet behind the voice.

Miller shuts off the tape. He pushes back and kicks his feet up onto his desk. The recording only troubles him more. *Why didn't you call when you could have possibly saved his life?* Miller needs help finding these people and pulls the glasses from his pocket. They are his connection to this case, though he doesn't know how or why. He puts them on, anticipating the next clue.

Ilysa is asleep from the exhaustion of childbirth and Callie is asleep in a small makeshift bed next to her. Elyse is alone with the silent child. She pulls something from her pocket and vigorously rubs the baby with it. Working quickly, she warms the baby with blankets. She takes a deep breath and breathes into the lifeless child's mouth. Elyse fills the lungs of the baby with her sheer desire for Cora to live. The baby jumps just a little. Elyse breathes into the baby again. The little limbs start to move just a bit more. Her little chest rises and falls as Elyse watches, and then baby Cora opens her eyes. She's breathing. Her color becomes a little less gray.

Elyse believes she may have smiled, just a little as if to say 'thank you for not leaving me' She takes this as a sign and creeps out the back door, babe in arms.

Miller's eyes widen with understanding. *There are two of them! The second one survived!*

AFTER TWENTY YEARS, Ilysa still grieves the loss of her baby girl. She has no idea Cora has grown into a beautiful—but Dark—duplicate of Callie.

Cora didn't have the attention or education her mother had provided for her sister. She grew up along the banks of the river, educated by Elyse. Elyse left school very early in life due to a complicated pregnancy of her own that had left her barren.

Cora learned a little of the dark art along the river banks. Her interest was not strong, but she dabbled in a few things. She hated hiding from the rest of her family, but Elyse would always remind her to watch for her sister or aunt. She told her that she felt, one day, Ilysa would come home.

"You have to be careful, Cora. If you're seen, we'll both be in danger," Elyse would say. What she could never tell her was, *'I brought you back from the world of the dead, stole you from your mother and sister, and raised you as my own'.*

At the age of twenty, Cora finds her own way in the world. She develops her patterns and haunts—places she doesn't think Callie will frequent. While Callie has no knowledge of her identical twin, Cora knows almost everything, but Elyse has never explained that night.

Cora and Callie look virtually identical. Their complexions are the same and the same dark ringlets fall below her shoulders. The only difference is the small scar Cora has on her left shoulder. If she put just a little effort into it, it might look like a shooting star, at least in her eyes.

Every time she looks at her reflection, she tries to imagine what it would've been like to grow up with a twin sister. As a small child, she remembers sitting for hours at a mirror, talking to her sister and pretending Callie was in the room. Elyse would walk in and catch her and scream her disapproval, but it didn't matter—her mirrored twin was her best friend.

One day… Elyse has her sister and one day, I'll have mine.

Cora takes her musing outside and decides to walk to the river's edge. The heat and humidity of Louisiana add a glisten to her clear complexion as she strolls to her favorite spot. There is a huge, toppled oak tree in a clearing. It's quiet. She can spend hours here lost in her thoughts. There is no Callie and no Ilysa. She doesn't have to hide down here. She's free to be unafraid.

The folks along the river know Elyse and Cora and she knows they'll protect them like they would their own. Others in Hammond know about them, too. It is hard to hide such a large, dark secret in such a small area. It's bound to peek out of the cracks and crevices of its confinement.

~~**~~

Miller continues his search for the face the sketch artist so skillfully created from his vision, but he no longer needs the pencil drawing; he now knows the face by heart. Those eyes haunt him in the darkness of his lonely apartment. The clear, chocolate-colored complexion and ringlet hair are hard to forget. Now he needs to know if he is seeing Callie St. Claire or her twin, Cora.

"Detective, hold your sketch up to a mirror," the caller said. *Now I get it.*

Miller is beginning to put the pieces of this puzzle together. He now knows the confused look on Edwards' face at the train station was because he thought he was watching Callie when it was her twin, Cora. She was so different. Maybe Edwards was starting to figure out that she was an entirely different girl. Maybe he had never seen *her* before. Maybe he didn't know there were two. His notes mentioned Ilysa and one child.

Edwards' client had spent fifteen years on his own, searching for a woman and child, not knowing the woman had birthed twins. That might be a secret worth killing over.

> *I think I may have a motive! But who would kill to protect that secret? Elyse? She faces jail time for kidnapping if Ilysa presses charges. Cora? She could've done it to protect Elyse, the only mother she's ever known, but it's hard to put Cora into the role of murderer. P.S. needed Edwards alive to find Ilysa. Ilysa? She could've done what she needed to do to protect herself and her daughter from the Edwards' client. Callie? His heart says, 'definitely not'.*

Maybe Edwards was getting a little too close? Too close to Callie; too close to Ilysa. *Using Callie to find the mother could've been his plan all along.*

Miller's thoughts are interrupted as he watches a young woman walking down the other side of the street. His musing has taken his brain off guard, and it takes several seconds for it to register, but even from the second floor he knows. He sees the woman who has been visiting him in his dreams. The walk is awkward, but the dark ringlets that cover her head and hang down her back are unmistakable. Miller almost falls backward out of his chair as he watches her turn into a small shop.

Snatching his jacket from the back of his chair, he runs out of his office and down the two short flights of stairs startling everyone on the office floor. He makes a crazy dash, zigzagging through traffic, across the street to the storefront. He peers into the window to make sure she's still there but sees no sign of her. Miller walks into the store, trying to look nonplussed as he wanders about. The store clerk glances up from her receipts.

"Hello sir, do ya need some help findin' somethin'."

He smiles and politely says, "no," but keeps watch to see if she will reappear. The clerk glances up and notices him looking around the store. After looking at almost every rack in the place, Miller decides he's waited long enough.

He turns to the clerk. "Which way did the young lady go?"

"Young lady, suh? There's no one here 'cept me and you."

"I saw her come into the store and I didn't see her leave."

"I never seen her come in. Jus' you," she says with a smile.

"What's in the back room?" He asks, pointing to the curtain behind her.

"Just storage, suh" She smiles again and goes back to doing whatever she was doing. "Have a nice day, suh" she says as Miller turns toward the door.

Miller walks back to his office. *Am I hallucinating? I know I saw her walk in here.* He lets it go for now. He decides to follow up on an idea that had come to him in the middle of the night. Daniel Edwards, P.I. out of Atlanta.

A quick check through a missing person's database turns up nothing. Someone has to know what he was up to, who he was working for, or why he was here. Miller pulls out all the stops and calls in old favors from his connections in Atlanta. He has an academy classmate that landed on the force there. It's worth a shot.

HE HITS PAY dirt when he locates Jeremy Hinds from the academy, currently working with the local P.D. in Atlanta. Within forty-eight hours Jeremy gets back to him with more information than he expected. He knows a guy who overheard a conversation between these two guys about a PI who was hired by this really rich guy that was set on fire by his girlfriend because he didn't want her to have his baby. The rich guy told her that if his wife ever found out about her or the baby, she'd have his nuts stuffed and mounted on the wall. She started ranting in some crazy language, tossed his drink on his hands, and followed it with the candle from the table. His hands lit up like a torch.

Jeremy goes into the archives to find the twenty-year-old police report. He finds the guy's name and description and reveals that Paul St. Claire filed a police report at the Emory University Hospital. Ilysa and her unborn baby disappeared without a trace.

Sources inform Jeremy that St. Claire spent ten years on his own and most of his assets trying to find Ilysa. He searched all of Atlanta and then all of Georgia without ever breathing a word to his wife. Edwards, being much better at tracking, would pick up from where St. Claire ended. It didn't take him long before he picked up her trail and followed her to Louisiana. *'Unburying the past sometimes wake up ugly things'. Edwards must have been close enough to really spook someone.* Miller has another clue.

Miller stops by his apartment for the file he's forgotten before going back to the river. He needs Elyse to answer more questions about the twins. He opens his door and finds Celia looking through his desk.

"Can I help you find something, Celia?"

"No-no, Sir. I was just dusting and—"

"You dust the inside of my drawers? That's very conscientious…"

"You're home early. Did you forget something?"

"Yes. I forgot what I came home for. Please leave my dust inside the drawers and finish what you need to do here." He does a brief visual sweep around the apartment trying to remember his purpose for coming, but his thoughts are derailed, and he turns to go back out the door.

"Yes, Sir."

Miller is really annoyed that he's forgotten what he wants from the apartment, but he finds Celia's snooping even more disturbing. *What is she looking for in my apartment?* When he leaves and heads for Elyse's house, he has a new determination that she will answer his questions.

The drive there is filled with the face of Callie St. Claire… or is it really Cora? Which one fills his dreams at night and his thoughts during the day? Is she a victim, predator, or uninvolved? Miller has to find her.

He also needs to find Paul to question him. He decides to call in an APB. The all-points bulletin goes out on the dispatch radio within minutes of his request. He's described as a "person of interest", but no one has seen him. *He's got to be staying somewhere.*

He calls Branson at headquarters, his voice sounding a bit more stressed than usual.

"I need you to contact every local hotel, motel, and Holiday Inn in Hammond and all outlying areas within a two-hour drive. We're looking for Paul St. Claire—white male, brown hair, brown eyes, and severely scarred hands. He's close; I can feel it. Edwards must have told him he had made contact with one and it was just a matter of time before he found the other." He disconnects the call and returns to his thoughts.

Financial reports on Paul show that he is not as wealthy as he was twenty years ago, but he still has a little money to kick around. His wife passed away five years ago, leaving him with a substantial life insurance policy, but no children. He seems to have put his business in the hands of a CEO and put his focus into finding Ilysa and the child he never knew.

He pools most of his resources and finds Edwards, P.I., through an old friend. Edwards is young, energetic, and good at what he does. He manages to follow Ilysa's breadcrumbs across two and a half states, yet he only finds Callie. Daniel's notes mention that he never sees Ilysa as if somehow, she is aware of and manages to avoid him. He watches Callie. He makes notes in the little notepad in his pocket. He watches to see if Ilysa will come out of the shadows.

Daniel tracks Callie into her mom's home state of Louisiana but somehow manages to lose her trail. He begins going shop to shop asking questions about the beautiful, young girl. His time is spent in the local diners and small shops downtown hoping to see her. He gets lucky one day and spots her just outside the African American Museum of History and again begins his surveillance from there. Edwards keeps detailed notes as he watches Callie. His research shows she'll be at the Museum of African American history every Saturday afternoon by three and she'll avoid the Marketplace. She loves to just sit at Hessville Park and read. She sits for hours. Edwards witnesses how she seems to be liked by those around her. Talking with people in the park comes easy and even the children that come with their moms smile and play without fear. Callie's smile is warm and friendly. She's beautiful and intelligent.

Callie doesn't mind people or crowded places, but she doesn't seem to like Laplace or the people there. They are a close-knit, closed-mouthed, and dark kind of people. Most are very suspicious of strangers. Callie keeps her distance. He follows her home every night biding his time, but no matter how long he waits Ilysa eludes him.

Hammond Louisiana will be the first face-to-face encounter between Edwards and Callie. He's grown tired of waiting and uses his southern charm to move things along a little faster. Getting closer to Callie might get him the information on Ilysa's whereabouts. Daniel moves into action because Ilysa knows how to stay one step ahead and Paul is getting agitated with his slow progress. Daniel knows he has to do something to draw Ilysa out.

7

MILLER STARES OUT of his window at the shop window across the street. How is he going to find Callie? The dark ringlet hair and brilliant smile take his focus away from the frustrating case for only a moment. His phone vibrates and breaks him from his reverie. Ted Branson shows on his ID screen, and he reads the text. *Paul St. Claire has finally been located in Bogalusa at the Sportsman Inn Motel.*

It's about time. Bogalusa is about an hour away. I knew he was close. He calls Branson back.

"Miller here. Have the local PD pick him up and bring him in for questioning." He hangs up the phone smiles at seeing the light at the end of the tunnel. He just needs to find Callie, Ilysa, and now Cora. *How are these people functioning in the shadows?*

~⁓**⁓~

The phone rings in the dusty little office of Edwards' landlord. He swats at the pile of newspapers on his desk, sending them flying to the floor, while he unburies the phone. He snatches it up just before the fifth and final ring.

"Hullo." The croaky voice is unmistakable.

"You gotta get a hold of Cora. This detective is picking up where Edwards left off. They're bringing Paul in for questioning as we speak. Miller already knows there's a twin and he's going to connect Elyse to Ilysa soon enough."

"Where's he getting this stuff from? Who's he talkin' to?"

"I dunno, but he's getting too close. They have to get out of there *now*. Once Miller talks to Paul St. Claire, he'll be coming back to the river. You'd better let Celia know what's going on, too.'"

"Celia told me she got caught snoopin' 'round his place."

"I told her to be careful. He can't find out she's been workin' for you."

"I know, I know. I'll tell her to be more careful. No more snoopin' for a while and I can get a warning to Cora and Elyse, too." The call ends with a click.

Just as he hears the click on the other end, Branson turns to see Paul St. Claire being escorted into the interrogation room by two officers and Miller. They briefly make eye contact and St. Claire looks away.

~ ~**~ ~

Miller leads St. Claire down the long brightly lit hallway and through a metal door where he is seated at a table in the small, barely furnished room. The typical gray paint does nothing to add to his mood. One officer remains outside in the hall while the other stands inside in the far corner. Miller sits at the table, unbuttons his suit jacket, and fishes through papers in a file. He tosses the sketch of Edwards onto the table in front of him.

"Do you know this guy?"

He barely looks at the photo. "No." His hands are on the table until he notices Miller looking at them. He slowly slides them back and puts them under the table.

Miller tosses a photo taken at the coroner's lab. "Maybe this one looks more familiar."

"Kinda looks like a guy I hired a few years back. He looked a little better then. What happened to him?"

"Somebody killed him and left him for gator food. Why did you hire him?"

"Lookin' for somebody. Isn't that why most people hire PIs? Lookin' for someone or something?"

"So, who are you looking for and why?"

"A woman I knew many years ago ran off carrying my child." Miller tosses the sketch of Callie on the table.

St. Claire brings his hands back onto the table. He takes the drawing and brings it closer to him. "Is that her? Is that my girl?" His voice is low and husky as if the words are having trouble coming out. "What's her name?"

"Edwards never told you?"

"No. I haven't talked to him since I hit Louisiana."

"Her name is Callie."

"Callie. She's beautiful. Ilysa named her after my grandmother."

"Mr. St. Claire, do you know a woman named Elyse?"

"Yes, she is Ilysa's sister."

"Sister? She's been acting like she doesn't know anything about her other than she helped her deliver the babies!"

"Babies?"

"Yeah. Ilysa delivered twin girls. The second baby was stillborn, but Elyse revived her and carried her off. She must not have told Ilysa about the baby, either." Miller watches him hard for a reaction.

"Where's the second girl?"

"Probably along the river's edge with Elyse." Miller goes to the door of the interrogation room and calls out to officer Branson. "Take a car to the Laplace and pick up Elyse and her daughter."

"Bring them both in."

"Yes, Sir. I'm on it."

~ ~**~ ~

Branson rushes out of the room toward his squad car and drives toward Elyse's home. Once out of sight of headquarters, he slows his speed, takes the long way around the city, and stalls for time, hoping Tom can get through to them in time.

Eventually, Branson arrives at the small cottage. There are no sounds or lights, except the one on the front porch. The rest of the house is dark. He knocks several times and announces himself. No answer. *Great, they're gone.*

He steps inside and looks around. The place is quiet. Furniture and pictures are there, untouched. There are dishes in the sink and the pot of soup on the stove is still warm. Most of their clothes are gone, but some are scattered on the floor. *They packed quickly.* Branson makes the call to Miller.

"They appear to have left the home recently, Sir. No indication here as to where they might be headed."

"I want an APB put out on Elyse and Cora James. Check the train station and bus terminal."

"What happens to them if you find them?" asks St. Claire.

"I'll have them brought in for questioning. I need to know what happened to Edwards and why. What exactly are *you* going to do, if and when you ever catch up to Ilysa and Callie, Mr. St. Claire? It's probably too late to press charges against Ilysa, and Callie is a grown woman, not a child. From what I've heard, you didn't want the baby. Why do you want her now?"

"Where could you have possibly heard such a thing? Ilysa? After I got released from the hospital, I tried to find Ilysa to apologize. I loved her and would have done whatever I could to make it up to her. She simply vanished. I have been searching for them for years because she and Callie are all I have left in the world since my wife died." He drops his head to hide his emotions.

Miller stands but turns back to glance at the individual seated at his table. He shakes his head and heads for the door. "Let him sit there for a moment then kick him loose," he tells the officer just outside the door.

Miller returns to his desk and stares out the window. The young woman he noticed before has returned to the store across the street. This time, Miller knows she's inside and rushes downstairs and out the door. He races blindly across the street, nearly colliding with a car whose driver doesn't see him coming. He doesn't hesitate this time but goes in and looks around. He heads straight for the store clerk, out of breath and pumped full of adrenalin.

"I just saw a young woman come into the store and don't tell me she didn't, or I'll arrest you for obstruction of a homicide investigation! Now, where did she go?"

The young woman seems startled and a bit nervous. She hesitates in answering as she tries to figure a way out then she straightens her posture and looks eye to eye at Detective Miller. Her whole demeanor changes. Her expression is not that of the pleasant store clerk from their past encounter. She stares at Miller as if she's in a trance. "Well, suh. You are still mistaken. There is no one here 'cept you and me and if you didn't come to shop, maybe it's best you leave now."

Miller feels that same churning in the pit of his stomach as he had when he spoke to Elyse. He leaves the store, and she immediately heads for the door, locking it tightly behind him. She briskly flips the closed sign over and pulls a window shade down as she walks away.

He now knows he needs help handling some of these people. This is getting weirder by the minute. He looks into the storefront window just as the clerk goes behind the register. She grabs a wool shawl and disappears through the curtain. *Why would she need a shawl? Even if she's going out the back door, it's seventy-two degrees outside today.* 'Just storage' is what she'd told him. He waits a few minutes, but she doesn't return.

~ ~**~ ~

The store clerk walks down a hall filled with metal shelves of her inventory and proceeds down a long, steep flight of stairs. She walks down another hall that is shorter and dimly lit. She sees her breath as she moves along. There is a large room to her left and she can see a brightly lit room in the corner to her right. Muffled voices, speaking in a language she doesn't know, can be heard. They get louder as she gets closer, but as soon as she appears in the doorway, they stop. The three turn toward her.

"That detective mus' be watchin' my shop. He sees you coming in." She says in Cora's direction. "Someone will have to get you out through the tunnel."

"Did you tell him anything?" Croaks a familiar voice.

"No, nothing, but that doesn't mean he won't be back. He's nosy, just like that other one."

"Elyse and Cora will be staying with another friend along the river for now. We have several homes there we can use." Celia's voice resonates from the hallway.

"How do we keep them safe without getting caught? Especially if he knows she's here." This is another voice, much deeper. The three turn to see officer Branson walking their way. "I *will* lose my badge if Miller finds out I'm involved in any way."

"You may lose your badge, but we're all facing jail!" Celia's voice rises.

"All right. Calm down. Everyone needs to keep their heads cool and their mouths shut. He has no way to connect us to Elyse or Cora. As long as they stay out of sight for a while, we should be able to keep this under wraps," Tom tells them.

"Mom and I are so grateful you all have gotten involved to help us. I don't want to see any of you get in trouble."

"It's too late for that," Celia says, looking at Tom.

The small group of accomplices disperses through the tunnel and the store clerk returns to her shop.

~~**~~

Miller watches from his office window as she raises her shade, flips her door sign back to "open" and unlocks the door. He makes eye contact with the clerk as the pool-blues smile back. It seems the pleasant clerk from before is back in the shop, but he has no idea the other four are leaving by way of the dark passageway beneath the store.

~~**~~

Branson appears back into the office moments later. He practically bumps into Paul St. Claire as he is leaving the building. Paul says something to Branson, but Branson doesn't respond. He just stops and watches as St. Claire walks out the door.

Miller watches the brief exchange. When Branson gets to his desk, he seems edgy and distracted.

"When you went to the home of Elyse James, what did you find?"

"Not much. It looks like they packed in a hurry. Clothes were thrown all over. Stuff in the kitchen looks like they just forgot about dinner and left. Everything else looks normal."

"I think I'll go take a look for myself."

"Suit yourself, but there is nothing there."

Miller slings his jacket over his shoulder and heads to the parking lot. The ride from Hammond to Laplace gives him time to clear his head and put his thoughts in order. *Find Ilysa.*

He picks up his cell and calls Branson. "Check the local Hammond real estate records. If Ilysa bought the home she's living in, there will be a record of the sale. I don't know why I didn't think of that *days* ago." *Maybe I was distracted by that face.*

"I'll see what I can find." Branson begins nervously typing on his computer. He gets into the public records for real estate transactions and finds nothing under the name Ilysa James. He tries for similar names and different spellings. Of course, the only James that shows up in the computer is Elyse, but he was expecting that one. He looks for St. Claire and he is surprised to find Callie is listed as the owner of the home. He jots down the address and immediately calls Detective Miller.

MILLER FINDS HIMSELF on the front porch of the home of Elyse and Cora James. The light is still on, and the front door is open. He pushes it just a little as his phone rings.

"Miller here."

"I found it. Ilysa bought the home but put it in Callie's name. I am sending the address to your phone."

"Great. Thanks."

Miller proceeds inside the home. It is as Branson described it. He slips into his rubber gloves and goes from room to room, sifting through all the things left behind. He remembers the night he spoke to Elyse and the room with the light shining under the door.

He heads there next. There isn't much left. He finds empty drawers and a few things left hanging in the closet. Miller spots something in the corner, on the closet floor —the small blue shoulder bag he remembers from the glasses. It wouldn't have seemed important to Branson. Miller opens it, but it's empty except for the faintest hint of a powdery white substance. Even with gloved hands, he is careful not to touch it. Miller bags it to take back with him for analysis and continues to look around.

The scent of jasmine lingers in the air, but there's nothing else here of interest and nothing to tell him where they might've gone. He stops on the porch and looks around as he prepares to make the long ride back to Hammond. He doesn't see anyone around but somehow feels as if someone is watching him.

He steps off the porch and warily moves to his car. He retrieves his mystical informant from his pocket. He still doesn't understand how the glasses do what they do, but he's grateful for the help they've given so far. He slips the glasses onto his nose and lets the images fill his head.

Miller watches as the people flow through the French Market. It's one of the city's most popular shopping areas, sitting right along the river's edge. His eyes scan the crowd as they move about. Suddenly, the dark ringlets of hair appear and pass so close to Miller's face that he steps back to get out of the way.

The woman passes by slowly, then suddenly turns her back to him and moves toward another vendor's booth. She is casually dressed in cotton pants, a cut-off top, and the same flats she wore in the train station. Though Miller can't see her face, he's pretty sure he's watching Cora.

The woman doesn't purchase anything; she just wanders from place to place. She's approached by a smaller woman who stands directly in front of her. Neither face is visible to Miller until a young man joins Them. After they turn to greet him, they move toward the closest exit. Now Miller can identify everyone in the small group.

As the images begin to fade, Miller slaps the top of his dashboard so hard the shock shoots straight up his wrist and into his shoulder. *What the hell?*

The rose-tinted informant has not disappointed Miller with its clue, but the secrets of Hammond are running deeper than he could have ever expected. Callie's whereabouts are still unknown. *Is she hiding or is she another victim?*

The ride home is difficult. The pain in his arm is minor compared to the fear that's jumped into his heart. Did someone get rid of Daniel and Callie to protect Elyse and Cora? Miller flips on his lights and siren and pushes his vehicle to the limit. He needs to get back to Hammond.

The lab for police headquarters is on the lowest level of the building and Miller goes straight there before heading to his office. He hands the lab tech the small handbag.

"There's a white substance inside. I need to know what it is, like yesterday."

"Yes, Sir. I'll get on it as soon as I can."

"No, you'll get on it now."

"Yes, Sir."

"Call me when you get a result." Miller turns to leave when his phone vibrates. "Miller here."

"This is Branson. Where are you?"

"Just leaving the lab. I'm on my way to the office."

When he arrives, he stops by his desk and checks his messages. One is from Paul St. Claire. *I'll call him later.* He types Ilysa's address into his GPS and leaves again.

Branson just misses Miller. He snatches up his phone. "Detective, I'm here at the office. Thought you said you were coming here."

"Change of plans. I'm heading for Ilysa's place. I'll let you know what I find." Miller is still a little disturbed by the last scene in the glasses. *Branson was at the marketplace with Cora and Celia. He never mentioned he even knew Cora. How does he know my housekeeper? What else isn't he telling me?*

HE GETS TO the address Branson sent to his phone. The home is a medium-sized, southern-plantation-styled home. It's an attractive and well-maintained place, very unlike Elyse's cottage along the river's edge. He climbs the short stairway in front and looks both ways on the long wrap-around porch before he rings the doorbell. He can hear the Westminster chimes play, then silence.

He waits a little longer before walking to the back of the home. The yard is neatly done with fragrant wisteria growing along the rear wall. A statue of Saint Francis stands tall and faces the house and there is a small wrought iron bench at the bottom of a huge Magnolia tree, inviting all to sit and relax a moment, but Miller has no time to relax.

He returns to his car and pulls out his phone. "Branson, I want round-the-clock surveillance on this house. I need to get an officer to keep an eye out and let me know if either Ilysa or Callie or anyone else is staying here. I also want Callie's sketch on the evening news tonight. Someone has to know where she is. If she's hiding, I want her found. Check hospitals and the morgue for any Jane Does matching her description."

Miller reluctantly returns to the car. The sky through his windshield is bright blue with a sprinkling of white feathery clouds. Callie's large bright eyes peer through the cloud to the right of him. The distraction almost takes him off the road, but he compensates and straightens his car just in time to avoid an introduction to the metal railing. His heart races from the near-miss, but his mind is still on Callie. He doesn't want to think of the unthinkable possibilities.

Headquarters is buzzing with activity when he arrives. He gets to his desk and finds another phone message from St. Claire. He hesitates but decides to call.

"Mr. St. Claire? Yes, Sir. How are you?"

"I'm okay. Any news on my daughter?"

"No, Sir. Nothing yet. I've decided to put her face on the news tonight to see if we can get some help from the Hammond residents. Something should happen within the next twenty-four to forty-eight hours."

"This waiting is the hard part, but I guess if I can wait for five years, forty-eight hours will feel like a walk in the park."

"Yes, Sir. I hope that's all it is."

The afternoon ticks away slowly, what feels like half the day is only several hours later. Miller watches the large-screen Tv through the glass window in his office. He can see the announcement about Callie and stops breathing until it's finished. His exhale sounds more like *where are you?* As the broadcast ends, he sees Branson at his desk. He's already on the phone, but Miller is suspicious about his intentions. Because no one else is aware of his connection with the glasses, he must be careful how he makes his information known. It's been a day or so since he's called upon his rose-tinted informant.

The next few days are filled with phone calls and tips of every kind—that is, every kind except the one that leads him to Callie. His heart gets heavier each day Callie is missing. He rifles through his notes, going over and over everything. *What am I missing?* He rereads all the messages on his desk and scours the files and pictures. He hasn't noticed the silence that has filled the office. When it finally hits him, he scans the room. Everyone is staring toward the entrance. When his long-range focus clears, the air is sucked out of his lungs, and he gasps.

The woman with the ringlet hair and tanned, clear complexion is standing in the doorway. This time, her headband is twisted behind her head to control her wild curls. Her dress—the color of a Georgia peach—is above her knees and hugging her like a straitjacket and her matching shoes only take her an inch and a half off the floor. If he didn't know her age, she would look to be about sixteen years old.

She leans toward the officer closest to her and speaks. He turns and points with a smile in Miller's direction. She speaks again and glides across the floor toward Miller. All eyes follow her through the room and once she reaches Miller's door, they return to their business at hand.

He catches his breath, quickly stands, and closes the door to his office. When he turns around, Callie is standing just inches away.

"I've heard you're looking for me." Her voice is soft and smooth, just like her skin.

He can hear just a hint of a southern accent with a current of highly educated and proper etiquette flowing beneath it.

"Yes, Ma'am. I'm glad to know you're all right." She makes him uncomfortable, so he scoots around her back to his desk. "Please have a seat."

"Why wouldn't I be?" Her voice has a musical lilt to it. She sits directly in front of his chair.

"We're investigating a possible homicide, but we didn't know if you were another victim." He pulls out the sketch of Daniel Edwards and passes it across the desk.

"Do you recognize this man?"

"It looks like Daniel. Daniel Edwards. He's been following me and mom since we left Mississippi."

"When was the last time you saw Mr. Edwards?"

"A few weeks ago. Has something happened?"

"He was found dead on the side of the highway. We don't have a definite cause of death yet."

Callie's face goes blank. The lids at the bottom of her eyes become pools as they fill and overflow.

"Why would someone want to hurt Daniel?"

"We don't know yet. There are a lot of peculiar things that are going to come out. I want you to be prepared."

"Peculiar? Like what?"

"Did you know he was a private investigator?"

"He told me his job was to find lost things."

"Yes, but did he tell you the things he was trying to find were you and your mother? Callie, have you ever met your father?"

Callie looks into Miller's eyes. The pools of tears threaten to overflow their banks again.

The look tugs at Jonathan's heart. He wants to offer a shoulder, but this was not the time or place.

"No. I just remember my mother would get very angry always tell me he didn't want me." The words catch in her throat. "We've been running from him since I was a child. My mother would tell me we were moving for other reasons, but after the fifth or sixth move, I kinda figured things out on my own."

Miller has to smile at her intuition. "He's here Callie, not far from Hammond. He wants to meet you. He sent Edwards to find you."

"I don't think my mother will like that."

"What would you like, Callie? You're grown and of age to make some choices of your own."

"I'd like to meet him. I have a lot of questions."

"I can arrange for you to meet him."

"Will you be there?"

"*Yes!* I will, if it will make you more comfortable," Miller says trying disguise his excitement.

"It will, thanks."

"Where are you staying?"

"I live on the west side."

"Leave your number and I'll make arrangements."

She picks up a pen and a notepad from his desk and scribbles her name and number.

"Thank you, Detective."

"You're welcome. I'll be in touch."

He doesn't have the heart to throw the twin sister in on top of everything else. She obviously cares somewhat about Edwards and now he's gone. The introduction to her father will be enough for now. He'll ask about Ilysa the next time they talk. He watches her almost glide across the floor as she exits the office, and his eyes stay focused on her until she disappears down the stairs. He immediately picks up the phone to call Paul.

"Hello, Mr. St. Claire. I have some good news."

"You found her?"

"Yes. She came to see me. I told her you were here, and she has agreed to a supervised meeting."

"Supervised?"

"Yes, Sir. She's a little nervous and will meet with you as long as I'm present."

"That's fine with me. Whatever makes her comfortable. Did she happen to mention Ilysa?"

"No, Sir. We didn't discuss her yet. Maybe when we all get together you can ask her."

"Set it up and let me know. I'll be there."

The phone call ends, and Miller is excited, for the moment. He still needs to connect the rest of the pieces to this puzzle to find his answer, but he'll sleep a little easier knowing Callie is unharmed.

He takes the rose-tinted glasses from his pocket and stares for a moment. *Do you know how he died?* He decides to wait until there is a little less traffic in the office before putting them on. Instead, he searches to find a suitable meeting place for father and daughter. It needs to be stylish like her, and still upscale for her dad.

La Provence. Perfect. I'll make a reservation. Miller sets things up for the following Friday night and makes both calls. Paul and Callie St. Claire are happy with the selection. He gives both the address and offers Callie a ride, but she turns him down.

"I'd prefer to meet you there."

He can hear the tremor in her voice. "Take down my number, just in case."

BACK IN HIS apartment, Miller leans back against the headboard of his bed and lets the rose-colored glasses lead him on his next adventure.

The images come into focus at the lower French Quarter in Jackson Square. It's the middle of the day and Celia, his housekeeper, is sitting on a bench. She is approached from behind by a man in a dark gray, expensively tailored suit. He stands behind her, but she never turns around. He simply puts an envelope on her shoulder. The hand holding the envelope is large, dark, and charred from burns. Miller immediately recognizes it.

Celia takes it and he turns to leave. Miller can't tell if they exchange conversation or not. She sits a little longer and, after opening the envelope to peek inside, puts it into her purse. When she stands to leave, she hears something or someone behind her and turns suddenly toward the sound. He watches as the stumpy little man rants and raves, waving his arms about as he approaches. Miller can almost hear the croaky voice as they talk. Celia pulls the envelope from her purse and hands it to him. Tom Bradley takes the envelope and scurries back the way he came. Celia continues in the opposite direction as the images fade.

The landlord from the apartment building is in cahoots with my housekeeper and Paul St. Claire? This is the second time Paul's passed a stuffed envelope to someone. He's shuffling out a lot of money for something. What could they possibly be working on together?

A chill runs down his spine. He's suddenly apprehensive about his evening with Callie and her father. He has to keep the information he's gained from the glasses his little secret, not that he could explain them anyway. He still has no idea how they work.

La Provence has the ambiance of a French inn with ceiling beams made of distressed oak. The atmosphere is warm and inviting. It's the perfect place to reunite a relationship… or even start one. The wine and food wrap guests in comfort like an old friend. *Yes, this is a perfect spot.*

Miller is the first to arrive. As the waiter leads him to a table set against the windows, he requests a bottle of wine be brought with water and menus. As he is being seated, he spots Paul and waves him over.

The two are only there for a few minutes before Callie appears at the entrance. Her floor-length cotton dress has a brilliant red design down the right side. Her short, red sandals are a wonderful complement to her outfit. She lets the ringlets fall where they may tonight, and she looks quite breathtaking.

She makes her way to the table and Jonathan realizes that, again, he hasn't taken a breath since she walked in. This time, his sudden inhale startles him and makes him cough uncontrollably. He laughs at his foolishness, which makes his coughing even worse. Feeling profoundly stupid and unable to stop coughing, he raises a finger at the two watching with concern and excuses himself to the men's restroom to gain control, leaving Paul and Callie alone at the table.

Paul looks at the young woman sitting across from him. "You look like your mother. Beautiful. Did you know you were named after your great-grandmother?"

"No. She never talked much about you or your side of the family."

"I guess she had her reasons."

"Her reasons? She was so hurt and angry and sometimes afraid. She thought you loved her! After the years you two had, special trips you took? After all the things you taught her. It's because of you we managed so well. Most of the money you gave her, she told me she saved it over the years. That's how she bought the house here, but she knew people would be looking for her, so she put the house in my name. If what you had then was so special, why did you tell her she couldn't have me? Look at me, Daddy. Why didn't you want me twenty years ago? Why did you send some young man to find me now? Did you know he's dead? And for what? You suddenly want to be a daddy?"

"No, Callie. I know it's too late for that. But I tried, Callie, for years. I looked, but I hit a brick wall every time. That's when I hired Daniel. He was good. He found things in months that I couldn't find in ten years. I know I missed out on 'baby' Callie, but can't I get to know you from this point on? I would love to get to know the lovely young woman sitting at this table. Can't we just talk and get to know one another? I *am* your dad."

Miller returns to the table. He sees he has interrupted a serious conversation. "Again, I apologize for that… whatever that was. I hope I haven't ruined the evening. Please, order whatever you'd like." He takes a second look at Callie and looks away.

The awkward silence is broken by a delightful waitress bringing water, wine, and menus. From there, the night passes as it should. The conversation stays pretty low-key and cordial.

Jonathan is pleased with the evening. *This is nice… kinda like a supervised first date.*

Close to the end of the meal, Jonathan turns to Callie. "Can you tell me about Daniel? When you talked to him, what did you talk about?"

"Daniel was charming. He was funny, polite, intelligent, and attentive. We talked about everything—our childhoods, schools, siblings, everything."

"Did he ever ask you about your mother?"

Callie's eyes get wide, like a deer staring at the headlights of Miller's car. She picks up her water glass and takes a long drink. "He did," she says, almost in a whisper, "but I would always find a way to avoid answering him."

"Callie, where is your mom?"

She takes in a long, deep breath. "I don't know. I haven't talked to her in weeks. She always finds a way to get me a message to say she's all right, but I haven't heard from her for a while." The pools begin to fill at the bottom of her eyes. "We got separated in Mississippi when she was avoiding Daniel. She knew he would follow me. She always told me if anything ever happened to her to make my way west. 'Don't stop until you get to Louisiana. I'll find you there when it's safe. There's a house there waiting for us,' she said. So that's what I did. She taught me how to travel and find safe places to sleep. She always gave me what I needed to get by. She's so smart—not just book smart, but street smart. She knew we were being followed. She showed me, Daniel, a long time ago. I knew who he was when he approached me at the le Café. I acted like I didn't, but I did. But I liked him… a lot. Somehow I just knew he wouldn't hurt me." She takes in another deep breath. The exhale is slow and almost prayerful; it may have been her goodbye to Daniel.

"My mother told me to try to find my Aunt Elyse who lives near the river's edge, but I don't like going down there. I was just going to wait to see if momma was going to get here."

"We think your Aunt Elyse has left the area."

"Why would she leave? This is her home?"

"She was trying to keep Daniel from finding out her secret."

"What was her secret?"

Jonathan reaches into a small briefcase and pulls out a picture of Cora. He can only tell them apart by the way they walk and dress. Cora seems a little awkward when she walks and is always more casual. Pretty, but her clothes are more worn, older, and sometimes tattered. She's still beautiful to look at and given Callie's clothes and posture, a person would need the shooting star on Cora's shoulder to tell them apart.

Miller watches her expression as Callie looks at the picture for a long time. She touches the little face, and her eyes fill. Her father sits quietly and watches. She looks up at Jonathan as she did in his office. "I've always felt like some part of me was somewhere else." The words struggle to come out as the tears finally leave the safety of their lids. "Do you know where my sister is, Detective Miller?" She hands the picture to her father.

"She was here in Louisiana until recently. Somewhere in Laplace. We aren't sure if she's still in the area, but I believe she is and she's usually with your Aunt Elyse. We're still looking for them."

She turns her gaze to her father. "You have gone from being childless to having twins. You didn't see that coming, did you?" She says with a little smile.

"No, Callie. I didn't. I had no idea. She's beautiful, just like you. I guess your aunt has some explaining to do to all of us."

Jonathan pushes his chair back from the table and stands. His five-foot, eleven inches look even taller from a sitting position. "You two will have to decide what to do. In the meantime, I still have a homicide to solve. Ms. St. Claire, will you allow me to walk you to your car?"

"Yes. Thank you, Detective. You've been very helpful."

As they exit the restaurant, they pause and say their goodnights to Paul, who passes them to get to his car.

Though the night air is not cold, the temperature has dropped enough to make the air too brisk for a sundress. Jonathan smoothly slips out of his jacket and softly drapes it over her shoulders.

She simply responds with a smile. "Do you think you will find her?"

"I won't stop until I do."

He lets her slide into the driver's seat and closes her door. Through the glass, he can see the beautiful eyes staring back at him as she brushes the dark ringlets out of her face. He gently taps on the glass and motions for her to lower the window. "Maybe when this case is over you might consider having dinner with me, without the watchful eyes of dad?"

"I might consider that." She laughs lightly.

He smiles as she raises her window and drives off. Watching her drive away is the hardest thing he's had to do since this case began.

Miller takes his time on the ride home. It's lonely for the first time. He's never really found someone he wanted to include in his life, given his line of work. *Callie St. Claire could be the first possible candidate.* He smiles at the thought. *First, I have to help Mr. Edwards. He deserves an answer.*

HE GETS INTO the office the following morning and finds Branson is already at work. He glances out the window at the storefront across the street. The sign in the window still reads "Closed". He'll call his apartment later to see if Celia is working at his place today and Bradley is second on his list for people to talk to. Somebody knows where Cora and Elyse are, and they are going to tell him.

"Branson!" He shouts, startling the young officer. "Walk with me. Now!"

"On my way, Detective."

Miller leads him down the stairs and outside the office building.

"Let's start with how you know my housekeeper, Celia Morales."

"Huh? How did you know?"

"I know more than you think. Answer my question. How?"

"Celia and I dated in high school. We've known each other for years."

"Why didn't you ever tell me?"

"You never asked me about Celia."

"Okay, let's get to more important matters. You never mentioned that Celia knows Tom from Edwards' apartment building. You also never mentioned that you know Cora James or that you, Celia, and Cora met at the Marketplace. Are you deliberately trying to end your career before you really get a good foothold? Because conspiracy to commit murder or accessory after the fact doesn't look good in your file when they start handing down promotions."

"I don't know where you're getting this stuff, but you've got me all wrong. Yeah, I know Celia. We're just friends. And I bumped into Cora at the Marketplace one day. I haven't known her very long and I don't know much about her."

"You'd better hope so because if I find any evidence of you aiding Cora and Elyse or linking you to the death of Daniel Edwards, I will personally take your badge and gun and you will never see a gold shield." Miller walks away, leaving Branson dumbfounded.

Back at the office, Miller's mind drifts back to Callie, but it is short-lived, interrupted by the vibration in his pocket. "Miller here."

"Yes, Sir. It's Dennis. From the lab. I have something for you."

"I'm on my way."

~ ~**~ ~

The forensic lab is bustling with science geeks of all ages. Test tubes filled with liquids of all colors are everywhere. Bunsen burners are heating up and containers are smoldering. Miller looks around at the extra little pieces to the puzzles these guys add-in. *We couldn't do what we do if they didn't do what they do.* He searches for Dennis and finds him in a corner lab.

"Whatcha got for me, Dennis?"

"I got a hit on the white substance you found in the purse. It wouldn't show up in a tox screen unless you were specifically looking for it. She probably smashed a berry in her purse. It's called Actaea Pachypoda, also known as doll's eyes or white baneberry, the consumption of which has a sedative effect on cardiac muscle tissue and can cause cardiac arrest."

"Good job, Dennis. Thanks." Detective Miller immediately calls the coroner's office.

"Hey, Doc! I need you to pull Daniel Edwards one more time and check for a toxin called Acta… Actapakypod something. White baneberry."

"Actaea Pachypoda? Yeah, I know the stuff. You can't eat it, and it makes a lethal wine." He laughs. "Okay. I still have a blood sample I can use. I'll let you know if I find anything."

"Thanks."

He may finally be able to connect someone to Edwards. Cora carried the same poison in her purse. He just needed to know how and when she would've been able to give it to him. She had a motive… and now means. She may have even had accomplices. *Find the opportunity and we have a slam dunk!* He still needs to find her.

Miller leaves the lab and heads back to his desk. Branson is at his desk, looking sheepish while talking on the phone. *Are you talking to Cora, Celia, or Elyse? You let them know I'm coming.* He stuffs his files into his briefcase and walks toward the exit.

"Detective Miller! Where are you headed? Do you need me to go with you?"

Miller stops and looks at the officer. He thinks for a moment and then walks to Branson's desk. He leans over and gets within inches of the man's face.

"Are you working *with* me or trying to sabotage my investigation?"

"I'm with you, Sir," he whispers.

"Then let's go. I'm going to go talk to that goofy landlord again."

"Let me get my things. I'll meet you at the car."

Miller turns to leave, but as he approaches the stairs, he turns back to see Branson on the phone. *I hope I don't have to shoot that kid.* "Branson! Let's go!"

Branson says something into the phone then slams it down. He rushes to catch up to Miller. He can't be surprised by the expression on Miller's face.

The drive to the apartment building is quiet, but Miller is not in the mood for games. He goes into the rental office and finds the disheveled Tom leaning back in his chair, feet propped up on the desk and reading the newspaper.

Miller comes straight to the point. "What kind of dealings do you have with my housekeeper, Celia Morales?"

The short legs come down off of the desk and he sits up straight. He looks at Detective Miller through soda-bottle glasses, then snatches them off of his nose. They make him look like an old cartoon character. "Huh? Well, she does little odd jobs for me."

"What kind of odd jobs? And do any of them have anything to do with Cora and Elyse James or Paul St. Claire or, for that matter, Daniel Edwards?"

"Uh…"

"What do you know about the death of Daniel?"

"All I know is somebody didn't want him gettin' too close to Callie. He was startin' to spend too much time with her. She didn't want time with her to lead him back to Cora."

"Who's *she?* Elyse? How could Callie lead Edwards to Cora? She didn't know anything about Cora until recently."

"You didn't hear this from me, but Callie bumped into Elyse about four months back. They're identical, you know, and without the other one, you might not be able to tell who is who. Even Elyse was caught off guard and called her Cora by accident. When Callie told her who she was, Elyse got nervous. Elyse knew that if Callie was in town, Ilysa wasn't too far away. Elyse thought she had to hide from Ilysa, but Callie was the one mad as a snake. She figured out that she had a sister that Elyse had hidden away. Don't let that pretty face fool you, Detective."

That whole scene at dinner was an act? Why'd she lie to me? "Do you know where Elyse and Cora are now?"

"Yeah. Some friends further down the river's edge are givin' them a place to stay. They didn't want to go too far."

"Take me to them. This time, no one warns them I'm coming. You lead the way and give Branson your cell phone."

The stubby little landlord hands Branson his phone and goes to his vehicle. Miller and Branson pull their squad car up behind him as he is pulling off. Driving down Route 55 and headed for Laplace, the landlord's phone buzzes. Branson reads the caller ID screen and then shows it to Miller. He shakes his head then puts his eyes back on the car that's leading him to his prime suspects. At least this time, he knows Branson isn't the one making the call.

It doesn't take them long to get the house along the river's edge. They pull up in front of a two-story house. The tall, stately columns give it the look of a southern plantation mansion, without the size.

Miller sends Branson around the back with a look that makes Branson's blood run cold. He knows the warning and proceeds around to the back door. Miller and the landlord listen at the front, and they hear voices. One female and one male. Miller knocks loudly and announces himself. The sudden shuffling inside tells him he's gotten someone's attention.

"Open the door. I'm looking for Elyse and Cora James."

He listens again. The shuffling gets faster and glass shatters. Miller signals Tom to stay still as Miller un-holsters his sidearm then kicks in the door to gain access. He looks around. The room is empty. He hears Branson coming in from the back door and signals him to look around the back rooms while he searches upstairs.

Going from room to room, he checks every corner until he sees a door off to his left that looks a little odd for the rest of the room. The paneling crisscrosses like the doors of a barn. All of the other doors have long, rectangular designs. He walks quietly to the door and turns the knob. *Locked!* He listens for sounds on the other side. Nothing. No footsteps. No voices. *People don't just vanish.* At that moment, Branson appears at the doorway.

"All clear downstairs," he says softly.

Miller turns his gun around and uses the handle as a hammer upon the doorknob. It doesn't take much force to knock it to the floor. Miller pushes the other end of the knob out and opens the door. They find a spiral staircase leading down into a very dark hole.

They look down the hole and back at each other. "Do you think that leads to Wonderland?" He asks as he walks past Branson and back downstairs. Miller goes to where he left Bradley and grabs him by the throat.

"Where'd they go?"

"I don't know."

"Where does the stairway lead?"

"I don't know!"

"You're the part of this group who's been hiding and protecting Elyse. Where would they go next?"

"I'm telling you; I don't know."

"Well, until you do know, I'm just going to hold you for conspiracy, obstruction of an investigation, and pissing me off! Get in the squad car."

"What about my car?"

"We'll have it towed to the impound lot."

"Branson, find out who owns this house."

"Yes, sir," he says glancing briefly at Tom.

Miller can almost feel the steam coming out of his ears. He can't believe he's this close to at least one of them and she's somehow managed to vanish into the wind. The ride back to headquarters seems to take forever. When they pull in front of the building, Miller notices the store clerk peering out the window. As they pull Tom Bradley from the backseat, she turns back to what she was doing.

Miller looks at Branson. "Find a holding room for this guy."

Branson takes Tom inside. On the main level is a hall with eight rooms. The rooms are only connected by a large window and speakers. A large table and several chairs are the only pieces of furniture allowed. Branson shoves Tom into one of the rooms and starts to close the door.

"You know, you not gettin' off this easy. You're just as guilty as the rest of us. When that detective finds out…." He starts to laugh as Branson slams the door closed. He leaves Tom in the room and goes upstairs to his desk. He finds Miller in his office. He's wearing the rose-tinted glasses.

"Hey, Detective. Aren't those Edwards' glasses? You like them that much?"

Miller ignores him as he carefully watches the scene in front of his eyes.

Elyse and Cora are in a field of bushes; some have the strangest-looking white berry dangling from the branches. The baneberry has a small spot in the middle that, at first glance, could look like an eye. Elyse, with gloved hands, puts a bunch into Cora's small blue purse. She makes sure the clasp is tight and tells Cora something before they leave. Right now, Miller would give anything for these scenes to have sound; he never learned to read lips. The two walk across the field and get into a small motorboat waiting at the edge of the river. Facing upstream, they ride for maybe two miles and pull the silver craft out onto the opposite side. Celia is waiting for them.

Cora hands her the purse and with gloved hands, Celia removes the berries. Some are damaged, but there are enough to do the job. Elyse and Cora take off in their boat back downriver. Celia takes the berries inside and begins working on them. Her back is to Miller, so he doesn't see what she does, but he sees her hold up two small, capped cylinders of liquid which she then puts in her pocket and walks out the door. As the images begin to fade, Miller removes the glasses and finds Branson still standing in front of him.

"You've really taken to the rosy view, eh Miller? At least they don't freak you out anymore."

"What do you know about white baneberry?"

"I know you can't eat them… and they make a lethal wine." He laughs.

Miller doesn't see the humor in his remarks and his expression leaves no doubt. His green eyes close to a slit as Branson moves to leave, stepping backward out the door.

Miller takes off the glasses and tucks them back into his jacket pocket. He goes downstairs to the holding room where Tom is waiting, standing with his back to a large window. *He knows more than he's telling.*

"Take a seat." Miller points to one of the chairs. "What do you know about white baneberry?"

"I know you can't eat the berries…" He laughs.

"…and they make a lethal wine, yeah, I know." Miller closes his eyes and drops his head back. *Must be the standing joke of Hammond.*

"Is there anything else you can tell me about Elyse and Cora? Who else is in on hiding them?"

"I don't know everybody. That's the way people like it. That way, nobody ruins it for everybody. We take care of our own here."

"Does that include helping someone commit murder?"

"Wouldn't you do anything to protect your loved ones?"

"Not murder someone trying to do a job!"

"His job was findin' somebody who didn't want to be found by somebody else. That's not a job. That's meddlin' in somethin' that's not your concern."

"Where would they go?"

"For the last time, I don't know. They could be anywhere along the river's edge or out of Laplace completely."

Miller gets up, snatching his folder in one fell swoop, and is out the door before Tom can utter his next breath.

"But…" His word falls silent.

12

MILLER GETS TO his leather swivel chair and plops his five-foot eleven-inch frame down with a heavy sigh. He swings around to the window overlooking the street.

The little store clerk from across the street is staring out of the shop window. Her pool-blue eyes meet his gaze just before disappearing from the window.

Miller picks his battles and turns around to call Callie. "Are you free to meet with me?"

"I can be free around 1:30 this afternoon."

"That would be okay. Can you meet me at the cantina on West Thomas Street?"

"Yes, I know where that is. I'll be there." *Click.*

Miller arrives early and sits out in front of the store. The aroma of coffee and pastries drift past his nose. He watches the people of Hammond passing by as he waits. He wants to put the tinted lenses in place just to see what tidbit of information they hold but decides to wait. He doesn't want to miss Callie's approach.

The sashay is unmistakable. The dark ringlets are held in order by a headband that matches the dress. The belted, button-down dress is a simple yet classy fashion statement for her; the royal blue is a nice choice and his favorite color. He opens the car door as she gets closer and stands there, one foot on the edge of the car and the other on the ground. He waits until she's next to the car to speak.

"Hello, Ms. St. Claire."

She turns toward the voice and smiles.

You are absolutely beautiful! He struggles to keep this encounter somewhat businesslike. Trying to keep his infatuation from showing on his face is getting harder for the young detective. For just a moment, Miller forgets she's here to answer more of his questions. He closes the car door and joins her on the sidewalk. With an underhand wave, he indicates to move inside, but when instructed to choose their table they locate one outdoors, away from the crowd, and make their selections.

"Why'd you lie to me at dinner the other night?" He comes straight to the point.

"She looks at him, her demeanor calm and her voice light and unwavering.

"Why do you assume I lied? What did I lie about?"

"You acted like you didn't know Cora, asking me if I knew where she was. You seemed surprised when you saw the picture of her... like it was the first time."

"I never said I didn't know about her." Her voice is as calm as a summer breeze. "I've known about her for months, but I've never met her. I've never seen her, so the picture you showed me was my first time. What I said was 'I've always felt like some part of me was somewhere else and I asked you if you knew where my sister was, Detective Miller. That is different from not knowing. And at no time was I lying about anything."

Her slight southern accent only adds to her allure, but he still needs to be Detective Miller until he closes this case. He can't let her get as embedded under his skin as she is in his head. He can't debate her explanation, so he moves on to something useful.

"You said you liked Daniel. What else can you tell me about him that will help me find who did this to him... or don't you care?"

"Honestly, Detective Miller, I don't care. Don't get me wrong, I liked Daniel. And under different circumstances, we probably could have had something good. But he and Paul were the reason I had to keep leaving my friends, my schools, and my homes. They were the reason my mom couldn't sleep at night. Daniel's job was to track down and find somebody who didn't want to be found. That's called meddlin' in other's affairs. Some people take their privacy very seriously."

"Some people take kidnapping very seriously, too. And taking a child across state lines is a federal offense. Even if it is a family member, it's against the law. Your aunt is looking at a lot of prison time. I have her on conspiracy charges, but when I add kidnapping, she may not get out. I also know your sister is involved, but if she was influenced by your aunt, they may cut her some slack. You may lose them both over this mess!"

Callie lowers her eyes and drinks her tea. He can tell she's wrestling with her emotions. "What do you want me to do, Detective?"

"Help me find them. That would be a great start."

"But I don't know where they are."

"Use whatever connections you have and figure out who's hiding them."

"I can ask around, but these people protect their own. I don't know if there's anything I can do."

Miller escorts Callie back to her car. He watches her until she is out of sight and returns to his office.

Branson is at his desk, phone in one hand and pencil with paper under the other. He is feverishly trying to dig his way out of his connection with this case and maintain his career.

Miller turns to his informant. With his back to the main floor of the office, he slips on the glasses. The images begin to emerge.

> *Edwards comes into view. Camera in hand, he leans against the waist-high wall and photographs from a small stone bridge at the park. When Miller tries to look in the same direction, he finds the images are too far away. He has little control over the glasses and can't bring the images any closer. He can barely make out the two people on the bench but continues to watch.*
>
> *Edwards is approached by someone from behind and when he turns around, Cora is standing there. She talks first and her movements are highly animated. She's angry. She points to the couple he's taking pictures of and yells even more. She slaps Edwards across the face and walks away quickly. He tries to follow her, but she turns to say something that stops him in his tracks. Then she leaves and so do the images in the glasses.*

"Man, why didn't you come with sound?" Miller screams at the glasses as he snatches them off of his face. It would be nice to know what these people are saying." He calls out to Branson. "Where are the photos from Edwards' camera?"

"They're all in a folder." He moves some things around on his desk. "Here, I have them here."

Miller flips through the pile of photos until he finds the ones from the park. He can see the couple he's looking for, but still needs the picture larger to see faces. He remembers his magnifier and digs through the drawer until he finds it. It enlarges the image just enough so he can make out the familiar ringlets. She's sitting with Paul St. Claire. He appears to be wearing the same dark gray suit as before. He takes the glasses from his pocket.

I thought you were showing me images related to Daniel's murder. Why would Paul St. Claire have anything to do with his death if he was the one that hired him? How is Daniel taking pictures of St. Claire and Callie together, if they just met at the restaurant? They lied about everything. Too many pieces of this puzzle are still missing.

Miller runs his fingers through his thick waves and turns toward the window. The strange little store clerk is in the window again.

He stands up to look down at her, but this time she doesn't run or look away. *What's wrong with you?* Miller decides to go to the shop to talk face to face.

She's waiting at the shop door when he approaches and opens it as soon as he steps up. She just as quickly closes and locks it again. The blue eyes speak volumes as they fill with tears and overflow. She's as tiny and thin as a rail; her black hair only makes the river blue eyes even brighter.

"You have something you want to tell me?" He asks softly.

"They say I can go to prison for helpin' Cora. She's been my friend for a long time. We grew up together 'long the river's edge. I just know she's scared, and Elyse isn't helpin'. It wasn't Cora's idea, ya know. Elyse put her up to it… sayin' she was going to go away for a long time if Cora didn't help her, but I didn't know she meant to kill that young man. He was kinda nice. Nosey, but nice. Always askin' questions 'bout folk here. I'm the one that called 911 after they dropped him in the woods. I didn't want to see him get eaten by the gators. He didn't deserve that. I tried to let you know where Callie was, too, and gave ya a hint about the twin, but you're a little slow." She snickers.

"Do you know where Cora and Elyse are now?"

"No. I do know they still in Louisiana, probably still 'long the river's edge, but I'm not sure who has them now. People takin' turns hidin' 'em."

"Do you know Paul St. Claire? What does he have to do with Daniel's death?"

"They told me Mr. St. Claire was Cora's daddy and he didn't even know she was alive. When Daniel found out there was two of them, he asked for more money, but Mr. St. Claire got madder than a snake."

Seems to run in the family. "Have you seen Ilysa James?"

"No, I don't think so. She never came back to the house they lived in. I live just a couple of houses down from them. Celia told me to keep an eye out in case she came back, but she never did. Just Callie. I was supposed to call her if Ilysa showed up."

"Do you know who cleaned up Edwards' apartment?"

"His landlord, Celia, and another man. I don't know his name. He helped get the body out of the apartment and into the woods. They also buried the car and cleaned it out. That's all. Am I still goin' to be in trouble?"

"Are you sure you don't know the other man?"

"Yes, I'm sure."

"Do you think you might recognize him again if you saw his face?"

"Definitely."

"If you keep helping me like this, I'll ask the judge for leniency. You call me when and if you get anything new on any of them. You may end up on probation for a year or two."

"That's better than prison. Thank you, Detective." She wipes her face dry and walks Miller to the front door.

Miller walks slowly back to his office, trying to process everything the little clerk told him. He's almost to the front door when Branson comes bolting out.

"I found Elyse! I know where she is!"

They sprint to their vehicle and speed off in the direction of the river's edge.

"Where are we headed?"

"She went home!"

"Why would she go back there if she knows we are still looking for her?"

"Guess she thought we wouldn't go back there since we already searched it. I don't know. Maybe she thought we were busy searching everywhere else."

"How do you know she's still there?"

"Someone saw her go into the house."

"Is Cora with her?"

"They didn't mention Cora."

Miller and Branson turn on lights and siren and push their squad car to the limit. The dust from the unpaved driveway fills the air as they screech to a halt. They arrive at the small cottage and find the door open. They announce themselves and enter the house. They find Elyse sitting at her kitchen table. Elyse watches as the men move about, a mug of teas in hand. She sips her tea as she continues to watch the men approach. She doesn't seem distressed by their presence. In fact, she seems a little too calm.

"Where's Cora?"

"She not here. Don't know where my baby girl is. You jus' remember she did nothin' to that boy. I did what I had to do to protect my baby, ya know? I couldn't let them take her away from me. Not after everythin' that happened. She was just a tiny, lifeless thing, but she came back … for me. It made up for all that man took away from me so many years ago. I tried to tell Ilysa, but she madder than a snake." Her voice drops low as she continues to sip her tea.

"She been my whole world for almost twenty-one years, but she grown now. I taught her how to take care of herself, my beautiful girl." Her eyes fill with tears. "She be all right without me now. She got her beautiful twin sister." Elyse smiles as her voice trails off. Her breath starts coming in short spurts and she holds her chest. Miller spots the vial on the countertop not far from the teapot and recognizes it as one of the same vials Celia had the baneberry in.

"Branson! Call 911 and get an ambulance here. Now!"

"What's wrong with her?"

"Same thing that killed Edwards! Call now!"

Branson makes the call. "Detective, what did she swallow?"

"White baneberry!" Elyse collapses to the floor.

"Hurry! She's dying!"

"They say you can't breathe for her without getting the poison in your mouth! Just work the chest compressions. It might help a little. Help is coming."

Elyse's glazed-over eyes are more than Miller wants to deal with. "Elyse, where's Cora?" Elyse slips quietly away. Her eyes close and her breathing stops.

Miller stops pumping her chest and sits on his knees, staring as the EMTs come to his side to check the body. They try oxygen and compressions for a few more minutes but pronounce her dead at the scene.

Miller tells them to bag the bottle on the counter for the lab. "Branson, do you have any idea where Cora might be?"

"I know a place I can try. She used to go there sometimes when she was sad. It's down along the river."

"Show me."

They watch the EMTs load Elyse's body into the ambulance before Branson leads the way to the river's edge. They walk a good half-mile along the river's bank before they see a teary-eyed Cora sitting alone on a fallen oak tree trunk.

Miller moves slowly so as not to frighten her. She's a fragile, less confident version of Callie. He sits next to her and waits.

"My momma?" She asks through tears still caught in her throat.

"She's gone, Cora. I'm so sorry." Cora leans her head over just a little until it settles on Miller's shoulder and cries. The scent of jasmine from her hair and skin floats up to Miller's nose. He sits there and lets her cry as Branson looks on from a distance. The sunshine bounces within her dark ringlets with each sob.

"What am I supposed to do now?" She asks when she finally catches her breath.

"First thing you have to do is remember everything your momma taught you. Then, I have someone who wants to meet you. Come with me."

THE THREE OF them walk back to the car and head for the office.

Miller makes a call along the way. When they arrive back at headquarters, Callie is there waiting. She's heard the news about Elyse and opens her arms wide to embrace her crying twin. Miller and Branson give them a little time before escorting them both to Miller's office. The girls sit quietly for a moment while Callie gently holds her sister's hand.

"Callie, have you heard from your mother yet?"

"Yes. I talked to her this morning. She's the one who told me about Elyse."

"How could she know? Elyse took her own life only ninety minutes ago. She couldn't have told you this morning. Maybe you misunderstood her?"

"No, Detective. I'm telling you the truth. She was crying when she told me. She said her sister's spirit whispered to her. A spirit can't talk to you unless it separates from the body."

"Where's your mother now?"

"I believe she's here in Hammond. She needs to be sure Paul is no longer a threat to her."

"Can you get in touch with her?"

"She'll get in touch with me when she thinks it's safe. Would it be all right if I take Cora home with me? She's got no one else."

"For tonight, but don't leave town."

"We don't have anywhere else to go."

The young women leave Miller's office having lost a mother and aunt to suicide. Ilysa is still MIA, but Detective Miller still isn't sure why.

Miller gets a compulsion to use his informant once again; it's as if the glasses are calling. He slips them on and lets the images come to life.

Daniel Edwards is in his apartment, seemingly going through his morning routine. He makes coffee then goes into the bathroom. He showers, shaves, brushes his teeth and combs his hair.

He starts preparing his breakfast then suddenly stops and looks toward the door. He peeps through the tiny glass hole in the door and sees a familiar face.

Edwards opens the door for Celia and invites her in, ushers her to a chair, pours two cups of coffee then goes back to the kitchen to cook breakfast. They're talking, but Miller hears no sound. Celia seizes the moment of inattention and slips the cylinder out of her pocket and pours it into his coffee. Edwards returns to the table with two plates of food and cream for the coffee. They chat over breakfast, but when Edwards tastes his coffee, he grimaces. Celia indicates hers is okay, so he adds more sugar and cream and tries again. After a second sip of the bitter coffee, he pushes it aside, but he's already taken in enough. They talk for another moment or two when he stops talking mid-sentence and is now having trouble breathing.

Celia looks on but offers no assistance. Daniel collapses onto the floor, clutching his chest. He looks to her for help, but she turns away, unable to witness the pain and agony she has just inflicted. She waits until she hears no more movement then slowly walks out the door, never looking back. When she gets to her car, she tosses the container behind a small bush and sits to make a phone call. Within minutes Tom appears with a tall, heavy-set man.

Miller only gets a brief glimpse of his face. They wrap Edwards in a heavy tarp and carry him out the back. The tunnel access will make it easy to get him to the basement of the little shop.

The images blur before Miller's eyes and he removes the glasses. He turns back to face his desk and sees a fellow detective standing in the doorway. "What?"

"What? What do you mean what? What's up with you and those glasses? The lights too bright in here or something?"

"No, they're not sunglasses. They—they help me think. Anyway, don't you have something better to do than stand around my office?"

Dismissed, the officer turns on his heel and walks out, closing the door behind him.

Miller picks up the phone. "This is Detective Miller. I need to get the cell phone records for Celia Morales spanning the last three months. Cross-check them with the phone records for Tom Bradley at the Treasure Cove Apartments." Miller hangs up, only to make a second call. "Branson, are you anywhere near the Treasure Cove Apartments?"

"I'm about fifteen minutes away."

"Do you have gloves and bags with you?"

"Of course. My kit is always stocked."

"Go to the apartments. There are small bushes near the parking area. I need you to check carefully for a small plastic cylinder. Handle it very carefully."

It's not long before he has the phone records in hand. He makes one more call to the coroner's office to verify the official date and time of death, then checks the phone calls Celia made on that date. As he scans the pages looking for the number that matches Bradley's office, he sees another familiar number. *That number!* He knows that number. He pulls out his notes. *Gotcha!*

~ ~**~ ~

The Louisiana sun is high, and humidity is even higher. Branson checks behind every little bush in the parking area until he finally finds the right one. "Detective Miller, I found the cylinder you were looking for. Should I take this to the lab first?"

"Yes, and tell Dennis we need results now!"

He calls headquarters, "I want arrest warrants for Celia Morales, Tom Bradley, and Paul St. Claire." Officers are dispatched to the residences and last known locations, respectively. Within hours, all are hand-cuffed, sitting in the back of squad cars, and on their way to headquarters.

Dispatch squawks on the squad car radio and announces, "Detective Miller, we have Celia Morales, Tom Bradley, and Paul St. Claire in custody."

Miller finally gets to make the call he's been waiting to make. His hands sweat a little as he picks up the phone. He calls Callie. "We have Celia Morales, Tom Bradley, and Paul St. Claire in custody for the death of Daniel Edwards."

"Why would my father want Daniel dead? He hired Daniel to find us!"

"Paul had a couple of reasons. He didn't like the idea that Edwards was getting so close to you. He was hired to find you and your mother, not get emotionally involved with you. Once Daniel found out there were two of you, he upped the price, got greedy, and your dad didn't want to pay. We know your dad paid Tom Bradley and Celia for their parts, and we also confirmed your father's involvement with Celia through their cell phone records. We know she called him right after she killed Edwards. We found the container she used for the white baneberry. The lab is checking for prints and traces of the poison. Once they confirm my suspicions, we can close this case. By the way, how's Cora?"

"She's fine; sleeping now. She took Elyse's suicide hard."

"I'm sure. I have nothing physical linking her to Daniel's death, and without Elyse's testimony, there is no one to say she participated. I don't think any of the people who did so much to protect her are going to put her in harm's way now. So, it looks like she's off the hook. If I hear anything else, I'll call."

"Thank you, Detective Miller."

He wishes he had something else to talk to her about but lets her hang up. With this case coming to a close, he wonders if she will talk to him again. His cell phone vibrates in his pocket. It's Dennis.

"Detective Miller, it's Dennis. I've got good news and weird news. Which do you want first?"

"Give me the good news."

"Okay. The cylinder found outside of Daniel Edwards' apartment had enough trace in it to test. It tested positive for Actaea Pachypoda, and the prints on it came back to Celia Morales. The weird news is the second cylinder found in the home of Elyse James came back positive for Actaea Pachypoda also, but the prints aren't hers so you might consider ruling out suicide."

"Whose prints are they?"

"Don't know. They're not in the database."

Damn!

Miller's View

A Look into the Darkness

Book #2

1

THE AGE-WORN FACE of Elyse James, as she gripped her chest and struggled to breathe, still troubles Detective Jonathan Miller. The possibility that Elyse did not commit suicide lingers like a bad dream, but his informant has yet to reveal another scenario. He keeps it close; protected, its unique feature remains his.

A year has passed since the murder of Daniel Edwards and no case since has left him with so many unanswered questions. Miller stares at the rose-tinted glasses that give him the fragments. They set, ominously quiet on his desk; he never knows when or what they will reveal. And though they helped him bring closure to one murder investigation, he is still being haunted by another.

"Detective Miller, line one!" Someone shouts from across the room.

"Detective Miller here, how can I help you?"

"Unburyin' the past sometimes wake up ugly things," the voice spoke softly on the other end.

Alarms resound in Miller's head. The words, he knows, the voice he knows, but it can't be her; she's been dead for a year. Who is this on the phone? No one had been around when Elyse said those words to him. Miller has never repeated them to anyone or added them in his report. Maybe Elyse is just making a plea, *don't forget me?* The print that they found on the vial of white baneberry doesn't belong to her, but they still don't have a match. Her daughter, Cora, was cleared of suspicion since she was the only other person in the home at the time. *I still need a few answers for Elyse James.*

The rose-tinted glasses set comfortably on Miller's desk and a stack of files block them from the prying eyes that peek inside. Miller glances into the lenses and sees his reflection for just a moment. Then they do something they have never done before. The lenses flicker with an image; then it disappears. Miller picks up the glasses, looking at them closely, but when they don't repeat the image, he slowly puts them in his pocket. He doesn't want to put them on in the office.

People still question his attachment to them, and he tires of the need for excuses. Things are a little slow this morning, so Miller packs a few of his case files and goes home. His apartment is conveniently close to headquarters and his status at work allows him more flexibility than some. Miller gingerly steps inside and looks around. He doesn't consider himself a slob but has to admit the place is a mess. *I gotta get a new cleaning lady. The place hasn't looked the same since Celia went to prison.* He tosses his case on top of the pile of magazines on the coffee table. He'll clear it later. He drops his almost dead weight into his favorite chair and takes a deep breath and removes the glasses from his pocket.

He takes another deep breath, puts them on, and lets the images play in front of him:

> *Callie St. Claire and Cora James are enjoying the sun in Hessville Park while catching up on the past twenty-one years. The identical twins, though the same in appearance, are like night and day in personality. They sit on a park bench just feet from a fountain. There is the slightest of rainfall and neither girl seems to mind. Callie has taken care to update her sister's wardrobe and Cora is looking more the identical twin than ever. Their laughter fills the air and things between them are as they should be. Someone taps Cora on the back of her shoulder, and it makes her turn. Her face shows surprise and recognition. The figure standing behind the bench is petite and also well dressed. When Callie turns, she too seems surprised. The look of relief is also evident on her face. Miller can assume with confidence that the person is Ilysa. She walks around to the front of the bench to sit between the twins and joins the conversation. Touching the face of her baby Cora is something she has waited so long to do, but she has been in hiding since the Edwards case — Miller has no idea where or why. She has her girls together again. Suddenly, Miller notices that all of the women have stopped talking. All three ladies catch the approaching long, large shadow as it glides across the grass directly in front of them and they lift their heads simultaneously.*

The images within the glasses begin to fade.

Detective Miller removes the glasses and stores them in his shirt pocket. *Ilysa is nearby. I still need to find her. Even if the girls know where she is, will they tell me?* He tries his luck with Cora first and decides to pay her a visit.

He goes to his squad car; the route to Elyse's cottage is still tucked into the recesses of his memory. As he drives the road shaded by moss-covered trees, Miller calls Branson at headquarters and heads for the river's edge.

"Ted, I'm on my way to Elyse's cottage to talk to Cora, meet me there. I'm leaving now."

"On my way, Detective."

~~**~~

Miller and Branson arrive at the cottage by late morning, but the smell of burnt toast and grits is still strong in the air. The screened porch and front doors are open.

"Wait here."

Miller approaches slowly because the steps are in no better shape than the last time he was here. The wood on the porch creaks with every step. No one could ever sneak up on these people. He is careful as he knocks on the splintered wood frame of the door. There is no answer. He knocks again and announces himself. Again, there is no answer. Miller grips his weapon in his shoulder holster and proceeds inside. He checks each room and finds nothing out of the ordinary. He turns to leave when he hears footsteps coming from the room overhead. He'd forgotten about the staircase at the side of the porch that lead to the attic. When he steps back onto the porch, Cora is at the bottom of the staircase. Miller glances up, Cora follows suit.

"Detective Miller, I stay up there now, I haven't been able to sleep downstairs since Elyse…," her voice trails off.

"Hello again, Ms. James. Your doors were open and…."

She cuts him off dropping eye contact and allowing the dark ringlets to fall into her face. "Yes, I know. Elyse did most of the cookin' and I had a little trouble with breakfast; 'sides, it's a beautiful day for just airin' out the house." Miller hears the voice of a child caught playing with the stove. "Would you like to come in?"

"Yes, that's fine, just for a moment." When he looks back, Branson is leaning against the hood of his car, watching.

~~**~~

"Why did he call me out here? He can't possibly need help with Cora. She's five-feet, one hundred-sixteen soaking wet."

~~**~~

Cora and Miller settle down in a small, but comfortable living room. He sits wringing his hands together, like a schoolboy about to ask a girl to dance.

"What can I do for you, Detective?"

He hesitates, not wanting to look up, but when he does, he looks at her face.

It's a mirror image of Callie St Claire; the honey-brown skin tone is offset by the dark ringlet hair. The dark-chocolate eyes and smile have a touch of sadness that Callie doesn't let show and Miller still believes that Callie is the most beautiful girl in Hammond. He never dreamed there would be two of them. His hint to their identity is the shooting star on Cora's left shoulder. Today, it peeks at him from under a short sleeve top. Looking at her makes him long for Callie again.

"I am hoping you've been in touch with your Aunt Ilysa, and maybe you can tell me where she is right now. I need to talk to her."

"You mean my momma, don't you, Detective Miller? Why do you still need Ilysa?"

"Yes, sorry, I just have a few questions about your mom, I mean Elyse, and I need Ilysa o help sort things out;she could shed some light on a few things."

"Be careful, Detective. Unburyin' the past sometimes wake up ugly things."

"Cora, did you call my office this morning?"

"Why would I do that?"

"Someone called my office this morning and used those exact words. Your mom, Elyse, said them to me when I first talked to her a year ago. I never told anyone else what she said."

Cora's face quivered. "I can tell you I didn't call."

"Where is Ilysa?"

"I don't know, I haven't seen her."

"You have seen her. You and Callie were talking with her at the Park; and who walked up on you three while you were talking?"

Cora jumps up from her seat. "What? What are you doin'? Are you followin' us around?" Her eyes are wide with fear and her voice shakes, "How could you know we were in the park?"

Miller isn't surprised by her reaction; she doesn't have the calm, unshakable façade of her twin. This one rattles.

"It doesn't matter how I know, where is Ilysa?"

"I think she is stayin' with Callie, but I'm not sure."

"The next time you see her, tell her she needs to come and talk to me. I want to help; I'm trying to help, but I can't if she doesn't talk to me." Detective Miller stands to leave. When he gets to the front door, he turns back to where Cora is standing. He scratches his fingers through his thick curly hair. She is almost the perfect twin.

He decides to give Callie a call. Miller searches his phone to see if Callie's number is still there. He never deleted it from a year ago during the Edwards case, why wouldn't it be there? He'd thought about deleting it but couldn't push that button. *Maybe she changed her number. Maybe she won't answer. Maybe… oh, Jonathan, just call the girl.* He finds her number and listens as the numbers sing out their tones. He steps away from Branson and within moments, he can hear the ringing sound of her phone and feel the sweat pooling in his palm.

"Hello." At the sound of her voice, Jonathan feels a wave of something he's never felt.

"Hello, Callie, this is Jonathan. Jonathan Miller… Detective Miller…uh, how have you been?" He responds, struggling for composure.

"I'm fine, Detective, how have you been?"

"Good, thanks."

"We haven't talked in about a year. What can I do for you?"

"Callie, I am trying to locate your mother. Is she with you?" There is a long pause before he tries again. "Callie?"

"I'm still here." Jonathan wished he could hear her say his name, but she doesn't.

"Callie, where is Ilysa? Don't tell me you don't know; I know you and Cora were with her at Hessville park recently."

"How could you possibly know that? Are you following me now, Detective Miller?"

She was the Callie he remembered; always calm, so unlike her sister. But Jonathan knew he couldn't answer her question.

"No, I'm not following you, Callie, but I still need to talk to Ilysa. Where is she?"

"This has been a trying year for my mom. Her lover is in jail, her sister is dead, and she is trying to get to know the daughter she thought was dead. Maybe you should allow her a little time."

"I just want to talk to her. There are some things about Elyse …."

"I'm pretty sure she doesn't want to talk about Aunt Elyse, but the next time I see or speak with her, I will pass along your request." Her voice is still soft and calm. She's completely unruffled by Jonathan's interest in her mother.

"Callie …." But Callie disconnects.

He cuts his losses and the two head back to his office. And though his conversation with her is over, his thoughts begin to roam. He remembers each encounter, every conversation, and yes, dinner with Callie and her father. He has to make sure Callie is not implicated in the death of Elyse, and then he can take it from there.

~~**~~

Callie's thoughts turn to Jonathan's face, the night of their dinner together. He was charming. She remembers the cologne from the jacket he put around her shoulders and smiles. *Could it be possible?* She tries to keep her mind on the road, but the thoughts of Jonathan keep interrupting. Young men have always been attracted to her, but it usually went nowhere because she and her mom were always on the move. She could never stay in one place long enough to have a relationship. Now, here she is again, running. *I have been running since before my birth. When is this going to stop?*

BRANSON GETS OUT of his squad car and goes inside, but before Miller gets out of his car, he pulls his informant from his pocket. Checking to see that there is no one around, it's a perfect time to see what they might show him. He holds open a file folder so anyone walking by would simply think he was reading. He gently glides the glasses onto his face and lets the images come into focus.

*The yellow banner overhead reads **12th Annual Tangipahoa Parish 4-H Pet Parade and Family Fun Fest at Zemurray Park**, featuring a country dance contest. People are gathering in a huge field. Musicians tune their instruments causing passersby to stop and look while folks in colorful costumes prepare for a night of competition. Smoke rising from the dozens of grills has others preparing themselves for the local cuisine. Vendors in aprons prepare the succulent dishes that the crowd will devour, with the spices that are Louisiana. Miller studies the faces in the crowd and recognizes quite a few. Karen is from his favorite coffee shop and Jesse works in the cleaners. As Miller continues to watch, he notices a young woman he has never seen before. She appears to be one of the dance contestants. She is tall, slender, with hair like Callie, only long and blonde. Her slender legs extend from the short skirt like a gazelle. He begins to notice how other contestants are watching her; especially one man, who can't seem to take his eyes off of her. It probably wouldn't have been a problem, except the expression of the short brunette beside him told another story. The brunette watches the man beside her, as he practically drools over this young woman, before turning on her heels and leaving in a huff.*

The images begin to fade as the man turns to pursue. Miller isn't sure because the image is cloudy, but the man resembles the same one from the Edwards apartment a year ago. The height and build would be about right.

"What was that about? Does this have anything to do with Elyse or Edwards?" Miller would like to put a nice pretty bow on his last case. He decides to make a note about what he just saw in the glasses and return to it later.

When he goes inside the building, he passes Ted Branson, several other officers, and another tall gentleman in a finely tailored suit Miller decides he can't afford even with his detective salary. The man's eyes follow Miller for a moment and then he returns to the conversation with the others. A bell, the size of a gnat, goes off in Miller's head, but he shakes it off.

"Too much free time, gentlemen!" He yells back as he takes the stairs by two to his office. "Branson, I need you in my office!"

"On my way, Detective!"

"Jerk." Someone from the group murmurs and they return to their conversation.

In his office, he closes the door, drops into his chair, and spins around a couple of times just as Branson pops in.

"Close the door, my caseload is growing daily, but we need to wrap this case up. We're close, I can feel it. I am determined to close Elyse's case before pursuing another investigation. What's the next step? Who else knows where I can find Ilysa? Paul St. Claire is still in jail; he's got another six months of his eighteen-month sentence. The landlord and Celia are still sitting behind bars for their role in Daniel Edward's murder."

"What about the store clerk. What was her name again?" Branson says jotting as he talks.

Miller finds his file and flips through his notes on the case. "Yeah, Avery Jarreau. The judge gave her just two years on probation. I wonder if she is still working across the street."

Miller turns 180 degrees and looks out of the window to the street below. He can see the shop window. The sign on the door says, "OPEN." He grabs his jacket and starts for the store.

"I'll be back," with a poor impersonation of Arnold Schwarzenegger in the terminator he laughs as he goes out the door.

Miller quickly crosses the street, pretending not to notice the loud voices coming from around the corner. He plays it cool and crosses at an angle. It's just enough to be able to see the men who are yelling. One has his back to Miller, but judging by the gray hair and uniform, he's an older officer and the other is the tall man from the group chatting inside. He glances up halfway and notices that the sign on the door now says, "CLOSED." He stops in his tracks, not noticing the approaching car.

The blaring horn and screeching tires make Miller turn and jump backward, landing on his butt; his arms and feet move him with crab-like quickness even further from the vehicle. Cars behind the first one screech to a synchronized halt as he gets to his feet, feeling quite the fool; all eyes are on him now, including the two men. He brushes the dirt from his hands and clothes, waves to the old geezer behind the wheel, and lets him go.

"Tryin' to git yourself kilt, son?" The old man yells as he passes.

The embarrassed detective gathers up what's left of his wounded ego and hobbles, as straight as possible, back to the building. He'll try his luck tomorrow morning to talk to the young clerk. He feels the laser-focus of people staring at him from the street back to his desk.

"You okay, Detective? We heard the commotion from the street. You trying to get yourself killed?"

"No, just got distracted. I shouldn't have stopped like that, another bad habit of mine. I'm fine though, thanks." He scratches his fingers through his curly hair.

Miller wraps his arms around a stack of case files and pulls them closer to his chest, trying to ignore the stares and whispers. *It wasn't that serious, people; move along.* Frustrated with the attention, he grabs a few more of his files, not caring which ones, puts them in his briefcase, and leaves for the day. At home, he'll be able to think and get his heartbeat back to a normal rhythm.

Miller makes the short trip back to his apartment. It's not even far enough away for the drive to calm him down or clear his head. He parks the car and realizes he has a white-knuckled grip on the steering wheel and when he lets go, his hands are still shaking.

Miller tosses his folders along with his cell phone, onto the kitchen breakfast bar. He fixes a small glass of scotch on ice to settle his nerves and sits comfortably on a stool to read. He takes the time to review and prioritize them in his objective way. He randomly points, *Eenie, Meenie, Minie, Moe*, then grabs file number three, and begins thumbing through it.

"This isn't one of mine. How did this get in here?"

The folder holds a picture of the man Miller saw by the front door at headquarters and again in the glasses at the festival. *Oh, there you are!* All the sightings start pouring back into his head. Now he has a name.

Victor Scott was arrested three years ago, for domestic violence. Pictures of his wife, Maryann Scott, are included in the file. Hospital records of her injuries show how her husband had brutally beaten her on more than one occasion. *She never pressed charges.* Miller is guessing, but without the bruises, she could be the brunette from the dance contest.

Of all the cases on his desk, he still manages to grab Victor Scott's file. *Something or someone seems to be pushing this guy in my face.* He reads up on Scott for just a few moments and is surprised to find that he was born in Miller's hometown, just two years earlier than himself. Miller felt his gut tighten for a moment and not finding anything else of significance, he takes Scott's file and puts it aside. It can wait.

MILLER'S PHONE VIBRATES and shimmies across the shiny breakfast bar. After the third buzz, he glances over to read the ID screen. It's Callie! He grabs for the phone and knocks over his glass of scotch, spilling its contents all over the bar and some of the papers from the file. It runs everywhere, including onto his clothing and the cold liquid makes him jump up from his seat. He grabs a kitchen towel to attack the spill and by the time he gets to the phone, the call has disconnected. He decides to get himself and his mess cleaned up before trying to return the call. And considering the kind of day it's been, maybe tomorrow would be better; he might say something he shouldn't and then he'd have to shoot himself. Miller calls it a night, hits a hot shower, and crashes as if someone has hit him over the head.

But the night passes much too quickly for Miller and the vibration on his nightstand bounces his phone until it nearly goes over the edge of the table. He snatches it up just before it can hit the floor.

"Miller here," he grumbles into the phone, not even bothering with the ID this time

"Detective Miller, this is Callie St. Claire."

Jonathan quickly awakens at the sound of her name. "I'm sorry to bother you at such an awful time, but I need to see you," she says in that same unruffled, in-total-control kind of voice.

"No, no, it's okay. I was, uh…, I should be getting up." Jonathan takes his first glance at the clock. It's 5:00 AM. He doesn't care; she's calling him. She wants to see him. He doesn't care why.

"Hessville Park, near the ice park on 173rd street. 9 AM okay with you?"

"Sure, I know where that is. 9:00 is good for me; I'll bring the coffee."

"Bring three cups." CLICK

Three cups? He is a little confused and a little disappointed but also wonders if he should be worried. Who is she bringing? And why? Miller realizes it's off the beaten path, especially for this time of year, but maybe she just wants someplace away from the frenzy of the morning rush. As he lays there smiling at the picture of him having coffee in the morning sun, with the beautiful Callie St. Claire, he senses he should arrange for backup.

Miller stops by the local café du jour and picks up three cups of coffee as promised, cream and sugar on the side.

"Three cups of coffee, Detective? Planning on a long day?" Asks Karen.

"Got a date, sort of."

"Umm, a threesome, and I wasn't invited." Miller smiles at Karen's daily flirtations.

"Thanks, Karen, maybe next time."

On his way to the park, Miller's inner voice tells him again to make a call. Hessville Park is pretty big and fairly empty this time of the morning; only moms and nannies with infants and toddlers are moving about. The ice park is closed, so privacy won't be a problem. Miller treks the quarter-mile into the park and arrives at the designated area. Even from a distance, he smiles at how attractive this young woman is. Her dark ringlet hair flutters in the soft breeze and her honey-colored skin softly shines in the sunlight. Miller's powers of observation kick in, noticing he has three coffees, and she is sitting there alone.

"You said to bring three cups; got a caffeine thing going on I need to be worried about?"

"No," she says with a soft smile and a slight tilt of the head, "she said she would come." Jonathan loves the sound of Callie's voice. Tranquil, like un-rippled waters.

"Who are we waiting for?"

But before she can answer, her eyes catch the walk of the petite figure, coming along the path. Miller turns around to see Ilysa coming towards them. Miller sets the coffee on the bench beside Callie and waits to greet the woman from the shadows.

Miller watches the smooth saunter of the woman as she approaches. Her calm expression makes him wonder if she will give him any information.

"Good morning, Ms. James. It's good to finally meet you. Your daughters look very much like their mother."

Ilysa gives Miller a soft, obligatory smile.

"I never had a chance to give my condolences for the loss of your sister," he adds as Ilysa settles onto the bench with Callie. She gently touches Callie's face before turning back towards Miller. She and Callie share the same clear, honey-brown skin, but hers has a few wrinkles left behind by the stress and worry of twenty years of running.

"My daughter says you need my help. What can I help you with, Detective?"

"I realize it has been a year, Ms. James, but I need to ask you what you remember about the events surrounding your sister's death," he says, taking the seat next to Ilysa.

"I don't remember anything about her death, Detective. I remember that I found my daughter that she took and hid from me; my sister, how could she do that? I remember that boy that was following us around, meddlin' in other people's affairs. I remember being afraid of that nuisance of a man, Paul, who didn't want me or his child when it mattered and then sent someone to track me. That's what I remember."

"A fingerprint, not belonging to your sister, was found on a small vial in her kitchen. We know it doesn't belong to Cora. It's not a match for Celia, the landlord, Tom Bradley, or Paul St. Claire. You two are the only ones left that had any connection to this case. I would like to fingerprint you both, to rule you out."

"No," Ilysa's answer is quick and firm. Her tone leaves no room for negotiation.

"I can have you both summoned by a judge for your prints. Unless you can tell me who else would have handled that vial of poison."

"I don't know; I don't care; it won't change anything. It won't give me back the twenty years I missed with my girl."

Miller looks at Callie with the obvious question on his face, but Callie just turns and looks off into the distance. No response. They all know that if either Callie or Ilysa agrees to be fingerprinted, it narrows the list of suspects down to one. Neither Callie nor Ilysa is willing to give up the other. Miller knows and understands, but Elyse, even after everything, didn't have to die because she was trying to fill a gaping hole in her heart. Miller's sworn duty compels him to close this case once and for all.

"Are you going to make me arrest you or are you going to tell me what happened?"

"I've told you all that I can and now I am leaving," says Ilysa. "That young man is dead; Elyse is dead; Paul is in jail, and those other two are in jail. Haven't enough people been punished, Detective?" Her voice is low and unwavering. Now he knows where Callie gets it.

"I appreciate you meeting with me, but I can't just let you go, Ms. James. Ten minutes down at headquarters and I will have my answer."

Ilysa stands up, poised to leave, but stops to look at Callie. Miller doesn't budge. Callie reaches for her mother's hand and looks up at her as the dark curls flutter in the breeze, but Miller can't interpret the look. It doesn't matter. Ilysa starts walking back down the path the way she had come. Before she can get fifty feet, she spots a uniformed officer coming from her left. She turns her back to him and begins to walk, and another officer is coming toward her. Ilysa does a slow 360-degree turn. There are uniforms all around her. There is nowhere to go. Miller is glad he made his call. He doesn't want to be the one to handcuff Ilysa in front of her daughter. Not this daughter; not Callie. He doesn't want to be seen as the bad guy in her eyes. When he turns to her, she is standing, watching, with tears in her eyes. He doesn't know what to say to her.

Callie St. Claire turns slowly and silently walks down a different path. She never looks back. He wants to talk to her; he wants to hold her. It takes every ounce of his self-control not to call her back instead, he watches her until she is completely out of his sight. If Ilysa's prints don't match the one on the vial of poison, then Callie becomes his prime suspect in the death of her Aunt Elyse. Miller isn't sure if he can handle that possibility. He's already watched her life turn upside down with the death of Daniel Edwards. That case landed her father in jail and returned an identical twin sister she never knew. Now, she has to watch as her mother is arrested for murder, a year later.

He turns his focus back to Ilysa, as she is being escorted to a squad car. She puts up no resistance at this point, but the cloud that has darkened her demeanor is huge and laden with emotion. Miller brings up the tail end of the cars returning to headquarters. Ilysa has been taken into interrogation room two to wait. Miller goes right in.

"Why, Ms. James? Why did you poison your sister?" He wastes no more time with pleasantries.

"You are mistaken. I didn't poison her."

"Are you telling me that Callie put the poison in her tea?"

"I'm telling you I didn't kill Elyse. I said nothing about Callie."

"But if you didn't, she is the only other possibility."

"Are you sure?" Her voice is incredibly calm. It's as if she has seen this movie and knows how it ends.

Miller runs through the list of possibilities again in his head. Callie is the only logical choice left. "I have to take you to be fingerprinted. I will get my answers."

"You're very handsome detective, you two would have made a handsome pair. It's a pity. Now, you will probably never see her again."

"What's that supposed to mean? 'Never see her again.' Is she going to run? If you are both innocent, why would she do that? Damn! You let us bring you in so she could have time to get away?" He reaches for his cell phone only to realize he must have left his phone in his car. He makes a mad dash out of the room, down the hall and up one flight, to the front desk of the building. He interrupts the officer at the desk. "I need roadblocks set up at all roads leading out of town. Look out for Callie St. Claire and apprehend, not assumed to be armed or dangerous!" He leans across the counter and watches as the officer calls in the order. Miller goes back to the interrogation room, where Ilysa is waiting, but when he opens the door, he finds an empty room. Miller sprints down the hall to the nearest exit door and finds it locked from the inside. He tries the stairway door. It too is locked. "How the devil did she get out of here? Where did she go?" Miller runs and checks every room on the floor. She is gone. Ilysa is in the wind. Again. And now, he is afraid, Callie is too. "What have I done?"

There are several officers in a small room, about midway down the hall. One of them is Branson. Miller opens the door and looks at the three.

"Did any of you see Ilysa James in the hall less than ten minutes ago?" They all shake their heads in response and continue their conversation.

Miller observes their behavior for just a moment and then closes the door. He looks up and down the hall, trying to find the crack that his 'wisp of smoke' just slipped through. *Someone had to let her out the rear door. There is no other way for her to have left this building. I will have somebody's butt in a sling for this!* Miller goes around to the back of the building, looking for anything. *She didn't just stroll away from here.* But as he reaches the rear exit, he sees a huge trash truck, more than halfway down the alley, making its weekly collections. It is now rolling over any hint of evidence of another vehicle being in the area, but he still goes to the exit door. He can see the tiny shoe print leading away from the building and they stop only feet away. Unfortunately, they stop where the tracks of the truck begin. The wide prints from the rolling dumpster simply blended with the tread of the vehicle. There's no way someone could separate them. Eyes closed, he leans his head back in frustration and when he opens them, sees his out.

Miller runs inside, bounds the stairs again two at a time, and rushes to the top floor. He goes to the building's security office looking for answers. He had spotted the rooftop cameras around the building from the alley and one of them should have caught her leaving. He puts his head in the door of the dimly lit office and sees two rows of cameras around the room: about eight or more. Many images of rooms, three floors, the alley, the front door, and the main lobby are all visible on one of these monitors. There is one monitor at the top and far left that is blank. There are only three uniformed personnel to watch all the monitors and one of those is asleep on his knuckles. Miller pounds loudly on the open door, causing the sleeping man to crash his forehead against the table. He aims his badge at the three and smiles. "Which one of you monitors the camera by the rear exit?" He held his breath, hoping it wasn't Rip Van Winkle.

"That would be me, sir," came the response from a petite, pony-tailed, brunette.

"Please don't tell me it's the one with the blank screen!"

The 'deer in the headlamps' look tells Miller she hadn't even noticed.

"Did you notice any activity near that exit, within the past twenty to twenty-five minutes?"

"No, sir, all has been quiet. Besides, someone would need a key to exit from that area."

"How many people have a key to that door?"

"You will have to ask maintenance. I don't know."

"Are you recording on these?"

"Yep, up to forty-eight hours at a time, and then they check to make sure nothing is out of the ordinary before they rewind and reuse."

"Good, rewind the tape, for that camera, back about thirty minutes."

"I'm sorry, sir; I can't without orders from Chief of Security, Captain Harrison. But if they find someone unauthorized to exit through that door, it will be reviewed. The Head of Security selects a few officers in the department to help review the tapes just in case we miss something. It may take them another day or so to go through them all."

"I'll be back," he says as he leaves the office. "She's got to be on that tape; she couldn't just vanish."

4

FRUSTRATED WITH THE disappearance of Ilysa, Miller goes to his desk and calls the head of security.

"This is Detective Jonathan Miller. I need to get clearance for the video feed from this afternoon's tape. A woman I was questioning was gone from interrogation room two when I returned. I need to see if someone let her out of the rear of the building."

"That shouldn't be a problem. We review tapes every forty-eight hours. If we see something out of the ordinary, there is an investigation."

"Is there any way to review the tapes prior to the forty-eight hours? It would be helpful to see them now."

"Detective, do you know what it takes to shut down this system? It takes Form-5433-8 to obtain an access code. A Form 3424-C to obtain an alternate tape for recording while your tape in question is being reviewed. A Form 1022 explains why you need to review the tapes and four signatures. It's Thursday morning, the team will see the tapes on Saturday morning. I will call you personally if we find anything."

"Fine, I will wait for your call on Saturday." Miller hangs up and raises his hand to slap his desk, but the memory of the pain from hitting his dashboard a year ago stops him within inches of the tabletop. His wrist took two and a half months to heal.

He walks around his desk and closes the door to his office. When he sits back in his chair, he glances through the big window to see if anyone is watching him and then turns his back to the door. He slips his informant from his pocket, with the hopes of seeing who is helping Ilysa move through the city undetected:

Miller lets the glasses fill his mind with the strange vision and sees Victor sitting with a thin young blonde at a local coffee shop. Miller recognizes the décor as Café Nola. He's been there several times for coffee. He doesn't recognize the young woman with Victor. Her long hair is pulled up into a ponytail and it gives her the look of sweet sixteen. But the thin-strapped dress looks like she just crawled out of bed. Victor's height, even sitting, makes her have to lift her chin to talk to him. His button-down shirt and slacks not only make him look semi-business but much older than she. She is grinning like a schoolgirl in love with the first-string quarterback, but Victor's expression is more annoyed than jovial. He looks distracted. He is leaning back in his chair, one arm hanging over the back and his dead gaze is on the chattering creature in front of him. The young lady moves closer to the table and says something to Victor. He lurches forward and backhands her across her face, making the young girl jump back in her seat with a look of sheer terror on her face. The sound startles the patrons around them as they all stop what they're doing and turn in the direction of the couple. The waitress approaches their table cautiously and asks to take their order. A couple passes behind her as they exit the shop and glare at Victor with the disdain small-town people have for shoddy behavior. Miller notices another pair of eyes on the couple from the plate-glass window of the café. A small brunette watches the scene; a mix of anger and sadness appear on her face. Victor looks at the waitress, looks at the girl, and tosses a small wad of cash on the table before he stands and turns to leave. The wisp of a white cloud blocks his view and Miller removes the glasses.

What are you showing me? These images have nothing to do with my case! What am I supposed to do with this? I need to know if this Victor character is connected to Callie and Ilysa. He grabs a picture from his file, jams it into a plastic protective sheet, and goes to find Avery.

Miller sees that the door sign says open, and watches traffic this time as he crosses the street. He doesn't need a repeat of that stupid incident. The store looks dark, but he palms the glass door and enters. The pool-blue eyes peer at him from behind the counter.

Miller goes to the counter and slams the picture down in front of her. "Do you know this man?"

Avery picks up the sheet and studies the picture. "Yes."

"How? From where?"

"That's the big guy that helped Tom Bradley move the body and clean up everything."

"You're sure it's the same man?"

"Yes, I'm sure."

"Thank you, Avery." *He knows Tom and Ted; probably knows Celia. I'll bet he knows Cora.*

Miller leaves as quickly and as angrily as he entered. Armed with another print and a little more against Victor, he is almost ready to book him for spitting on the sidewalk.

MILLER STOPS BY the lab and finds Kevin donning safety goggles and a lab coat. He startles the young man with a pat on his back. Miller pushes the plastic sheet onto the table in front of him and looks him in the eye.

"There are prints on both sides of the bottom of this sheet, mine are at the top, see if any are a match to the print from the Edwards case. Log them in for Avery Jarreau, a twenty-year-old, Caucasian female. Call me as soon as you get a hit."

Miller's nerves are on high alert as he paces in his office. He's not waiting for Saturday; he can't. He makes a phone call to maintenance and has someone with keys to the back-door downstairs in minutes. As he waits for the janitor to find the right key, Miller searches the surrounding area. He glances up at the camera that's generating the blank screen. It's been angled towards the wall. Miller taps the old gentleman on the shoulder and points. The old man looks at Miller.

"I ain't do it," he says as he shakes his head and goes back to finding the key.

"I believe you," Miller laughs briefly. "How would someone get the key to this door?"

"Dey hang on a hook in da office. If you know dey dere, you jus' go git 'em. Trick is knowin' which one fits 'cause dey not marked." He fidgets with the keys a little longer before finding the right one. When the key slips easily into the hole, the elderly man cocks his head towards Miller and smiles.

The janitor opens the door to the alley like it's the door to a grand ballroom. Miller begins by checking the door sill to look for clues. Prints on the ground are from a small foot, toe and heel are narrow and probably only a size six. Perfect for the petite Ilysa. He looks up and scans the tops of nearby buildings.

There is a camera at the far end of the alley that is pointing his way. *Worth a shot.* He thanks the old man, walks into the tiny mom-pop mini-mart, and looks around. At least he knows where to come to fill his junk food cravings.

"I need to speak to the owner," he says to the young man behind the counter.

"My dad owns the shop; he won't be in for another hour."

"Do you know if your security camera in the alley is working?"

"I think so, but my dad will have to help you."

"No problem, I will be back."

Miller leaves but turns back just as he steps outside the door. The young man is already on his cell phone, talking in whispered tones. *You're a bit paranoid, Jonathan; he could just be talking to his girl.*

Miller returns an hour later, and the owner makes the tape available; it shows the hood of the SUV in the adjacent alley. The driver of the vehicle has a clear view of the door of the building and just waits. It opens quickly and Ilysa rushes out. Windows on the SUV are dark, so the driver is unidentifiable. The gray-haired officer opening the door is in uniform but is turned so that you can't see his face. The SUV pulls a quick left and stops just long enough for her to get in and then speeds down the alley. They are careful with everything except the car. The tags are clear enough to read and Miller calls it into the office.

It is only minutes later when dispatch gets back to him. "***TRBLMKR*** is registered to a Victor Scott," the dispatch agent responds.

Why does this guy keep popping up on my radar? "Get an APB out on those tags. And send me his home address. Somebody find this idiot and bring him in! Every officer on the street had better keep their eyes open for that car. If I find out he passed them on the street and they don't report it, I'm gonna have somebody's badge!"

Dispatch makes the broadcast. "All officers on patrol, be on the lookout for a silver SUV; tag Tom-Robert-Baker-Larry-Mitchell-Karl-Robert. The driver is wanted for questioning in the disappearance of Ilysa James. Warning: Detective Miller is out for blood on this one."

Miller goes back to the office. Feeling the heat rising from his collar, he curbs his urge to punch something. He goes back to the security office with the monitors. Looking at all the screens, he spots the one from the basement. It still shows nothing. Miller pounds on the door again.

"You!" He yells and points, scaring the bejeezus out of the young woman in front of the monitor. "What's your name?"

"Officer Jennifer St. John, sir," the young woman sputters.

"How long has that screen been blank?"

"Well." She stops and looks at her equipment, then at the monitor. "It seemed to be functioning when I came on duty. So about one hour."

"Is that NORMAL?!" Miller screams "No, sir."

"What is the procedure for cameras that are showing blank screens, miss?" Miller feels the veins in his face and neck bulging past their normal boundaries.

"A report is made, and security checks it out."

"Has *this* camera been reported?"

"I didn't notice until you mentioned it. I... I didn't."

"Who do you report to Officer St. John?"

"Chief of Security, Captain Harrison, sir." Her voice trails off as she watches Miller's back round the corner. "Man, he looks madder than a snake." Her coworkers nod in agreement and return to their monitors.

Miller strides into the office of Captain Harrison. The older man looks up from his desk, into the eyes of a crazy man.

"Detective, what the devil is wrong with you?"

"I just came from the security room. They haven't notified anyone about a misaligned camera. There is a camera in the basement, near interrogation, which has been facing a wall for at least an hour and no one has tried to correct it. It needs to be dusted for fingerprints, to see who has handled it and I don't want to have to wait forty-eight hours for answers. I need to know what that camera caught if anything. You're Head of Security. It's your job to handle this, but if I need to take this to Internal Affairs, I will. Someone let my suspect out of here before I could even get her processed. I want to know who, and I want to know today!"

"I'll get someone on it."

Miller tears out of the office mumbling, leaving the only intelligible word *'incompetent'* hanging in the air.

AS MILLER STORMS through headquarters, **TRBLMKR** is taking exit 50 off of the 55 and making its way onto a dirt road that leads under the highway. A white Mercury Mountaineer is waiting there in the shadows. Ilysa walks to the waiting vehicle, turns, and waves as the SUV speeds off, leaving a cloud of dust behind. She opens the door and just sticks her head inside. The smiles from her girls are all she needs to feel better.

"Where are we goin', mama?" Asks the voice from the back seat. Cora looks at Ilysa with the face of a child starving for love. She has her mother, her real mother, and Callie, and Elyse's death is a fading memory.

"North, baby, I found a place up north where we can stay."

"Do you think they will come looking for us?" Comes a question from the driver.

"I don't think for a moment that that young, handsome, Detective of yours," she looks right at Callie, "is going to let this go." She sits and straps herself into the car and the three get back onto the highway and drive two and a half hours northwest of Hammond. Ilysa believes she has found a place small enough to get off the radar. Pineville is a city in Rapides Parish. It nests close to Alexandria. They should be able to mix in well with a population of 15,000.

~~**~~

"Detective Miller, this is dispatch, Victor Scott has been located at his residence; silver SUV, tags **TRBLMKR**, is not at the scene.

"I'm not far, hold him there. I'm on my way." *Where's your car, Victor?* "Ted!, let's go!"

Miller and Branson arrive at the home of Victor and Maryann Scott. The entire driveway is overhung and shaded by huge oak on both sides. The large, two-story Victorian spreads out in front of Miller as if it has no beginning and no end. He can feel the hairs on the back of his neck rise as he looks around. The manicured landscaping, in the full bloom of magnificent colors, brings out the beauty that is Louisiana, but it does nothing to ease his agitation. He climbs the short staircase and stops in front of the eight-foot door. He looks up and down as Westminster Chimes play on the other side. It's not long before Maryann appears at the door and Miller's eyes are as wide as an owl.

"You look surprised, Detective."

"Yeah, I was half expecting someone in black and white to open the door."

Maryann giggles. "No, Detective, no servants here. Please, come inside." She opens the door wider and two large Russian Borzois are standing in the entrance to the corridor. Suddenly, the larger of the two is growling, showing large teeth, but Miller notices that the dog seems to be more focused on Maryann than him and Ted. The noise from the dog startles Maryann and she yells out. "Victor! Call the Rock!"

Victor whistles and both dogs run toward the sound.

She looks at Miller and then back at the Rock, "I hate that dog. The other one is so sweet, but the Rock is just mean. I think he wants to eat me or somethin'. Come with me, the other men are in Victor's office. This way."

"Thank you." Miller looks around as they walk behind Maryann.

She opens the door to the elaborate office, and they find two of Hammond's uniforms standing near, and Victor is seated at his replica of a presidential desk. Miller picks up on all the ostentatious artifacts surrounding this man. A replica of Caravaggio's 'Death of a Virgin' hangs on his wall, while Milo's 'Aphrodite' stands in mid-center of an adjacent wall. Even the rug in front of the desk was probably worth thousands. Miller is careful to stop just before stepping on it. He approaches slowly as he takes it all in. He can feel his eyes, trying to roll around in their sockets, but closes them long enough for the sensation to pass.

"Mr. Scott, I'm Detective Jonathan Miller. Sir, first, where is your silver SUV tag…"

"I know what my tags say detective, but I don't know where the car is now. I've told these officers; it was gone when I woke up this morning."

"And what time was that."

"I slept in, so around eleven."

"Did you call it in?"

"I haven't gotten around to it."

"It's four in the afternoon; your car is missing, and you haven't gotten around to it?"

"I have four more vehicles in the garage."

"Mr. Scott, what is it exactly that you do to afford all of this?" He says, waving his finger around the room.

"I'm a diamond broker, working with a group in Belgium, I dabble in Artwork and Antiquities, but mostly diamonds and yes, the desk is a replica of the Resolute Desk given to President Rutherford Hayes by Queen Victoria in 880."

"Excuse me?"

"You had that question on your face when you walked into the room."

"Oh. I wasn't aware that I cared. Well, here's a question I know I care about.

How do you know Ilysa James and her daughters, Callie St. Claire and Cora James?"

"I don't believe I do."

"You're sure you don't know them? Maybe if I show you some pictures." Miller pulls out pictures of the three ladies. Callie's picture is the last to come out and putting Callie's picture on his desk is difficult. Miller is slightly distracted and watches as her face slides slowly across the surface of the shiny desk. He wants to reach out, grab her back and protect her from this arrogant, annoying individual.

"I'm sure, Detective. Faces that beautiful, I would remember. No, I'm sorry, I don't recognize any of them. On the other hand, these two are quite beautiful, so maybe, if you find them, you could make the introductions." The smug look is a little too much for Miller to handle.

Miller's eyes narrow to a slit and his jaw went taut, but he's never been great at keeping his emotions off his face. "Okay, Mr. Scott, if I have any more questions, I will be in contact."

"Oooh, I see, you've got your eyes on one of them. Okay, I'm willing to share, maybe I can have the one you don't want," he says with a laugh.

Miller turns away before saying what he's thinking.

Branson and the two officers are dead on his heels. "That guy's a piece of work."

"Yeah. Dig up whatever else you can find on this guy. Let's see if diamonds are all he does. I got a bad feeling about this guy."

They get back to headquarters and Branson immediately goes to work on his computer. Victor Scott's life is about to go under the microscope and Miller is sure he won't like what he sees.

Six months later…

MILLER BELIEVES HE has lost Ilysa, but what hurts him, even more, is that he's probably lost Callie too. He's only seen her once since Edward's case. There has been no word on their whereabouts in months. She and Ilysa simply vanished, taking Cora with them. Miller has released photos of all three women. He pulled one of Ilysa from the internal monitors, from when they brought her into headquarters. Cora's picture was retrieved from the home. The photos went out to all law enforcement agencies in the state of Louisiana and beyond the borders, just in case they have crossed the state line. He just needs some idea whether they went north or south. Miller thought watching Callie walk away from him was hard. Not knowing if he'll ever see her again is tearing him apart inside.

He tries to focus on some of his other cases, including taking a closer look at Victor Scott, when early one morning on his way to work he gets a radio call from Hammond dispatch.

"There's been some activity on a credit card for Callie St. James. The name seemed a little questionable to the officer, but the sighting gives a pretty good physical description. It's in Pineville, northwest of Hammond. It should take you approximately two hours and fifty minutes to get there."

"I'm on my way." *Finally! I know where you are… Pineville!*

Miller's heart threatens to beat right through the walls of his chest. Partly because he can now move forward with his case; partly because he now knows where to find Callie. The drive to Pineville gives him a chance to calm his nerves and sort through the details of the case, but there is something about Victor Scott that is scratching at his moment of peace. He glances at the GPS and it tells him he is less than half an hour away. He flips on the band radio in the car and listens to the local chatter. The usual reports come over the waves and he almost tunes it out until he hears, "This is unit 231, single female spotted, possible suspect in that Hammond case." Miller perks up and listens closely. "Yeah, I pulled up the pictures of the three women they're looking for and she could be one of them. She's having coffee and reading a book at the Pelican Café on Esler Field Road. Are we supposed to contact Hammond?"

Miller quickly punches in the new location for his GPS. He is less than twenty minutes away. He picks up his handset and identifies himself.

"Dispatch, this is Detective Jonathan Miller from Hammond, I am less than twenty minutes from that area. Advise the officer to maintain visual, but do not approach. I repeat, do not approach. Miller out." When he arrives on the scene, he slowly approaches and finds a place to park where he can see her. He sits and watches her taking a deep breath of relief at the sight. The sunlight and breeze play with the dark ringlets and put a smile on his face. She is wearing the buttoned-down, royal blue dress he loves, and her poise and attitude are unmistakable. He is looking at Callie; he doesn't need the shooting star to be certain.

"Dispatch, Detective Miller here, I am on Esler Field Road with my suspect in sight. You can pull your guys back with my thanks. Miller out." He listens as the dispatch operator repeats his order. And now he simply waits her out, but at least can breathe again. He notices the glass of water on the table. *That's just what I need.* He reaches into the glove box and pulls out a pair of rubber gloves and a bag.

"Dispatch, Detective Miller here, can you get your lab, guys, on the phone?"

"Sure, Detective, I can patch you through."

Moments later. "Sir, this is Dorian in the crime lab, what can I do for you?"

"Dorian, if I brought you a glass, could you run a set of fingerprints for me?"

"Certainly, if they're in the system, it shouldn't take long."

"Thanks, I'll call when I'm on my way."

Miller waits for Callie to finish. He loves seeing her again. She lifts her face to the sun and smiles; she seems relaxed and enjoying her time alone. After another ten minutes, she signals to her waiter. The young man comes, check in hand and after Callie pays him, she takes one more sip of her water and collects her things to leave. Miller is already out of his car and moving slowly. He doesn't want to spook her; he just wants the glass. Miller stays on the opposite side of the street until she has passed him unaware. He crosses over just as the busboy moves towards her table and then Miller picks up speed. He swoops in and flashes his badge before the busboy can clean the table. Smiling at the waiter, he grabs the glass, tosses the remaining water, and places it in a bag. *I can get the answer I've been waiting for.* He goes back to his car and calls Dorian.

The crime lab is a quick twenty minutes away from the café and Miller is excited and scared. He is either going to find the one piece of evidence that clears Callie of Elyse's murder or sends her to prison. He hands over his treasure to Dorian, watches, and waits, while he works his magic on the glass. He uses a small air dryer to remove any moisture before dusting and removing the prints one by one.

"I have three good fingers and a thumb, the only one missing is the pinky. Must be a woman," he laughed.

"How did you decide that?"

"Raised pinky," he says, demonstrating, "guys don't usually do that." He laughed again. "Which finger do we have for comparison?"

"Right index," another small bell sounds in Miller's head.

"Great, I'll start with that one," says the tech.

Dorian takes the print and runs it through a database. It runs for what seems an eternity to Miller, but then he hears a beeping noise.

"You got a hit?"

"Well, not exactly. I didn't find a match in our database. Maybe I should try a different print."

"Run them all!"

Dorian sets the machine to run all the prints he had collected. After another thirty minutes. BEEP!

"Sorry, Detective, zilch."

"Enter the prints into the database for a Callie St. Claire, twenty-two-year-old, black female from Hammond, Louisiana. You can add a note that lists me as the contact detective. I will sort this out from home. Thanks for your help."

"No problem, and good luck."

Miller walks back to his car, not sure of how he is feeling. On the one hand, he now knows, it was not Callie's print on the vial. That moves Ilysa back into first place on the suspect list, but now, he needs to find her again. Pineville isn't huge, but there are plenty of nooks and crannies in which to hide. He will still need the help of the local PD. There is a bell clanging in his head that gets louder. He calls the lab at Hammond headquarters.

"Kevin, Detective Miller here. I need you to check something. Pull the Daniel Edwards file. Look for the lab work on the vial. How many prints were on it?"

Accessing the digital file, Kevin finds the information he needs. "One, Detective. Just the right index finger."

"Not even a partial print on the other side? Who can hold and squeeze a vial with just one finger?"

"It would be next to impossible."

"Thanks, Kevin."

"Oh, Detective, wait! I got one more for you. The plastic sheet you brought in got a hit to the vial — the index finger of Avery Jarreau is a match. Though, it still doesn't explain the one print."

Miller makes the long trip back to Hammond and with a starting place to looking for the three. He doesn't want to spook them into running any further. He will let them sit in Pineville until he can figure out how to proceed.

~~**~~

Branson is at his desk when Miller walks in.

"Help me sort something," Miller says as he sits in the side chair of Branson's desk. "I've just come from Pineville, where the local crime lab helped me run Callie's prints. They are not a match for the print on the vial from Elyse's case. Her prints were not in the system until today. We know it's not a match for Paul, Celia, Tom, or Cora and we still don't have a print for Ilysa. Am I still on track?" Branson is typing fast and furiously as Miller talks.

"Well, yeah and no. We have everyone else, but how do you know it's not a match for Cora? She's not in the system either."

"Why wouldn't she be in the system as part of the Edwards case?" Miller's glare unnerves the young officer.

"When we brought her into headquarters, we kind of introduced her to Callie and sent them home. We didn't charge her or Callie with a crime. Therefore, neither one was booked or fingerprinted. We don't have Cora's prints on file."

Not taking his glare from the young man, Miller stands and goes back to his office.

Branson continues to peck at his keyboard until suddenly he jumps up and runs to Miller. He goes in without knocking and his face has the wide-eyed look of a kid on Christmas morning.

"Detective! The old house, the one they left. There's no one there. Ilysa and Cora had to have touched something in the house. We have to find a print somewhere!"

"I've been so crazy with this case. Why didn't I think of that? I might not shoot you after all. That's using your head, Ted. Now you're starting to think like a detective. Let's go."

They grab their gear and head for Ilysa's home.

For a moment, Miller is excited. This puzzle is only a piece or two away from being complete, but he is still anxious, and the drive feels longer than it should.

~~**~~

Arriving at Ilysa's two-story home, Miller's heart, again, is pounding in his chest. He grabs his bag from the trunk and darts inside, leaving Branson still fidgeting for something in the car. The yellow crime scene tape is still across the door; he snatches it down and uses his lock picking tool to open it. He steps in and looks around for the best place to start. *Bedrooms?* Excited, Miller takes the stairs two at a time. He pokes his head into various doors and starts with the biggest room. He hears Branson coming through the front door and yells, "I'm upstairs in the Master!"

Branson sticks his head in the door and looks around. "I'll take the bathroom," he says, pointing to a smaller room.

The two put on their gloves, break out the dusting powder and get to work. Miller is all over the small bottles and knick-knacks on the dresser. He knows there has to be something there. He lifts and holds every bottle up to the light. *This woman has to have prints!* "Branson, are you finding anything?"

"Not yet, checking the medicine cabinet next. How are they not leaving prints, no one cleans that well."

How does someone move around the house and not leave a print? Miller looks at the dresser drawer knobs. Dusting all of them completely, he shines his flashlight and sees something on one. He pulls out a pocketknife and unscrews the drawer knob. There is a partial print on the bottom. "I may have something!"

He drops the knob into a bag and continues his search when he hears Branson yell from the bathroom. "I have a couple of prints on a prescription bottle of trazodone."

"An anti-depressant?"

"Yep, with all the confusion in her life, I can kinda understand it. Callie mentioned she was afraid and angry. Depression would probably fit in there somewhere, but why leave it behind?"

"Copy down the name and number of the doctor that prescribed it and keep looking. We need to make sure we have one print for Ilysa. If we only get Callie, we're back to square one."

The two spend the next two hours going through the kitchen and other rooms in the house. They collect over a dozen prints in hopes of getting Ilysa's and Cora's and then head back to headquarters.

Miller hands all the prints over to Branson and sends him straight to the lab. "Tell them to run them as quickly as possible." He turns and walks away.

"Yes, sir, I'm on it." Branson walks the long hall with the strides of a man on a mission. Carrying his bundle of baggies, he makes his way to the lab. The lab lacks the usual commotion and Branson notices only three techs moving about. He calls one over. "Where is everybody?"

"They needed extra help over in Ponchatoula, something big. Left us to run the place. What can I do for you?"

"Can you run some prints?"

"What am I matching them against?"

"A print on the vial from the Daniel Edwards case," Branson says as he jots down the case number for the tech. "If you could do this quickly, Detective Miller would appreciate it. Call this number when you get some answers."

"I'll see what I can do."

MILLER WALKS SLOWLY back to his office. The weight of the case is on his shoulders and closing it is key to lightening the load. He closes the door and walks behind his desk. His worn leather chair welcomes him like an old friend as he takes a moment away from his files and waits for his call from the lab tech. The vision of Callie lifting her face to the sun brings him a moment of peace.

He enjoys the leads from his informant, taking the bits and pieces as they come. He needs the answers; he can follow the breadcrumbs and they always help, even if he can't explain them to anyone. He lifts them from his pocket and places the glasses on, letting the images flow:

Miller watches as the small brunette enters the front door to her home; the door opens wide and lets the sunlight flood the foyer. She sets everything she has in her arms down next to the door, not bothering to close it. She stops moving and looks towards a long staircase to her right. Something has captured her attention. Her steps are slow and quiet as she moves towards the bottom of the staircase. She stands there for what seems to Miller an indeterminable amount of time before she begins to walk up, gripping the banister like a lifeline pulling her to shore. She slowly opens the door of the room to her right and cautiously pokes her head inside. The bed is bumping madly against the wall and the bed linen is losing its grip on the mattress. The woman in the doorway, Miller clearly sees, is the same from the festival and the photo in the file, less the bruising and swelling. It's Maryann Scott. She quietly closes the door, goes back down the stairs and out the front door. The glasses give Miller one last glance inside the bedroom as the linen flies backward uncovering a man and woman. He recognizes Scott and the young blond from the café as the images fade.

As Miller removes the glasses, a nasty taste in the back of his throat makes it swallow hard, and he reaches for a bottle of water on his desk. Victor is proving to be an unpleasant character.

He had some part in the Edwards case, no matter how small. Now, he is entwined in the James case and bound up in his life's confusion. Miller needs a name for this blonde.

Miller prepares to leave the office when his cell phone rings. The ID screen lets him know that the lab is calling.

"Miller here."

"Detective Miller, this is Willy from the lab, about those prints you wanted us to run. I didn't come up completely blank. The partial print is not enough to make a match. The usable prints, well, none are a match to the vial, several are not in the system and only two of the prints match a Callie St. Claire. The good news is, I got a hit on a set from the living room. They matched a domestic violence case a few years ago, for a Victor Scott. I logged all of them in just in case we get something else to compare them to."

"Thanks, Willy." CLICK

He lied about knowing Ilysa and the girls, but that's not surprising. Scott is back in my scope.

THE ROSE-COLORED INFORMANT rests comfortably on his desk and Miller still hasn't figured out how they do what they do. He grew up with the strange stories of the south, but never took them too seriously. Could he be dealing with magic? *Naw, Jonathan, get a grip!* He stares intently and the glasses begin to flicker, like a movie reel on the fritz. As soon as he picks them up the images go quiet. *Oh, you're toying with me now. What was that?*

The wheels within Miller's head go into overdrive and he begins his search through Daniel Edwards' file. *There has to be a reason they worked for you and no one else.* He digs through Daniel's history and finds his mother, Beth Edwards. Beth was a student of Philosophy and Religion, with a strong curiosity for African American religion at Piedmont College in Georgia. Piedmont's archives have all the past yearbooks and as he flips through page after page, Beth makes her appearance. Yearbooks are always fascinating reports of history and Miller continues to flip through, looking at the images of old. The gatherings of the students for various events fill the pages. He studies the faces, the youthful energy he remembers from his days at school shows on the faces in front of him. He sees Beth actively involved and seemingly normal, and his eye catches another young woman. She is much younger than he saw her before, but he knows her. He continues as his heart rate climbs; she is in every picture he finds of Beth. He finds another and marks the page, as he flips back to the book of students, to see if he can find her. Page after page, he tries to match this face. His eyes begin to blur after what seems like hours of staring. He makes it all the way to 'H' without any luck in finding her before he bookmarks his spot and closes out the website. He needs a break from the computer screen and stands to stretch his long frame. *That face: I know that face, it is so familiar to me.*

From his desk, he can see Branson at his desk, excitedly working on something. He doesn't even notice when Miller approaches his desk. His fingers are flying around the keyboard faster than the assistant at the main floor entrance.

"What do you have going there?"

"I've got good news and bad. The bad news is, I'm still digging things up on Victor and none of it is good. Born in Atlanta to Emma Scott, single mom, dad is not on record, but I know where to go to get his name, just haven't gotten it yet. Victor spent most of his childhood there, but they came here when he was in his early teens and he went to the local high school. In trouble for fighting in school, but he's got a sealed juvey record. I got into it and found out he beat up one of his teachers, Ms. Julia McClain. Seems our boy has a bit of a temper. He was ordered for psych evaluation and anger management classes. Ha, doesn't appear to have helped him."

"You are going to love this. I finally got a hold of the doctor on Ilysa's prescription, a Dr. Feldman and she has been on them for a few years now. Her doctor diagnosed her as clinically depressed with a side order of bipolar disorder. That was shortly after the birth of the twins. She was facing the death of one child on top of the rejection of the father, Paul St. Claire. Her sister vanishes with the baby and never speaks to her again. Every possible link to family and relationship vanishes before her eyes and Ilysa is left alone, with a baby to raise, for the next twenty years."

"No other family members?" Miller asks.

"No, as far as we can tell, Elyse was her only living relative."

"Okay, thanks."

"Wait, Detective, one more thing. She just had her prescription renewed. It came up as a pharmacy in Pineville."

"Can we narrow that down a bit?"

"Yes. We now have her address," he says with a smile.

"Oh, okay, that's narrow. Since she doesn't know that we know, I don't think she has any other reason to run. We will pay her a visit in the morning, go home and get some rest."

"Great, see you in the morning, Detective."

"Right. Oh, Branson… Good work."

Miller watches as the young man smiles and gathers his things from his desk and heads down the stairs. Over the past two years, Branson has redeemed himself and chosen which side of the law he *really* wants to be on. Miller has submitted the paperwork for his promotion to detective. He looks around the office and most of the lights have been turned off. The light of only two or three desk lamps gives the room a gloomy glow. He will continue his research later. He clicks the chain on his desk lamp and goes home. His career keeps him busy, but he wonders what it would be like to open his apartment door and find Callie waiting for him inside. When he opens his door now, he sees an apartment in need of a cleaning service. *I'll add it to the other 200 things on my 'to-do' list.* But no Callie. He reaches for his phone, stares at her name and number, and can't seem to push that button. He wants to talk about the case, any case; he just wants to talk to her. He pours a glass of golden 'screw the world' and tries to relax.

It's quiet, and Miller takes advantage of the solitude as he slips into the comfort of his thickly padded chair. He takes the glasses from his pocket and slides them onto his nose. This time, the focus on the images begins to sharpen.

> Miller is confused by these images. *There is a large group of people gathered in the middle of the street, looking down at something he can't see. He takes in the surrounding area as quickly as possible, trying to determine the location. They are in front of a store, but Miller can't make out the logo. He doesn't recognize the place or anyone he sees there. Suddenly, a man runs up and breaks through the crowd, frantically pushing people aside as he makes his way to the center. Anguished, he looks up at the faces surrounding him and pleads for help. He reaches down to lift the head and torso of a woman. All Miller can see is the long, blonde, curly hair falling to the ground. Her breathing is weak and shallow, and her nightgown hem is all but shredded and dirty. She is missing both shoes and resembles a rag doll in the man's arms. When the glasses shift their view, Miller can see her face. She opens her eyes to look at the man and a tear rolls down the side of her face. Pulling her close to him, he cries, as her eyes close again. The paramedics arrive and after a few minutes of CPR, they stop; it is too late for the woman. There is nothing they can do for her. As emergency personnel talk with the man, Miller gets a better look at his face. It's Victor! But who is the blonde woman and what has happened to her? Possibly the blonde from the café?* The images fade.

Miller knows he can't approach Victor with this situation just yet. He needs to know who the blonde is. And now he needs to know why she's dead. Are these visions past, present, or future? He decides to make Café Nola his first stop of the morning. Maybe someone there will know who she is.

It doesn't take him long to get there and his luck seems to be making a turn-around. He sees the same waitress from the glasses on duty and waits for her at an outdoor table. He reads her badge as she comes toward him.

"Hi Tara, I need to talk to you, can you break away for just a few moments?" He asks as he discreetly shows his shield.

"Yeah, sure, I'm due for my fifteen minutes. What can I help you with?"

"Do you know Victor Scott?"

"Yeah, I know Victor. Comes in two or three times a week."

"Have you ever seen him come in with a young blonde?"

"Lizette, sure. They have been coming in together for a couple of years now."

"Does this Lizette have a last name?"

"Umm, shucks. Hey Casey," she yells towards another waitress, "Hun, what's Lizette's last name?"

"Babineaux, Lizette Babineaux," she screams back.

"There you go, Detective."

"Is she from around here?"

"No, sir, she's from the lower French Quarter. Been here maybe a year."

"Thanks, Tara, you have been extremely helpful."

"Glad to help. You'll know where to find me if you got more questions. Better yet, you could probably get more information from her aunt, Maryann."

"Victor's wife, Maryann?"

"Yep, that's the one."

"Wow, thanks again."

"One more thing, have you seen her recently,"

"No, now that I think about it, I haven't seen her for a couple of weeks." Miller's trek to the car is short and he has a few more answers to his questions. Unfortunately, most of his answers always lead to more questions. Like whom would want the young Lizette dead. When it comes to these scenarios, the first suspect is typically the jealous spouse. Miller takes a brief moment in his car to sport his tinted informant.

The images fill the glasses and Miller sees Maryann Scott milling around the house. She nervously looks around as if she is trying to move about unnoticed. The dogs are sleeping on the kitchen floor. She snips a little hair from the smaller dog and strokes his coat gently, almost tearfully. And then she approaches Rocky slowly, cautiously. Miller notices the position of the small scissors in her hand. The look on her face as she approaches says she could kill the dog, if the opportunity ever presented itself, but instead turns the scissors and snips a piece of fur from his coat. The dog jumps up and begins to snarl and bare his teeth. This noise wakes the smaller dog, but when he sees Maryann, he returns to his nap. Rocky is still growling, and he is stanced to attack, but Maryann backs away just as slowly as she had approached. Putting the hair into a small bag, she slips through a side door and makes her way into the garage. A large silver SUV is sitting unlocked. She opens the passenger side door and looks around carefully until she spots one long blonde strand between the two seats. She puts the strand in a separate bag just as the kitchen door to the garage opens, spilling light onto her activities. When she looks up, the large physique of Victor is standing in the doorway. He says something to her as she closes the car door slipping the bag into a pocket and she responds when she nervously slips sideways past him into the house.

The glasses are forcing Miller to pay attention to images that have nothing to do with Elyse. He is grateful for what they show him but sometimes wishes for a remote control to change the channel. Miller needs to know who poisoned Elyse's tea. He jots down a few notes about his last two scenes and puts them in Victor's file. He looks at the rose-colored glasses. "How do I get you to show me what I need?" He tucks them back into his pocket and goes home.

Miller reaches into his pocket and grabs his phone; he's got Branson on speed dial now and he just hits a button.

"Ted, Miller here, I need you to check to see if anyone has reported an accident involving a Lizette Babineaux, check the hospital…morgue…. See if her name pops up."

MILLER FEELS LIKE he's on a roll with getting clues he wouldn't get anywhere else. Though he's never needed this kind of help before, it adds a level of intrigue to his work.

> *As the images come into focus, Miller can see into a private room with monitors and tape players; the review team is at work. Captain Harrison is in the room with two other officers, and Officer St. John. No one has a view of the other's monitor and Harrison is floating around the room. After hours of viewing, St. John approaches the day and time that Miller needs to see. She notices the slight, slow movement of the camera, the time stamp reads ten minutes before Ilysa's disappearance, and stays very quiet. But as Harrison gets closer to making a pass by his monitor, she rewinds the tape a little. Once Harrison clears her area, she lets the tape run. The recording goes blank as it points to the wall just above the door. Miller's view shifts just enough to see the male figure return to the lounge and realize he didn't return the camera to its original position and the janitor's key is still in his pocket. Jeremy Riggs, being in a hurry to aid in Ilysa's escape, didn't catch the camera at the opposite end of the hall. Though the figures are distant, it shows Riggs using the key he borrowed from the maintenance locker and opening the door as Ilysa slips out of the interrogation room and out of the rear door. Riggs quickly locks the door, slips the key into his pant pocket, and returns to the lounge area down the hall. It's only after Miller enters the room to inquire about Ilysa and leaves again, that Riggs finds the perfect moment to return the keys to the maintenance room.*

Jonathan connects the older, grey-haired officer talking to Victor, the officer reviewing the monitor tapes, and the one opening the door for Ilysa. *RIGGS!!!! Can I just shoot him! All right, all right, calm down Jonathan, because now you have to find something that ties him to Ilysa and her escape. I'll get tech support to tap his phone and the lab should have the prints from the door handle in the basement.*

Miller calls tech support first. The tap is easy and fast. Then he calls the lab; If only everything could be simple for a change.

"Hammond Police Department Crime Lab, Kevin speaking."

"Kevin, Detective Miller here, Captain Harrison should have sent you prints from the doorknob to the back door of the building. Anything come back on those."

"Detective Miller, those prints were layered on because so many people touch that handle. It's processing, but it's going to take a while to sort through the layers and make them individual prints if we even can."

"Do what you can with those prints; I have to know if he is on there."

"Detective, are you looking for someone in particular? Because if we have something to compare prints to, it will make it a little less daunting."

"Well, you should have the prints of all maintenance workers in the building, but also check Jeremy Riggs."

"Officer Jeremy Riggs?"

"Yeah, that one. And keep it quiet, just in case."

"Okay, I will let you know if I get anything."

"Thanks."

~~**~~

Miller looks across the room and Riggs is sitting with his back to him, at his desk. He wants to reach across the room and grab him by the throat, but instead, calls him into his office.

"Have a seat. Riggs, how long have you lived in Hammond?"

"I have been in Hammond for about thirty-five years, before that I was in Laplace."

"So…. You know a lot of the people here in Hammond?"

"Hammond's not an itsy-bitsy place, but I know a lot of people here. I've seen a lot of young people grow up and I've been to a lot of funerals. Why you askin'?"

"I guess you're about fifty-six or fifty-seven? Did you go to high school here?"

"Well, fifty-nine and yeah, I went to Hammond High. Detective, why are you asking me all these questions?"

"I'm still connecting some dots. I'm trying to wrap my brain around why people would stay silent, go to jail or possibly face other serious repercussions over the James/St Claire family?"

"I don't know what you're gettin' at!"

"You don't know? What does this family have on you, to make you risk your badge, your reputation as a good, clean cop, and possibly your pension?"

"Nothing, they got nothing on me!"

Miller goes over and pushes his office door closed, a little harder than needed, and catches the attention of a few people.

"What I'm getting at is why Ilysa's family circumstance is important enough to get so many people involved? What is she to you that you would risk your career over her?"

"I don't know what you're talking about!"

"Who was driving Victor Scott's truck?" Riggs shifts in his chair and stares at the floor.

Miller gets up close to his ear, and his angry whisper makes Riggs inch away. "Let me explain something. I'm not asking you questions I don't already have the answer to. It will just come off better for you if you tell me. I know you and Victor are mixed up in this situation; I even know how; I just don't know why. I know you let Ilysa out of the basement door, and I will find a way to prove it. They are working on the fingerprints as we speak. And I will get the video from the other camera that you forgot to move and when I get what I need, and I *will* get what I need, I will have your badge and gun. Then I'm going to find the blonde and I will get him or her too. The dominoes are going to fall Riggs and the top domino, Victor, he's going too. The question left to ask is, do you want to share a cell?"

Riggs looks at Miller, wide-eyed and confused, stands and walks to the door. "I don't know where you're gettin' this stuff from. I can't lose my badge. I didn't do nothin' wrong." Riggs continues to look at Miller as he backs out of the office. He doesn't even stop at his desk but goes straight to the staircase and disappears.

I think I rattled him a little. Now, I need him to make a mistake … and he will.

MILLER LOOKS UP and sees Branson pick up the phone again as he makes headway in his search. He laughs as he watches the young man jump from the phone to the computer and back and is shocked when he sees him jump up from his desk and head his way.

"I found her!" He says with a big grin.

"That was quick."

"Yeah, well, there was a police report filed at the hospital. She was taken into the North Oaks Medical Center a week ago after she collapsed in the middle of the street. A crowd saw her running barefoot in her nightgown and then she just fell; she was pronounced dead at the scene by the EMTs and she's still at the morgue because no one has claimed the body."

"I think I will go and talk to the coroner."

"Mind if I ride along, asks Branson."

"Sure, you found her, might as well stick this out."

The entrance to the morgue is dark and they aren't sure anyone is there until they hear voices in the distance. Looking through the thick window of the door, they notice two men in lab coats, gloves, and glasses, working on some severely battered individual. Miller taps on the glass, attracting their attention and the taller of the two removes his gloves and comes to the door.

"I'm Detective Jonathan Miller; this is Officer Ted Branson and I understand you have an unclaimed, Caucasian female, approximately twenty years old. Lizette Babineaux."

"I believe she is still here. Give me a moment to get out of this and I can probably help you. I'm Dr. Maxwell, Coroner. You can wait for me here."

Maxwell speaks to the other man in the lab, who nods his head in agreement. He proceeds to remove his gown and returns to the waiting men. Miller and Branson follow Maxwell down the hall to a storage room. Miller flips up the collar of his jacket as he enters the room. The temperature must have dropped about thirty degrees from the already air-conditioned hospital. Maxwell flips through a clipboard filled with papers until he locates Lizette.

"Got her, drawer # 233," he says as he leads the men across the refrigerated room. He pulls the handle and out slides the cold slender body of Lizette. Her grayish color skin is still flawless.

"I don't see any wounds. No cuts or scratches except on her lower legs. Do you have a cause of death?"

"You're right; there are no wounds, no defensive wounds, nothing. We recorded her COD as cardiac arrest."

"She's kinda young for a heart attack, isn't she, Doc?" Branson asks.

"Anyone at any age can be scared to death," he says bluntly. "Here, look at her feet. She was running barefoot, through God-knows-what. She didn't care about the pain in her feet or on her legs; it appears she was running for her life."

Miller looks at the doctor, then back at Lizette. *So, what was chasing you? What scared you to death? I know it wasn't Victor, you were running to him, not away.*

"What will you do with her?"

"She can stay here for another twenty-four to thirty-six hours, we need the drawer. If no one steps in to claim her and cover the costs, the county may give her a simple box and burial, or they may decide to cremate. I don't know yet."

"Thanks, Doc, I have an idea about that, but I'll get back to you when I know for sure," Miller says as they leave the refrigerated room. Miller believes another visit to Victor is in order. Leaving the morgue, he is deep in thought and Branson is busy jotting notes, so the trip seems fairly quick. They approach the home of Victor Scott, and Miller again takes in the vast estate of this man. He could fit his one-bedroom apartment a dozen times over in the space. Maryann opens the door and the shadow that infidelity has cast over her marriage darkens her face and her spirit.

"Hello, Detective Miller, Officer Branson, what can I do for you?"

"We need to speak to Victor."

"He's not here; he is away on business. Is there something I help you with?"

"Do you mind if we come in," he says as he steps across the threshold. "Maryann, when was the last time you saw your niece, Lizette Babineaux?"

"Lizette?"

"Yeah, twenty, pretty blonde."

She's not *really* my niece and it's been months, I guess. Why are you askin' me about Lizette?"

"Did you know she is dead?"

"No, I just told you I haven't seen her in months."

"I would like to see Victor's office again?"

"I guess it will be okay, but is there something I can help you find?"

"I'm not exactly sure."

"Come this way, then."

Miller realizes that the largest of the dogs isn't at the door, growling and snarling as they enter the home. "Maryann, where are the dogs?"

"I lock the big one in a kennel when Victor isn't home. The Rock freaks me out and I can't control him. He only listens to Victor. The little one, Timber, is asleep in the kitchen."

Miller takes his time looking around. Mostly old, black and white family pictures hanging along the wall show the faces of Victor's family. Victor's childhood is portrayed only with his mom. *Maybe Dad is the one taking the pictures. But don't most couples take turns.*

"Do you know anything about Victor's parents? Are they still living? Maybe even in the area?"

"His mom is living in Atlanta somewhere; moved in with her sister a couple years back. His dad is still here, but he doesn't see him much. They split up when Victor was a young teenager; he's an only child. He used to rant about his mom being 'the other woman, but then his dad left her too."

"It's just that there aren't many photos of the dad and even hers are very old, nothing recent. It's like he doesn't like his life, past a certain age."

"Victor's kinda bitter 'bout a lot of things."

They walk into the office and Miller moves towards the bookcases; he studies the surroundings. There are smaller pictures scattered around the bookshelves and on his desk. He takes a closer look at one on the shelf. Victor is a small boy, approximately six years old, on a sliding board; the open arms and smile of his mother await him at the bottom. *That playground.* Miller had seen it before, in another picture, or was it a dream. He continues his search and notices a folder on Victor's desk for CARVELE Shipyards. Miller thinks twice about opening the folder without a warrant. If there is anything in it detrimental to Victor, he won't be able to use it to convict him. *The* dock *must be where he brings in his diamonds and artwork. Mental note Jonathan, check out CARVELE shipyards for connections to Diamond brokers and Victor Scott.* They leave and make the drive back.

"Did you notice, she didn't ask how Lizette died? What happened to her? Nothing. She didn't even seem surprised."

"Yeah. No love lost there."

Miller pulls up in front of the headquarters building to let Branson out and continues to his apartment.

ALONE IN HIS car, he waits until he is in the parking area of his apartment building and then tries to pull a little more information from the rose-tinted glasses. They don't disappoint him.

Miller watches himself as he stops by Claire's local café and picks up three cups of coffee as promised, cream and sugar on the side. He sees himself for the first time within the glasses. It feels like part movie scene and part memory. He watches himself having a conversation with Karen and grinning at her comment. He sees himself pick up his car radio and begin talking. He remembers what he said, even though the glasses still offer no audio. It's like reading lips, except he never learned how. 'This is Detective Miller and I need four available units at Hessville Park. Tell them to take up crosshair positions out of sight, close to the ice-skating rink. Instructions are that they don't move if I stand and walk with the suspect, but if I stay seated and she begins to walk away, they are to move in slowly. The suspect is not assumed armed or dangerous. Do not come weapons drawn.' The glasses shift to show the grey-haired Jeremy Riggs in his squad car as he reaches to turn up the volume and hears the repeated orders over the radio and then realizes Ilysa is about to be apprehended. He makes a call to Victor, who in turn makes a call. Moments later, Victor hands his keys off over his head, and through the window of his office, he watches the silver SUV speed out of the driveway. It stops in the alley just across from the back door of the building. The tinted windows hide the driver from an outsider's view, but as Ilysa gets into the car, the glasses show the top of the back of the blonde-haired driver before the images fade out.

The glasses point Miller in the direction of the clues he needs to close the case. Loaded with the right ammunition, he knows what to say to get confessions. But he has to be careful about discussing the information he gets through the glasses. He can't explain them. No one else can see what he sees, and he would come off sounding like an absolute madman. People would have him fitted for the stylish wraparound jacket if they knew. He pats the pocket that holds his secret and smiles. Now if he could only find their origin and possibly learn to control them, then he could have some fun.

He still needs more to connect Riggs to the release of Ilysa. He needs a motive for the dedicated officer to put his badge on the line.

Miller starts to walk but stops near his building and turns slowly to look over his shoulder. The eerie feeling you get when someone is watching you washed over him like a wave. Looking around and seeing no one, he walks inside. The feeling doesn't immediately go away, and he looks out of his balcony window. For a brief second, he thought he saw a pale face watching him from the tree line.

Miller pours a short scotch and relaxes with a glance into the rose-tinted informant.

Miller watches a young couple as they keep vigil over their three-year-old son; he is playing only yards away. Miller can also see another young woman, alone on the opposite side of the play area. She sits just out of the view of the couple. Her glance darts from her son of about age five, back to the couple. Her face clouds over a strange shade of gray, but Miller can't determine if it's sadness or anger in her eyes. He looks back towards the couple; their faces are only vaguely familiar. Their conversation is becoming more and more animated, and the young boy climbs into a play tube and peeks through the opening.

13

MARYANN LOOKS AT the horrific toys in her bag. The hair from each dog is stitched strategically onto each dog-shaped doll. The one strand of blonde hair is on the girl doll. Maryann shakes just looking at them and needs to work up the courage. Reliving each humiliating incident that Victor and Lizette have put her through doesn't take long. She's never done this before, but she has to do something. She wants to make sure the dolls work the way Daeva says they will. Maryann finds the small dog-shaped doll to use on Timber, the smaller of Victor's dogs. The little dog likes her, and she likes him, not like the Rock. When she sticks the doll and sees the pain the dog is in, she decides to spare him; he cries out and is sick for a moment, but recovers quickly when she removes the pin. She has a successful practice run.

Victor freaks out and files a police report. Maryann stands off to the side and watches as Victor rants and raves about how someone hurt his dog. Nothing they can do without witnesses, evidence. Maryann bides her time and then goes after Victor's favorite dog, Rocky, the one she hates the most. She takes the dog-shaped doll with The Rock's hair glued on and a long pin. She knows what to do. The first stick makes the dog squirm fiercely; the second one makes him howl. Maryann would love to torment this beast the way he has tormented her, but she can't. Timber is nearby, trying to comfort his friend and it is too much for her to see. She decides to issue the fatal prick and end both their discomfort. She heard the dog fall to the floor right on the priceless office rug. Victor's favorite dog is dead. Victor calls the police, and they send Miller in to investigate; Miller, in turn, calls the local Veterinarian, but he finds nothing obvious. No clues, no sign of injury. The Vet says there is nothing, but he can do an autopsy. "It looks like a heart attack."

~~**~~

Maryann waits until things cool down a little bit. Then she gets up the courage to pull her blonde-haired doll from its hiding place. She tracks down Lizette and finds her in a small trailer park just outside of town. Parking her car near a wooded area not far from the trailers, she peeks inside her bag and takes one more look at the small doll. She winds her way through the parking area to find Lizette's trailer and knocks softly. Her young niece opens the door excitedly in a sheer nighty as if expecting someone else. When she sees Maryann, she tries to close the door, but Maryann forces her way inside.

"I know what you been doin' with my husband, you little tramp! Your momma must be turnin' over in her grave watchin' you."

"My momma didn't care what I did when she was alive, why would she care now?"

"I'm givin' you one last chance to stay 'way from Victor; he's married to me, not you."

"Sorry, Antie, can't do that. I'm crazy about Victor. 'Sides, he's so ready to dump you."

"What are you talkin' about, Victor loves me."

"Not anymore, says he loves me more. Look at yourself, you look like an old woman. You dress like an old woman, and you smell worse than you look. This is what Victor wants," moving her hands up and down her body. She laughs at Maryann and turns her back to her aunt. Maryann is tired of Victor's foolishness and Lizette using her youth and beauty to taunt her. All reasoning goes out the window when dealing with this foolish girl, but Maryann is fighting for her marriage. Maryann grabs her by the stringy strands down her back and starts to punch.

The two fight, but the animal sounds coming from the two women escape the neighbors. Maryann has her pinned down on a small couch, with a tight grasp of her throat, until Lizette pushes her backward with both feet and makes her bump her head on a nearby table. Maryann falls to the floor and lies there motionless. Lizette takes this as her chance and out the door she goes. Once outside of her trailer, she runs through the wild brush, bare feet, and sheer nighty, until the first stabbing pain comes. She falls and scrambles to get back to her feet. The fear is filling her as she tries to run to Victor. She can feel her heart beating faster and harder as she heads for the only person who's ever cared, even a little. The next pain hits, then another, and then another. Each one makes her stumble. The briars rip at her legs, feet and hem of her nighty as she tries to maintain her footing. Another stabbing pain grips her.

Maryann has regained consciousness and has the doll and a long pin in hand. She slowly pushes the pin in and then removes it. She repeats this over and over, enjoying the pain she is inflicting on the young girl. *Stupid bitch, I tried.*

Lizette is now running through the street, dirty and tattered, catching the eyes of everyone in town. She tries to make her way to Victor, but before she can reach him, Maryann makes one last pinprick, straight into the heart area of the doll. Lizette collapses in the street, only yards away from Victor's office. People start running past his window towards her and the commotion catches his attention. He gets up to see why everyone is so excited. As the crowd is moving about, Victor catches a quick glimpse of the long blonde hair, and his pace accelerates. He overhears the name Babineaux and he begins to run. Breaking through the crowd, he makes his way to her, lifting her gently as he implores the crowd to call for help.

EMTs arrive and briefly give aid to the victim, but it is too late, Maryann has finished the task. The EMTs cover Lizette's body and load it into the ambulance. Hammond local police arrive and have Victor set aside, away from the crowd, as they attempt to calm him. Meanwhile, Maryann is watching from nearby, awaiting her chance to leave without being seen. When she thinks it's safe, she slips into the darkness of the brush and back to her car. The grip on her steering wheel is precarious and her heartbeats are thunderous against the walls of her chest.

~~**~~

Miller calls Branson into his office. "Close the door and have a seat."

Branson sits in the chair beside Miller's desk and tries to make himself comfortable on the hard, wooden seat.

Miller looks Branson straight in the eye. "What do you know about voodoo?" He tries to keep his voice calm and low; trying not to appear nervous as he steps through *that* door.

Branson sits straight up. "Not a lot, just enough to know I want no part in it."

"Do you know about any of the local women who practice?"

"I have heard about quite a few. What exactly are you looking for, Detective?"

"There is just something bugging me about the illness of one and the death of another perfectly healthy dog, in a short amount of time. I don't believe in voodoo, but I know many people in Hammond do. You only need something personal from the victim, right?"

"Yep, something personal and sometimes just some hair will do."

"Hair?"

The scene from the glasses of Maryann with the dogs and in the garage finally makes sense to Miller.

Branson continues. "I know of one that is popular around here. They call her Daeva Keket. I was told it roughly translates to the evil spirit of darkness or death or something like that. They say her hair is as dark as night, but her skin is as pale as the full moon. Her fingernails are six inches long and curl around your arm when she touches you, but I think they were just trying to creep me out. They say all she needs is a broom and a pointed hat, and she would forever be the wicked witch. If you want to get rid of someone, she's the one to turn to, they say. Just her name gives me the heebie geebies."

"Do you know where I can find her?"

"Why would you want to do that? They don't call her that because she is light, bright, and grants wishes. When her name comes up, things die!"

Miller turns in his chair and faces the window. "I need answers that only someone like her can give me. I don't know anyone else. And unless you can put me face to face with another one, then she will have to do."

"I don't know about this detective; do you *really* want to take a look into the darkness? You might not like what you see."

"She's got the answers I need. How do I find her?"

"I don't think this is a good idea, but I will make some phone calls and see what I can dig up. I know some people, who know some people. Somebody will know where she is, but you might regret finding her." Branson gets up and goes back to his desk, shaking his head.

As the images become clear, Miller can see two women sitting in a dimly lit room. Ilysa and Avery are alone in the basement of the store. He notices two cups on the nearby table, as the ladies sit and talk. Ilysa, always in her poised, calm, and controlled manner is facing the young woman when she quickly turns towards the door. Avery moves towards the door to investigate. Stepping into the long dark hall, she looks both ways and walks out. Ilysa pours the powder contents of a small packet into the girl's cup, quickly stirring to help it blend. When Avery returns, Ilysa quickly encourages her back into drinking her coffee while they talk. Only minutes pass before the young woman's eyes look heavy with sleep. Ilysa convinces her to sit in a small, thickly padded seat and watches as the girl drifts off. Ilysa slips on a pair of gloves and then pulls out a vial. Taking the girl's index finger, she places it on the vial, then wraps it and returns it to her pocket before she leaves. Ilysa slips out through the tunnel access, unnoticed. She takes the wrapped vial to Cora and puts it into her hands. She says something just before she turns to leave.

Miller looks out of the window at the store where Avery works. The door sign says 'CLOSED.' His questions will have to wait. He looks around the office and people are starting to file out for the day. He slips the glasses back on and turns towards the window. There is nothing. It has *never* not shown anything. He relaxes, sets his head back against his chair, and closes his eyes. *Maybe I'm just tired, maybe we both are.* The brief respite is all he needed. When he opens his eyes again, the glasses are flickering.

Images start to appear and even though he is facing the end of daylight through his window, the images are in the dark. It takes a moment for Miller's eyes to focus.

In the darkness. The glow from the streetlamp illuminates the mist of rain falling. He can see the steam rising from the hot pavement below. The evening cools as Maryann pulls a shawl tightly around her shoulders while she walks toward the gate. Darkness creeps around every corner, the shadows reach for her when she passes and the tombstones of every size and shape give Maryann the willies. She peeks down pathways, looking for Daeva. She looks as if she wants to call out, but fear catches her by the throat. When she finally finds her standing in the doorway of a mausoleum for Stanley Parks, she hesitates, but the spindly fingers with the long curly nails beckon her to come. They talk, but Maryann's eyes can't take in the appearance before her for more than a moment at a time. After a while, Maryann hands her a thick envelope. Looking quite pale herself now, she walks back to her car, hoping no one sees her. She sits there, gathering her composure. Her hands tremble as they try to grip the wheel.

Miller slides his cell phone from his shirt pocket just enough to see the ID. Cora James is calling.

"Miller here."

"Hello, Detective, this is Cora. I need to see you." Though the year has matured her a little, she still sounds more like a little girl than her sister.

"Hello, Cora, what's going on?"

"I need to talk to you. Can you meet me? I will be at the playground in Hessville at 1:00 today."

"I can be there."

Miller arrives at the park and is waiting when Cora walks up. She's in her flat shoes; her jeans are worn and her top hides her shooting star. She's pulled her hair up on her head and the bazillion ringlets are, for the moment, contained. Miller notices that she won't look at him, appears more nervous than usual, and has the awkwardness that is not his Callie.

Cora turns her back to him as she speaks. "Ilysa gave me the vial and said, 'handle it carefully, don't use it unless you need to.' That night, Elyse came home. She was really scared, sayin' Ilysa was back and madder than a snake. She wanted me to leave with her again, but I told her I was tired of runnin' and hidin' from people. I wanted to be all together again like a real family, but she screamed that Ilysa wouldn't let us." She began to cry. "She said Ilysa would take me away from her and send her to jail." The teary-eyed girl tried to explain. "I just wanted to be with my sister and Elyse kept sayin' we had to leave. She was runnin' round like a crazy woman, screamin' at me to get my stuff. I didn't want to hurt her. I swear to God, I didn't. I wouldn't even be here if it weren't for Elyse. She blew part of her soul into me so I could live! You gotta love someone a lot to give them part of your soul. I just didn't want to let go of Ilysa and Callie, not again." She stopped to take a deep breath as if reliving the moment. "I convinced her to let me make her a cup of tea to calm her down so we could think up a plan. I used the vial Ilysa gave me and poured it into her tea. I told her I was gonna go for a walk to clear my head and then we would talk. I went out and stayed. Celia told me how Daniel died, and I knew couldn't watch that. That was just before you got there." She stops and briefly looks up into the face of the handsome detective the pools in her eyes reflected a fear Miller had seen before. "I won't confess to no one else and you don't have anythin' to prove I did it. I just want my family. Please." Miller looks at Cora's face, but all he can see is his beautiful Callie. The same dark ringlets flutter with the breeze. The same eyes fill to the brim with fear, guilt, and maybe even a little remorse.

Miller takes just a few steps away from her. He remembers the first time Callie walked into his office and his heart softens just a little more. *She's right; I have nothing tangible. Ilysa is the one that put Avery's print on the vial, but I can't prove that. I can't use what I saw in the glasses against her. I have nothing, except Cora's word, that she was the one that essentially poisoned Elyse. It is ironic that Elyse's life was ended by the person she brought back from the dead. I don't know, maybe she's telling me the truth, or she could be saying it to protect Ilysa.*

Miller turns and walks back toward Cora, stopping at her side. His look makes her drop her gaze; "Cora, how's Callie?"

"She's just fine, Detective; I'll tell her hello if you like."

"I like, thanks," he says, then continues past her, leaving her breathing hard with her eyes closed. He walks back to his vehicle; gets in his car and pulls off.

~~**~~

She turns and watches as he pulls away. Once he is out of sight, she smiles as she straightens her posture, releases the bazillions of dark ringlets from their band, and pulls out her phone.

"It was worth the drive. It's done; he believes me. Yeah, I think my next career move will be acting," Callie laughs as she strolls back to her car.

"I'll be home in a few hours. Bye." She feels bad having to trick him, but Cora and her mom are all the family she has, and he needs to let this go. At least until her father is released.

14

MILLER IS SEETHING a bit, over the encounter with who he believes was Cora. Even if he can't get definitive proof, he has to clear things up in his head. Before going back to his office, he makes a detour to see Avery. The door sign now says 'Open'. He walks in and finds the pool-blue eyes fixed on him, no smile, no surprise, no fear

"Hello, Detective Miller."

"Hello, Avery, you got a minute to talk to me?"

The young clerk waves her hand around. "It's not like I'm busy."

Miller looks around the store, "Got a point. I just want to ask you about Ilysa James. Do you remember talking to her?"

"I think so, but I'm not sure. I thought it was a dream. It all felt so surreal. I believe we were right here, downstairs in my break room; we had coffee and talked. Then suddenly she was gone."

"Do you remember what you talked about?"

"Ilysa called me first, to see if it would be okay, her stoppin' by and all; she wanted to thank me for helping Cora, but she didn't want to do it over the phone. When she came in, she was acting weird. I mean, she's always been nice to me, but that day she was nicer than usual. I don't remember why, but I was so tired. I must have fallen asleep and when I woke up in my chair, she was gone. Everything was gone. My head felt like I was in a fog and the day was over, so I locked up and went home. That's why I thought it was a dream."

Ilysa is trying to set you up to take the fall for Cora.

Miller has no way of knowing how many people are willing to sacrifice for this woman or why. Who is she that Riggs would be willing to give up his badge? Victor, his lifestyle and business? Celia and Tom are already in prison for aiding her in the murder of Daniel. Now, they're helping her evade the law.

Miller goes to his squad car and radios the Pineville local PD.

"Pineville Dispatch, this is Detective Jonathan Miller from Hammond, I would like the local PD in Pineville to watch for the same three ladies from my previous case. I will resend the pictures for ID purposes. This is just to verify that the women are still in the area. I have a possible residence they can confirm. They are not to apprehend, but if they are in the home, please contact me. My number will come with the photos."

"Detective Miller, this is Pineville Dispatch, we will do what we can to help."

"Thank you."

Miller gets the photos from his file and scribbles his number on the picture of Callie. He wonders if she still has his number in her phone; he has hers but calling seems such a daunting task. He sends a facsimile of the photos, hoping the women are staying put in Pineville. The locals will find them again; he's sure of it

The Pineville dispatcher puts out a request for all officers to be on the lookout for the women. She also gives the suspects' residence, and the on-duty officers begin to scribble it down.

"Dispatch, this is unit 390, we are about five minutes from that location and can do a drive-by."

"Great, unit 390, this is just a confirmation of the location, do not apprehend."

"We understand."

The officers make the short trip and approach the home. The one-story home is well maintained and adequately landscaped. Nothing too showy to attract attention, but better than the appearance of just squatters. There is one car in the driveway and the officers make note of the make, model, and plate. They calmly walk up to the door and rap firmly on the storm door. Ilysa peers through the peephole and takes a deep breath before opening the door. "Hello, officers."

"Hello Ma'am, we are looking for a Conner Stephens, does he live here?" The officers peer over her head and see another female sitting at a small table.

Ilysa slowly exhales the fear that was welling up inside. "No sir, just a house of women here. I'm sorry; I don't know the person you're looking for."

"Thank you for your time, sorry to disturb yawl."

"No need to apologize. Have a good day."

The officers leave and Ilysa closes the door, leans her back against it, and closes her eyes. *That damn detective, I can smell him all over this. He's gettin' to be as bad as that PI.*

Miller makes use of the glasses one more time, before going home for the night. They have been treating him like a ping pong ball, bouncing his information between the two cases. Maybe he'll wrap them both up and be done with the craziness. Then he can focus on Callie. As he slides the glasses on again, the images are back in the dark.

The shadowy figure becomes more discernable as Maryann approaches. The stark black hair against fish-belly white skin makes Daeva Keket look like a resident of the boneyard. The light breeze catches her loose clothing, and the coldness of the tombstones makes Maryann regret the decision to meet here. Miller recognizes the large ornamental gate that she walks through. They are in Parklawn Cemetery. She steps gingerly through the area as if she is afraid she may wake the dead. Darkness surrounds the two women as they talk and Maryann's glance darts back and forth, making sure the shadows are staying put. The woman shoves a bag into Maryann's hand, but doesn't release it and begins pulling out small objects Miller can barely see. She shows each one, says something to Maryann, and then drops them back into the bag. Maryann turns to leave, and the woman grasps her arm; the long-curled nails scrape her skin and make her shudder. She speaks again and waves one of the long-curled nails in her face. Maryann pulls something from her pocket to hand her, snatches her arm away, and runs back the way she came. She sits in her car and peeks into the bag, with another shudder she quickly closes the bag and pulls away. The images fade as Miller's cell phone vibrates in his pocket and calls him back to reality.

It's tech support. "Detective Miller here."

"Detective, we got something on your tap. Officer Riggs placed a call to a cell number registered to Victor Scott within minutes of us placing the tap on his line. Would you like the audio sent to your computer?"

"Yes, that's fine, thanks."

Miller plugs in his earphones and within a few moments, he is listening to the audio recording of the conversation between Victor and Jeremy.

Riggs: I just left his office; the guy is creepy. I don't know where he is getting his information, but he knows I'm the one that let Ilysa out of the building. He also knows about the blonde driver in the truck.'

Scott: Did you admit to anything?'

Riggs: No, but I'm telling you, we gotta get rid of this guy. He's getting too close.'

Scott: How do you propose we do that? If he turns up missing, someone else will come around asking questions. He's a little too well known, not like that nosey Private Investigator.'

Riggs: It's only a matter of time before he figures out Lizette was driving the truck and connect her to you."

Scott: You haven't heard, Lizette is dead, and he can't hurt her now. You and I are the only ones who need to worry.'

Riggs: What do you mean, Lizette is dead! What happened?'

Scott: They say it was a heart attack; they say she was scared to death.'

Riggs: You know there is only one thing in these parts that can do that! You've heard the
    stories.'
Scott: But why would someone want to hurt Lizette? 'Who?'
Riggs: How you been in business this long and be so stupid? That little lady was a troublemaker
    at the age of twelve. Now she's known for sittin' right in the middle of your marriage.
    Tell me you can't think of one person who would want her gone.'
Scott: I gotta go, I'll talk to you later'.

The conversation ends and Miller is more determined than ever that these two are going away. Miller calls his contact in the District Attorney's office.

"Sam, Miller here, I need a search warrant for Victor Scott's home."

"What have you got?"

"I believe Maryann Scott is responsible for the death of Lizette Babineaux. I need to take a team to search the entire property for the murder weapon."

"I can have it for you in the morning."

"Thanks, Sam. Can you have someone meet me at Scott's home in the morning, I don't want to waste any more time?"

The next morning, Miller gathers a team of six officers in front of the home of Victor and Maryann, waiting for a warrant to show up. He begins giving instructions to the officers when a large black SUV speeds up the driveway. One eager young officer jumps from the vehicle and runs towards Miller.

"DA Smith said you needed this right away."

"Thank you for the speed, son."

"Umm, Detective, do you need any more men? My partner and I have time to assist."

"Sure, kid. I'll take all the help I can get."

The young man looks back at his vehicle and with a huge smile on his face, waves his partner over. Another young officer leaps from the truck and runs.

~~**~~

"Listen up! I need you to be sharp, attentive, look for anything out of the ordinary. Something strange happened to Lizette Babineaux and I want to know what. She didn't die from a gunshot, stab wound, or strangulation. So, what killed her? Coroner said she was 'scared to death'. We have one photographer among us, so when you find something 'scary', call him before moving it. I don't want to have someone screaming about planted evidence. If these people are connected, I want this clean and documented."

As the team approaches the house, Maryann is already standing in the doorway. Miller backs her up and pushes the search warrant into her hand as the remaining officers enter the home and begin to fan out in all directions.

The wide-eyed Maryann screams in protest. "Detective, what's going on?"

"Maryann, where's Victor?"

"He's in his office. What is this all about?"

"We have a warrant to search your home." Miller begins walking towards Victor's office. He doesn't stop as he pushes his way into the doors. Victor is on the phone and is startled at the intrusion.

"Detective, what's going on? Why are you barging into my office?"

"Tell me what your relationship was with Lizette Babineaux."

"We were friends. She used to work for me at my warehouse."

"You were friends? Friendly enough to cry for her in the middle of the street? Friendly enough for her to run barefoot and half-naked through the street to get to you? Are you sure you were just friends!"

"Yes! She was having a rough time at home, didn't have anything when she came here. She needed a job! So, I would find little odd jobs for her to do there."

"Was being your lover one of her odd jobs?"

"NO!"

"Why do you think someone wanted her dead? My men are searching your home as we speak, if I find anything connecting you or your wife to her, I will have you prosecuted to the full extent of the law. Do you understand me? Now tell me what happened the day she died."

"I don't know. I heard a commotion in the street. I saw the crowd running and when I got outside, I heard someone scream her name. When I got to her, she was too weak to tell me anything. She tried. She was trying to say something, but she couldn't. Then the ambulance came, but it was too late."

Maryann stands in the doorway listening, not saying a word, and staring at the floor. The officers are looking through everything, in every room, finding nothing.

Miller turns his ranting in her direction. "What about you, tell me again how you knew Lizette?"

"Of course, I knew her, she was my first husband's niece, but we weren't close or anything. There's no tellin' what that child got herself mixed up in. She was always in trouble, ever since she was young. Nobody could do nothin' with that girl."

"Where were you the day she died?"

"I was here."

"Alone?"

"Yes."

"You're lying, Maryann!"

MILLER TAKES A break and goes to his vehicle, a little spooked by Maryann's action, and his respite is quiet until he gets a call.

"Detective Miller, this is Pineville dispatch, we have a confirmation on your suspects. They are currently still at the address you provided. Officers report one vehicle, Mercury Mountaineer, plate 583 Vincent Thomas Baker. Two females reported in the home at the time of the visit."

"How do they know that?"

"They approached the home under the pretense of inquiring about a young man. They got a visual on the mom and one other female matching your photos."

"Thank you dispatch. If they could maintain loose surveillance, I would appreciate the assistance." *I just hope they didn't spook her and make her want to run again. Ilysa is used to being tracked; she may get nervous. If she thinks for a moment that I'm still looking for her, she may take the girls and run. I can't let her run with Callie, I just can't.* He pulls out his cell phone and searches for Callie's number. His thumb hovers above the send button but hesitates. He misses her voice, he misses her smile, and every so often her face creeps into his dreams. He relives the visions of Callie in the glasses; her encounters with Daniel Edwards still sit in the back of his mind. Seeing her face to face, in the park the morning he met Ilysa is probably one of his favorites. The breeze and the sunlight intermittently played with the ringlets.

Circumstances being a little different could have made for a beautiful start to the day. No other woman has sweetly occupied his thoughts and dreams the way Callie has, and he's ready to include someone like her in his life.

16

MILLER HEADS BACK inside as the officers are all over Victor's home; the photographer is waiting for the call to go to work when the first scream rings out. He scrambles toward the sound and finds the caller in the master bedroom. He is on his knees, beside the bed, and makes the photographer get on the floor with him. Flashes from the camera brighten the floor beneath the bed and the officer reaches in and grabs a small gold bracelet. Engraved on the bracelet is the name, Lizette. He puts it into a small plastic bag and takes it to Miller.

The young officer that delivered the warrant is on the team searching the lower level. They are rummaging through the kitchen cabinets and he discovers the cabinets below the window seat. When the doors don't open, he looks at the cushions and then lifts one. It's empty. He moves to the next one. Also, empty. The last one he opens makes him jump back, knocking over the items on the table

"Hey! Hey! In here!! Bring the photographer!"

Several other officers and the photographer run into the kitchen. When they look over into the seat box, they get nervous. They recognize the things that are in there and they know what they can do.

"Somebody get the Detective!"

Miller is in the office with Maryann and Victor when he hears the noise and is already on his way. Victor and Maryann follow close behind him. He looks over into the seat box and is mesmerized. He's never been this close before; the strange dolls are hideous and he's heard, powerful, if you believe. Miller knows where they came from and who they belong to, but he still can't say. He looks at the young officer.

"Bag all of them. Get them to the lab and check for DNA. Let's see if we can get any information from these things." He looks at Maryann and Victor, "These belong to either one of you?"

Victor looks at the dolls and notices the two dog-like dolls; each one has a tuft of hair that he recognizes from his pets. He is quick to deny ownership. Maryann looks thunderstruck. He turns to face his wife.

"Maryann? You! Did you kill my Rocky? You know how much that dog meant to me. And Lizette? Your niece? Why?"

Everyone in the room turns to look at Victor in disbelief.

"You treated that beast better than you treated me. I hated that nasty dog, and she wasn't my niece, the little tramp. If you have to ask, 'why Lizette,' then maybe I should have had one made for you too." Victor lunges for Maryann, hands outstretched and ready to latch onto her throat. Several officers grab him in restraint. Miller points to an officer in the room. "Cuff her and take her in, don't forget to tell her her rights."

"Yes, Detective." He leaves with Maryann in tow.

The other officer comes in and hands Miller the bag with the bracelet. "I found this under the bed in the master bedroom."

Miller turns his attention back to Victor. Distraught over his dog and Lizette, he was six foot, 230 pounds of misery.

"Okay, Victor, you have a little more explaining to do, look familiar?" He asks, holding up the plastic evidence bag. "You're a very busy man, but how did you manage to land yourself right in the middle of so much crap? You lied to me about not knowing Ilysa James and her girls. You have been helping them clean up and cover up their mess since Edwards. We found your prints at her home!" His statement gets Victor's attention, and he looks up. "I know you gave Lizette the keys to your silver SUV to pick up Ilysa from headquarters and Jeremy Riggs let her out of the building. Now you have gotten a young girl murdered and your wife imprisoned because you lack a little self-control and respect for your marriage. Victor! Please! Explain this mess to me."

Victor gets up and walks over to a small bar in the wall. He drops a couple of ice cubes in a glass and pours himself a glass of scotch, then looks at Miller with the question. Miller just shakes his head no.

"I wasn't lying to you when I told you I didn't know Ilysa or her girls, I had never met them. I know Tom Bradley. Tom called me a year ago, said he needed help to clean up the apartment. Me and Tom go way back. He's helped me through a lot of stuff, so I couldn't say no when he asked me for help. All I did was help him move the body, empty and clean the apartment, and clean out the car and wipe it down. He said if I helped him, he would keep my name out of it. I was helping a friend who was helping a friend. But then Ilysa got here, and the shit hit the fan. She found out about Cora, and she went crazy. She came lookin' for Elyse with fire in her eyes. I've never seen anyone as mad as that. I didn't want to be the one to get in her way, but I didn't want to see her hurt Elyse either. We tried to hide her and Cora. We kept them away from Ilysa for as long as we could, but she was like a huntin' dog with the scent of blood. Nothin was going to keep her from Elyse."

Miller let him continue to dig his hole, "How does Riggs figure in this? Why on earth would he risk his badge?"

"Why don't you ask him?"

Miller slaps the table and the sound echoes around the room. "I'm asking you! Stop pissin' around and answer me!"

"Riggs owed Elyse's dad. He got into trouble a lot back in high school. This one time, some kids were selling drugs in the school, and they almost got caught, but they slipped the stuff into Riggs' backpack before the authorities got there. Elyse's dad just happened to be nearby and saw the whole thing. He saved his bacon, and those kids went to jail for possession with intent. Riggs was on the law enforcement track early and that would have blown his whole career before it even started. Riggs promised to return the favor, but that James guy died before he needed anything. However, Elyse knew about it and never let him forget. He had to help her or lose his job and his pension."

"Do you realize that that makes you both an accessory after the fact? I know you didn't *actually* kill Lizette, but your actions are directly responsible for someone causing her death. Unfortunately, I don't believe I can arrest you for being an adulterous asshole, but I can arrest you for Daniel Edwards. Officer, please cuff him and take him in. But before they take you in, Lizette is still waiting at the coroner's office, unclaimed. She needs to be buried, Victor. You can still do right by her." Miller hands him a piece of paper with the office phone number on it.

Victor looks at Miller and before he is cuffed, he takes the paper and makes a call to Jefferson's Funeral Home.

"Done."

Another officer takes Victor and escorts him to a squad car. Miller walks to the front door of the house and leans against the doorsill as he watches the car with Victor drive off. Pulling the door shut behind him, he goes to his squad car and radios dispatch. "This is Detective Miller. I want Officer Jeremy Riggs picked up and brought in for booking." He sighs with a sense of relief and heads home. *They can all sit in holding until morning. I'm done for the night.*

He walks into his apartment, thankful for the calm. When he walks past the bookshelves, a photo catches his attention. He looks to be about seven or possibly eight. Dressed in his favorite blue jeans, he and his mom are having a picnic under a tree. He lifts the frame from its resting place, letting the dust rain down. He studies the picture from corner to corner. The hairstyle. The dress is the same as from the playground in Victor's photo. If that was his mom, then it could very well have been his dad; he hasn't seen him in 24 years, so the face is a blur. The three-year -old on the playground must have been him.

A picture of a small photo album flashes in his memory. His mom gave it to him four years ago, just before she passed. He ran to his bedroom closet. Down on his knees, he rifles through the stuff on the floor until he finds a box. He hasn't touched it since the funeral. He pulls the box reverently into the light and sits on the floor as he opens it. Small pictures, letters, and mementos of his mom brought back memories he'd fought so hard to bury. It was just the two of them; his mom never remarried or had other children. They were each other's best friend.

He finds what he's after and lifts the small album out, and before he can even open it the dam breaks, and 24 years of tears spill over their embankment. *Mom, I miss you so much! I'm all alone!* He waits until the pain subsides and then slowly turns the first page.

Miller flips through the pages of the book as if his life depends on it and one by one, a tear or two rolls with each image. Though the life in the pictures shows a very busy kid and Miller sometimes still feels the sting of being without a father, his mom kept him surrounded by strong role models that guided him through the rough patches. His little league coach was the closest thing to a father any boy could ask for. Even after he grew up, Coach Evans was there to listen. He had his spot in the photo album. There were only a few gaps where even mom was not around, but he was always safe. She made sure of that. Miller flips the next page and loose papers fall to the floor. He carefully sets the album on the floor and picks up the folded, yellowed sheets.

OMICRON GAMMA THETA SPREADS FEAR ON CAMPUS

The headline of the newspaper clipping names Beth Edwards and classmate, Tracy Jackson, among seven others, were caught in the basement of the Arrendale Library, almost in the center of campus. The group seemed to be practicing some strange type of ritual. Most have been put on temporary suspension, others have been expelled.

The article went on to describe the scene when police arrived, but the thought of his mother being in the midst of something like that is unthinkable. Miller has to put it down, but there were several more just like it. Miller picks up the box and takes it to his bedroom, dropping the box and spilling the contents onto the comforter. Pictures, clippings, and old letters scatter everywhere. When Miller goes to right the box, he notices the Piedmont College yearbook that had been at the bottom of everything. He notices similar clippings from the school and glances at the names. Beth Edwards is among them. He looks for his mother. *Mom's maiden name was Jackson, Tracy Jackson.* He scans the article and finds her picture. She and Beth are in every article. This face is the same one from the yearbook photos. His mom and Daniel Edwards' mom seem to have spent a lot of time in the same activities. *How small is this world going to shrink this week?* As he is examining one of the articles, he notices another possible familiar face. He flips back through the others; she too is tucked in and behind various structures in a lot of the pictures. "Damn, are you kidding me, her too?"

He closes the box with all of its contents and goes to bed. His thoughts are all over the map. They bounce from Victor to Daniel to Daeva and Callie, but then exhaustion takes over and he closes his eyes.

"What's wrong with me today, I just feel like I'm losing my mind." Miller kicks off his shoes and sits on the side of his bed --- Exhausted, he lies back against his pillow and closes his eyes. I'll just catch my breath and then change for bed. His mother's face comes clearly into view. He is in a small townhome with his parents and they are screaming at the top of their lungs. Little Jonathan is curled up in the corner of the living room sofa, eyes squeezed tightly shut and hands over his ears when suddenly he hears the loud SLAM! He can't move for several seconds, but when he finally gets the nerve to open his eyes, he can see his mom seated at the table crying. He jumps and runs to the window in time to see his dad walking down the concrete steps of the house. Miller runs out the front door and sits on the stoop of his home as he watches his dad walk away from the house. He's only three and doesn't realize, dad won't be back in time for dinner.

Streams of sunlight wake Miller from his wanderings into the past. He rubs his eyes while making his morning adjustments to the long skeleton that would be his six-foot frame. Flashes of the strange dream come back to him. He remembers the stoop in front of his home as a child. The faces of his parents, as they argued and screamed, came and went through his mind. He remembers as the feelings of wanting to be somewhere else, with someone else, re-emerged in his spirit. He is wholly committed to never making his child feel like that.

MILLER IS FEELING pretty good about last night and turns his attention back to Ilysa. It's been 48 hours since the officers made their disguised visit, and he doesn't know what she will do. She's smart, intuitive and she was able to stay two steps ahead of Edwards for years. He can't make the same mistakes. He doesn't want Callie to leave the state, but she may have a stronger loyalty to her newfound family than to her future. Miller's thoughts of Callie press on him until he has to do something. He reaches for his phone and listens for her voice, but all he hears is the ringing tone. He doesn't realize that on the other end of that ringing, she is staring at the ID screen. He doesn't know that the longing to answer is there, but she waits too long. By the time she hits her answer button, Miller is gone. *Maybe she was away from her phone; maybe she's busy; she could have lost it. I should try again. I'll try later.* If only he could hear her thoughts, as she sits and stares at her phone. *Wow, he still has my number; I wonder why he called. Maybe he'll call back. I hope he calls back.*

Miller gets in his vehicle and heads for the office. He just needs to finish the paperwork on the Scotts. Suddenly, he gets a radio call.

"Detective Miller here."

"This is the Pineville dispatcher. We want to let you know there is some possible activity going on at the residence you were inquirin' about. Officers noticed one of the females, they think it's the mom, loading suitcases into the car."

"Dispatch, please advise them to maintain a watch. If she leaves alone, wait until she is away from the house, out of visual range, before stopping her. Then call me. If all three women get into the car, then take them all in."

"Will do, Detective, dispatch out."

I knew it! She's going to run again, but is she going alone? I've got to get her to stay. He has to do something.

"Why are you leavin', we've been through so much to try to be together? Where will you go?" Asks Cora.

"They are looking for me. I'm sure of it. That Detective from Hammond did not fall for your ploy. He may leave you two alone if you stay here."

Callie is sitting in their living room listening when her phone rings. It's Miller and this time she doesn't wait to answer

"Hello."

"Hello Callie, I'm glad you answered. I want to talk to you, alone, but for now, it is important that I speak to Ilysa. I know she's there, I know she's getting ready to leave, but I can help her. She doesn't have to run anymore." Callie looks up as Ilysa stands in the doorway.

"They must be watching us, he already knows you're getting ready to leave. He wants to talk to you. He says he can help, and you won't have to run anymore." Her large eyes are tear-filled and imploring. "Please, momma."

Ilysa looks into the chocolate-colored eyes of her beautiful daughter, her student, and her friend. They've been running from someone all of her life. Ilysa slowly, reluctantly takes the phone.

"Hello, Detective Miller."

"Ms. James, please let me help you. If you come back to Hammond, I will speak to the DA on your behalf. I will do my best to keep the girls out of harm's way because I know that is your ultimate goal. But if you try to run again, with or without the girls, Pineville PD will be waiting to take you in. Promise to talk to me, give me your word and I will call off the locals. Today is Wednesday and I can give you a couple of days to gather your things.

"I will be there on Friday."

"Thank you, Ms. James. Would you please let me speak to Callie?"

Ilysa looks at Callie and smiles as she hands her back the phone. She turns to leave, and Callie settles back into the soft cushions of the sofa. "Hello again."

"Callie, I believe your mom is coming to Hammond. I'm trying to trust her, but Callie, even if she changes her mind, don't leave with her. The truth is, I would like to see you sooner rather than later and if you say yes, I'll come up there this evening and get a room. Then we can meet for breakfast or coffee, or whatever you like in the morning. Just don't go."

"Ok, Detective Miller. I think I'd like that."

Miller smiles. "First, just call me Jonathan. Second, thanks and I will call you in the morning around nine."

"Okay, bye"

"Bye."

Ilysa comes back around the corner.

"He's driving all the way up here to see me."

"Of course, he is, baby. I told you he wasn't going to let this go. I could see it in his eyes when he looked at you. I remember that look on the face of a man that loved me once. At least yours isn't married."

Callie just smiles and Ilysa disappears back around the corner.

"Does that mean you're not leavin' us, momma?" Cora asks excitedly.

"No, Cora, I'm not leaving you. I'll go to Hammond on Friday and speak with this detective. I will hear him out."

"Good, I'll help you bring your suitcases back into the house." And Cora runs out to the car. When she closes the door to the car, suitcase in hand, she sees a squad car pass by the house. The officers inside just nod and continue on their way. Pineville dispatcher has updated the alert and they have already received word to cease their surveillance.

HAMMOND HEADQUARTERS IS all abuzz with the arrest of Officer Jeremy Riggs, Victor Scott, and his wife. Jeremy is facing conspiracy and accessory charges. Maryann is facing a homicide charge and Victor, if felony stupidity was a charge that would stick, Miller would smack him with it, but accessory charges and aiding a suspect will have to do.

Miller finishes his paperwork and rushes home to pack a small overnight bag. Though Pineville is close to three hours away, Miller is excited at the thought of seeing his Callie. The excitement is better than coffee to keep him awake on the drive. It's late when he arrives and he is lucky to find a room available at the Magnuson Hotel. He's less than ten minutes away from Callie's home. The clerk gives him his key and he retires to his room. He opens the door, and his room is clean, fresh, turned down for the night, and the first thing that comes to mind is *Who's your cleaning service? Maybe I should move that to the top of my to-do list.* He unpacks his few things and hangs up his shirt and pants in the closet. He looks out of his window overlooking the pool. There is just one lone swimmer. It's tempting. He could use the chance to relax, instead, he heads for the bar and grill next door. He thought he had the place to himself until he spotted a couple at a table in the back. It's quiet and dark. He orders a scotch and stares out of the window. With two cases wrapping up, his thoughts are free to fill with the young woman he will see in the morning.

The sun rises on a new day with so many possibilities. Miller showers and quickly changes into a simple, clean, white linen shirt and black pants. He calls Callie.

"Good Morning, Callie. Are we still okay for this morning?"

"Yes, I'll be ready."

"I know where you are and you're close, so I can pick you up. Can you be ready about nine o'clock?"

"That's fine."

Nine o'clock rolls around and Miller drives up in front of the house as promised. His two-seater convertible, thank heavens, is much cleaner than his apartment. He knocks on the door as he raises his sunglasses above his head. Ilysa opens the door and smiles.

"Good morning, Ms. James. How are you?"

"Just fine this morning, Detective and yourself?"

"I'm well, is Callie ready?"

"I believe so, you can wait inside if you like."

"If it's all the same, I'd rather wait on the swing."

"Suit yourself. I'll tell her you're here." She closes the door and Miller sits and rocks gently on the porch swing. He rises the next time the door opens, and Callie steps out in a pale blue sundress. Her dark ringlets are held back from her face by a matching headband. Her smile is bright upon seeing the man standing before her. Being the gentleman his mother raised him to be, he offers her a bent elbow and she shyly accepts. Ilysa and Cora peek through the sheer curtains in the window and watch as he opens the door for Callie and moves around to the other side of the car. As he buckles himself in, Callie catches her mom still at the window until Miller pulls off.

"I'm glad you decided to come. Do you have a favorite place here or should I just pick one?"

"No, favorites. Over the years, I've learned to eat just about anything." They drive for just a little while when Callie sees a large Ryan's restaurant sign looming above the buildings. "There, the Ryan's, I've been there once. It's not as fancy as La Provence, but it's got decent food."

"Ryan's it is, but if you don't like it, we can find someplace else."

They get inside and get seated by the tiniest blonde hostess Miller has ever seen. Upon first glance, you might think she was thirteen years old, but she is pleasant and seats them in a private booth near the counter. She is soon followed by a waitress who pours two cups of coffee and quickly takes their orders.

Jonathan's eyes never leave the face of the woman in front of him, but at least this time he remembers to breathe. They simultaneously begin to talk and then laugh at the moment.

"You first," he offers.

"Do you *really* think you can help my mom? Cora and I need to make peace with all that has happened."

"I promise to help your mom as best I can. I can't promise she won't have a short jail term. We are talking conspiracy to commit murder and evading the law. The one good thing she did was not cross the borders. Then it would have become a federal case and completely out of my hands. Your dad managed his short stay. You know he is due to be released soon."

"I know, the time has passed quickly in some ways and yet seems like an eternity in others Detective Miller."

Jonathan cuts her off. "Please, Callie, call me Jonathan."

"Jonathan, okay, when you called yesterday, you asked me not to leave. Even if my mom wanted to go, you would want me to stay. Why?"

"I was afraid if she continued to run and took you and Cora with her, I might not ever see you again. Honestly Callie, when you first disappeared, after Ilysa's arrest, I almost lost my mind. I want to get to know you. I need time to get to know you and I can't do that if you leave."

"What's wrong with you?"

"What do you mean," He says laughing, "what's wrong with me?"

"Well, you're handsome, stable in your job and known in the community, you drive a nice car, you don't live with your mother and you seem to know how to treat a lady. So, why isn't there a Mrs. Miller? Or is there and you just want a side chick?"

"Okay, I guess that is a fair enough question. First, there isn't a Mrs. Miller, and second, a man would have to be psychotic to make you a side anything. I've been pretty focused on my career since high school. I graduated and went straight into the academy. I wanted the gold shield my father, grandfather, and great-grandfather had. I never found the right time or the right woman that made me want to change that…. Until now."

Callie blushes at the compliment.

"Are you rushed to get back home?"

"No, there isn't anything I have to get back to that can't wait."

"Great, I saw a park nearby, maybe we can talk more there." Jonathan pays the check and helps Callie up from her seat. The park is a short drive and though the activity level is busy on the side where they enter, Jonathan finds a walking path through the trees, where they can take their time and stroll. He reaches for her hand and she hesitates for only a moment before gently interlocking her fingers into his. The warm breeze plays with the loose ringlets Jonathan has come to love and it makes him smile. They walk, talk and laugh well past the lunchtime hour. Their first day together is perfect and Jonathan is pretty sure this will not be their last.

He has spent most of the day in Pineville but now has a three-hour ride back to Hammond. He gets Callie home and part of him doesn't want to leave her. He also doesn't want to spook her and move too fast. He walks her to the door and kisses her on her cheek.

"You know you can come back, back to Hammond I mean, whenever you want. There are no charges against you", he explains gently.

She drops her gaze.

"Tell me you will think about it."

But before she can speak, Ilysa opens the door. "Callie? Well, did you two have a nice day?"

"Yes, it was a very nice day. Thank you. Ms. James, I will see you tomorrow. Callie has my number if either of you needs me." He smiles at Callie and turns to leave. Jonathan looks up at the two when he opens his car door and Callie nods with a smile. As he drives off, he looks in his rearview mirror and they are just walking inside. His smile is across his face and as bright as the moon. *She's going to stay*

His drive home is filled with promise. Ilysa will finally tell him what he wants to know, and he can stamp 'Closed' on Elyse's file. And Callie, his beautiful Callie, the future looks hopeful.

MILLER WAKES THE next morning feeling better than he has in years. He dresses and prepares for work, and though he doesn't believe he has much of a singer's voice, he belts out his favorite song all the way to headquarters.

The place is buzzing with activity and the path to his office is a labyrinth of people and officers. *It's too early for this.* But Miller will soon have his anticipated confrontation to deal with.

"Holding, this is Detective Miller, I need Victor Scott escorted up to my office."

"Yes, Detective, I'll have someone bring him up."

"Detective Miller," Branson calls from the doorway. "You got a moment?"

"Sure, Ted, come on in. You got something for me?"

"Yeah, but I'm not sure if you want it. I'm digging around in Victor Scott's files and his mother, Emma, never married. The father, I told you wasn't listed on the birth record, but there are ways of finding out who he is. I traced him back to Atlanta. Is it my imagination or is everyone from Atlanta moving to Hammond?"

"So, you found him, who is he?" Miller asks, annoyed.

Branson shuffles papers in his hands and stares at his sheet. He hesitates, then looks up at Miller.

"What is it, Ted?"

Branson looks back down to his papers just as the officer walks in withVictor, no longer donning his tailored suit, but grey county overalls. His glance shifts to Victor, then back to Miller.

"We'll pick this up later, Ted. Excuse us. Victor, have a seat."

"But detective…," Branson says.

"Branson, later."

Branson leaves and closes the door behind him but looks back in through the large window.

"I understand you are originally from Atlanta, what part?"

"I grew up in Little Five Points, that's before it became one of the hotspots of Atlanta."

"I was born not too far from there myself. I'm finding a lot of Atlanteans in Hammond." Miller looks up from his conversation and Branson is still at the window.

"Excuse me for just a moment." He pokes his head out of the door. "What is it Branson, do you need me for something?"

"Yeah, I need to tell you something. Did you notice any family resemblance?" Miller steps out and closes the door. "Excuse me.?"

"Victor's father, his name is Lawrence Miller. Detective, his dad, is your dad."

"Are you sure?"

"Yeah, pretty sure."

"Thanks, Ted." A bit stunned, Miller goes back into his office and closes the door. He sits and stares at Victor

"Detective, you look like you've seen a ghost."

"Do you remember much about your childhood? A playground at Lake Claire Park?"

"Yeah, spent a lot of sunny days there as a kid."

"Tell me about your parents."

"Mom and dad never married. The way I hear it, he was already married and had a thing with my mom. When I was about two, the wife got pregnant. Things were okay for a while and then the wife found out about me and my mom, and she filed for divorce. That was great because now I had my dad. That lasted another year or so, then one day he just walked out."

Yeah, he seems to have gotten a lot of practice at that.

"Is your father still living?" Miller queried.

"Alive and well and living in La Place, LA," came the sarcastic response.

AS MUCH AS he would like to continue this conversation with Victor, Ilysa and the DA have both come into headquarters. He gets the officer to escort Victor back downstairs, without mentioning the fact that they are half-brothers. He needs time to absorb that fact himself; and his dad, 'alive and living in La Place', is unbelievable.

He's brought in his contact and friend, Allen Smith from the DA's office, in hopes of finding the lesser charges for Ilysa. He seats them in his office and Ilysa gets to tell her story. From the affair with Paul St. Claire to the death of Elyse —the details Miller hadn't heard before are coming out.

"Why did you use Avery Jarreau's print?"

"She's young. She's never been in trouble with the law, therefore, no record. Her prints wouldn't even be in the database. I didn't expect you to connect her to any of this. And even if you did, I would be very disappointed if you convicted a young woman because you found one print. But that got both my girls out of harm's way and I will do whatever it takes to keep them safe."

"And your sister?"

"My sister was my whole life after our parents died. She was there for me when I needed her. She helped me hide from Paul and that P.I.; helped me deliver my babies. Why didn't she say anything? She left me believing my baby was dead. She never, in twenty years, tried to contact me to let me see her." This is the first time Miller has seen Ilysa even remotely emotional. She's always been calm and in control. But the memories of her life were flooding in on her and Miller could see the tiny cracks in the dam. "I would never have done that to her. I remember the pain she was in when that doctor messed her up inside. I remember the nights she cried. I was there when they told her she would probably never have children. She cried like a wounded animal. I held her hand and tried to comfort her. So, when we found out I was pregnant, she was thrilled. She could at least be an aunt if she couldn't be a mom. Then later we discovered there were two and I thought Elyse would pop with excitement," she laughed through her tears at the memory. "Then she stole my child."

"You didn't poison Elyse, but you are the mastermind behind her death. There is no physical evidence that will make a case. There is no solid evidence connecting your daughters to either homicide. There is no evidence other than your confession to putting the print on the vial. As far as evading the law, we can work with that. I can't say you won't spend a day in jail, but it probably won't be life. Let me see what I can do. I will get back to you in twenty-four to forty-eight hours. But if you try to leave the state, you will only make yourself look guilty. Then I won't be able to stop them from trying you in court," explains Mr. Allen.

"I won't leave the state. Thank you."

"Don't thank me yet. Jonathan, I will talk with you later." Smith stands and leaves

She turns to Miller. "Thank you too."

"I think this will swing in your favor, Ms. James."

"Are you going to hold me here?"

"As long as you are working with me, I can release you on your own recognizance and you could stay at your home here in Hammond. You won't have to drive to Pineville. Do you want to call the girls?"

"Yes, thank you, Detective. You've been very helpful. I told you once before that you and Callie would make a handsome pair. I still think so."

Miller smiles. "I will give you a moment. Just make sure you leave me a way to reach you." Miller also stands and leaves.

Ilysa calls the girls and lets them know what's happened. They are excited that their days of running are over. They look at each other, smile, and prepare to go home to Hammond.

MILLER CHECKS IN on Maryann in her holding cell. She's been processed and her new outfit and living quarters are not as fashionable as the home she left. The dark circles under her eyes and streaks down her cheeks make her look a little crazy, but the tears don't stir Miller. The ugly secrets and lies of Hammond are slowly being uncovered, but he isn't prepared for the craziness of voodoo.

"What the devil were you thinking? Voodoo dolls? Where did you get them, Maryann?"

The small brunette sits quietly, ignoring the detective. "Where did you get the dolls?"

She stands and paces the small room, fingering the graffiti on the wall. "I tried to get her to leave Victor alone. She laughed at me. She said Victor didn't love me anymore, that he wanted her because she was young and beautiful." She turns around and wipes her face on her sleeve. "I love my husband, Detective, but he made me look like a fool, messin' around with that little tramp. Everyone in town saw them together."

"Did you ever try just talking to Victor? Did you try anything else? She was only nineteen. There must have been some other way."

"You don't understand!"

"I understand she was a kid, young and dumb, maybe, but still a kid. Victor was just as much at fault as Lizette. He had to play his role in this mess. Why didn't you kill him too?"

"I was trying to save my marriage, why would I want him dead?"

"Maybe because he made you look like a fool. Maybe because he made you feel like less than a woman. Maybe because you know deep inside that if he's done this once, he'll do it again."

Maryann turns back to the wall and plays with the graffiti. "Maryann, where did you get the dolls?"

"You don't want to find her, Detective. She's scary."

"Can you tell me her name and where to find her?" His tone was not indicative of fear

Maryann says nothing and continues to play with the signs and symbols before her. Miller shakes his head and goes back to his office. He passes Victor's cell, at the end of the hall and looks into the small window. He's just sitting there, looking like the end of the world is imminent. He's lost his wife, his lover, and his business is in a questionable state without his presence. Miller continues but doesn't even manage a hello. *I'm not sure how I feel about having a half-brother. The weird thing is, neither of us grew up with a dad. He left both of us.*

Miller reaches his office and takes a deep breath when he sits. His rose-tinted informant is on the desk, and he notices almost a motion picture. Images are flickering in the lenses as if they aren't sure what to show first. Miller looks at them nervously. *You're being a little weird right now. I'm not sure I want to look.* But the images continue, calling him to pay attention. He puts them on to see what's going on and one person is standing before him. This is the same pale skin and dark-haired figure from the articles. The deathly appearance is a little unnerving. She turns sharply and Miller finds himself looking into the soulless eyes of a woman. Suddenly, he can hear the sound of the wind blowing in the background. He's never heard any sound before.

"I am Daeva Keket. I know you are in possession of something you don't understand. Come to me."

"How is it that I can hear you? I've never been able to hear things from within the glasses?"

"Find me and I will answer your questions."

"Where can I find you?"

"You know where to find me, Jonathan, you've seen me here before. I felt your eyes upon me when I spoke with Maryann. Look for me here, but make sure you are prepared for what you hear." She turns back around and walks away into the shadows

Miller takes the glasses off and sets them aside. He remembered the visions of Maryann's meetings with her; the shadows, the tombstones. *I'm not going out there at night.*

THE NEXT MORNING, Miller gets a phone call from Sam Smith asking him to be on the lookout for a fax coming into his office. It gives all the details related to Ilysa James.

"Jonathan, this one is going to cost you a bottle of Loren. I've worked my contacts and given her a sweet deal. I hope she takes it because the alternative is not good."

"You got it, thanks, Sam. I'll talk to her."

Before he can hang up, the papers start to flow out of the machine in the corner. Sheet after sheet. He reads through them and calls Ilysa.

"Good morning, Ms. James. Can you come to my office this morning? Let's say eleven. No, there's no rush. I'm glad they're coming home. One o'clock will be fine. Tell the girls I said hello." *She's coming home today!*

Miller is just finishing a phone call with his new cleaning service when he turns his wrist to see that it's 12:55 PM. He glances up in time to see Ilysa walk up the stairs, but his surprise comes when Callie and Cora follow just behind her. He can't take his eyes off of Callie as she glides across the floor in his direction. He opens the door and allows the three to come into his office and then he steps out to grab an additional chair.

"Please, have a seat ladies. I have some good news and some bad news." He takes a seat at his desk. "The DA has pulled some incredible strings. Okay, the bad news is that the law tends to frown upon poisoning people, even under the circumstances of this case. But since the evidence is not concrete and definitively not pointing to one individual, we have only your confession. They are sentencing you to one year in prison, but they are dropping it to six months probation.

You will be able to stay in your home, not leave the state without notifying your probation officer and just keep in touch. Can you do that?"

"I can do that. Thank you, Detective."

"You're welcome. I'm glad it worked out so well." The ladies stand to leave. "Callie, can I talk with you before you go?" Ilysa looks at Callie. Then she and Cora leave the office.

"It's nice to see you again. Do you think I could pick you up for dinner tomorrow night?"

"I'll check with momma to make sure, but I don't think she'll object."

"That's great. I'll pick you up around seven."

Callie leaves and catches up with Ilysa and Cora. Her smile tells her mother everything she needs to know. The three walk downstairs, arm-in-arm to go home. Having her back in Hammond and being unafraid of the future offers him a sense of relief he hasn't had in a long time. He finishes his paperwork for the case decides he has enough time and daylight to make it to Parklawn Cemetery, so he grabs what he needs for the evening and leaves. The hairs on the back of his neck start to stand as he nears the entrance. Its enormous gates sit wide open and Miller is thankful for the little daylight that remains. He begins his search for the empty-eyed spirit, half hoping she isn't here. Wandering in and around the huge cold tombstones and monuments, he peeks around corners praying she doesn't jump out from somewhere. He would rather not die of a heart attack here in this place. The walking paths are wide enough for processions to make their way through and Miller looks down each one. He turns a corner and is startled by the pale face and black hair standing at the end of the path. He doesn't feel a breeze, but he would swear that her hair and clothes were being moved by one. Daeva Keket uses one of her long-curled nails to summon him closer. He slowly moves down the path, his heart racing unbelievably.

"I didn't think you would come," she says.

"I have a lot of questions…"

"I know," she stops him in his thought, "You don't understand how you and Daniel are the only ones able to use the gift. Come walk with me. I made them for his mother many years ago, but he learned at an early age that he had a connection to the arts, through her. He was such a sensitive little boy; he was so easy to teach."

"Why am I able to use them? I didn't know Daniel or his mother. My mom would never have been involved in this kind of stuff."

"She and your mother were also excellent students, eager and willing to learn. They had a natural connection and were good at the Dark Arts. And even though your mother tried to keep you away from it as best she could, you are almost as sensitive as Daniel. You are connected through your mother; connected to the glasses, to me, and the darkness and so the glasses will show you many things, some good, some not so good. They may show you images in the present, past, and after you learn more, maybe the future."

"I don't believe you. I don't believe in Voodoo. I'm not trying to learn more about it. The glasses, I have to admit, are kind of interesting, but I'm not trying to get caught up in this creepy world."

"As long as you are using the glasses, you won't have a choice."

"Why am I able to hear sounds now? I could hear you talking to me when I couldn't hear anything before?"

"Did you ask to hear?"

"Yes, a long time ago."

"Well, maybe they find you worthy of the change. Your connection to them is gradually growing stronger. They will continue to change for you as long as you have them and use them. You just have to keep yourself open so they will show you what you need, but beware, they may sometimes show you things you don't want to see."

Miller is so interested in his visitor that he hasn't noticed how the time has slipped away. He glances around and notices the sun has set, and the shadows are starting to creep around him. He would rather be staring down a 200-pound criminal with a firearm, than standing in this cemetery with these shadows. He has more questions but asks the next two or three as he begins walking backward.

"You know where to find me," she laughs as she takes in his movements. "I am among many friends here." She fades into the shadows.

Miller turns toward the main gate and quickens his pace.

His apartment is a welcome sight again. Not only is it away from the Priestess and the cemetery, but the new cleaning service has done a marvelous job in his place. *It's clean enough to invite a special guest. Yeah!* He falls asleep, dreaming up ways to impress Callie and the next morning, Miller rises with a new sense of excitement.

"Good morning, Callie, would you have coffee with me?"

"Good morning, Jonathan, how patient are you? I'm just waking up."

He laughs a little, "Okay, how much time do you need?"

"Just an hour. Will that make you late for work?" she asks.

"Whenever I show up, I'm on time. I'll see you in an hour."

The coffee shop is a little busy and the usual 'Hello, Detective' is coming from different tables as they walk. Jonathan smiles politely and with his arm behind his back, guides Callie with the tips of his fingers to their table. He allows her to sit first and moves to the opposite side of the table.

"I know I asked you out for coffee, but if you have time and want breakfast just order what you want."

"I don't have to rush back," she says with a smile.

Jonathan waves at a waitress and she returns with coffee and menus. As she pours over her choices, he watches her face. *You are beautiful!* "Callie, I have an ulterior motive for asking you out this morning. I just want you to see my face when I ask you to my place for dinner Friday night. I'm cooking, so if your favorite things include more than four ingredients, well then, I might have a little trouble."

She laughs at him and he drops his head.

"I'm sorry. I'm not laughing at you, I think it's kind of cute that you want to cook for me. I like a lot of things. Simplest would maybe be pasta, seafood, or salads. I'm sure anything you fix will be fine." She flashes his favorite smile, bright, easy, and sincere.

"Great, I will pick you up around five and that will give me time to get stuff done by six."

"That's fine. Is there something I can bring?"

Jonathan reaches across the table and takes one of her hands in his. "You and an open mind."

Her quizzical look makes him laugh this time. With breakfast finished, he takes her home and heads to work, feeling like a schoolboy. He only has two days to plan and shop for the dinner he will prepare. He's so excited. He doesn't believe anything can dull this feeling.

He arrives at work and checks his internal mail. It's business as usual until he finds the memo informing him that Paul St. Claire is scheduled for release in two weeks and Victor Scott by the end of the month. *I refuse to let even this bring me down* His mind turns back to his plans with Callie.

He calls his cleaning service, informs them of his plans, and asks them for a few special things to clean in the apartment. He knows he will need help and wants everything just right. He starts by picking a few things up on his way home and all the while running through, in his head, what he wants to say to her.

By Friday morning, He just wants to hear her voice. "Good morning, Callie, how are you?"

"Good morning, Jonathan, I'm okay. Nice to hear your voice."

My thoughts exactly! "You too. I'm at the office and I just got a memo you might be interested in."

"What about?"

"Your dad. Callie, he's due to be released at the end of next week."

"That's great, will it be okay if I am there?"

"I think he might like that. So, I will see you at your place around five?"

"Let me know which day and I'll be there for him, and yes, I'll be ready by Five."

He decides to leave work early and go home. He has everything he needs. The cleaning service came in this afternoon to work so when he walks into the apartment it is not only clean and neat, but the service has set the table with a tablecloth, place settings and candles. He quickly mixes his salad ingredients in a bowl and covers it. He finds a vase for the flowers he picked up and places it in the center of the table. He changes into something a little less official and drives to get Callie.

She is ready as promised; the white short sleeved dress, low heel and bright smile are a perfect combination for the day. Her dark ringlets and brown skin are perfectly set in the yellow color. The glow on her face matches the one in his heart every time he sees her.

"Hi Callie! You look wonderful."

"Thanks."

The typical small talk fills the car ride to the apartment; so far, it's light and easy, and he loves her laughter. When he opens the door to the apartment, she smiles

"You have a nice place."

"I'm glad you like it. Here, have a seat. Would you like a glass of wine now or with dinner?"

"I'll wait. Thanks, but don't let me stop you."

"I'll wait but let me get started with dinner." Jonathan moves into the kitchen. "I found an old recipe of my mom's and combined it with the things you said you liked, so I hope it comes out as well as I think it will. I have a salad to get us started," he says as he lights the candles and gently kisses her cheek.

He dishes out salad, then prepares and serves the main dish creole shrimp and pasta and white wine. He serves a dessert of warm apple pie, topped with vanilla ice cream and hers sparkles at the top. She looks at her bowl and her mouth opens wide with a smile. Then she looks up at Jonathan as she removes the diamond ring from the ice cream.

"Callie, I have a confession to make. You touched my heart the first time I met you. Watching you walk down the path at the park was harder than you could understand. And when you disappeared with your mom and I thought I would never see you again, I almost lost my mind. I decided I never want to feel like that again. If you accept this ring, you can take your time. I won't rush you. I will wait until you are ready to marry me. You won't have to leave Hammond again, unless you want to, or we are leaving together, never again out of fear. I just don't want to be without you anymore. This ring belonged to my mom, but when the time is right, we will pick out our own. For now, it's just a promise to you that I will always be here for you and if you want, my future is your future."

Callie stares at the ring, then stares at Jonathan. She is so very quiet that he worried she would run out of the room. Her eyes water- like the banks of the Mississippi and threaten- to overflow.

"I accept, Jonathan."

~~**~~

The following Friday morning Miller stands at the top of the stairs leaning against the wall as he watches Callie and Cora greet Paul at the front door. Callie introduces Paul to Cora and

Miller notices the slight hesitation as the two hug. It's the first time he's seen her, and he steps back to view them side by side. He smiles and the three leave the building the picture of the trio walking out remains with Miller and he gets little done for the rest of the day.

23

MILLER LEANS AGAINST the banister of the stairs and watches as they process Victor for release, handing him all of his belongings and paperwork. Even though he's out of jail, he's on a short leash for another two years.

Victor turns to leave and Miller steps into his path. The men are eye to eye and Miller sees a small resemblance to the father in his pictures. He still hasn't clued Victor in on their connection.

"You are clear on the fact that you are restricted to Louisiana?"

"Yeah, I got it. My partner will handle my overseas stuff."

"That's fine. I have another matter I need to speak with you about, but that's for another time." He steps out of Victor's way and lets him pass but continues to watch him as he walks out.

Miller goes upstairs to his office and closes his door. Branson steps in moments later.

"You okay, Detective? I saw Victor leaving."

"Yeah, I'm good."

"Did you tell him?"

"No."

"Why not?"

"Not the right time, I guess."

"Okay, you know what you're doing," he says as he steps back and closes the door

Yeah, I know what I'm doing.

"Jonathan." Miller looks up at hearing his name, but there is no one at the door.

"Jonathan." He hears it again. It's very soft, but he knows someone is calling his name. He just can't tell where it's coming from.

"Jonathan, look into the glasses." The whisper of a voice belongs to Daeva. He turns his back to the door and puts the glasses on. The pale face from the cemetery is standing before him.

"Jonathan, you haven't been back to talk to me."

"I've been a little busy."

"There is so much I can teach you, just like I taught your mom, Beth, and Daniel. I can teach you more about the glasses you possess. I can teach you more about the gift hiding inside of you."

"What gift? What are you talking about? I've never been able to do anything before I picked these things up."

"It's because your mother shielded you. Unlike Daniel's mother who encouraged her son. But I can bring it to the fore, sharpen it and make it stronger. The glasses will be able to help in other ways, and eventually, you won't need the glasses."

"I will think about it," he tells her as he removes the glasses. *There's a snowball's chance in hell that I will study anything with you.*

Weeks pass and Miller is ready to make his move, but he needs Victor to help him pull this off. He makes the drive.

"Victor, this is Detective Miller, I am on my way to your place. I will be there in about fifteen minutes."

"Well, you know where I'll be."

Fifteen minutes with his thoughts running amuck, Daeva's words come back. All efforts to turn them off are futile. 'I can sharpen it, make it stronger' the words reminded him of the six-million-dollar man, 'we can rebuild, make him stronger, faster, blah, blah, blah.' Miller has little interest in making it 'stronger'. He is almost grateful when he finally arrives at Victor's place. He can take care of the here and now.

Miller listens to the chimes on the other side of the door and waits "Hello, Detective, what is it I can do for you exactly?"

"I want you to call your father, make sure he is home and tell him you are coming to see him. Don't mention me."

"Why would you need to see my dad?"

"That's not your concern. Make the call."

Victor calls and finds his dad at home. Then he and Miller make the drive to Laplace. The small house with half of a wrap-around porch sits only yards from Lake Pontchartrain. Miller wonders who manages the upkeep of the property and grounds. He soon learns it's in better condition than the man who answers the door. "Hi dad, I brought a detective from Hammond, who wants to meet you," Victor says as he steps aside for Miller.

Miller moves in front of the tattered man and studies him from head to toe for a moment "Hello, Dad."

JONATHAN QUICKLY SNAPS his arm back and his fist flies across the jaw of the older man. Lawrence Miller stumbles backward and falls onto his butt

"Hey, what the hell are you doing?" Victor asks. "Dad? What are you talking about, Detective?"

The man, still on the floor, rubs the thick whiskers on his chin and looks at Miller. "Oh, hello Jonathan. Maybe I deserve that." Victor steps past Jonathan and helps the old man off of the floor.

"Someone want to let me in on what's going on? Dad?" Lawrence just looks at Jonathan and Jonathan's silence speaks volumes.

"Victor, meet your brother, I guess half-brother, Jonathan Miller." Victor turns to Jonathan. "You knew…"

"I just found out a few weeks back, when they brought you in for the Babineaux girl."

"And you still didn't say anything? When you were asking all those questions about my parents, you knew then, didn't you?"

"Yeah, that's when I found out. I wanted to make sure you would bring me here. I didn't want him to know or leave." His father could see the anger in Jonathan's eyes and watched as his hand slid upwards toward his sidearm.

"Jonathan, don't do nothin' stupid, we all make mistakes in our life."

"You just left us. That wasn't just a mistake! You didn't call, you didn't visit, and you didn't even bother to send birthday or Christmas cards. Nothing! I can still see you walking down the street. You broke her heart and left her alone with a little kid." Jonathan's hand was now resting comfortably on his gun and positioned to unsnap the holster.

"Jonathan, can we sit and talk like adults here?" Victor asks. "Please, take your hand off of your weapon. He's just a broken old man."

Jonathan turns to Victor. "You should be just as angry, you were born first. Then he had the gall to walk away from you and your mother for us, and then come back, only to leave again. "Here", he says handing Victor the gun, "you want to shoot him? Go ahead, shoot him."

"No, I don't want to shoot him. It won't change anything, especially the past."

He turns back to Lawrence. "How do you have the right to ruin four lives with your 'mistakes' and not be held accountable for them. Twenty-five years, and not a word. You didn't even show up for her funeral."

"I didn't know about her funeral."

"Enough people you both knew were there, I'm sure somebody mentioned it to you."

"Drop it, Jonathan, he didn't care about either of them or us."

"What do you mean?" Interrupted Lawrence. "Maybe I wasn't part of your life, but it's not like I didn't care. I watched you from a distance most of your life. When you graduated High School and entered into the Academy, I knew. When you got your Detective Shield and solved your first case...."

Jonathan drew back again poised to punch again and Lawrence flinched. "What the hell are you talking about?"

Lawrence walks over to a small table in the living room and pulls a book from the drawer. He hands it to Jonathan and sits down on the sofa. Jonathan looks at the thick, leather-cased book. He drops into another nearby chair and fingers the casing.

"Go ahead," prompts Lawrence, "open it."

It takes Jonathan another moment, but he slowly turns the pages. Similar pictures of him on the playground as a young boy are the first ones he sees. Grade school pictures, scouting, him with Coach Evans, and all of his high school activities. Everything. There were pictures of him graduating from the Academy. There is a page with pictures of Jonathan and Victor side by side, and for the first time, he sees the likeness. They both strongly resemble their dad.

Jonathan didn't know if the tears in his eyes were from the sentimentality of what he was seeing or the pure, unadulterated anger that was threatening to erupt like Mt. St. Helen. "How did you get all of this?" He said through clenched teeth. "You can follow my life, but you can't call to wish your son happy birthday? If you had all of this, you can't even lie and say you didn't know where I was. I remember hearing mom crying in her room. I did everything I could to make her happy; to make up for you not being there, but I was just a kid! Why didn't you come back?"

"I'm sorry Jonathan, I didn't know how to come back. I didn't think she would take me back. I didn't know if you would."

"You could have asked, Damn you!" Jonathan takes the book and throws it across the room. Papers and pictures sprinkle the floor like snow as Jonathan storms out of the house. Victor looks at his dad, then follows Jonathan outside. Jonathan hears the door close and turns to see Victor coming toward him.

The orange sun is setting low in the trees along the river's edge. The fall breeze carried the scent of Cajun cooking reminding Jonathan he hadn't eaten.

"How long have you known he was here?"

"Oh, I found him about six years ago. I was talking with one of my warehouse foremen about my dad being a decorated detective on the force and how I didn't see him much growing up. When I said his name, my foreman told me he knew my dad. They attended AA meetings together for a while, then dad stopped coming. He's the one who told me where to find the old man."

"Victor, why aren't you angry?"

"I suppose I was angry when I first found him, maybe not as angry as you," he laughs, "but angry. Anyway, I've had six years for my anger to subside. Maybe in six years, you won't be so angry either. I come to check on him once in a while, just because. Hell, I've been an only child for thirty years. And now I have a baby brother. I think we should go get a drink. And discuss how you put your big brother in jail," he laughs again. The brothers get back into Victor's car and head for Main Street Bar and Grill. They don't notice the car parked down the street. The figure inside the long dark sedan watches as they pull out of the dirt driveway.

THE POUNDING ON the door makes Lawrence drop the photos he had just collected. "Damn!" He jerks the door open. "Do you have to bang? I thought you guys were …., oh, it's you. What are you doing here?"

The burly foreman steps past Lawrence. "What's Victor doin' with that Hammond detective." He slams the front door. "That detective is going to be a problem."

"That detective is my son, and you're gonna keep your hands off of him."

"I thought Victor was your son, now you tellin' me we got two problems?"

"No, Victor still doesn't know anything about what we're doing, and we can find a way to keep Jonathan out of our hair. Leave my boys out of this."

"Have you heard from Ilysa?" asks the Yeti standing before him.

"Not in weeks. That little lady is strange. Kinda like Jekyll and Hyde, but I have to admit, she knows her diamonds."

"We need to contact her. Maybe she can help."

"I heard she is on six months' probation; she has to keep her nose clean if she wants to stay of jail." Lawrence lifts his head to find the man's face.

"You'd better come up with another plan then. If he connects her to you…."

"He has no reason to connect me to her. He doesn't even know that I know her."

"What if he starts snoopin' around the warehouse, he could screw up a lot of stuff."

"So, we need to make sure he doesn't go to the warehouse."

"Go back to work tomorrow and stop worryin'."

"You can talk about not worryin', you're not the one trying to run that entire operation with half your crew missin', your boss on lockdown, and clients crawlin' up your butt for their precious stones!"

~~**~~

The next morning at CARVELE Shipyards, Clayton Woodstock is flipping pages on his clipboard muttering to himself as he walks. He's not watching where he's going and bumps into Victor's partner Mat Preston.

"This is not exactly a good place to wander around with your head in your butt, and what the devil are you mumbling about?"

"Ever since Victor got locked up this job has been crazy. I got overseas orders I can't fill, and stateside orders are coming in faster than we can manage. I can't be in two places at one time. I need Victor on the job. This business is going down the toilet without him. I wish somebody would teach that guy a lesson, messin' round with people's livelihood."

"I'll get a hold of Victor, maybe some things he can do from home. He still has his overseas contacts."

"Yeah, but he needs a crew to inventory, pack and crate that stuff. We lost most of his guys after he got busted, including the other foreman and the rest don't take orders from me."

"They were his guys, maybe he can get them back. Just relax, I'll talk to him."

Preston walks through the warehouse taking note of the activity. There are guys there, some working, some not, but they're in the arts and antiquities side, not the diamonds. Victor had hand-selected his guys for that job. His trust was given sparingly, and if you lost it you never got it back. With Victor, revenge was usually swift and painful.

Preston makes his way back to his office, stands in front of the plate-glass window, and looks over the park below. The sun plays with the subtle colors in his silver suit as he calls Victor Scott."

"This is Preston, we got a problem. Your foreman Woodstock is losing it. None of your diamond crew is on the job and only half of your arts crew is in. Nothing is moving on that side. He needs you to make some calls. Your overseas orders are lagging and he can't let arts crew work the inventory without your signature."

"I can see who I can get back in there, but they still have this fancy piece of jewelry around my ankle, so I ain't going anywhere. Let me make some calls, I'll get back to you."

Preston disconnects and stares out of his window. He makes one more call before leaving his office.

"Hey, this is Preston, got a job for you. I'm sending you a name, get me anything you can on him. No, just keep an eye on him for a while, let me know what he's doing."

~~**~~

Reflecting off of the wall, Jonathan can see flashing lights, but they are not the lights from his squad car. He cautiously peers around the corner, and at the end of the alley he can see the lights but can't make out what is producing them. He stealthily moves toward the lights, careful to avoid the broken glass, cans, and other trash scattered about. He gets closer and sees his rose-tinted glasses on the ledge of a window. In disbelief, he pats his jacket pocket hard enough to hurt and it makes him jump up in his bed. It takes him a moment to get himself oriented, but when he looks over to the last place he set glasses and they are still flashing and flickering with such speed Jonathan gets a little nervous.

"'You've never given me weird dreams before, so what's up?" He says approaching slowly.

Jonathan steps slowly as if he is trying for a sneak surprise. The glasses suddenly go dark. He picks them up and puts them on only to see pitch black, but then moving toward him is the pasty white face of Daeva Keket. Her hair and clothes blowing in the wind that Jonathan can now hear. She gets closer and he can see the empty eyes. He can almost feel the cold radiating from her like the burial chambers around her. He now understands why she gives Branson the heebie geebies.

"What's going on?"

"Jonathan, I've been sensing something you should be aware of. Be careful, someone means you harm."

"What are you talking about, Daeva? Who?"

"I'm not sure, the images are always in the shadows. Watch your surroundings," she warns as Daeva begins to fade back into the darkness.

26

JONATHAN AND CALLIE laugh and talk over their lunch break. They spend as much time together as possible and it's always good.

"Callie, have you ever wanted a house of your own?"

"Of course, most people want to settle down someplace and call it home."

"Close your eyes and tell me what it would look like," he says smiling, but

She hesitates. "Go on, close your eyes. Tell me what you see."

Callie closes her eyes and describes her home, the colors, the covered front porch, the fenced yard for kids or pets, the large windows to let the sun in, but with light blue drapes for privacy when needed. She rambles on for quite a while as Jonathan takes mental notes of everything, including the way her face brightens with every detail.

"It sounds perfect," Jonathan says smiling. "It suits you. Come now, we both have to get back to work."

They leave the café and after a warm, tender kiss go their separate ways, unaware that from the same black sedan someone is watching on the adjacent corner. The charred hand reaches for a cell phone on the dashboard and makes a call. "I think I have a solution…"

When Jonathan returns to work people notice the smile on his face and the weightless stride, but he's still concentrating on the details Callie provided and the stares go unnoticed. He goes into his office and is immediately followed by Ted Branson who is now wearing his silver detective shield thanks to Miller.

"Lunch with Callie, *again!* That's the third time this week," he says laughing.

"Yes, and it will be three times next week and once on the weekend. Now close my door please." Branson laughs as he backs out and closes the door.

Miller picks up his cell phone and calls an old friend. After a few minutes. "Thanks, I would appreciate any help you can give."

"I'll let you know what I find. Talk to you later."

Miller stands and stretches. His thoughts drift back to his lunch with Callie, and he smiles

"Man, you got it bad," laughs Branson as he sticks his head in the door.

"Get out of here!" He laughs and throws a wad of paper towards the door. His cell phone rings and Victor's number is on the screen.

"Miller here."

"I got a problem, can you come to the warehouse?"

"I have plans for the evening but, I can be there first thing in the morning."

"That's fine, thanks."

~~**~~

"Preston here. Really. Ilysa's girl? That's almost too easy. Maybe we can control two dogs with one bone. Okay, thanks, I owe you big."

Miller's View

The Case of the Blue Diamonds

Book #3

MILLER HAS BEEN planning this evening for weeks, but keeping his poker face will be the hardest challenge of his life. Right after work, he will get to see his Callie. Miller finishes the last of his paperwork. He neatens his desk and stacks his case folders into tidy piles, then brushes the few crumbs from lunch to the floor. He tugs on the chain to his desk lamp and waves to it with a smile as if it were an old friend.

"Goodnight, see you tomorrow," he says softly, so no one will think he is truly losing his mind. But Miller is in such a light-hearted mood, he's not sure if he would care. He grabs his jacket and heads out the door. The smile on his face is bright enough to illuminate the room as he exits, but if he wants to play his hand, he will have to drop it.

Miller arrives at Callie's in his little sports car. He gets to the front door and rings the bell; the smile drops from his face when Ilysa is the first person to respond.

"Good evening, Jonathan," she speaks with a warm, soothing tone, but it is the first time she has called him Jonathan.

"Good evening, Ms. James," he returns the tone. Though she is always calm, always pleasant, there is an undercurrent, within her spirit, similar to her deceased sister, Elyse, which Miller can sense. A Mount St. Helen just waiting for the right moment to erupt.

"Would you like to wait inside tonight? Callie should be down shortly."

Jonathan accepts her invitation as she steps aside. "Please, have a seat anywhere."

Jonathan sits on the edge of a chair and takes in everything around him. They are back in the house near the river's edge. It's cozy and well kept. Small, unique pieces scatter the room. *Ilysa must be a collector.* Jonathan recognizes a few things, and he also knows their approximate value, but what he doesn't know is how she can afford them. Miller's mind is spinning but comes to an abrupt stop when Callie walks in.

Callie appears, wearing a royal blue, floor-length sundress, her dark ringlets fighting against the confinement of a headband. The sight of Callie stops his wandering thoughts. She seems so small, even in her heels, she has to crane her neck up to see the top of his six-foot, runner's body.

Jonathan looks down into the deep chocolate brown eyes; the smile he had when he left the office hasn't returned. He runs his fingers through the short, thick curls on his head. "Are you ready?"

"Yes, I'm starving." Callie hesitates, a little put off by his tone, but she has her taste buds set for the succulent flavors of DON'S Seafood. The drive is pretty quiet. Jonathan acts like he's in another world.

"Are you all right?" she asks, but Jonathan doesn't respond. He maintains his stoic expression as he continues past the restaurant Callie is expecting. Out of the corner of his eye, Jonathan catches the priceless quizzical look in his direction, and it was the last straw. He could no longer hold it in; the mischievous little boy's laughter burst through his demeanor. "Jonathan Miller, what are you up to?"

Jonathan is determined not to mess up his plan, but he is about to burst at the seams. The drive takes another twenty minutes before he pulls into a driveway. He parks in front of an adorable, little, two-story home. A manicured lawn and colors popping from the flower beds welcome them.

"Jonathan, are we picking someone else up for dinner?"

"No, it's just us." He hops out and runs to her door. "Come on, get out," he says, excitedly.

"Why are we here?"

He walks her up the short flight of stairs and to the large, covered porch. There is a swing sitting still; quiet, patiently awaiting its guests.

Callie looks around as Jonathan pulls a key from his pocket and opens the door. Stepping aside, he lets her in first. Callie steps inside, cautiously eyeing everything around her.

"Do you remember the conversation we had at the cafe a while back? You closed your eyes and rambled for ten minutes," he laughs. "Well, I made a phone call to a friend in real estate, and after looking at several places, he found this one. Told me he thought it was perfect for us. I took one look and saw you sitting in that swing. Another friend decorated for me; I think she's got great taste in furnishings."

Callie recalls the conversation in her head as she glances around. Jonathan takes her hand and leads her into the kitchen. The warm shade of yellow makes her eyes sparkle. The sky-blue curtains match the tablecloth perfectly. In the center of the table are yellow roses and blue irises, a card, and a small box set against the vase. Callie looks at Jonathan.

"You did all this for me?" She slowly moves to the table and makes a quizzical glance at the card, looks at Jonathan, and when he nods his consent, she opens it. Then Callie lifts the lid to the small box and discovers the most beautiful diamond ring she has ever seen. When she turns back toward Jonathan, he is on one knee, looking up at her. The levees holding back her tears threaten to break and flood the house.

"No one has ever done anything like this for me before."

"Callie, I love you. I can't imagine my life without you. So this is ours," he says, standing and waving his arms around the house, "and I am yours if you'll have me."

She hesitates. Callie is quiet; so very quiet. She walks around the room a little. She stares out of the large picture window and into the fenced backyard. Jonathan becomes nervous.

"Callie, what's wrong? Don't you like it? You can change anything. It's yours to do what you want." He laughs trying to hide his nervousness.

"No, Jonathan, the house is perfect." She starts walking toward him.

"It's the ring. If you don't like it, we can exchange it. I should have let…" By this time, she is within inches of his face and before he can finish, her lips are pressing against his.

"The ring is beautiful; I couldn't have picked a better one."

"So is that a yes?" He laughs again, not quite so nervous.

"That's a yes, Jonathan Miller." Her smile is bright, but the dam has cracked, and the tears are flowing.

Jonathan just pulls her close, laughing softly. "You scared me for a moment."

She laughs too.

He puts her at arm's length long enough to remove the promise ring and slide the engagement ring on her finger and then looks into her tear-stained face. "Are you still hungry?"

"No, but I could use a glass of wine. Give me a minute to freshen up, I can't go anywhere looking like this."

"Take your time. There is a bathroom around the corner to your right." He watches as the love of his life saunters off. He can't believe the feelings that are running through him. When she returns, she is his beautiful, tear-streak-free fiancé.

Arm in arm, they leave the place they will soon call home and head for DON's to celebrate the beginning of their new life.

THE NEXT MORNING Miller arrives at the warehouse as promised to meet Victor. The cavernous warehouse is strangely quiet, and Miller begins his hunt for Victor. He winds his way through the long hall lit by low-wattage ceiling lamps and spots a door at the top of a long metal stairway at the back of the building. A glimmer of light comes through the small window. Miller heads straight for it.

Victor is muttering to himself and doesn't even notice Miller when he approaches. So he knocks on the open door, startling Victor just a little.

"Jonathan! You're here, great."

"Sooo, what's the problem? Where the heck is your crew?"

"I sent everybody out of here today. Gotta figure out what the hell is going on."

"What are you talking about, Victor?"

Victor stuffs his hand into his pocket and removes a fist full of exquisite blue diamonds. "I came in today to work my overseas inventory, and I found these inside the dust cover of a piece of art I was getting ready to ship.

"Oh man, if I had known you were moving stones like this, I would have waited to give Callie her ring."

"Well, that's great, except they are illegal! Wait, what? Did you say you gave Callie a ring? When?"

"Last night, those were the plans I told you about."

"That's great, congratulations!" He says, patting Miller on the back.

"Yeah, thanks. Now back to these beauties," Jonathan says, taking one stone from Victor's hand. "Got any ideas?"

"A few, but I don't know how to prove it; not without getting my butt thrown back in jail," Victor says. "These aren't coming from Belgium with my usual shipment, and I need to know where they're coming from. There aren't that many people in the area dealing with stones of this value, so I have to be careful who I ask. Ask the wrong person, and I tip my hand that I know." Victor's distress is showing on his face.

"Okay, calm down, there's gotta be a way. Let me dig and I will get back to you. Just be careful in the meantime. If they find out that you know about the blue diamonds, your life could be in danger," Miller says.

Jonathan leaves the office and finds his way back down the long staircase around the winding halls of low lights, and to his car. He looks back.

"This whole place gives me the willies," he says, spinning 360 degrees.

Jonathan doesn't notice the dark sedan parked in the back of an adjacent warehouse, waiting, watching. As Jonathan pulls off, the scarred hand reaches for the phone.

While the dark sedan watches Miller, Clayton Woodstock is in the shadows of the warehouse, keeping an eye on Victor. He rubs his fat fingers across the four days of growth on his chin then grabs his phone.

"Hey, that detective just left Victor's office. I couldn't hear what they was talkin' about, but I could make a wild guess or two."

"They don't have any proof to connect us, so there isn't anything to worry about."

"You mean they don't have any proof to connect you and Ilysa. But I'm not going down alone. My hands are all over this, and so are Preston's. But you two are just as involved."

"Well, they can't connect us unless you open your big mouth," says Lawrence.

"And you better believe, if this mouse gets caught in a trap, it's gonna squeal!" Clayton threatens.

"Stay calm. It will be fine." Lawrence Miller tries to mask his fears as he calms his friend down.

"It's been two days. I gotta get back in here if I'm gonna move this inventory. If you don't call Preston, I will!"

"Okay, I'll call him! Go somewhere and cool down."

Lawrence is staring at his phone. If he calls Preston, Victor and Jonathan could be in danger. He makes a different call.

"Hey, it's Lawrence. I think I need your help. Can we meet at Nola's tomorrow at six?

"Sure, I can be there," says Ilysa.

~~**~~

Meanwhile, back at his office, Miller is making phone calls of his own. He still has one of the stones that Victor found, but he needs someone with the right tools to see if there are any markings. He carries it to his lab tech, Kevin, who is working on something brown, wiggly, and a quarter of an inch long.

"What the hell is that?"

"It's an aphid, or more commonly referred to as a tick."

"And why, exactly, are you looking at it under the microscope?"

"Well, a bunch of these little guys were found on a recent homicide victim. They may be able to tell us where he's been. If he bit and sucked some blood from our victim, we'll know if he is withholding evidence or if he is an accomplice. In the process of feeding, they can regurgitate nasty stuff like bacteria and viruses, and crap that can kill you. So I'm going to extract its blood with this needle and run another test. I'm hoping this little guy will tell me what killed our victim."

"You can do that? Run a toxicology screen on a bug?"

"Sort of."

"Wow, who knew? Right now I need to know if there is some way to identify the origin of a valuable diamond. Is there anyone you know that you can trust implicitly?"

"I'm afraid the world of diamonds is beyond my means," he says, pulling the linings of his empty pockets out and laughing, "but if I needed to ask someone about diamonds, I would call The Diamond Boutique on West Main. The owner is Elena Guy. I've heard she knows her stuff."

"Great, thanks, I'll check with her in the morning." Miller turns to leave. "Uh, good luck with your aphid thingy."

Kevin just smiles and goes back to his microscope.

"Hold still little guy, this is gonna hurt a bit."

Miller gets back to his desk and his cell phone rings.

"Miller here."

"Hello, Detective."

"Wow, it's my favorite voice in the whole world," he says, "How did your mother take the news?"

"She and Cora are so excited. She wants to know how soon she can start planning the wedding," Callie laughs.

"That's between you and her, all I have to do is be there."

"You mean you aren't interested in planning it?"

"I'll tell you what, when you want my opinion, I will give it. If not, go with what you want, I draw the line at pink ruffled shirts, but I'm easy."

"Okay, I'll let her know."

"I only have one person on my invite list. Well, maybe two."

"That keeps things small and intimate."

"That's okay with me."

"Me too. I like the sound of that. Just the important people."

"I have a more pressing question," he speaks softly but tries to sound serious.

"What?" Her tone reflects more concern than curiosity.

"When do you want to move into the house with me?"

Callie smiles with relief. "How about this weekend, I'm off?"

"Yes! That's what I'm talking about." They both laugh at his enthusiasm.

3

"JONATHAN."

Miller looks up from his desk. There is no one at the door.

"Jonathan!" The voice is familiar. *Oh, right.* Jonathan turns his back to the door and pulls the rose-tinted informant from his pocket.

"Daeva, uh, what do you want?"

"Jonathan, meet me at the cemetery tonight by nine o'clock and be sure you have the glasses with you."

"You're crazy if you think I'm coming out there in the dark; that place gives me the willies!"

"Um, who are you talking to, Detective?"

Jonathan snatches the glasses off and spins around quickly to find Detective Branson standing in the doorway.

"No one, just thinking out loud. Close my door on your way out, thanks."

Jonathan turns back towards his window and places the glasses back on and speaks a little softer. "Daeva, are you still there?"

"Yes, you have to come. Tonight." Daeva fades into the shadows.

I don't think I trust that…, that…Priestess. But Jonathan reluctantly shows up, shining his flashlight and inching his way past headstone after headstone, crypt after crypt. He looks past the tall marble engraved vault with the name Henry White and sees Daeva at the end of the wide path.

"Don't be afraid Jonathan. Nothing will harm you here as long as I'm around. You haven't used the glasses in a while. I sense you are losing your connection; this is not the time. Things are stirring around on the dark side, and they have you in their sights."

"Who are you talking about? What are you talking about?"

"The 'snowball in hell' is melting quickly, Jonathan, and you need my help. Now, where are they?"

How'd she know about the 'snowball in hell' comment? "Here, in my pocket. I never leave home without them." He tries to sound funny, but the strain was obvious.

She takes the glasses, folds them closed, and slides them into her bra.

"Hey, wait a minute! I want those back."

"And you will get them. Follow me." They walk into the crypt of Henry White. Henry died in 1892, but the smell inside tells Jonathan that something has met a more recent demise. If it isn't Henry, he isn't sure he wants to know. The crypt is large; large enough to add several more members of the White family, but Daeva has set up a temporary training site in the open space.

Daeva removes the glasses from her blouse and lays them on a small wooden table. Candles light the room from all corners; Henry White has a single row of candles the length of his casket, and there are two on the table. She looks at Jonathan and turns back to the glasses. Taking a small bottle of purple liquid, she pours it over the glasses.

"Hold out your hands." She puts the glasses in his hands, still dripping with the purple concoction, and backs away. Jonathan's heart is racing as he watches the Priestess begin to shake, slowly at first, and then violently. Words spew from her lips, but most of them he doesn't understand; a few Cajun-French words he catches because he has heard them before; something about the light, and spirit, and help. But the rest is gibberish. She rambles and shakes for ten minutes before Jonathan sees any sign of her slowing down, and then he hears her say his name.

"Jonathan."

"I'm still here."

"Put the glasses on."

He wants to say, 'Hell No!' but doesn't dare. He places the glasses on his face and watches as the images flow. The images are clear, much clearer than before, images of faces from his case files. He sees himself with Callie at the local café the day she describes the house. The glasses show him the day he took Callie to the house and gave her the ring. They are showing him his life just like they showed him the life of Daniel Edwards. He starts to freak out, takes the glasses, and tosses them across the room. He watches them fly; already regretting the act. The lenses hit a wall and shatter, making Jonathan cringe with guilt. He looks at Daeva with the apologetic eyes of a six-year-old. Daeva returns his look with a smile and points to the glasses. When Jonathan looks again, the glasses are not only intact, but they are also not scratched, not even smudged with a print.

"How?" he stammers.

"I had a feeling you would lose it." She lets out a low, creepy laugh. Branson was right, she could be the wicked witch with no problem. "The purple solution prohibits their being damaged by anyone or anything. Now, let's try it again. Put them on."

Jonathan does what he is told and refrains from any more overreactions. Daeva shows him everything about the glasses, even things she never had the chance to teach Daniel, their previous owner. She is thrilled. Once he lets go of his inhibitions, Jonathan proves to be a quick study.

The clock tower strikes midnight before Jonathan leaves the cemetery. The sense of dread he had when he entered is no more. He glances back at the Priestess.

"Jonathan, be careful. I sense a different spirit working and take care of that beautiful girl."

"How do you…never mind."

"We are connected through the darkness, through the glasses, Jonathan. What I don't see or feel, I sense in other ways. When you need me, call me through the glasses."

"Goodnight, Daeva, and thanks, I think."

Jonathan quickly makes it back to his car and heads home. *'Call me through the glasses.' I wonder if she meant that literally.* Though his head is spinning, his heart has successfully returned to a normal rhythm, and he arrives at his apartment a little excited about what may come next. He's still wide awake at two A.M. and wants to call Callie. *Are you nuts? And say what? Are you trying to get into the World Book as the shortest running engagement in history?* He opted for a glass of scotch and went to bed.

MILLER CAN'T WAIT to see what else these glasses can do. He rushes to work and opens the first file on his desk.

"Elizabeth Waterman, a sixty-five-year-old, Caucasian female. Originally from Brazil, married to Maurice… Hmm, this looks like a random car accident. Why did this end up on my desk?" A strange sensation comes over him, and he takes the glasses from his pocket.

--**--

The images are instant and clear. No more wisps of smoke. Miller sees an elderly gentleman sitting across a table from another man. Papers scatter the table top and the elderly man is signing page after page. Then he sees the same elderly gentleman on the street corner, engaged in a conversation with a seedy character dressed in a soiled jumpsuit. He's in great need of a shave and haircut. The name badge, below his left shoulder, reads Hammond Waste Management, Anderson. The glasses are not making Jonathan wait for anything, not like before. They are just feeding his impatience with bite after bite.

Jonathan continues to watch the scenes unfold, and he sees Anderson hop into a waste collection vehicle and start to drive. It's dark, and not many agencies have their trucks on their routes at this hour. The truck proceeds down West Coleman, picking up speed as it passes Spruce and Pine. The light at the intersection with South-West Railroad turns yellow as he approaches, but he doesn't relinquish his speed. Traffic seems almost nil, and Elizabeth Waterman, unaware, enters the intersection when the truck slams full force into her car. The car spins, crumpled metal flies, shattered glass, and car parts litter the street. Elizabeth's head is slammed into the window, sending shards into her head.

According to the file, Maurice Waterman was trying to collect on the insurance policy he had recently taken out on his wife. He used the excuse of funds being in offshore accounts and not readily available, and that he needed to cash in the policy for burial expenses. Waterman collected his three-

million-dollar payout. As he sat in the chauffeur-driven sedan, Jonathan heard him laugh. 'I'm sorry, I failed to mention, I had her cremated and scattered in her favorite flower bed in the backyard.'

~*~**~*~

"Damn! Insurance fraud? Elizabeth was born into money, but Maurice Waterman is a millionaire in his own right. Why off the wife for insurance money?" He takes the glasses off and looks at them. "You, my friend, are incredible!"

The feeding of information goes on, file after file. Jonathan is jotting clue after clue and leaving notes in the files as he goes.

He now has the answers to five cases in front of him and decides to go for an even six, but when he opens the next file, the glasses begin to show him something else.

~*~**~*~

The images are clear, and Miller recognizes the cargo palettes and shipping containers. He is looking at the CARVELE shipyard. The warehouse is two buildings away from Victor's office. There are two dark sedans and one large, dark, SUV parked by the opening. Matt Preston is standing outside of the sedan talking to a younger woman. Her reddish-brown hair is cut short except for the side that covers her left cheek. But her style of dress and shoes indicates that she does well for herself in whatever she is doing. The conversation is in whispered tones, so Miller doesn't get any of it. He can get a close-up of the tags, and when Preston pulls his hand from his pocket, Miller can see he is holding only a few of the flawless blue stones. The woman slowly reaches for one and holds it up to the sun. The expression on her face is sheer delight.

~*~**~*~

"Well, it won't take long to finish up these other cases, so I'll see what else I can get on these stones." Miller grabs his jacket and heads for Elena Guy's Diamond Boutique. When he walks into the elegant salon, brightly lit and shimmering with gold and glass cases; several customers are sitting at tables in plush cushioned chairs. Each personal assistant is wearing a gold, satin smock engraved with his or her name, not one hair out of place and a smile plastered on that looks like the Cheshire cat. Jonathan pretends to be a buyer, glancing around from case to case. Not one blue diamond in sight. A smocked individual approaches him.

"Hello, welcome to Elena's. My name is Sybil, how may I be of service?" Her South American accent is unmistakable.

"Hello, is the owner of this establishment available?"

"I believe she is in the back. Can I let her know who's asking for her? Or maybe what your needs are?"

"My name is Jonathan, and a co-worker referred me to her for a special engagement ring."

"I'll see if she is free to speak with you. You may certainly look around if you wish."

The young woman spins on her heels and disappears behind a white and gold curtain. The large E and G catch the light when they move. When she returns, she smiles at Miller. "Ms. Guy will be with you shortly," she says, as she waves toward a chair.

The next time the white and gold curtain moves, a five-foot, five inches, seductively tanned woman comes through. She has a lively step in her heels and is wearing a pencil skirt. Her fitted jacket with gold and diamond trimmed buttons hugs her like a straight jacket. But it is the haircut that makes Jonathan's jaw drop. Cut short except for the front that covers her left cheek, just like the woman at the warehouse with Preston. He's not sure how well he can hide his surprise.

"Hello, I'm Elena Guy. How can I help you?"

"Well, I was in the market for a special engagement ring, and a coworker suggested you were the go-to person for diamonds. I need a stone to match the flawless, and exquisite beauty of my young lady. I want something different, unique in style, setting, maybe even color."

"I see and have you considered a karat size or price range you would like to stay in?" she says, as she motions Miller to follow her.

Miller picks up a slight South American accent. She's not from Hammond, but perhaps she's been here longer than Sybil.

"For my lady, if the ring is right, the price is right. Show me what you have."

"So, for me to fit you with something appropriate, tell me a little about her. What she does, what she likes, favorite color, that sort of thing."

"I can tell you her favorite colors are bright blue and yellow. She is always fashionably dressed, much like yourself," he says, waving his hand over her clothing. It makes her smile. "She is outgoing; she's funny…"

"Okay," she laughs at Jonathan's description.

"Let's start over here. Everything, in this case, is two karats or more; we can change the setting or customize it to your liking."

Miller sees plenty of things he likes, but the blue diamonds are not in the case.

"Are there any naturally colored diamonds? I've seen ads for chocolates and blacks but are they authentic?"

"Gems like those are rare, hard to get, and very expensive, but yes."

"Any other colors?" he asks.

"Yes, your lady's favorite yellow, also called Canary."

"But no blue, huh?" Miller keeps pushing. "Before I make a final decision I'd like to see all of my options."

"Well, I've heard of them, but I've never seen one. I could make some phone calls and see if any of my connections have come into any. If you leave your business card, I will call as soon as I know something. Your young lady is a lucky girl."

Miller thinks quickly. "I don't have one on me right now, let me just jot down my information." He pulls a small pad from his jacket pocket and writes his first name and cell phone number. "Thanks." He flashes a smile and leaves. When he gets back to his car, he pulls a business card from his pocket and stares. *Yeah, Detective Miller, that probably wouldn't have gone quite the way you wanted it, even though you did catch her in her first lie.*

He drives to his office but calls Victor along the way. "I've got good news and bad news."

"I could use the good news, but throw the bad at me first," Victor says.

"I can tell you that Matt is involved, and I'll work on the concrete proof, but I can also tell you at least one person who is working with him. Are you familiar with an Elena Guy? She owns this rather sophisticated boutique on West Thomas Street. She's going to 'see if any of my connections have come into any' of the blue diamonds." He tries to repeat in her mild accent.

"I know Elena. She is one of my local customers. She buys high-end artwork and my Belgium stock of diamonds. That's probably how Matt connected with her. So, which part of that was supposed to be the good news, Jonathan? On the one hand, my partner of seven years is dealing behind my back, and on the other, my business connection of the past ten years is dirty right along with him. I'm happy Jonathan, ecstatic! Thrilled! Can you hear how thrilled I am?"

"Calm down before you blow a gasket!" Jonathan attempts to soothe his brother. "Don't worry, Victor. We'll get him and everyone connected with him. You may be able to help."

"You name it, little brother."

~~**~~

Jonathan, thinking that he has played his hand pretty well, doesn't realize Elena is on the phone before he has even started his car. She's been in this business longer than he knows and suspicion is the name of the game.

"Preston, this is Elena. Seems there's some curiosity about your blue diamonds."

"What do you mean, curiosity?"

"A young man stopped in to query about diamond engagement rings. He wanted to know if I had blue for his young lady."

"Would he have happened to be tall, good-looking, African-American?"

"Yes, that sounds like him. He only left his first name and number"

"Detective Miller. Jonathan, I believe."

"Detective?"

"Just be careful what you say around him."

"I understand." She hangs up, hoping she hadn't let the cat out of the bag. "Detective Jonathan Miller?"

~~**~~

Preston calls Lawrence Miller. "Yeah, this is Preston. We all need to get together. We need to talk."

"I'm headed to meet Ilysa now. We'll be at Nola's by six; You want to join us there?" says Lawrence.

"Yeah, I'll call Elena back and tell her to come too," replies Preston.

"Okay, see you there. We'll hold a table for four."

Preston calls Elena. "Meet Ilysa and Lawrence at the Nola Café. I'm on my way."

But Elena makes one more call. "It's Elena; I had someone come in asking questions about blue diamonds."

"Do you know who they are?"

"Yes, I've already talked to Preston and he knows the young man as Detective Jonathan Miller. We're meeting at Nola's tonight, Lawrence Miller and Ilysa James will be there. You should come."

By the time Preston arrives, the three are seated in the corner of the restaurant having a heated whisper of a conversation.

Preston walks towards the frantic group the rest of the café customers have done their best to ignore, but when the trio at the table notices Preston, they stop mid-sentence.

"Are we trying to bring the rest of Hammond into our circle, ladies, and gentleman? We all know why we're here. We have a new concern to deal with."

"That's my son you're talkin' about," says Lawrence.

"I'm not talking about Victor," Preston informs him. "I'm talking…"

"I know damn well who you are talkin' about- Detective Jonathan Miller, he's my son, too."

"Oh, for the love of Pete, are you kidding me? I was hoping the last name was a coincidence." Just before Preston can pop a blood vessel, his eye catches the doorway, and in walks Maurice Waterman. He stands at the door looking around.

"Who called him?" asks Preston looking around the table.

"Guess that would be me, he is my boss you know," Elena smirks.

"Have you lost your mind? That old man is crazy!" He whispers as Waterman approaches then jumps up from his seat as he gets closer. "Maurice, good to see you!"

"Sit down and shut up. Preston, did you *really* think you were going to have this talk without me?"

"I certainly would have brought you up to speed." Preston knows the truth about Elizabeth Waterman. He remembers Maurice vowing to silence her when she threatened to expose him. Elizabeth was always nagging him about his other secret. Maurice was furious at her disloyal attitude and Preston was witness to people who ended up on Maurice's bad side. He wasn't even sure if Waterman had a good side, so he kept a big, safe distance between them.

"Somebody tell me how this detective found out about the blue diamonds," Maurice insists."

"We're not sure, but he did visit Victor at the warehouse," Lawrence jumps in.

"So now Victor knows? I thought we were keeping him in the dark."

Ilysa adds. "We were doing so well."

"He must have just stumbled on them. No one is stupid enough to make that mistake," says Preston.

"As for Victor, I think if he knows now, we cut him in and see if he bites. And if you four can't come up with a way to get rid of that detective, I can give him a couple of extra homicides to keep him busy!" Waterman spews.

"We'll come up with something, Maurice," Elena flashed her Cheshire smile, but Maurice had already turned to leave.

"You'd better."

Preston turns to the three at the table and looks straight at Elena. "Are you happy now? He will do anything for his diamond business.

Maurice did not become a millionaire just with the death of Elizabeth. His diamond business was doing great before then, but it exploded with the discovery of the blue vein in South America. People can't get enough of them and don't care that children were kept out of school to work the mines for almost as many hours as their fathers."

"I don't know what you plan on doing, but it better not involve hurting my boys," Lawrence says.

"What about that girl he's been seeing?" Preston asks.

Ilysa glares at Preston but maintains her calm. "That girl happens to be my daughter. Touch her and you will deal with me, and I will make anything Waterman could do to you look like a prom date. Excuse me." Ilysa leaves the group and exits the café.

"Any other ideas?"

"We could use the girl as leverage, to control the detective, just give strict instructions to hold and not harm," Elena suggests.

"Do you know any thugs with integrity, Elena?" asks Preston.

"I might be able to help in that department. I have some friends who owe me a favor." Lawrence stands to leave as he reaches for his phone and dials the number. He leaves Elena and Preston to finish their conversation.

"Ilysa's going to be a problem. I've known her for a while, and she's a bit strange."

"Why do you say that?

"I know her sister was into voodoo, and I can't say that Ilysa doesn't have a dark side to her as well. I don't know for sure if she uses it, but I don't want to find out. I just feel like there is something else under that cool, calm voice."

"Well, if Lawrence can get his people to do the job, then we'll have him to blame."

"If he screws up and something happens to her daughter, she's coming for all of us. Just get someone to keep an eye on both of them."

"I'll make the calls," she says.

They leave and go their separate ways, but none of their departures go unnoticed.

THE WEEKEND COMES and Jonathan arrives to take Callie away. She has packed several suitcases and a few small boxes, and she is wearing the brightest smile he has ever seen.

"Are you sure you're ready for this?" she asks.

"Callie, I've been ready for you for a long time. I didn't think I could be this happy." He opens the door for her and loads the car; the two drive off to their new home. When they pull into the driveway, Callie notices the small, sporty, yellow car parked under a tree.

"We've got guests." She sounds disappointed.

"No, no guests," he laughs.

"Well, whose car is that?"

Jonathan hops out and goes to open the door for her. "It's yours," he says, handing her the key.

Callie's eyes light up, yet again, as she runs to the 2005 Audi TT.

"Mine?" she yells back. "Thank you, it's so cute!" She opens the door and sits behind the wheel. "Jonathan! I love it!"

Jonathan is already up the stairs with the suitcases and headed back for the boxes, grinning from ear to ear. "I'm glad you like it. I didn't want to have to take it back. I think the salesman would have cried."

Callie closes the door, runs into his arms and they tumble into the soft, plush grass. "How did I ever get lucky enough to find you?" She playfully kisses all over his face and then lands on his lips, lingering softly, breathlessly. It turns into a hard press and Jonathan sits up and deftly lifts her from the ground. He manages the stairs and the door with her still in his arms but stops on the soft padded carpet in the living room. For the next two hours, passion lights up the new home.

"I would love to continue this, but I should get back to work. A couple of things need my attention. You can stay and get acquainted with your new home, or if you need more from your mother's, you can take your car. Whatever you like. I won't be too long."

"It's Saturday! Do you have to go back?" She pretends to be a pouty face.

"Don't give me that face." He laughs. "I promise, a couple…three hours tops." He heads for the bathroom for a quick shower before leaving.

"Okay, maybe I will just go and show her the car." She is still smiling brightly.

~,~**,~

Callie watches from the upstairs window as Jonathan drives off. She stands there long enough to notice the black sedan only moments behind him. She looks, but she's too far away to read the plates. She cleans up, straightens the room, and hops into her new car to go to Ilysa's. Callie's years of living on the run have heightened her survival skills too. She remembers when she had to watch for the P.I. from Atlanta. So when she feels the chill run through her and knows that the 68-degree weather isn't the cause, she places the blame on the dark sedan with the tinted windows three cars back. That's two within hours of each other. Callie gets to her mom's house and sees an identical car parked on the next street. She pretends not to notice, but once inside, she calls Jonathan.

"Hi, Jonathan. I think I'm being followed; maybe you too. When you left the house, there was a black sedan that left right behind you. And I noticed one behind me on the 55. Now it's parked about a block and a half down the street."

Jonathan stands up and looks out of his office window to the street below.

"Yeah. Four doors and tinted all around. I see it. Callie, please stay at your mom's tonight. Let me see if I can get to the bottom of this."

"Okay, call me later and be safe."

"Will do. And don't worry. Bye."

Ilysa walks into the room at the end of the conversation. Callie hangs up and turns to see her mom.

"Callie, what's going on?"

"I don't know. It seems as though Jonathan and I have someone interested in our business."

"Who? Why? I don't understand."

"Neither do I, but Jonathan wants me to stay here for the night. He'll find out who's behind this." Her excitement over her new car dims.

~,~**,~

Jonathan is at his desk looking through the information collected by Branson. Elena Guy looks to be about thirty-eight years of age and of South American origins. He is plugging away trying to find anything on her. No one in the U.S. Database with that name. No birth certificate, no social, not even a driver's license. He tries the international database with the same results. He'll put Branson on it first thing Monday morning. He is so much better at the digging than Miller. Someone moving merchandise with that much value has to be in somebody's system.

He decides to go back to his apartment instead of the new home; he is glad he made the call not to give it up. It is so much closer. Miller cautiously watches the movements of the sedan. It always stays two or three cars behind him, but its nondescript appearance stands out like a sore thumb. Miller pulls into the parking area of the apartment and doesn't see the sedan, but he gets that sensation of being watched. He gets inside and looks from his balcony window. Not only is the sedan sitting in the corner of the lot, but he sees the pale face and dead eyes of Daeva standing in the trees, looking at the sedan and then back to the window.

But at least Jonathan believes he knows the good guys from the bad guys.

He calls Victor.

"Hey, it's Jonathan, looks like I stirred a hornet's nest."

"What do you mean?"

"They've taken enough of an interest to tail Callie and me all around town. There is a sedan sitting outside my apartment tonight. I just don't know who's behind it, Preston or Guy. When I find out, I will let you know."

"Jonathan."

"Yeah?"

"Be careful."

"Oh, how touching, big brother sounds worried."

"Seriously, you fool," he laughs nervously, "watch your back."

"Okay, okay, will do." Jonathan backs away from the window and cuts off the light. He's worried about Callie but having her alone at the house would have made him worry even more. At Ilysa's, she's not alone and he can focus on who and why. He stretches across his bed, but he can't sleep. With the lights still off, he goes back to the window. Daeva is no longer in the tree line, but the sedan is still in the corner. Jonathan grabs his old boy scout knife from his nightstand and goes down a different staircase, out through the basement entrance, and hugs the shadows like brand new friends. Hiding behind the other cars in the lot, he makes his way to the trees. Six feet and one hundred sixty pounds is a lot to sneak through a wooded area. The snap of the wrong branch and they will know I'm coming. He gets to the side of the vehicle and sees the guys are sound asleep. He pulls the small blade and after jotting down the tag, punctures both rear tires without waking either sleeping beauty and makes his way back the same way he came. Pleased with himself, he goes to sleep.

The next morning, he gets in his car. The sedan is still sitting. He waves and takes off, leaving them in the lot. He looks back in the rear-view mirror in time to see them jump out to inspect their damaged tires. Jonathan laughs all the way to headquarters.

Its Sunday, but still, a minimal staff is on duty including Branson. After he calls in the tag number to get a registrant's name, he scribbles a note and takes it to Branson. "I need to see if you can dig up anything on Elena Guy. She runs a diamond boutique, and I get nothing. U.S. nor Interpol have that name in their system. She has a South American accent so there may be something there."

"Yeah, no problem, I'll let you know what pops."

"Thanks." He goes to his desk, and the name Elena Guy stares back at him from his notepad. *Ten to one that's not even your name.* He also noticed that the tag number he wrote down last night is in sequential order to the tags from the warehouse.

Branson puts what he is working on aside and starts punching keys. He looks up South American diamonds. He reads through article after article and the words, Santa Elena, Guyana, and Brazil keep slapping him in the face. He does a search for Elena Guy and Miller was right. Nothing. He searches the boutique's Internet page and finds her picture. He gets to use the newly installed facial recognition software. They are years behind everyone else, but Hammond is trying so hard to catch up to the 21st century, but a small town and big funds are hardly ever used in the same sentence. Letting the program run in the background, he goes back to the Internet page, to continue his hunt, digging through telephone records, banking records, overseas connections, local connections, and old newspaper articles. Scribbling notes as he goes; Branson gets excited and works at a feverish pace.

Miller looks up and watches him jump from computer to paper and back. *How does he do that? Youth!* He laughs. Miller knows he only has a few years over Branson, but he doesn't spend nearly enough time in cyberspace.

Miller steps outside to clear his head. Something about Elena is nudging him. 'Jonathan, look to your right,' the soft voice from his pocket says.

He recognizes Daeva's voice, and it no longer freaks him out when his pocket starts talking. He casually glances in both directions so that it doesn't seem obvious, but when he looks to the right as directed, he sees the dark sedan parked at the corner two streets down. His pocket makes another noise. This time, it's his cell phone.

"Miller here."

"Detective Miller, we did a run on the plates you gave us, and the vehicle is registered to a Maurice Waterman of Waterman International Corp. located in LaPlace."

"Great, thanks." A large gong goes off in his head, but he's not sure why. He looks down towards the sedan again and then turns to go inside almost colliding with Branson, who is coming to find him.

"I got it!" he says, waving papers in his face.

Miller spins him around by his arm. "Control your excitement, Jr. we've got an audience." Branson tries to turn to look, but Miller jerks him back. "What did you find?" he asks, stepping back into the building.

"Who's watching? What? Um, okay, so Elena Guy's Diamond Boutique is owned by a millionaire businessman named Maurice Waterman. Waterman has been moving diamonds, both legal and illegal, from a place close to the border of Brazil. This is one of those places under investigation for the use and abuse of child miners. A man going by the name Oliviera stumbled on a vein in the mountain where the stones are created through volcanic activity and tumbled through a naturally occurring water flow similar to the first riverbed. The alluvial diamonds were discovered in India, around 800 B.C. They are rare and naturally blue, and just need the cut and polishing process; it's phenomenal. That's where the real money is. When the Venezuelan government found out that brokers were bypassing the KP, they tried to keep the rare and precious stones in Venezuela, but the owner of the mine started to make triple the value. The money got too good, and they had to find a way to get them out of the country. They move them from a place called Santa Elena and then into Guyana, hence the name Elena Guy. They give them fake certifications and push them through around the world. When I put Elena's face through the recognition software, I get a Safira Santos. She's been working for Waterman for over twenty years. She's moved up the ranks and now, though she owns her storefront and a little part of the business, the diamonds still come from Waterman International Corp."

"They informed me that the sedans following Callie and me today are registered to Waterman International Corp., but why do I know that name?" Miller pauses. "I remember! He's in a case file on my desk. His wife died in a crash with a maintenance truck. They ruled it an accident, but I think I have another idea on that. Well, now it looks like I have two reasons to visit Waterman."

6

MILLER GETS TO his desk the following Monday morning and finds Branson already at work. Again, he is working at a feverish pace on the keyboard. Miller goes over and sits in the chair beside him. Branson looks up and grins.

"What the hell is wrong with you this morning, too much coffee?" Miller asks.

"I had a very interesting Friday evening and a more interesting morning. I happened to be at Nola's café Friday night and watched an interesting conversation. At first, it was Ilysa James and your father, which I found interesting enough, 'cause I didn't even know they knew each other. Then it got more interesting when Elena Guy showed up and sat down at their table. When Matt Preston came in and walked up to them, I almost got nervous, but then he sat down. Old friends, maybe. I tried to give them the benefit of the doubt. But when Maurice Waterman went to their table and his wrinkles were not sitting pretty on his face, I knew something was up."

"So what did you find this morning?"

"I have been pulling phone records and cross-matching numbers. Elena, Matt, Ilysa, and Lawrence have been talking off and on for at least a year, and that's only because that's as far back as I can get."

"Ilysa and Lawrence are involved in the smuggling of illegal diamonds?" Miller says, more thinking out loud than talking, but Branson responds.

"I'm afraid so. So how do you arrest your dad and future mother-in-law without destroying two families?"

"I don't particularly give a rat's behind about Lawrence, but Ilysa is another matter." Miller goes back to his office shaking his head and muttering. "Ilysa? How do I talk to Callie about this? Dinner and wine, lots of wine," he says to himself.

Lawrence is chattering on the phone; trying to find the right guys to do this job isn't easy. Either they want way too much money, or they want to control the situation. He decides to call Jack Chandler. He's known him since he's lived in Hammond. Chandler was someone he could talk to when he was in AA, and they touch base every now and again. Chandler was not only a recovering alcoholic, but he also did some time in the Hammond Correctional Facility.

"Hey Chandler, this is Lawrence. How's it going?"

"Hey Lawrence, goin' pretty good for a change, sober eighteen months now. How about you? How you doin'?"

"I'm doin' good. You workin', Chandler?"

"Naw, kinda between jobs, why you ask?"

"I need some help. This job needs someone who can follow directions and keep a cool head."

"Ain't gonna land me back in the facility, is it? Cause I got no plans on ever goin' back."

"If we all play our parts, and nobody gets hurt, then we should be fine."

"Okay, I'm in. What I gotta do?"

"I'm gonna give you directions to my place; you can crash here. It ain't the Hilton, but I got a spare bedroom."

"When you want me to come?"

"The sooner, the better. I'll fill you in on the job when you get here."

"Okay, see you tomorrow."

"Great, I will let my team know."

It's a balmy evening and the light, warm breeze gently blows. Miller takes Callie to her favorite place and orders a light rosé. He needs to talk to her about this case without discussing too many details, but can't find the right time or the right words. Callie is enchanted with the house and car; she's making plans for the wedding. Jonathan tries to listen, but his mind is on the bad news he's about to deliver. One of her favorite songs begins to play.

"Dance with me," she says, reaching for his hand and letting him lead her from the table. He'll let her have this evening; they can talk later.

The song is slow and romantic. This certainly is not the time. He holds his Callie close and enjoys the moment. After a delightful dinner and a few moments on the dance floor, they decide to take a walk on the boardwalk of the seaside restaurants. The aroma of the surrounding kitchens fills the air replacing the usual smell of marine life. The street is empty save a few cars. Jonathan and Callie are lost in each other and don't sense the approaching danger.

THWACK! Darkness fills Jonathan's head. As one hand covers Callie's mouth, another wraps around her waist. Someone tall and heavyset drags her in one direction and after placing a sack over her head, shoves her screaming into a vehicle. Two others grabbing Jonathan under each arm drag him away in a different direction.

~~**~~

Slowly, Jonathan's world begins to return. He has no idea how much time has passed. He blinks trying to focus on the white planks of vinyl spread out before him. It's daylight, but just barely. Maybe 6 A.M. Then he remembers. *Callie! Where's Callie?* He hears loud voices and there is a strong smell of fish. There is a life preserver with the name 'Wave Goodbye' out of LaPlace, LA. He lay there listening, trying to think through the pain in his head. When he hears footsteps approaching alongside him, he quickly closes his eyes and pretends to be still unconscious.

"You must have whacked him pretty hard.

He is still out cold, you sure you didn't kill him," the male voice says, as he uses his shoe to nudge the body.

"Yeah, he's breathing, but he's gonna have a hell of a headache when he wakes up."

The voice was right. Jonathan's head did hurt and whoever did it is gonna pay. He doesn't recognize the voices, but glancing upward as much as he can without moving his head, he can only see the sky and a string of lights. He doesn't remember the sensation of moving, though he could have slept through it. They must be docked at a marina, but which one? And where is Callie? He slowly and carefully moves his hand to his back waist. *Damn! My gun is gone!* He always carries it, but when he is out with Callie, he never wears it at his shoulder. He checks for his cell phone. He silently grumbles when he realizes it's also missing. Lying face down he can feel the glasses still in his pocket. Guess they wouldn't have any reason to take those. They don't know what they do. He listens again for voices; he picks up on three distinct. One is American, and the others have voices hidden behind a Cajun-French accent. He hears the ringtone of a cell phone. *Drifting downstream? Oddly appropriate for a boat.*

"Yeah, yeah, he's still out," says one of the Cajun-French voices. "What you want us to do with him?" Miller tries to listen in. "In that case, the price just doubled." The voice is silent as it waits for the caller's response.

"NO! 'Cause, he's a cop! I ain't killin' no cop! I got one more strike, and I'm locked up for life. I ain't rotting in a cell for you." The call is decidedly disconnected.

"What's he sayin', he wants the cop dead? And what about the girl?"

"He ain't sayin' nothin' about the girl, man. Somebody else got that job, but he's crazy if he thinks I'm killin' a cop."

"Maybe we can just throw him overboard and let the crocs do the dirty work."

The ringtone plays again. "Yeah. He's still faced down on the floor." The others gather to listen.

"No, not yet. We was just talkin' about it."

There is a heavy sigh of frustration in the next statement. "Now you want us to bring him to you at the warehouse. Fine."

Jonathan is listening closely and hears the motor begin to roar. Then the boat begins to move slow and easy, possibly in reverse. He maintains his position on the floor of the boat until he can determine whether there is a chance for his escape. He must stay alive if he is going to find and help Callie.

Jonathan takes the opportunity to rest, hoping the pain in his head will subside. If there is a chance they will take him to where they're holding Callie, he needs to be ready. He lay still, but he can feel the boat move, turn and then accelerate. The voices are barely audible over the engines. He calms a little with the glimmer of hope that for now, she is still alive.

The boat he is on travels for a while. When it docks again, two men lift Jonathan by his arms and drag him off the boat. His eyes cast downward; he takes in the details he can see. The combat boots and camouflage pants they wear; the grassy terrain they walk across; the reasonably clean floor of the warehouse. They drop him on the floor and walk away. Within minutes, Jonathan can hear the large, heavy metal door closing. He waits and listens. No voices. Nothing. He sits up and shakes his head, trying to clear the fog, but it only reminds him of his headache. He wanders the place to get a feel for where he might be. The preserver on the boat said, 'Wave Goodbye' LaPlace, LA. Nothing on the walls of this tin can. The windows are too high. Jonathan goes to the metal door, but not knowing what's on the other side, he's reluctant to try to open it. He tries several other doors in the place finding one that leads upstairs. The door at the top says rooftop. *Damn, it's locked.* He grabs the fire extinguisher and breaks the cheap padlock. Jonathan steps out onto the roof and looks around the area. He's not in La Place. He's still in Hammond. Victor's office is three buildings away. He finds the fire escape at the far side of the building and makes his way down to the ground. As he looks around the corner of the building, he spots Callie as she is shoved into the back of a dark sedan similar to the one that was parked outside his apartment.

He doesn't recognize the big guy climbing in beside her.

'Call me through the glasses,' the words just ran through his mind. "I wonder." Jonathan decides it is worth a try. He backs up a little from the corner and pulls the glasses from his pocket.

"Daeva, can you hear me?"

"Yes, Jonathan, I can."

"I could use a little help."

Jonathan waits. Nothing. Then someone taps him on his shoulder. He thought it might be one of Preston's thugs, but he looks down into the pale face and lifeless eyes of Daeva Keket.

"They have Callie. I have no phone, no gun, and no way to get backup. Do you have a way of seeing where they are taking her?"

"Do you trust me?"

"Uh, is this the right time for this conversation?"

"Jonathan, do you trust me?"

"Do I have a choice, right now?"

"Yes, you do. You can choose to trust me to help you or not."

Jonathan, worried about Callie, looks into the dead eyes and sets her straight.

"I will treat you no differently than anyone else. I will trust you wholeheartedly until you prove to me that you can't be trusted."

Daeva smiles. "Put the glasses on. Think of Callie. See her face in your mind. Then watch the glasses work."

Jonathan does as he is told. He sees the sedan turning out of the warehouse area and onto the main road, then turning onto Highway 55, headed south.

"Daeva, I see her. I see them."

"They will give you what you need. Just give them a starting place."

"Thank you, um, do you need to get back in the glasses?"

Daeva laughs her dark laugh and fades away. "I'm not even here, Jonathan."

Okay, that's probably perfectly normal for her. Jonathan shakes it off and runs for the building where Victor's office is. The place is back to its usual tempo and noise level as Jonathan makes his way to the metal staircase.

He bursts in and finds Victor on the phone.

"They've got Callie."

Victor stares at him for a moment. "I have to go. I'll call you a little later," he says into the phone. "Who's got Callie, and do you have a clue as to where they are taking her?"

"She is in one of Waterman's sedans, and I don't know the guy with her. I've never seen him before," Jonathan responds.

Victor can see that Jonathan is worried, even if he is forcing calm to make an appearance. "Don't worry little brother, I'm not letting anyone keep you from your wedding day."

Jonathan tries to smile, but he doesn't pull it off very well. "I need to make a call, and I'll need a ride to headquarters for my spare gun."

"No problem, you can use the phone on my desk. I'll wait for you downstairs by my car."

When Victor leaves, Jonathan calls Branson and fills him in. With the glasses on and following Daeva's instructions, he can now see that they are taking the exit to La Place.

"It's Victor, yeah, he's here. He somehow made it out of the warehouse. I'm taking him back to his office, so your head start just got cut a little. Get moving and hide the girl."

Jonathan gets to the car. "Okay, let's go."

The two ride silently as Jonathan drums his fingers against the door. "Man, calm down, please. She's gonna be alright," Victor tries to sound reassuring.

"She might be. But if you don't stop driving so slow, you will be a new road rage statistic."

"Glad to see you haven't lost your sense of humor."

"I'm not kidding! Victor, pick up speed. "They have my girl, and I need to find them!"

"I'm already doing more than the speed limit, and I have one of Hammond's finest in my car, I don't want to risk getting a ticket."

"Damn it, Victor, do you want a ticket or a funeral!"

"Okay, okay." He picks up speed and gets to headquarters.

"Thanks, I will let you know as soon as I have something." Jonathan jumps out and runs inside. His spare gun is in a lockbox inside his drawer. He grabs it and a key to his squad car.

Victor's phone rings. "Yeah. No, I tried to slow him down, but he's worried about the girl. He's getting his things now and headed for his patrol car. Of course, I didn't tell him anything. He can't know I have any part in this. Where are you headed? Good, he won't think to look there." Miller gets behind the wheel and tries for a moment to settle his nerves. He removes the glasses from his pocket and puts them on. The images don't wait. They are almost as anxious as he is.

He can see Callie in the car. Her dark ringlets are free of the headband she was wearing the last time he saw her and tears are streaming down her face as she looks out the window. The sedan pulls into the driveway and Lawrence steps out onto the front steps. Chandler gets out first and opens the back door, grabbing Callie by the arm. He pulls her from the car. Lawrence smiles when he sees her. Chandler brings up her to the foot of the stairs.

"My son has great taste in women," he says.

"You're Jonathan's dad? Why are you doing this? Why am I here?"

"Well, darlin', you're here because we need Jonathan to back off and stop snoopin', and we're kinda hopin' you will convince him to do that."

"You're as stupid as you look. Jonathan loves me, which means he's only going to keep coming until he finds me. Then he's going to find the idiots who took me and what you're planning. In short, you just locked your jail cell," she looks into Chandler's eyes. "And he's already madder than a snake at you," she says right at Lawrence. "So when he finds out you're in the middle of this, he may skip the cell and land you straight in a coffin." Callie's face is tear-streaked but, Jonathan can hear her speak in a still calm, unshaken tone. She refuses to let on how afraid she is.

Jonathan knows where she is. He calls Branson to give him the address; then he calls for more backup.

"Victor! I know where they are. I'm on my way now."

"How the hell did you find them that fast?"

"I'll explain another time. I gotta go."

"But…" Jonathan disconnects and heads for La Place.

"Lawrence, he's coming your way. I don't know how he found out! Just get the girl and get out of there. Go back to the warehouse area and keep her quiet."

Lawrence looks at Chandler. "We gotta go, my son is coming for this little lady, and Victor couldn't slow him down."

"I know how to slow him down."

7

JONATHAN ARRIVES ON the road leading to his father's house. The tree line and underbrush are thick and will make a great cover for the approaching officers. Branson is there, and two additional squad cars are behind him. Miller gets out and meets up with the group.

"There are at least two men and they're holding one female. Please use caution when entering, and watch for the girl, she's my fiancé and if she gets hurt…try not to shoot; but if you have to shoot, shoot men. You two branch out around that way and come in from the back. The rest of you come with me."

There is only one car in the driveway. The sedan is gone. *Maybe Callie is still inside with my father.*

They slip up the stairs without a sound and peer through the windows. One of the additional Officers signals that he has eyes on one individual. Jonathan tries the door knob, but when it doesn't turn, he signals for the other officer to kick in the door. The four men rush in from the front and the noise brings the two from the back. They find Lawrence sitting in his favorite chair. The TV is on, and he appears to be sleeping, but when they try to rouse him, he doesn't move. Jonathan rushes over and feels for a pulse.

"You two, search the house. I need to know who has Callie and if they left a clue as to where they are taking her next. He's still alive, call for an ambulance. Branson, go to your car and wait, I'll call you from my car." Miller dashes to his car and grabs the rose-tinted informant from his pocket. He focuses his thoughts on Callie and watches for the images.

Callie is back in the sedan. The tinted windows are no shield for the glasses. She seems calm, but she is laying in the backseat and this time her hands and mouth are bound. The big guy Jonathan doesn't know is driving and moving pretty fast.

"Hey, it's Chandler, Victor just called, said we needed to move the girl because the detective was coming. He doesn't know how he figured it out. I kinda left him a gift to slow

him down a bit. No, no, he'll live. I'm headed back to the shipyard where they dumped the detective and taking the girl there."

"Branson, head for the CARVELE Shipyard, wait for me near the North entrance and when these guys finish up here, tell them where to go."

"How do you know that's where they're headed?"

"Call it a hunch."

"Where are you going?"

"I'll meet you there; I won't be too far behind you. I'm going to come in from the south side, but I have a stop to make first. VICTOR!" Miller disconnects his call and picks up the glasses.

"Daeva?"

"I can hear you, Jonathan."

"They've moved her down to the shipyard. I don't know if this guy is crazy or not; he's already hurt my father."

"I will do what I can."

"Daeva?"

"Yes, Jonathan."

He can feel the words trying to catch in his throat. "Please….don't let them hurt her."

"Easily done, Jonathan."

Inside of Warehouse 27 stacks of wooden crates are in row after row.

Various sizes are stamped in codes no one else is supposed to understand. There is walking space between the stacks and the tin wall. Nooks and crannies everywhere give Daeva plenty of play room. She sees the room where they are holding Callie and lines up with the large window. Smoke begins to appear from the stacked crates, and Callie brings it to their attention.

"What the devil is that?" shouts Preston. Chandler runs out of the office to investigate but finds nothing. Daeva makes a brief appearance at the corner of the window startling Preston to look outside the room.

Whoooooooooo! The howl of a coyote echoes through the massive warehouse. The noise seems to be coming from different corners of the warehouse, and both men scramble for refuge back inside the room. Daeva makes another brief appearance and fades away. The pale skin and dark hair are unnerving, but the legend of the Priestess is known throughout Hammond.

Her presence is enough to distract them from Callie.

Jonathan arrives at the shipyard and heads for the building that houses Victor's office. His car is not around, and the huge doors are closed. He goes to the warehouse where he was dumped, but the windows are high; too high to see inside.

He calls Branson, just in case the radios are being monitored.

"Where are you?"

"We're at the main entrance. Where are you?"

"Warehouse 27, come in quiet."

He slips around to the back of the building trying to get a sense of where they might be holding Callie. There is no one in sight when he looks into the huge building. He moves inside, using whatever equipment or box he can find to hide behind. *Voices!* He moves closer to them.

Miller sees Callie through the large glass window. Her makeup streaks her face where tears have fallen, and the position of her upper arms tells Miller that her hands must be tied behind her. She is watching something or someone and is facing away from Miller. There is a sound of movement, and he sees her eyes and head start to move back in his direction. Miller darts back around the nearest corner just as Matt Preston and Jack Chandler step through the door. They don't see Miller peering from a short distance. He lets them move out of sight; then moves closer to the door to check for others. With no one else in sight, Miller goes inside the room. When Callie turns and sees him, and starts to mumble, he immediately puts a finger to his mouth.

"Callie, hush baby, I'm here." He moves behind her to undo her ties.

"I'm going to get you out of here. Are you okay?"

Callie just shakes her head. He moves in front of her and wipes the tears from her face. "It's okay, if you need me to move mountains for you, I will," he says with a smile. "Stay here for just a moment. Let me see where they are."

Clayton Woodstock spots them moving towards the entrance and yells and shoots in their direction. Miller moves in between him and Callie, shielding her from flying bullets. He aims and returns fire just once, hitting Clayton in the leg. The noise alerts the others, and the sound of heavy steps is moving in the direction of the gunshots. Preston reaches the area ahead of Chandler and fires at Miller but misses. When Miller turns to fire at Preston, Clayton takes another shot. He hits Miller directly under the armpit sending him crashing to the ground. Callie runs to his aid, but she sees the others coming at her. She grabs Miller's gun and fires until the gun clicks and clicks. Both men are on the ground, and Clayton has just stopped shooting. Callie taps Miller's pockets looking for his phone.

"911, what's your emergency?"

"I'm here at the shipyards with Detective Jonathan Miller; he's been shot. Please send help!"

"Where are you?"

Callie looks around for any identifying marks. There is a stack of crates nearby. "Warehouse 27 at the CARVELE shipyards, Please, hurry, he's bleeding a lot."

"What's your name?"

"Callie, Callie…my name… is Callie."

"Okay, Callie, try to calm down. Help is on the way, just stay on the line with me until they come. Can you see the wound?"

Callie unbuttons Miller's shirt and searches. "I can see it."

"I want you to apply pressure to the area with any clean cloth you can find. Just hold it there."

"Jonathan, stay with me, please! Please don't go! Tell them to hurry!"

"They're coming. You're doing great. Just hold on."

Jonathan has a handkerchief in his jacket pocket, and Callie makes use of it.

"They're dead! I shot them!"

"Who's dead, Callie?"

"The men who kidnapped me. I shot them."

"Don't worry, it will be okay. I'm glad you weren't hurt. So who are you holding the cloth on?"

Callie looks down at Jonathan. His eyes flutter as if he is in a dream. "He's my fiancé, Detective Miller."

It isn't long before she can hear sirens coming in her direction. The backup team and EMTs reach Callie and Miller at the same time and then she hears the voice saying, 'Miss, you did great, but you can let go now.'

They patch Miller up and put an oxygen mask on him before pushing him and his gurney into the ambulance. Callie hops in and rides by his side. Branson calls in for additional wagons for the bodies and several officers assist Woodstock to a squad car. The police are at the emergency room entrance waiting to take her statement. Callie stops and watches as they roll her fiancé down the hall to a room. She glances down at her hands and clothes stained with his blood and collapses from the exhaustion into the arms of an officer. He scoops her up and settles her onto a cushioned sofa. A nurse rushes to her aid with a cool cloth for her forehead and something to help clean her hands. The coolness on her head brings her back slowly. Callie awakens to watchful eyes and realizes where she is.

"Jonathan! Where's Jonathan?"

"He's still in surgery. They just need to stitch him up. The doctor will be out to speak with you momentarily."

In the meantime, Callie recounts the entire 48 hours to the officers. "Miss St. Claire, can you think of any reason for them to do this?

"No, but they underestimated Jonathan's determination to get to me. Whatever he did, he *really* made them mad."

The surgeon approaches them, not looking at all happy, but a small smile appears when he stops and takes a breath. "He lost a lot of blood, so he's a bit weak. Fortunately, the bullet went straight through and missed his lung by a few centimeters. He'll be good as new in a few days."

"Can I see him?"

"He's under heavy sedation. He'll be out for a couple of hours. Go home and get some rest."

"I could go and get cleaned up, but I don't have my car here."

"We can get you back home, Miss St. Claire. No problem."

"Thank you."

Callie is dropped off at the new home. She looks at the dress covered in Jonathan's blood and wonders if it will ever come out, but doesn't care enough to wash it. She heads for the bathroom and steps out of everything and into a hot shower. The emotions of the last two days flow from every pore. As the water pours over her head, the tears pour from her eyes. With no one to watch or hear, she cries and moans like a distressed animal holding nothing inside.

She wraps herself in a towel and curls up on her bed, her skin still shimmering a little with water. She tries to sleep, but she needs to see Jonathan. She dresses in light blue linen pants and top, pulls her still damp ringlets up high on her head, and heads for the hospital. Jonathan's fourth-floor room is private. She stands in the doorway and looks at the man she loves. He appears to be sleeping, but as she turns to leave he opens his eyes.

"Callie?"

She turns back to him. "I thought you were sleeping. I was…"

"It's okay, come in. Are you okay?"

Callie moves closer and sits on the bed. She lays her head down on his abdomen and her dark ringlets fall over his chest. He strokes her head, and her tears flow again. "I almost lost you. I was so scared," she whispers.

"I know me too. I'm glad they didn't hurt you. The officers were here earlier. I hear you saved my life! I didn't know I was marrying an undercover cop! Ha-ha," he laughs at her.

Callie sits up and laughs too. "I don't know what made me do that. I've never fired a gun before."

"Well, for someone who has never used a gun, you were pretty precise. Callie, do you remember the guy with Preston?"

"Yes, they called him Chandler. Jonathan, he's a friend of your father," she says softly.

"Baby, it's not just my father involved. Your mother is somehow connected to these people too. I don't know how, or why, but she was seen talking among their group."

"Why would my mother be involved with these people?"

Ted Branson sticks his head in the door. "Hello in there! Is this where I might find Mr. and Mrs. Bond!" They all laugh as he steps inside the room. "Hey, Ms. St. Claire. Glad to see you're doing okay after your ordeal. Man, headquarters is buzzing about your girl. I wouldn't be surprised if you make the evening news! They're calling you a hero for saving the detective."

"Please call me Callie and it was just a reaction. I didn't think about what I was doing." She turns and looks at Jonathan. "You were hurt; I had to do something."

"You did great, I'm proud of you," Jonathan says, smiling.

"So how long are you going to be out of commission, Detective?"

"I should be out of here by the end of the week, and if I get cleared, I'm back to work on Monday. In the meantime, I want some eyes on Elena Guy, Maurice Waterman, Victor, and my father." He looks at Callie, "You and I will talk with your mother. I don't believe that she would have any part in this."

"Well, why would your father have any part in kidnapping your fiancé? Maybe they were planning to use her to control you. Or Ilysa. Or both. They didn't plan on the power of your feelings for this young lady. I'll get the guys on watch duty, and you two take care." Branson leaves the room and goes back to headquarters.

He calls in Miller's orders.

Miller is released on Friday and is immediately on the prowl for Victor.

"This is Detective Miller; anyone got eyes on Victor Scott?"

"This is Unit 728; we're at CARVELE Shipyards. There is a silverSUV registered to Victor Scott parked in front of Warehouse 31. Warehouse doors are open wide."

"This is Detective Miller; I'm on my way. Thanks"

Miller arrives at the warehouse and makes a fast trek to Victor's office. With no warning, he kicks the door in and charges full speed at the man he called brother. He draws back his arm and slams into Victor's jaw before he is aware of what is happening.

"Why Victor?" he yelled.

"I'm…"

"Don't you dare say you're sorry!"

"They promised they wouldn't hurt Callie, and then they would cut me in on the millions. All I had to do was stall you and keep my mouth shut. They hadn't considered how fast you would get out of the warehouse and track them down."

"They almost killed me!" Jonathan turns to leave but turns back. "I was okay with being an only child, but I let myself accept the idea of having a big brother. Now I guess I will be okay again as an only child."

"I'm sorry, Jonathan," Victor finally gets out.

"What was the point of holding her? What did they hope to gain?"

"They were trying to get you to back off of this investigation into the diamonds."

"And Chandler? How much control did they think they had on that guy?

"Chandler? He's a friend of dad, so I guess he thought he could trust him."

"Yeah, some friend, he put dad in the hospital."

"What?"

"You didn't know? We found him unconscious in the house."

"Is he okay?"

"Yeah, nothing serious. They should release him tomorrow, but he still faces a list of charges including accessory to kidnapping. He'd be going back to jail with Chandler if Callie hadn't shot him.

"Oh my God, Chandler is dead!" He plops into his chair.

"Yeah, and Preston is hanging on. Callie is a pretty good shot. Last I heard he has survived surgery and is upgraded from critical to a stable condition."

"Man, I hadn't heard."

"Victor, why would you agree to get involved with these people? You've only been out of the scope of HPD for ten months, and you let them suck you into this?"

"The diamonds are exquisite, and the money is unbelievable. People can't get enough of them. They sell themselves. People see them and have to buy. Price doesn't seem to be a problem either."

"Is going back to jail a problem? Because this time it won't be eighteen months, it will be eighteen years! I don't want to have to arrest you again. I have to talk to my future mother-in-law about her role in this mess. I'm not looking forward to that conversation," Jonathan tells him.

"I can tell you she plays a small but significant part of Preston's team," Victor informs him.

"Well, I can't believe she has any part of a team of people who would kidnap her daughter. She treasures her twins."

"Yeah, maybe, but everyone has a weak spot. Precious blue diamonds, well could be Ilysa's," says Victor.

"You're trying to tell me that you think Ilysa would put her daughters in harm's way for a blue gem?"

"I don't know. I don't know Ilysa that well. What I do know is that these stones, especially in the larger karat, make people do ugly things." Jonathan turns to leave the warehouse and makes a quick call to Callie. "I'm on my way."

They enter Ilysa's house, but she isn't there. They wait in the living room. When Ilysa arrives, she notices their somber look.

"What's wrong with you two? Did someone steal your centerpieces?"

"Let's just say the past two or three days have not been a lot of fun," Miller responds.

"I'll make some coffee, and you can tell me all about it." Ilysa goes into the kitchen.

"Jonathan." Callie looks at Miller. "Are you going to arrest my mother?"

"Callie, I can only do so much. If your mother has anything to do with these illegal diamonds, I'm not sure there is much I can do. If she was aware of the kidnapping escapade…"

"Kidnapping!" Ilysa screams, "What are you talking about? Who?"

"Preston, Lawrence, and a couple of others grabbed us after dinner a couple of nights ago. They worked together in holding Callie."

"Callie, are you all right? I told that S.O.B. Preston if he put a hand on Callie he would have to deal with me," says Ilysa.

"Like mother, like daughter," Miller laughs.

"What's that supposed to mean," asks Ilysa.

"Callie dealt with Preston and that guy Chandler well enough."

"Callie?" Ilysa repeats.

"Yeah, she shot them both. Killed Chandler, and Preston is still in the hospital."

Ilysa drops onto an ottoman. "You shot Preston? My Callie?"

"Yeah, mine too. I was coming to rescue her, and she saved my life."

He looks at Callie, and she smiles. "Ilysa, tell us how you are involved with Preston and the diamonds." Ilysa has to catch her breath and regain a straight thought.

"I met Preston when he and Paul worked together in Atlanta. One night Paul caught Preston giving me the full-court press and ended their working relationship on the spot. I never told Paul, but Preston and I kept in touch, and when I left Paul, it didn't matter anymore. When Preston got into the diamond business, he brought me in; I saw the gems and the money we could make, and I was hooked. Have you seen them? They're as addictive as some drugs! I have been working with him ever since."

"You knew they were illegal! You knew people, children, were dying to mine these!"

"I didn't know anything about the mining process until a few years ago when I overheard Preston and Waterman talking. I only knew that they were rare, beautiful, and very expensive. I have a special gift. I can look at them and tell which ones were flawless with my bear eye, whereas others need a scope, so I became a necessity so they wouldn't get worthless stones. Waterman needed Preston and Preston needed me."

"What can you tell them about blue diamonds?"

"I learned early on, working with Preston, the difference between the stones. I can look at Type IIB diamonds, which account for 0.1% of gem diamonds, and tell you which are flawed. They are usually light blue due to scattered boron within the crystal matrix; these diamonds can also be used as semiconductors, unlike other diamond types. Sometimes a blue-grey color will occur in Type IA diamonds and be unrelated to boron. Have you ever seen a naturally occurring green diamond? Their color is caused by GR1 color centers in the crystal lattice produced by exposure to varying quantities of radiation."

"Wow, that's fascinating. You're a very intelligent woman, Ilysa, so how is it that you didn't know they were being smuggled out of Brazil?

"No, you don't understand. I saw the diamonds; I saw the certificates. I didn't read them, but I saw the stack that came with the stones. It wasn't until much later that I found out the certificates were fake."

"I couldn't find one blue diamond in Elena's Boutique. How is he selling such large quantities?" Miller asks.

"Mostly by word of mouth. He has private clients around the world. Sometimes they even sneak small amounts into the settings of pieces that look like fancy costume jewelry. If you didn't know how much someone paid for a piece, you would never know the precious blue diamonds are among them."

"You could be facing a long time in a Federal prison. I don't know how to keep you out of this, Ilysa."

"I appreciate your help, but I can take care of myself. Excuse me. I will get some more cream for the coffee." Ilysa walks back into the kitchen leaving Miller and Callie drinking coffee and talking. It takes them a while to realize that Ilysa has not returned.

"I'll see what's keeping her," Callie says, but it's not long before he hears her calling, "Mom. Mom! Jonathan, she's gone!"

ILYSA JAMES HAS never spent time in a cell, and she wasn't about to start now. She slips out of the back door without a sound and disappears. She will contact the girls later to assure them she is fine.

The topic of conversation with Miller had to change. She could look at his expression and tell he was expecting more like he knew her secret before she had a chance to say it. She wouldn't do it with Callie present. She wouldn't dare admit that the one night with Preston was so much more. Ilysa couldn't look Callie in the face and tell her that the man she shot could very well be her father. She was never sure, and she never told anyone except Elyse. Thankfully, Elyse carried Ilysa's secret to her grave.

Ilysa waits until sunset to move. She is comfortable in the shadows only because she is unaware of the eyes that watch. They watch her as she opens the gate to the garden. They watch and follow as she reaches for the spare key that Preston left under the yellow rose pot; and again as she opens the door of the dark house, moving around as if it were her own. She slides into the bed where she has spent many a night wrapped in the arms of Matt Preston. Ilysa sleeps here, undisturbed, unconcerned, yet unaware.

Daeva Keket is also in the shadows. She watches and knows.

On the run again. Ilysa had almost forgotten what it was like. Her home was comfortable again, filled with the constant chatter and laughter of her girls. Now, this. What is she going to do? Ilysa takes a chance on visiting Preston in the hospital. He's not under a police watch, so she goes to his room and finds him asleep. She stands at his side and takes his hand in hers.

"Hello," the nurse greets her.

"Hello," Ilysa responds. "How's he doing?"

"Better. His Doctor upgraded him to fair, and he's healing well from the surgery."

"That's good."

"Yes, at this rate of recovery he could be out of here in a week or two."

The nurse finishes with her routine and leaves. Ilysa looks at Preston.

"Thanks…for not leaving me. I would have been madder than a snake." Ilysa wasn't sure, but she thought she saw the corners of Preston's mouth turn up into a smile.

She pats his hand and quietly leaves the room. She avoids the eyes of the staff in the hall and the guards on duty. She leaves the hospital unnoticed by everyone and returns to Preston's home. It's quiet and clean, but it's not home. Her girls are not here. She calls Callie and gets her voice mail.

"Callie, it's mom. I just wanted to let you know I'm okay. Tell Cora not to worry, I will call her soon. And tell Jonathan, I'm..I'm sorry. I feel like I've let him down. I will call again soon, okay, baby. Bye."

Hours later Callie glances at her phone. A missed call is reflected on the screen because the noise of the café masked the sound. She listens to the message and tears fill her eyes. She wonders if she should call Jonathan. She decides to wait not knowing what to say.

Jonathan is in his office, fuming, pacing, and muttering; how could he be so stupid. I should have known she would ditch. I let these relationships get to me. I would never have done that with any other suspect. I would have had backup. She could be anywhere by now. Jonathan's phone buzzes in his pocket. The ID screen reads Medical Center. "Detective Miller here."

"Detective Miller, this is Irene Houser from North Oaks Medical Center. I am so sorry I didn't see the note on this chart until now. You wanted a call if Matt Preston had any visitors.

Well, a woman came in to see him earlier today."

"Did you ask who she was? Or can you describe her?"

"I didn't ask her name, but she was maybe five-foot-four inches, petite, well-dressed, attractive woman in her mid to late forties."

"Thank you for calling."

"Your welcome, if she comes back, I will call again."

"So she didn't leave! Because of Preston?"

Miller heads for the hospital, with hopes that Preston is still there. The nurse on duty is chattering a mile a minute at someone on the phone. The person on the receiving end of her rant is not understanding the difference between visiting hours and 'come whenever you want hours.' Miller was clearly out of the visiting hour range but hoped his shield would pull some weight. When the nurse hangs up after thanking the person for being so understanding, Miller watched the sarcasm drip from the receiver.

"And what can I do for you at this hour, sir?"

"Hello," he says, trying a little charm. "I'm Detective Jonathan Miller. I need just a few minutes with Matt Preston; I was told he was on this floor." Miller flashes the gold badge and crosses his fingers.

"Is it so important that you speak with him now? Visiting hours were over three hours ago."

"It is important, and I promise I will only be a few minutes."

Miller smiles again, holds his breath, and waits. The nurse lets out a heavy sigh and points a long painted nail at Miller.

"Room 226, ten minutes, just ten!"

"Thank you very…."

"Nine!" she calls out, pointing in the direction of the room Miller takes off to find Preston. He stops at the door to listen, and hearing nothing walks inside. Preston is lying, bandaged around his chest and upper abdomen, but when Miller looks just below the bandage, he is shocked. He's seen the little mark before. He takes a moment to glance at his chart. Pieces of this puzzle begin to flow together.

"Matt? You awake?" A groggy Matt Preston opens his eyes.

"What do you want, Detective?"

"I want to know what's going on with you and Ilysa James."

"Nothin', now get the hell out of my room."

"She's on the run, Preston, where would she go?"

"I don't know, and even if I did, what makes you think I would tell you."

"I know she's been here to see you and…"

"Yeah, so what? Friends visit friends in the hospital, Detective. Didn't friends visit you when you were here? Ilysa and I are friends, that's all."

"You have no idea where she might have gone?"

"No!"

The nurse from the desk sticks her head inside the door. The scowl on her face told Miller his ten minutes were up.

"I'm leaving. Thanks." Miller stops at the edge of the door, "I'm gonna find her, and whatever you are hiding, won't stay hidden much longer."

"Yeah, goodnight."

Miller walks the hall wondering what they were trying so hard to protect. Thoughts are winding their way through his synapses so fast he isn't paying attention to where he is walking and bumps into the nurse.

"Pay attention to where you're going, you don't want to end up a patient on my floor."

"Well, no, but I could think of worse places to end up," he says, leaving her with a smile on her face.

I need my files. Miller stops past his office grabs a file on Matt Preston and one on Paul St. Claire.

Ilysa said they worked together years ago. He stuffs the files into his briefcase and goes home. He opens the front door of the new house, and he hears music playing. He sets his things down near the door, "This can wait 'til morning." He climbs the stairs, bypassing his typical glass of scotch, and the fragrance of rose petals is slipping from beneath the bathroom door along with the music. He taps softly.

"Callie?"

"It's okay, Jonathan, come in." He enters to find Callie soaking in the rose-scented bubble bath, candles illuminating the room cast a heavenly glow on her face and wet skin. Her bazillion dark ringlets are tied high on her head with a sheer white scarf and the smile on her face is just what he needs to make the ugly secrets of Hammond disappear. He's so glad he's found her. He knows he'll never love anyone the same way again. "How was your day?" she asks softly.

"I forget," he answers, half-jokingly. Seeing her like that did make him almost forget everything before walking in the bathroom door. "You're here, you're breathtaking, I love you so much, and right now, that's all I want to think about."

"In that case, care to join me? Water is still warm." She smiles as Jonathan kicks off his shoes, unknots his tie, and falls into the water. They burst into laughter at his antics and then kiss as Callie helps unbutton his soaked shirt. Jonathan leaves his eyes closed and enjoys the feel of her hands on him. He relaxes with her like no one else in Hammond. Once they leave the tub, it's his turn to thrill her from head to toe.

The smell of coffee stirs Miller from his dreams even before his alarm. He opens his eyes to the sunshine with a light Louisiana breeze fluttering the curtains at the open window. It's all so picturesque he's not sure it's not a dream. When he looks up and sees an angel dressed in a long white gown, her hair still balanced on the top of her head, standing over him, holding a cup of freshly brewed coffee. *Ahh, it's not a dream.* Miller sets the cup down on the nightstand and takes her by the hand and pulls her playfully to the bed.

"Your coffee will get cold," she laughs.

"Ice cubes, haven't you ever heard of iced coffee?" He kisses her passionately until she moans with delight. They are in their special place, together.

Jonathan lets Callie shower first while he does a quick review of his files. There are five by seven pictures of the two men and Jonathan lays them side by side. Maybe Paul can shed some light on the subject. Jonathan showers and dresses for work. The biggest smile lights his face from the memory of this morning, but when he gets downstairs again, Callie has already left for work. He moves to where he left his folders and discovers a note stuck to Paul's file.

'Jonathan, I hope these two aren't up to no good. But one will probably know where to find momma.' Love, Callie

Miller has already tried Preston and gotten nowhere. Paul St. Claire may be a little more open to talking since Miller spoke as a character witness in his favor at his trial, but he doesn't know where Paul is staying since his release from jail. He calls Callie.

"Hello."

"Hi sweetheart, I need to talk to Paul. Do you know where he is staying? Did he go back to Atlanta?"

"No, he said he didn't have anything to go back for since his wife died. He had someone there handle his real estate, and he moved in with Cora. She had space and wanted the company."

"I guess that all worked itself out, huh. You haven't heard from Ilysa, have you?"

"She left a brief message on my phone saying she was all right, and she would be in touch later."

"Callie, you will let me know when she calls again. Right?"

"It's my mother, Jonathan."

"I know. And you know that if there is anyone who is going to do everything possible to help her, it's me, right?"

"Right."

"Right. Okay. I'm going over to talk to Paul to see if he knows anything."

"Okay, tell him I said hi. I haven't had a chance to see him much since he was released."

"I'll tell him."

Miller takes the road leading to Elyse's old cottage. The deep tree-lined path brings back unwanted memories, but arriving up to the front of the place, Miller is stunned. New wooden stairs have replaced the rickety old staircase, and the entire screened-in porch looks brand new. The splintered wooden door and frame have been replaced and painted. Colorful flowers make a straight line at the front edge of the house, and it has a refreshed look to it.

Jonathan steps onto the first stair and listens. No creaking! He moves on to the next step and then the porch. Quiet and sturdy! Miller knocks on the door without fear of injury. Cora opens the door, and Miller catches his breath at the sight of the young woman before him. She could very easily be Callie. Cora has her dark ringlets gathered tightly to the back of her head, and Miller detects a little makeup on her face. A light shade of green accents her eyes to match the top she is wearing. He's never seen her in makeup before. She is looking more and more like her sophisticated sister.

"Cora, wow, you and the place look great! Who worked on the house?"

"My father is pretty handy with this kinda stuff. And people been kind enough to help or give us what we needed."

"And you! Look at you."

"Yeah, I'm trying. Callie helps me a lot. It's nice having a sister. Even though she's only minutes older, she's like a big sister. She's smart and brave."

"You were pretty brave the way you confessed to me about poisoning Elyse. That took a lot of courage."

"Huh? What are you talking about?"

"That day we met at the park… and…"

Cora turned her back to Miller. "That wasn't you… was it Cora? Callie pretended to be you."

"I wanted to do it, but I was scared! Callie said she could act like me enough to make you believe her. It would have been the same story, just me tellin' it, so nothin's changed."

"I'll deal with you two later. I need to see Paul."

"He's out back. You can go-'round this way."

Cora led Miller around to the back of the house to find Paul working on a small garden area.

Shading his eyes with one hand, he reaches his other out in front of him as Paul removes his working gloves.

"Hello again, Mr. St. Claire. How are you doing?"

"Hello Detective, I've been keeping busy 'round here. This is a nice place, but it needs some work. I'm getting used to this Louisiana humidity. It's different from Atlanta, but it's okay. What brings you 'round to the river's edge?"

"Ilysa's missing, you got any ideas where she might be?"

"If I know anything about Ilysa, it's that she's not missing. She just doesn't want to be found. She's gotten to be the best I know for staying underground, in the shadows, or right under your nose without you knowing it." Paul laughs. "You won't find her til she's ready to be found unless you got some help like a street informant."

"Hmmm, well, if you hear anything, please call me."

"I'll certainly do what I can, Detective. You have a good day now."

"Yeah, thanks. You too." Miller turned to leave, and Cora meets him at the front.

"You won't tell Callie what I said, will you?"

Miller looks down into the worried face, "I will think it over." He returns to his car and heads back to headquarters, but the drive gives him time to relive the scene in his head and he doesn't like the idea that she felt like she needed to pull a stunt like that. Why couldn't she just talk to him? Even then he loved her enough to listen to her. Miller didn't know whether he was hurt or angry. It's the first and only time he can recall her ever playing that switched twin game on him. Without seeing the 'shooting star' birthmark on Cora, he can't tell them apart. Miller goes to his office; he and one other officer are on the floor. He closes the door and plops his numb body into his chair. No sooner does he hit and close his eyes, than his phone vibrates in his pocket. He stares at the ID screen reading the name Callie as if all brain matter has ceased to work.

"Hello."

"Hello. Jonathan? Are you okay?"

"I guess so… yeah."

"Where are you?"

"I'm at my office. I got some paperwork to catch up on, so I might be late. Or maybe I'll be here all night."

"You sound strange. You're sure you feel okay?"

"Yeah, go on to bed, I'll see you in the morning."

"Okay, I love you. Goodnight."

"Goodnight." This is the first night, since meeting Callie 3 years ago, that he hasn't wanted to be with her. It is a feeling Miller didn't like. He closes the files on his desk, clicks off his lamp, and stretches his long frame on the sofa in his office. His thoughts race around like thoroughbreds on a track.

CALLIE!

JONATHAN WAKES THE next morning, stiff and achy from crunching up on his office couch and not in the best of moods from the agitated sleep. Branson is the first to get the brunt of his bad mood as he sticks his head in the door.

"Late night, Detective?"

Without a word, Miller throws the first thing he can find which happens to be a shoe and Branson ducks it and closes the door. Through his window, Miller can see Branson shaking his head. Miller retrieves his shoe and sits to put them on. He waves Branson back inside.

"Yeah, sorry about that. Do you think you could grab me a coffee and let me get my brain back to the train station? It might take two or three to get it on track."

"Sure, be right back." It doesn't take him long, and he returns with two cups. "Do you need an ear?"

"I don't know."

"Is it work-related, or Callie related?"

Miller looks up at the question. "Do you know any twins?"

"Well, yeah, I went to school with a pair. The Callahan twins. Boys. Always in the middle of the trouble. Not jail kinda trouble, but mischief kind."

"Did they ever pull the old switcheroo trick?"

"Once or twice, maybe. But we learned how to tell them apart, so that ended pretty early. Uh oh, the girls? Callie and Cora?"

"I went to talk to Paul St. Claire, and Cora let it slip that she never confessed to me about Elyse's poisoning. So Callie pulled the twin switch, clothes, posture, speech, everything."

"Oh, I see. Well, did she tell you something that wasn't true? That would be more important than the fact that she told you instead of Cora."

"Cora said she wanted to tell me, but she was scared. Callie thought she could pass herself off as Cora and make the confession. She did. She was too convincing. Cora said the story wouldn't have changed."

"You know how bashful Cora is, so maybe her sister was helping her out."

"But why did she feel like she couldn't just talk to me?"

"It was a crazy time, she didn't know you as well as she does now, she didn't know how you would react."

Miller feels a little calmer after talking to Branson. Talking to Callie would be his next step and hopefully end this ache he has inside. His cell phone rings and interrupts his thoughts.

"Miller here."

"Detective Miller? This is Thomasine Kitner. I'm an RN at the North Oaks Medical Center. I understand you've requested a call when Matt Preston has visitors. One, in particular, a middle-aged woman."

"Yes, yes I did. Is she there now?"

"Yes sir, she just went to his room about ten minutes ago. I can see if I can get her to stay a while if you want to come now."

"I'm on my way." Miller had almost forgotten about Ilysa. His thoughts and emotions are so wrapped around Callie. This distraction is unusual, and he somehow has to balance the two worlds if he plans to have both. For now, he has to focus on the underground mother-in-law. North Oaks Medical isn't far away, but he uses the siren to get through traffic. Miller races up the stairs bypassing the elevator wait and makes it to Preston's room stopping just outside the door. He listens for a moment, and there are two voices. One must be the nurse he spoke to on the phone. Miller steps inside. Ilysa and Nurse Kitner are at the bedside talking to Preston.

Miller catches the release of hands on the bed.

"Ladies. Gentleman. Nice to see everyone this evening." Ilysa and Preston turn to Miller with anxious faces. He looks at the nurse, "would you please give us a moment?"

"Certainly," she responds and gives Miller a soft smile as she exits.

Miller closes the door behind her.

"Ilysa, your disappearing acts have to stop. Whatever this is?"

Ilysa interrupts. "Whatever this is, is none of your business."

"Unfortunately, you keep making it my business. You keep getting caught with your hand in the middle of the illegal cookie jar. So, tell me, what's the story with you two?"

"I already told you; Matt and Paul worked together."

"Yeah, I know that part. But why are you here?"

"I can't visit a friend in the hospital, Detective?"

"You're going to hang on to that story? Okay. Preston, when are you going to be released from here?"

"They told me I could leave by Monday. So I got another four days. Why?"

"I just want to make sure my guys are here to escort you to your new home."

"What new home?"

"Hammond Detention. Didn't they tell you when they brought you in here? You're under arrest for smuggling illegal diamonds, kidnapping, attempted murder of a police officer, conspiracy, scaring my fiancé out of her mind, and a shit load of other charges I will think of later." Preston drops his head back onto the pillow and closes his eyes. "As for you, come with me," he says looking at Ilysa. They leave the room and exit the hospital. "Your daughter is worried sick; please call. Let her know you'll be in temporary holding at headquarters until I get some answers." Miller picks up the car radio. "This is Detective Jonathan Miller, I need a babysitter at the North Oaks Medical, room 226, starting tomorrow morning. Matt Preston is set to be released on Monday morning, and I want to make sure he gets a personal escort and a warm, welcoming reception at Hammond Detention Monday afternoon."

Ilysa sits in the back seat of the squad car, silent. She's like this for most of the ride. Obstinacy with a hint of arrogance, hidden by a calm façade, fill the back of his car. But Miller lets her ride quietly. He'll be patient a little longer, but it's getting late and he wants to go home. Headquarters is settling down for the night, and the officer on duty takes Ilysa to a private holding cell for the night. She goes reluctantly, but she goes without a fight.

"Ilysa," he calls out. "I'll see if I can arrange for adjoining cells." Jonathan watches as she is led down the hall, signs off on the sheet that lists occupants, and turns to leave.

Jonathan pulls into the driveway, and Callie is sitting on the swing. The dark ringlets fall to her shoulders, and the breeze plays with them all. He sits and watches her, captivated as always and suddenly unsure. He climbs the stairs and makes his way to the swing. Neither says a word and Callie lays her head on his shoulder. The evening breeze is cool, and she pulls her shawl around her shoulders and Miller brings her closer to him.

"You know you can talk to me… about anything."

"I know."

"You know you can trust me too."

"I know." Her voice is as soft as the whisper of a butterfly. She melts away the disturbance in his soul. "If I need you to move a mountain, you will," she says with a smile, remembering his words. "Does this have something to do with why you didn't come home last night?"

"Maybe, a little. It's going to be okay." In the back of his mind, he still plans to talk to Callie about the switcheroo later, but his anger and hurt have dwindled.

He takes her hand and leads her into the house, up the stairs, and to the bedroom. He showers and dresses for bed, but before Callie can join him, he is sound asleep. She kisses him and pulls up the sheet, turns out the light, and goes to sleep.

CALLIE WAKES TO the sunshine, an empty bed and a rose on the pillow beside her. Bringing it closer to her nose, she can smell the scent of the rose blended with the scent of her fiancé. She smiles and slips into a simple sundress and straw hat as she prepares to work in the gardens at the back of the house. She has the touch for making things grow. Colors are popping every season and offset with the lavish greenery. It's quiet, peaceful, and relaxing and Callie can think about wedding plans. The Hydrangea Blue has to be one of her favorite shades, and she lays a yellow Calla Lily next to it. The flowers make her match-up color combinations and decide the Calla Lily would also make great table arrangements. She smiles as she lays a single white tulip in the middle, on either side of the tulip are two yellow Calla Lilies, and then she lays three hydrangeas on both sides.

Callie suddenly feels something around her neck. She struggles to get her fingers in between the cloth and her neck, but it's too tight. It's hard for her to breathe; she can't scream. She thinks of Jonathan as she kicks and struggles against the force behind her, but she can't get any leverage. She tries to get to her feet, but the perpetrator of her horror is lifting her off her feet. Fear again has gripped her.

POP! POP! POP! The noise is sudden, unexpected, and Callie feels the grip around her neck slacken, and someone's arms around her as she drifts to the ground.

"911 what's your emergency?"

"This is Detective Ted Branson. I'm at the home of Detective Miller. I need an ambulance and a coroner's bus. Twenty-three-year-old female in need of assistance."

"Detective Branson, EMTs are on their way. Who's the bus for?"

"Gunshot victim is a Caucasian male, approximately thirty to forty years of age."

"Coroner says he's sending a wagon for transport, he's not available for another thirty minutes."

"That's fine, I'll make sure the victim goes to North Oaks Medical and I will wait for the transport. Please contact Detective Miller and have him meet them at HMC."

"I will notify the detective."

"Callie? Callie, can you hear me?" Branson tries to stir her.

There is a flutter of her eyelids, and Branson knows that she will probably be okay. A few minutes more and this would have been a very different situation. The EMTs arrive and load Callie, complete with an oxygen tank and IV fluids. Branson watches, knowing Miller is going to piss a brick when he finds out. Now he needs to know who the clown on the ground is. He takes a quick photo for use later at the office. Within minutes, he hears the coroner's bus pull up, and the men roll the gurney around to the back of the house. Branson secures the gate when they leave and heads back to headquarters.

Miller arrives at the North Oaks Medical Center minutes after Callie and goes into the ER. The nurse at the front desk points him in the right direction.

"Callie, it's Jonathan, can you hear me?"

A soft-toned voice behind him says, "We have sedated her. She woke up a little frantic, so we gave her something to calm her down."

"Is she okay, was she….?"

"No, she wasn't raped. The redness on her neck suggests he tried to strangle her. She's going to be fine, thanks to the detective that stopped the attack. The bruising on her neck will go away in a few weeks."

"Do you know who the detective was?"

The nurse flips through her notes. "Yes, the EMTs noted a Detective Ted Branson."

"Thanks. Is she going to be admitted?"

"The doctor wants to keep her overnight for observation."

"Have someone call me when she moves to a room and when she wakes?"

"Yes, sir, I can do that." The nurse says as she leaves the room.

Miller kisses the forehead of his sleeping lady and turns to leave. He stops long enough to glance at Callie's chart, and he's on the phone with Branson before he even reaches the doors of the hospital.

"What the hell happened?"

"I was looking for you and stopped by your house. Callie didn't answer the front door, so I went to the back gate. When I entered, this guy had Callie by the neck, up off her feet. I saw him, figured he wouldn't answer any of my questions anyway, and put three rounds into the back of the S.O.B."

"It scares me to think of what would have happened if you hadn't come by."

"Well, then don't think about it. We'll set up precautionary measures for when she's home alone. We aren't going to let this happen twice."

"Why would someone try to hurt her?"

"My guess is you ticked someone off."

"Who?"

"Well, my brain automatically goes to Preston, Waterman, or Guy, to name a few. You did kinda mess up their business. There are all kinds of agents sniffing around in their stuff. You're the one who used to say, 'relationships make you vulnerable.' You and Callie are going to have to watch your backs. I'm running his face now on the software to get an ID on him. Then we'll connect him with somebody."

"Ok, thanks. Let me know when you get something. You're right, this won't happen twice." Miller immediately picks up the phone and calls a security firm; explaining in detail what he wants.

"No problem, Detective. Is tomorrow convenient for you?"

"Tomorrow is fine. Thanks."

~~**~~

A White Van arrives early the next morning. Dozens of boxes are unloaded and placed in the living room. A crew of four men works inside and a crew of four more works outside. Miller has finally found the woman he's waited a lifetime for; he is not about to lose her to the craziness he faces every day. The men work quickly and cleanly. By the time they finish cameras are covering the front and back of the house, alarms on ground-level windows and doors, and one on the garden gate. If any go off, the neighborhood and half of Hammond will know it. Miller can rest assured that when she is home, she is safe. Everything is in place before he goes to pick Callie up from the hospital.

He knocks lightly on her opened door. Callie is dressed and sitting quietly on the bed. Jonathan moves closer and takes her in his arms. "I'm so sorry. Are you all right?"

She hesitates. "No, Jonathan, I'm not all right. This is twice someone has tried to hurt me. Why?" she asks, as the tears run down her cheeks. "Is this what it's going to be like being married to you? Someone is going to come after me because of a case you're on?"

"No, Callie, I'm going to keep you safe. Branson is tracking the ID of the guy, and we'll figure out who he was working for."

"What about your next bad guy, and the one after that? Jonathan, I'm scared."

"It's going to be all right. I promise. Let me get you home. I've already started putting things in place."

Jonathan starts to move and notices Callie hasn't budged an inch. She looks at him, tears still trickling down her face. "Jonathan, I want to go to my mom's for a while."

"But Callie, I've…"

"Stop! Please, just take me to her house. Please." Callie's even tone, unwavering calm, voice has found its tipping point. Jonathan has never heard it before, and it scares him a little. He doesn't want her to be afraid, but he can wait to show her the house. It is setup and ready for whenever she comes home.

"Okay, I will take you to Ilysa's. Maybe spending time with Cora will be helpful."

~~**~~

The ride is quiet as Miller takes her back to Ilysa's home. He makes sure she settles into her old room before leaving.

"Take as much time as you need. I will make you feel safe at home; you'll see. But for now, rest. I will have your car dropped off here, so you'll have it." He reaches out for her, and she quickly lets him fold her into his arms. "I didn't find you to lose you this soon. I will find the people responsible. I promise. And you can promise me just one thing."

"What might that be?"

"Promise me you will continue to plan our wedding. Do you even have your dress picked out?"

"I have it narrowed down to three. I just haven't decided which."

"Great, now promise me. Please."

"Okay, I promise to keep planning."

"That's my girl. I'll see you soon, but I'll call you later."

"Okay." And she gives him the 'Callie' smile he loves so much as he heads back to headquarters.

DETECTIVE BRANSON SMACKS his computer and mumbles obscenities as his software program sorts through the images.

"That never works for me," says Officer Atkins at the next desk. "How's it working for you?"

"The software is great and usually works faster than this," Branson responds.

"Actually, I was referring to the smacking and cursing," the young officer laughs.

"Oh. This guy is not coming up in the database. We need to know who he's working for and why they attacked Miller's fiancé."

"Sounds like the kind of creep who has a history. Keep fishing, he'll pop up. Have you tried Interpol?" Atkins asks.

"I can't run both the National and Interpol at the same time. I'll have to do it if or when this one ever finishes," Branson responds.

"Hey, I got some time, give me the face and I'll run it on my computer. I need more practice with this new-fangled software myself."

"Thanks for the assist. Sending to your computer, now."

In minutes, the officer has the image and is running it through the Interpol Criminal Database. Both computers are searching millions of faces. Branson walks into the break room for coffee and sits at the small table. He looks up as he takes his first sip and sees the officer waving him back to the desk.

"Hey! I got something! Look, he's from Brazil. Marcos Cartier. He's got a record a mile long. This is one nasty character!"

"Waterman and Elena Guy/Safira Santos are from there. I need to dig more into the two of them. What's their connection to Cartier?"

Miller arrives as Branson has his computer searching the names. "This is what I've found so far. Maurice Waterman was detained in Brazil according to police records. He was questioned for hours regarding the diamonds and people involved, but when he denied knowing anything his position and money allowed him to walk. Once free, he picked up Elizabeth and the young Safira and just left Brazil. They came to America where he continued doing what he was doing, just using others to keep himself out of the light."

"What do we have on this new guy?"

"We found him in Interpol. His name is Marcos Cartier. We know he is native to Brazil, but still digging to see how he connects to Waterman or Guy. It's gotta be them. Unless there is someone else you may have ticked off lately."

"What about Preston? A gunshot and hospital stay makes me mad enough to go after somebody. I just wouldn't go after a woman. I like to take my fight straight to the source."

"Yeah, me too. We'll check Preston too if this doesn't pan out."

"Branson, guess who made the news in Brazil? Waterman was named primary suspect in the death of some woman named Carlita Santos. But check out the picture of the chauffeur. Does that look like that Cartier guy?"

"So Cartier worked for Waterman in Brazil? Did he go from being Waterman's chauffeur to his goon? I told you. You put a kink in their business; that's why they went after Callie."

"Like I said, I take the fight right to the source."

"Detectives, would you like just one more bullet in your gun. I looked up a birth record for Safira; Carlita is her mother. Anyone want to take a stab at who's the baby daddy?" the officer says, with a wide grin.

"Waterman!" Miller and Branson say together.

"He probably killed Carlita off like he killed Elizabeth, brought the child back to the states with him. He's a millionaire with a private jet, so he bypasses all kinds of legal documentation for the child. So she's gotta be in the legal system under one name or the other. Check both!" says Miller.

"I've got Santos," says the officer.

"I've already looked under Guy, so let's try this," says Branson, as he types another name into the database. "Damn. There you are. He has her in this country under Safira Santos Waterman. So she must only be using Elena Guy at work because nothing comes up under that name. No social, no driver's license, nada. So other than the boutique, what is she doing?"

"Somebody get eyes on these two, NOW! At least I know where Preston is." He says as he walks out of the office. Preston was escorted to Hammond Correctional straight from the hospital.

Branson is on his phone calling dispatch and cars in the immediate area of the boutique respond; cars in the vicinity of Waterman's residence respond."

"Detective Miller, this is Unit 27, we're about a block and a half away from Ms. Guy's Boutique. A limo just arrived and let her in. She is leaving the boutique now."

"Well, that would explain why she doesn't have a license. She doesn't need one. But she must have a residence."

"Unit 27, find out what her destination is for me."

"Roger, Unit 27 out."

They allow the limo to leave and after a few moments turn to follow. They turn towards the upper east end of town and duck into the new gated community of Country Club Estates, valued at a quarter of a million and up.

"Branson, get into the computer and get an address for Ms. Guy/Santos whatever the name is she's going by."

"I got a feeling you may find Waterman first," says the young officer.

"If she doesn't have a social or driver's license under the name of Guy or Santos, then she probably doesn't have real estate."

"He's right, but I found something, Maurice Waterman has two half-million-dollar homes in this community. I've found his addresses; now we just have to get into the gate."

Miller thinks for a minute and remembers his friend, Mitch, in real estate. "Let me make a call."

"Well, technically, we don't get a gate code unless there is a house for sale, but let me see what I can find out. I'll give you a call back shortly." Twenty minutes later Mitch is on Miller's cell ID.

"Okay, here's the deal, there is a home that's been on the market for a while, and the code to show it is still available. I can get you in, show you a million-dollar property, and you can still put eyes on the property you are interested in."

"Great, how soon can you meet us out there?"

"It will take me about thirty minutes from here, how about you?"

"About the same, see you there."

Miller looks at Atkins, "Appreciate the assistance, you interested in seeing million-dollar homes?"

"If you don't mind, I'll tag along."

Miller, Branson, and Atkins arrive at the gated complex in an unmarked police car. The two cars arrive within minutes of each other and Mitch waves as he pulls up beside them, code in hand.

"I'm going to drive past the address you gave me, then we can circle back."

"That's fine. Just make it quick. I don't want her to leave again."

"Ok, follow me," Mitch says.

Driving through the community Miller checks to make sure he hasn't mistakenly picked up ten-year-olds in his car. The oooh's and ahh's sound like kids in a toy store. Miller laughs and shakes his head as the two younger officers drool over homes their pensions will never cover. They drive past Waterman's house. The lights are on. They continue as planned, quickly glancing at the property for sale. Branson is typing on the mobile computer bringing up information on the first Waterman home. "He's only owned this home since the death of Elizabeth," he says.

"He certainly didn't cash in on insurance to bury his wife," Miller mumbles.

"How do you know that?" asks Atkins.

"Insider secret," Miller laughs. "So where was he before this house? I heard she had a garden that she loved. If she didn't live here, where did she garden?"

"Second address for Waterman? Let's see," says Branson. He begins typing again. Branson begins laughing. "You are not going to believe this." He looks up at the street signs. "Turn left at the next corner. Okay, two blocks, make a right. This home was purchased about ten years ago. I bet Waterman is in this one. A gated home within a gated community. Paranoid, just a bit?"

"My first guess… is that he orchestrated Elizabeth's 'accident' after she ranted against his affair with Carlita and then she threatened to expose his illegal child and diamond business. He used his wife's insurance money, to buy a home for the child of his Brazilian mistress, that she told him to get rid of. He is a real piece of work." Miller explains.

"Think she's interested in getting married?" asks Atkins. Miller and Branson turn to look at him. He throws up both hands. "I'm just asking," he laughs.

"Branson, make a note of both addresses, we'll get warrants and come back to search both."

"When you come back to search Safira's home, can I come?" asks Atkins, still smiling from the back seat. They all laugh at his persistence.

"Yeah, okay," Miller agrees as they follow Mitch back to the main gate.

"Thanks, Mitch. I owe you one," says Miller.

"No problem, you know I will collect," Mitch laughs, "Did this help?"

"You have no idea," says Branson.

They separate and the three men head back to headquarters. Miller drops them off in the parking lot. "You guys go home. I will see you tomorrow."

"Good night, Detective," Miller hears almost in unison.

MILLER PULLS UP into his driveway. The soft orange glow of the porch lights welcomes him home. Callie's home! He can smell the remnants of dinner when he rushes through the door, but there is no sign of Callie. He rushes upstairs to see if she is in her bath but finds every room empty. He returns downstairs; peeks into the kitchen and sees a small plate over low boiling water. Callie's been here. She's left dinner warming for him tonight. He washes his hands and sits to eat, but as he stares across the table at an empty chair, he loses his appetite. It's late, he's emotionally exhausted, but instead of going to bed, he carries a small glass of scotch outside to the swing.

It's been three weeks since Callie was released from the hospital. And though they talk, Miller hasn't seen her. His favorite cocoa-colored eyes and dark ringlets, his honey-colored baby, has stayed away. The house is eerily quiet without her music, and he hasn't smelled her rose-scented bubble bath. Things were busy at work, so he doesn't even get to hear the soft sound of her voice. Tomorrow. He promises himself as he finishes his drink and goes to bed.

But just like the nights before he knew her, Callie stares at him from the ceiling. She crashes into his dreams like a freight train. Miller sees her trashing the wedding venue, throwing glasses and ripping her dress. He wakes with sweat on his brow and calls her before he even gets out of bed.

"Good Morning, Baby, how are you?" He says.

"Good Morning, Jonathan, I'm fine, I guess."

"How are plans coming?" he asks trying not to sound nervous.

"I haven't done anything since I left home. We have to talk."

"Okay, breakfast, lunch or dinner?"

"We can do an early breakfast. I have to be at work by eleven."

"That's fine, meet at PJ's, it's close to work, and you won't have to rush."

Miller knows that if biting his nails was a habit, they would be down to the knuckles by now. He doesn't recall a conversation he's dreaded having more than then the one he is facing.

~~**~~

When he arrives at PJ's, Callie is already seated at a table. The sunlight coming through the window lightens her eyes a bit but makes her skin glow, but there is a cloud casting a darkness over her spirit, and her smile is not the same. Jonathan's heart sinks.

"Hi Callie, I've missed you so much."

"I've missed you too." She says, but she doesn't meet his glance.

The waitress approaches and takes their order for coffee then leaves. Jonathan reaches for Callie's hand, but she withdraws.

"Jonathan, I've been thinking. I'm not sure I can marry you. Everything that has happened has made me terrified."

"Callie, I know it was scary. I'm sorry. I love you, and I'm not going to let anything happen to you. Come with me, let me show you." Miller slaps a ten-dollar bill on the table and takes Callie by the hand to his car. "I'll bring you back before your shift begins." Miller takes her to the house.

"First, there is a new set of keys. If something doesn't look right before you go in, push this button, and it sends an alert to a monitoring service that automatically calls headquarters." They go inside. "There are alarms on the windows and doors on the first level; alarms on the windows upstairs and rear of the house. Look here, there is a special alert button by the side of your bed in case something happens when you're here, just get to that button. It will scare the bejeezus out of anybody. Follow me," he says, grabbing her hand again. He takes her to the backyard and, to the back gate. "See, the gate is secured so no one can walk in uninvited. This will sound off just like the one next to your bed. They make a hell of a noise. Callie, if this isn't enough, I will get you a dog. A big dog! Or a bodyguard. You name it sweetheart; I'll get it. I just want you to feel safe, and I want you home with me."

Callie says nothing. She walks back into the house, out the front door, and gets into his car. Miller follows not knowing what to say. He gets into the car and starts to drive.

"Callie, please say something."

Before she gets out of the car back at the diner, she says, "I like what you did to the house; I'll think about it." Before he leaves, she looks into the window. "I get to pick out the dog?"

He laughs, "Of course. See you later?"

"Maybe."

"You do still love me, don't you Callie?"

"Of course I do, Jonathan, that won't change. I just ..."

"I know, you need time. I will give you as much time as you need as long as I know you're coming back."

~~**~~

Jonathan goes to his office with less of a sense of doom in his soul. Maybe now he can face Ilysa. He signs in at the holding area. The officer leads him to a separate room where he awaits her arrival. When the door opens, Miller notices she is wearing the latest in-house attire for her stay. The gray color doesn't flatter her, and the jumpsuit even rolled up at the ankles, drowns the petite figure. Needless to say, her demeanor is somewhat challenging to overcome.

"Good morning, Ilysa. I hope you're sleeping well," he begins.

"I'll sleep when I go home."

"If you don't start talking to me, you may never get home. They are looking to file Federal charges against you and Preston. The blue diamonds you are selling are as bad as the blood diamonds from Africa. They cost families their lives and the lives of their children. Their certification is fake and they are transported out of the country against the orders of the local government. How can you be a part of that and not feel some sense of guilt when you look at them?"

"Is there something specific you would like to talk to me about, Detective, if not, I would like to return to my cell?"

"Sure, Ilysa, let's start with this. Do you happen to know your blood type?"

"Why are you asking me for my blood type?"

"Do you know it or not, if not I can take you to the lab."

Ilysa's eyes meet Miller's and she hesitates. She knows where this is going. "I do believe I'm what they call a universal donor. I'm type O. Anything else, Detective?"

"Yes, I would like to talk about Preston."

"Your friendship with Preston, would you say it's been about twenty-one and a half years?"

"I have told you numerous times; he worked with Paul. So probably closer to twenty-three years. They were together for close to two years before I even met the man," Ilysa tells him.

"So Paul's only reaction to the affair was to terminate the working relationship. Or did he put two and two together Ilysa? Is that why he told you he didn't want the baby; because he suspected all along?" Ilysa's eyes are wide with anxiety.

"Paul is the father of my girls!" She slaps the table in frustration.

"Ilysa, I saw the birthmark on Preston. The 'shooting star' is very similar to the one Cora has on her shoulder. I also looked at Preston's medical chart while I was visiting. Because of his gunshot, he lost a lot of blood. Hence, transfusion. Need I continue?"

Ilysa lowers her gaze and grows very silent. The gray in her jumpsuit matches the gray that washes across her face. "You're right," she finally confesses. "That's what the argument was about so long ago at the bar. When I told Paul I was pregnant, he questioned me about the affair. Asked me how sure I was that the baby was his and not Preston's. I flipped. After being with Paul for so long, loving him the way I did, and in one night I get pregnant after being with Preston, I didn't know what to do,"

"That's how Paul's hands got burned?"

"Yes. They don't know. You can't tell them. Can you imagine their reactions when Preston realizes he held his own daughter captive, or Callie's when she finds out she shot and almost killed her father?"

"They will have to know eventually."

"Eventually is not now, please. Can I go back to my cell now?" Miller stands and taps on the door. An officer unlocks it and escorts Ilysa down the hall. She carried that burden for over twenty years. You might think that telling someone, anyone, would make your walk lighter. But not Ilysa, at least not yet.

"We'll talk again soon," he says. How do people get so wrapped up in lies? Their lives are one lie, one secret, and one unspoken word after another. Elyse was right, 'Unburyin the past sometimes wake up ugly things'. This is going to be ugly. Miller signs out of the holding area and goes back to his office. The bright red hair of a young boy peeks from the edges of his helmet when he pokes his head in the door, "Detective Miller?"

"You found him."

"You requested search warrants for two homes in the Country Club community?"

"Yes, you got them?'

"Yes sir," the Courier says, laying them down.

"Thanks," Miller says, slapping a ten on the desk and making the kid smile as he exits.

THE GATES OF the Clubhouse Estates are closed, but Miller calls the Waterman home. "This is Detective Jonathan Miller; I'm here to speak to the owner of the house. I'm at the main gate and need access."

"Give me a moment, Detective."

Miller hears a buzz and watches as the gate opens. Miller and the squad car carrying Branson and Atkins follow. They pull up to the first address. A home to accommodate a family of five or six and guests. It made Victor's mansion look like a dollhouse. Miller rang the bell and a tiny brunette dressed in black and white opened the door.

"Hello, may I help you?"

"Good morning, my name is Detective Miller, this is Detective Branson and Officer Atkins. We need to speak to the owner of the house."

"I'm sorry, Ms. Waterman is left for work already. She be back 5:30."

"Ms. Waterman? I'm sorry, I thought Elizabeth Waterman was deceased."

"Si, Elizabeth is, but Ms. Safira still lives here."

"Isn't Safira's last name Santos?" asks Miller.

"Her name is Safira Santos Waterman," responds the woman.

"Does anyone else live here?"

"No, no, no. Just Ms. Waterman and me."

"We have a court order to search the home. May we step inside?

"I should call Ms. Waterman first."

"You can call, but in the meantime, does Ms. Waterman have an office here?"

"Si, but you can't go in there. I can only clean the office when Ms. Safira is home. If she not here, I wait."

"I understand. You just show me where it is. I'll explain everything to Ms. Safira."

The small woman shakes her head as she leads the detective down the hall. Branson and Atkins are working their way around the house, checking for safes, hidden rooms, and doors that need skeleton keys to unlock. Branson looks up and sees Officer Atkins outside wandering the pool area.

"Why are you out here?"

"I saw it through a bedroom window. Man, this is awesome. This is where I would be spending my free time…."

"It's nice, but what are you doing?"

"I had a thought. Well, I saw it in an old movie. They hid a valuable diamond in the pool." He tapped his index finger against his temple trying to remember. "Oh yeah," he says, and runs to the drain basket. He removes the cover and turns to smile at Branson when he finds a plastic bag. Atkins pulls the dripping plastic out and unties the cord that secured it in its hiding place. He opens the bag to discover another plastic bag. Inside were several smaller white plastic bags. Branson is photographing the entire discovery on his cell phone.

"I think we got something here," says Atkins. When he opens the first white bag and looks in. "A gold key?"

"Anything written on it?"

"Just a number. 1020 could be a house number, a locker, a safe, or lockbox."

"Check the other two," says Branson.

"Two more keys, two different numbers," Atkins responds.

Miller is in the home office of Safira Waterman. He can hear the frantic phone call of the housekeeper, but he continues to search the files. She has well-organized, meticulous details. He picks up on references to Matt Preston, Lawrence Miller, and Ilysa James. And though he knows not one word of Portuguese, he understands some and can read a few words in Spanish, but he is not fluent in reading, speaking, or understanding either. He finds it strange that most of the documents are in English, and the Spanish and Portuguese words are scattered intermittently throughout. He makes a list of the words. He can look them up later. The nervous little maid walks back into the office, and this time she doesn't seem so timid.

"Ms. Waterman says you are to leave immediately; you should not be here when she gets home."

"I was just about to leave. Thank you." As she leads him back towards the door, they bump into Branson and Atkins still carrying the plastic bags.

"We found something interesting in the pool drain," says Atkins.

"The blue stones?" asks Miller.

"No, better," says Branson.

"You better not say, 'Beans, magic beans.'

"No, not beans, why would you think they were magic beans. They're keys," says Branson.

Miller shakes his head. "Keys to what?"

"Heck if I know but must be something important if you need to hide them in your pool. They have three different numbers and nothing else."

"How are we supposed to find what they open?"

"Well, we can start by asking," says Branson. He is looking out of the front window as Safira Waterman steps out of her car. She is still wearing the white and gold EG smock from the boutique. Miller notices she is also wearing a long white scarf, similar to the one Cartier used on Callie.

They all watch the elegant sway of her hips as she walks to the door. Miller opens it, surprising her a bit.

"Ms. Guy, or should I say Ms. Santos, or is it Ms. Waterman?" Safira looks like a deer caught in the headlights.

"You!"

Miller shows her his shield and ID, "Detective Jonathan Miller. I'm glad you made the trip. Maybe you can answer some questions for me."

"Questions? Like what?"

"Let's start with these," he says, handing her the three gold keys. "What do they unlock, and why were they hidden in your pool drain?"

"I'm not sure what kind of people you are used to dealing with, Detective, but we don't answer questions without the presence of legal counsel. I don't know what you're looking for, but if the search warrant doesn't include my pool, then you have until I count to five to return my property to exactly where you found it. One…"

All three men look at one another, "Well is it included?" Miller asks.

"Two…" Safira continues.

We didn't know there was a pool, so we didn't think to include it."

"Three…"

"Atkins, please, put them back; Branson, please, photograph the keys, numbers, and location."

"Have a nice day, Detective. Anything else you need, please call my lawyer before scaring my housekeeper."

Safira hands Miller a business card with the firm Courington, Kiefer & Sommers, L.L.C. written in gold. They are probably the most elite firm in Hammond. Waterman would have the best. Miller puts the card in his pocket and walks out.

Safira calls after him, "Detective, if you are considering going to Maurice's home, I would strongly suggest that you skip that plan. He is a most unforgiving sort of man."

"I'll take my chances, thanks," Miller responds. Atkins and Branson are walking through the door just as he turns back towards his vehicle.

They sideways slip past Safira and catch up.

"Detective, are we going to Waterman's?" asks Branson.

"Call for a backup team, and you two search Waterman's home. I'm going back to the office to follow up on some things I saw in Safira's office. Atkins makes the call, and Branson drives in one direction while Miller pulls off in another.

Back at headquarters, Miller takes out the notes he scribbled from Safira's files. His computer translator should come in handy, and he tries the first word.

Piedra(s) means stone(s); probably talking about the diamonds. The second word he types is muerte meaning death. Could be related to the death of the miners. He goes through the rest of his list.

Mina, mining; gobiero, government; persianas, blind; apuntado, targeted…

What about the government? Who or what was targeted? Who was blind? The government or just someone in the government? The questions roll one after the other in Miller's head. There are always more questions than answers.

BRANSON AND ATKINS find themselves at Waterman's residence with an ugly situation Miller will be glad he missed. The mansion has a fence on four sides with eight feet high of wrought iron, but when the men approach they are not so welcomed by four massive Dobermans. They drive up to a speaker in the driveway and identify themselves.

"Mr. Waterman is not expecting you," says the voice on the box.

"We have the warrant to search the home," says Branson.

"If you can get through the gate, past the dogs, across the yard, and to the front door blood-free, then he might talk to you. Mind you Cyrus and Milo are champion racers." Branson and Atkins look at one another.

"You thinking what I'm thinking?" asks Branson.

"How much trouble do you think we'll get into?"

"We have a job to do, they are impeding an investigation, Miller will have our butts if we don't get in," says Branson.

"Let me try something else," says Atkins, as he steps out of the vehicle and walks up to the speaker. "This is Officer Anthony Atkins; these are some very handsome dogs you have here. I'm betting you spend a fortune on their food, training, and upkeep. It will be a shame if I have to put a bullet in them so that we can have a civilized conversation." Atkins pulls out his sidearm and acts like he's checking his rounds. He looks up at the camera facing the gate and points at the dogs. "Which one did you say was a champion racer?"

Seconds later, the dog's ears stand erect, and all four take off running towards the back of the house. There is a buzz, the monstrous gates open, and small lights illuminate the driveway like an airport landing strip.

"The Wizard awaits," laughs Atkins and he hops into the car.

"You wouldn't have shot his dogs, would do?"

"Would you have rammed the gate?"

"Only as a last resort."

"Well, there you have it, as a last resort." Atkins chuckles to himself.

A tall, but frail, grey-haired man opens the door. The arrogant voice from the speaker doesn't match the character before them. "Mr. Waterman is waiting in his study. This way please." The old man leads them down a long hallway.

"Why do these offices always have to be so far away?" whispers Atkins.

"Maybe they don't want their secrets too close to the main entrance, how the hell am I supposed to know?" Branson whispers back.

The gentleman opens the ceiling-high ornate wooden door to Waterman's office, and once the men are inside, he closes it to leave.

"Officers, this better be good."

"We have the warrant to search your home," Branson responds.

"What might you be looking for, if you don't mind my asking?"

"I'll let you know if or when we find it. It will include your office, so if you can wait in the living room, it will be appreciated," Atkins chimes in. They wait until Waterman exits the room. "We need to look at his files." Atkins starts going through desk drawers, but none have what seem to be business files.

"I have a locked cabinet here. I'll be nice and ask for a key." Branson finds Waterman sitting quietly reading. "My warrant says I can examine your business files, and there is a cabinet that is locked. If you would prefer I not break the lock, then please give me a key."

Waterman lets out a heavy sigh, digs into his pocket, and pulls out a small gold key. He gives Branson a stern look before giving it to him. Branson makes his way back to the office. He finds Atkins feeling his way around the bookshelves.

"What are you looking for?"

"Hidden passages, safes; You know, the stuff rich people use to hide things."

Branson goes to the locked cabinet. "Hey, over here. Look at these," says Branson. Atkins makes his way to him and looks over his shoulder.

"Do you read Brazilian Portuguese?"

"No, sorry. Let's pull some files with at least some of the names of the players and get pictures. We can cross-reference back at the office."

"Good idea." They gather more files and get photos of several key pages. Some mention CARVELE shipyards, Elena, and Preston. Insurance files on Elizabeth and Carlita are there, but one file they knew Miller would want is Waterman's Brazilian contacts and overseas clients for the blue diamonds.

Atkins looks Branson in the eyes, "I feel a promotion coming on." They find Waterman still sitting and reading, "We are finished for the evening, but we will let you know if we have any further questions," Atkins informs him.

They go to headquarters and retrieve their cars to go home. "Nice work Atkins, thanks again."

"You too, and thanks for letting me help. See you Monday, this is my weekend off," he says, with a sudden shudder.

"You okay?" asks Branson.

"Yeah, just a strange feeling on the back of my neck like someone is watching us."

"It sounds like you might need this weekend off. Relax and enjoy it. You got plans?" Branson asks.

"My lady and I are driving down to Lac des Allemands for the weekend. I rented a cabin. Hey look!" he pulls something from his glove compartment. "I haven't told anyone else yet, not even my folks, but I'm going to ask Renee to marry me!" he says, showing Branson the engagement ring.

"That's fantastic, congratulations. I'll know how she responded when I see your face Monday morning," Branson laughs.

Atkins shakes his head and laughs too. "See ya." He gets into his car and pulls off. Branson sits in his car and watches Atkins drive off wearing the biggest smile.

'I guess I'll be doing that one day,' he thinks to himself. He drives to his apartment. 'Atkins has Renee; Miller has Callie; I don't even have a pet. I've always liked Cora but asking her out has never come up. Yeah, that would be weird now. Cora and I are on a double date with Miller and Callie. Yeah, weird.'

Neither notices the sedan at the corner.

15

"WELL HELLO, WHAT can I do for you lovely young folk?" asks the clerk. The blonde bun on top of her head could have served as a bird's nest. But it was the cat-green eyes behind the super thick glasses that made Atkins smile.

"We have a cabin reserved for the weekend; the last name is Atkins."

"Okay. Says here you have a two-bedroom cabin reserved, are you going to be sharing with anyone else?"

"No, it's just us," he replies, smiling.

"I have a one-bedroom cabin; it will save you a chunk of change."

"It's fine; we'll keep the one we have." Atkins pulls out his credit card and police identification.

"Oh, Officer Atkins from Hammond, is it? Welcome to Lac des Allemands, you're in cabin #6. Take a left out of this lot, make a left at the stop sign, and drive just a quarter of a mile down. It's on the left. Y'all enjoy your stay here."

"I believe we will, thanks," he says, looking over his shoulder and smiling. He grabs the key from the counter, and he and Renee set off on their weekend. Finding the cabin was as simple as the clerk said. They found a quaint, cozy cabin with queen size bed and a two-seater hot tub in the back. There is a small fireplace in the corner and a small load of wood nearby. Atkins is watching with a smile as Renee moves about the cabin, unpacking the champagne, fruit, and cheese he has bought. He taps his pant pocket; the small box from the glove compartment is now safely at his side. He wants to pick just the right moment to pop the question.

"Anthony, I'm gonna take a quick shower and change for dinner," Renee calls out from one of the rooms.

Atkins has already chosen the restaurant for the evening; he just hasn't decided if presenting the ring at dinner is too cliché. He's been practicing the words in his head, in his mirror while shaving, and even in his dreams. He's ready. He cleans up and changes. Pats his pants one more time. Oh, geez! Where? He scares himself for just a moment. He put his surprise inside his suit jacket just in case the time is right. He breathes a sigh of relief.

Dinner comes, and Renee carries the conversation. Atkins is trying hard to be a good listener, he waits for her to break, but she doesn't. Desert comes and goes, and her family disputes are still the topic of conversation. He's content to let her vent and get it out. Maybe he'll try over champagne, fruit, and cheese a little later.

Back in the room, he tries again to create an ambiance. He lights the fireplace, a couple of candles on the table.

POP! The cork to the champagne flies and he pours two glasses. The sound brings Renee out of a room dressed in silky loungewear. The firelight flickers in her eyes as she looks at Anthony.

"Champagne? What's the occasion?" she asks.

POP! POP! The Ruger Predator releases two .270 bullets from their chambers. Confused, Atkins looks at the bottle in his hand and then looks up again as Renee's stunned expression drops to the floor. Atkins drops the bottle and the glass he was about to hand her and starts to run to her side. POP! POP! The Remington 700 in turn fires two .223 bullets into Officer Atkins. The Atkins drops just inches away from Renee's face; the small box tumbles out of his pocket.

All is quiet in the woods. The creak of the solid cabin door should have sounded like an alarm. The heavy combat boots clomped across the floor as if too big for the feet they were on, careful to avoid the crimson flood of the two victims. Proof of the completed task is required if payment is expected, and a camera phone would have to be enough. More than enough proof is collected before the boots clomp out the door.

~~**~~

It's 10:00 AM on Monday.

Branson has been at his desk piecing together a few things about Safira Waterman, and he is looking forward to hearing the exciting report from Atkins, but he hasn't come in yet. Miller is at his desk with the door shut. Branson can see him flipping through files. Branson decides not to concern him yet and try calling. The phone rings and rings before going to his voicemail.

By noon, Branson's head is back in Miller's door. A shade of concern shadows his face. "Detective?"

"What's going on Branson?"

"It's Atkins. He is supposed to be on duty this morning, but he hasn't shown. I've tried calling, but it rolls to voicemail."

"Maybe the weekend was better than he expected."

"Well, I hope so, he is supposed to have proposed to his girlfriend Renee, but he said he would see me on Monday."

"Maybe he needed some extra time; he'll show up." Branson closes the door and returns to his desk. He tries to focus on his work, but his mind keeps drifting to Atkins. He watches the door for his arrival. But there is no sign of Atkins.

"Detective Miller, you have a call on line one," someone calls out.

"Miller here," he responds.

"Detective Miller, this is Karlie Marsh at Lac des Allemands, I am sorry to have to tell you that one of your police officers was killed here over the weekend. The local police are here, but they thought I should call you."

"What is the officer's name?"

"His ID says, Anthony Atkins."

"Did they say how?"

"He was shot. My staff found him this morning."

"Please let them know I'm on my way," Miller tells her. He disconnects and calls Branson into the office.

"Did Atkins tell you where he was going?" he asks.

"Yes, we talked just after work on Friday. He and his girl were going to Lac des Allemands. He showed me the ring he was going to give her. Why?"

"I just got a call from Lac des Allemands. Officer Atkins was shot; they found him dead this morning. I'm heading down to find out more."

"What about Renee, did they mention her?" Branson asks.

"She didn't mention the girl. Get your stuff, let's go."

The ride to the Lake resort takes them about forty-five minutes. The locals have a barricade on the road entering the campsite. Cabin #6 is streaming with the bright yellow crime tape. Miller and Branson approach with their badges showing and enter the cabin. Miller scans the scene, the blood on the floor, the bullet holes in the screen, and no broken glass. He looks through the hole in the screen to see if the area provided a clear shot. He turns to the officer at the door, "I understand he was not alone. No one mentioned his guest when I got the call."

"Yes, there is a Caucasian female victim, her ID says Renee Vacherie, twenty-five years of age. She was also shot twice. It appears she may have been shot first. He was standing closer to the table, dropped what he had in his hands, and was shot trying to get to her. He also took two bullets."

"Did anyone recover a diamond ring?" asks Branson.

"No sir, not that I've heard mentioned."

Branson catches Miller's eye, "I wonder if the killer took a trophy?" he asks.

"If it doesn't turn up, we'll know. Do you think you will recognize it again?"

"Yes, I think so."

"Why?" Miller questions still glancing around the room. He spots a clump of something on the small area rug and goes to investigate.

Using a gloved hand, he lifts it and deposits it into a baggie. When he looks around outside of the cabin, he doesn't see anything similar. "We'll get this to the lab and see if they can match it.

"Officer, did they find shell casings?"

"No sir, the shooter must have cleaned up afterward. But they did find one bullet, the girl has one entry and exit wound. The .270 caliber bullet stopped here in the wall. I believe another officer bagged it."

"I'll see if I can find it," says Branson. He steps outside and finds several officers gathered around Atkin's SUV. He opens his ID. "Hey guys, can anybody tell me what caliber weapon we might be looking for?" He searches the inside of the car then around it and then under the carriage. When he gets to the rear tire well, he finds a surprise. Using his camera to record his finding first, he snaps several pictures and removes the device.

"Yep," chimes in one officer, "Shooter has a .223 Remington rifle. We pulled one slug from the wall. Our lab will check it for prints."

"No one reported hearing rifle shots?" asks Miller.

"No one we've talked to remembers hearing shots at all, but shots in these parts wouldn't be so unusual. People hunt up in these parts all the time."

"Yeah, maybe, but how many people hunt at night?"

"Great, please let me know what your findings are. Officer Atkins was working with us on a case. I need to know if that slug and rifle belong to someone connected. We'll make arrangements to have his car brought back, too."

"We'll be in touch, detectives."

After wandering the surrounding area of the cabin, Miller and Branson head back to Hammond. "Do you know anything else about Renee?"

"No, I just found out about her on Friday. Atkins was so excited about this weekend but look at what I did find." Branson pulls out the tracking device.

"Someone was tracking him. Why?"

"Right, why him? He's only been on the case for a few days."

"Is there anything we can find out from that box?"

"We can dust for prints, but the serial number may be our best bet."

"We'll find the ones responsible. Both families have to be notified."

The rest of the drive was silent. Each is dealing with the loss of the young officer differently. As soon as they arrive back at headquarters, Branson pulls Atkin's personnel file. With his address and emergency contact information in hand, they leave again. His parents reside in Ponchatoula, it's a short ride, but a dreaded one. They pull up to a small log cabin-style home; two steps and four by six-foot landing stick out in front of the door; just big enough for two wooden rockers. Miller rings the bell. A rotund blonde with an extra chin answers the door.

"Hello, Mrs. Atkins?"

"Yeah, what can I do you for?"

"My name is Detective Jonathan Miller; this is Detective Ted Branson. May we come in? It's about your son, Anthony."

Miller can see the list of possibilities run through her mind and her efforts to not panic. She lets them in and leads them to the living room.

"Frank! Frank, come out here! Somethin's happened to Tony!" she screams. Another rotund individual appears from a back room and stands beside her.

"What happened to Tony?"

"I'm sorry, Anthony was shot and killed this weekend," Miller manages to get out through the wailing of his mom. He gives them a few moments to process the loss. "I have to ask you a few questions if you don't mind. Did you know his girlfriend, Renee?"

"Yep, they been seeing each other for the past couple of years," his dad responds. Renee, she's a sweet girl. She's gonna be devastated."

"I'm sorry, you don't understand. She was with him. She was also killed."

"Oh, good Lord!" they both cried out. "Who would do such a thing? That girl never hurt a fly!" says Frank.

"We need to find her family. Do you know her parents?"

"Yes'ir, they live in Hammond. They have a little flat on West University Ave. I'll write down their address for you," Ms. Atkins tells him.

"Thank you very much. And again, we're sorry for your loss." The two detectives leave the sobbing couple and make the trip to find the Vacherie family. They deliver the devastating news to another set of parents, inform them that the person or persons responsible will be found, and go back to headquarters. Miller takes the clump he found on the carpet of the cabin down to the lab.

"Hey, Kevin, how'd the aphid thing come out?"

"Turns out the little bugger had a healthy bite of our victim. They shared a common toxin. What can I help you with today, Detective?"

"I found this clump of something at a crime scene. I'm hoping you can tell me what it is."

"Sure, I can probably have an answer for you before the end of the day."

"Thanks, Kevin."

Miller goes to his office and closes his door. The weight of the day makes him fall into his chair. He can't get the senseless death of the young couple out of his head. He turns his back to the door and retrieves his tinted informant from his pocket. He focuses his thoughts on Anthony Atkins, and the glasses do the rest.

The image of Atkins at the front desk comes in as clear as if he were right in front of Miller's face. The young Renee stands not too far away anxiously awaiting the romantic weekend ahead. Miller can see them at dinner, Atkins nervously planning his move and Renee chattering and again back in the cabin. Atkins is preparing the fire, champagne, and snacks and Renee walks into the room. He sees her take her first hit, the expression of surprise, and the second hit. Then Atkins dropped the champagne, moving towards Renee, and taking two hits. He sees the combat boots enter the room dropping the clumpy substance. Show me his face! The view begins to move upward as the person prepares to take the picture. The fatigues are baggy, and the hat and camera cover the face. The flash goes off, SNAP! The boots pause for only a second on their way back out of the cabin.

Miller is almost sorry he used the glasses. He didn't necessarily want to watch the murder of the young officer. But he now has to find out why Atkins was a target.

16

MILLER IS IN desperate need of his Callie. Her smile is the best pain reliever in his world. He decides to drive over to Ilysa's to see if she will spend the evening with him. When he arrives, he finds Callie in the front yard tossing a ball to a large, German Sheppard. He gets out and just watches them for a moment.

"Jonathan! I'm glad you came. Watch this. Jagger, sit," she commands the dog, and he obeys. "Jagger, heel." The dog moves to her side. When Callie moves towards Jonathan, the dog moves with her. "Isn't he wonderful? He's retired K-9 police. They let me have him for a few days on a trial basis. "Jagger, sit. Jonathan, meet Jagger, Jagger, shake." The dog lifts his paw. Jonathan laughs and shakes with the dog. Jonathan likes the animal and vice versa.

"Great choice Callie, he's perfect."

"They said he took a bullet protecting his handler in the line of duty, so he can't be on the team anymore, but he is healthy, he's fast, and should be a good protection dog. He's got a purple heart, to prove it. When I went in to see the dogs, he was sitting beside another officer. He just walked up to me and sat at my feet like he's been waiting for me. He took to me so easy." The dog is licking Jonathan's face. "I think he likes you too."

"He's a handsome guy. So how long will you have to make a decision?"

"I have to let them know tomorrow if I want to keep him."

"If you keep him, will you come home?"

"Yes."

"I love it. Do you have a leash for him?"

Callie removes it from her pocket and dangles it in front of him.

"Great, wanna go for a walk?"

The three of them stroll the neighborhood and Jonathan keeps her close.

"When I go back to the K-9 Unit, they will give me his attack commands. And they will work with me, so I'm comfortable giving him commands, and he can get used to me."

"He seems to listen to you already, so it should be easy. Just make sure he knows I'm one of the good guys," he laughs.

They walk a little longer before going back to the house. They sit on the porch swing while Jagger stretches out on the floor beside them. "I'm ready to come home, Jonathan. I miss my house. I think with everything you've done and with Jagger there by my side when you're not home, I will feel better. So, after I make him an official part of the family, I will get my stuff." Jagger looks up at the couple as if he knows that they're talking about him.

"And the wedding?" he asks.

"Is back on, I have my dress. I want to use the Blythewood Plantation for the ceremony, but I want you to see it first."

"Callie, I would marry you in the back alley of the headquarters' building. All I want to hear you say is 'I do'. So if Blythewood is what you like, then Blythewood it is. You can even make Jagger the ring bearer."

"That might be cute. I don't have a ring bearer yet."

"Sure, he can carry like a little basket or something. We can put a black bow tie around his neck," he laughs.

Callie laughs too, and Jonathan revels in its sound. It's enough to make him tuck his sadness away, if only for a moment.

"Jonathan, do you think we can get permission for my mom to attend the wedding?"

"I can make some calls, but I can't promise you. The judge was lenient with the help of the DA. But Ilysa was supposed to keep her nose clean. Our families just don't seem to be capable of staying out of trouble."

"What about Victor and your dad? Are they going to come?"

"My dad definitely won't be invited. I am straddling the fence between having Victor as my best man and shooting him. He called me, concerned about the diamonds being moved around through his company. Now, since they have offered him a share of the income, he's walking around with blinders. He's the one who alerted them that we were on our way to my dad's house. All along he's acting like he's helping me."

"I can understand you being mad, but do you have an alternative best man?"

"Yeah, I'm thinking of asking Ted Branson. He's been like a kid brother to me over the past few years."

"Okay, if you can find one more guy, then I will have Cora and the only friend I have at work. A small party is just as nice."

"Just tell me we aren't in pink cummerbunds!" he says, covering his eyes and laughing.

"You know my favorite colors are blue and yellow, silly," she responds with a playful punch on his shoulder.

"Hallelujah!"

"Did you pick a date? Blue and yellow sound like spring colors, but I don't know if I want to wait that long."

"Jonathan, spring is only six months away. I want to be a May bride. April may be rainy, and June may be too hot. Besides, I have to cross my fingers that I'm not too late for a date at the place. As soon as I know what's available, I will call you. I'll make the call in the morning. Once I have a date, I have to find a caterer, cake, and an official to perform the ceremony."

"Okay, okay, I get it. Anything I can do to help, just ask. I wish I could sit here all night, but I have to work in the morning. I love you, baby; goodnight." He kisses her softly and stands to leave.

"I love you Jonathan, goodnight."

"Night Jagger, take care of our girl!" he calls back from the foot of the stairs. Jagger raises his head and lets out a loud bark.

Jonathan gets into his two-seater and looks around the car; there is a little space behind the two front seats. "I think I'm going to need something a little bigger. Jagger will just barely fit in the back."

As he pulls off of her street, he glances around. No sign of any dark sedans. Callie throws the ball for Jagger a few more times before going in for the night. She can't wait to tell the adoption agency that she will keep him. She can picture the bed she will get him for Christmas with his name on it.

THE PHONE RINGS.

"Miller here," he says.

"Detective, this is Kevin. I got the results you wanted. It's a basic kind of dust, but it does have a sawdust component. It's going to come from wooden shipping crates like you would find in the shipyards."

"Thanks, Kevin that helps."

"Branson! Get an APB out and get Clayton Woodstock in here!"

Miller prepares to go home for the night. Still saddened by the loss of Atkins, but mad as a snake, he leaves all of his files on his desk. No case will take priority over getting Woodstock and whoever put him up to killing those kids. Branson takes a backup team to CARVELE Shipyard to track down Woodstock.

It's been a long day; Miller is updated with details of Atkin's funeral service, Jagger's successful adoption, a May 10th wedding date at Blythewood Plantation, and the conditions under which Ilysa will be able to attend the wedding.

~~**~~

It's Friday morning, and Jonathan is on his way to work when the chatter on the car radio gets very busy; the animated conversation is loud and chaotic, and he's not sure who's speaking. Something is distorting the transmission, and it's not just static. He listens carefully.

"This is Detective Jonathan Miller, what's happening?"

"De..tive, We …..Woodstock, he's..the..run."

"Where are you?"

"Car…vel… down by Pier 30. Nee…b..up."

Miller quickly makes sense of the transmission and drives full speed to the shipyards. He arrives to dust flying about, and once he finds the direction they are headed in, he makes a quick left picking up speed and a quick right through the middle of a warehouse. He comes out as the car carrying Woodstock is moving toward him.

Miller spins sideways blocking his path, but Woodstock makes a wide spin, crashes through the wooden guardrail on the pier, and lands on top of a small boat tied there. Officer Branson and his team retrieve him from the wreckage. EMTs are arriving by the time they get him out of the crumpled mess of metal and plywood. Miller watches from his car until they load and transport Woodstock to North Oaks emergency room under police escort. He knows it will be days before he can question him so Miller, exhausted, goes home to prepare once again for Callie's arrival and grabs a bag of dog food on his way.

The next morning, he stops by North Oaks Medical Center to check on the status of Clayton Woodstock. He runs into his favorite 'Nurse Kratchet' at the nurse's station, giving someone else the time of day. He waits.

"Hmm, Detective Miller, who are you here to upset today?"

"Good morning to you too," he tries for affable in his voice. You have a patient under police guard, Clayton Woodstock. Which room? Please," asks Miller.

The nurse flips through a file rack, "256, that way," she points. She watches him walk down the hall. "Why you gotta be so young?" She laughs and shakes her head.

Miller finds room 256 and the guard assigned is sitting and reading.

The officer catches Miller's approach. "Detective."

"Officer. I want to see how he is doing."

"I don't think he's awake more than a few moments at a time. They have him on some serious medication. But I hear him babbling in his sleep, but they say you can't hold that kind of talk against him."

"If you ever hear him 'babble' the names Preston or Waterman, I want to know."

"Yes, sir."

Miller steps into the room; the man has a bandage around his head, and his left arm is in a cast. He is black and blue around his face, but Miller feels no sympathy for the man; He searches the room for his clothes. The staff has put his belongings into a small closet, and Miller sees the shoes. Lifting them and turning the soles upward, Miller finds the same material that is being analyzed in the lab. It's stuffed into almost every gutter of the tread in the boot.

If Woodstock is not the shooter, then he is certainly connected. Miller doesn't see anything other than clothing in the closet. He makes his way back to the nurse's station.

"Excuse me, can you tell if Mr. Woodstock has any other personal effects that might not be in his room?"

The nurse goes back to her charts, "Yes, Detective, he came in with a wallet; ID, a little cash, that's it."

"No cell phone?"

"Did I read off anything about a cell phone? No."

"Okay," Miller says, throwing his hands up in surrender. He turns to leave. Where did you leave the phone? First thing Monday morning, I need a search warrant for his residence. Miller can feel his blood boiling at the thought of these guys. He's ready to lock up Preston and Waterman with enough charges that they will never see another day outside of prison. He leaves the hospital and prepares to say goodbye to a fellow officer. Services for Atkins are only a couple of hours away. Miller makes his way downtown, the street is blocked off for the funeral participants and the long black cars that line the street. He shows his shield and is allowed on the street and directed to a spot to file in with the cars ahead of him. Taking just a moment to take in the majestic façade of the church, he sends a short prayer to the saint above the doorway. When Miller steps inside the entire right side of the church is filled with men and women in uniform. He joins the ranks and spots Branson in the crowd; he is unashamedly tear-streaked.

The service is beautifully arranged from its musical selections to its personal input from those who he touched during his life. Miller even learned some things about him since they'd only worked this one case together. He wished he had connected a little earlier, but Miller makes it a practice not to get too close to too many people. Branson and Callie are the closest people in his life, though he technically has a brother, he has not established a close relationship with him. He leaves the church after promising his parents and his God, that the murderers of this young man will be caught.

HEADQUARTERS IS BUSY Monday morning when Jonathan gets a call.

"Detective Miller here," he answers.

"Detective Miller, this is North Oaks Medical. We were told to inform you when Mr. Woodstock was able to talk. He's awake and somewhat alert. This might not be a bad time for you to come if you can."

"Thanks for the call." Miller made the promise, and he intends to keep it. He moves everything out of his way and drives to the hospital. As ordered, there is an officer still at the door. The blue curtain around the bed is drawn, and the voices coming from the other side are low. Miller taps on the door and announces his presence.

"Just a moment, Detective. I'm almost finished here," a female voice responds. Miller hears the curtain begin to move, scraping the metal hooks against the metal rod above their heads. The open curtain reveals a young nurse removing a bundle of soiled bandages and Clayton wrapped in fresh white linen. "He's all yours, Detective."

"Do you know how much longer he will be here?"

"I will have to check with the Dr., but I will let you know."

"Great. Thanks."

Miller sticks his head out the door. "No one is to come in here, is that clear?"

"Yes, sir."

He closes the door and walks over to Clayton. The bruises on his face have begun to change colors, the awful purple and green make him look a bit alien.

"Woodstock? Woodstock! Open your eyes and look at me! Who hired you to kill Officer Atkins and his girlfriend?"

"I ain't kill nobody," he mumbles.

"You didn't? You didn't go to Lac des Allemands and kill a couple in their cabin?"

"I told you I ain't kill nobody."

Miller pulls two pictures from his briefcase. The lifeless faces of the couple lying on the floor of the cabin fill the pages. Woodstock turns his head when he sees them.

"Don't act like you're sensitive to this! This is your handiwork! You shot them in cold blood, and when I find the weapon and match the bullets, it will be two more nails in your coffin. You're going down for two counts of murder one that brings the death penalty."

"I ain't kill nobody! I just drove the car!" he yells.

"Who did you drive up there?"

"I can't tell you that," he answers. "They'll kill me."

"Hmmm, electric chair or bad guys, or I could just let you go and let the families of the victims have you? Seems like all of your choices are ugly ones. And either way, you die." Miller turns to leave.

"Wait! What do I get if I tell you?"

"Maybe a few extra hours on this planet, because frankly, I'm ready to shoot you myself."

"That's not enough. I'm going to need to leave town."

"You tell me what I need to know, and I might find enough money in my pocket to buy you a bus ticket."

Clayton lays his head back and closes his eyes.

Jonathan tries to give him to the count of ten, but by five his patience has run thin.

"Clayton! Who hired you?"

"Waterman!" He finally screams out. "He got so mad at that Officer Atkins guy after they searched his house. Waterman said he was rude, arrogant, and disrespectful; the officer threatened to shoot his champion dogs. I swear the old man was the color of a hot chili pepper when he was talkin'."

"He had them killed because Atkins was rude? But Atkins wasn't alone, he was with Branson when they searched the house."

"Yeah, but Branson wasn't rude."

"What about the girl, why did you shoot the girl?"

"I didn't shoot her! But I think she was just payback for aiming his weapon at Waterman's Dobies."

Miller was at his boiling point. "Who shot Atkins and his girlfriend? Who else was there?"

~~**~~

The shooter stuffs the baggy clothes and boots into a duffle bag while running through possible hiding places in their head. The bag is tossed along with the dismantled rifle into the back of the long black limo where they can be dispensed of later. The completion of the task yielded a nice reward, but knowing the task will please another will likely bring a bigger reward. In the corner of the trunk lies the hideous doll representing the last loose end.

Miller is seething. Waiting for Clayton to finish a damn sentence is making him feel homicidal, which is bad for a homicide detective. He holds his hands behind his back to restrain them from choking the rest of the life out of this man. "Clayton!"

"Yeah, well, I was paid to attach the tracker and drive the car. But I didn't shoot them."

"Who did; who shot Officer Atkins?"

"Waterman."

"Maurice? I don't believe…"

"Not Maurice, Safira. She was supposed to shoot the guy. I don't know which one shot the girl."

"Safira Waterman used a Remington rifle? That's what you want me to believe?"

"I'm not lying! She shot them and then went inside. I just saw a couple of flashes, like a camera, then she came out. So you still gonna help me get out of town, right? I helped you; now you gotta help me."

"You didn't tell me who the second shooter was. You helped them kill two innocent kids! For what?" Miller fumes. "I'm gonna help someone all right. I'm gonna help them smack you with the book, the whole book, from the hospital room to your jail cell! Someone will come to take your statement!" Miller walks out.

"But I told you who shot them!" Clayton screams after him. "If you don't help me, Waterman will have me killed!"

"Shut up in there," the officer yells from the hall. "Maybe next time you'll choose your employer more carefully."

Another nurse comes in with medication for Clayton. She pours the water and hands him a small cup with several pills. While he swallows, she injects a syringe filled with a clear liquid into his IV line. Clayton leans his head back against the pillow then jerks forward with such a force he almost knocks his nurse over. Fluid erupts from his mouth, and his eyes are completely rolled back into their sockets. The young nurse hits a button on the side of his bed.

"CODE…CODE…I don't know what this is, room 256! STAT!"

The man is flailing around in his bed as a team of nurses and a doctor arrives. Even the officer at the door rushes in to assist. They try to restrain him, but he begins to scream. The agony in his voice is almost pitiful, and the officer calls Miller. The commotion in the background is loud.

"What the hell is going on?" Miller asks.

"It's Clayton, sir. He is having some kind of attack. They can't restrain him."

Miller can hear him through the phone and turns the car around to head back to North Oaks. He makes a mad dash across the parking lot and up the stairs.

When he enters the room again, Clayton is sitting on the bed, quiet, still, and staring blankly. Suddenly his head turns quickly to the left, and everyone in the room knew the sound. The nurse screamed as Clayton fell backward onto the bed. The Doctor felt for the pulse, checked his eyes, and looking up at the people in the room announces, "He's dead!"

"What just happened?" Miller asks.

"I don't know… He snapped his *own* neck. I've never seen anything like that before."

The nurse is in the corner of the room shaking. Miller turns to her. "He was fine just forty minutes ago."

"I came in to give him his medication. He put the pills in his mouth and as soon as he swallowed the water he went crazy. He vomited like a volcanic eruption and then he started flailing around and screaming like a mad man. I called everyone in, and he went ballistic! Is he *really* dead?"

"Yeah, says another nurse. He's dead; weirdest damn thing I ever did see." They clear the room and call for the coroner. He calmly examines the body and looks at the nurse sitting across the room.

"This man has a broken neck! Who could do that right here in the hospital?"

"He did," she responds.

19

THE SCENE IN the hospital room troubled Miller for the entire drive back to headquarters. What would make a man spontaneously snap his neck? It was a scene from the Exorcist. Exorcist! Dark Arts! Voodoo! That's it. Daeva said she sensed another spirit working. Maybe it was working on him, but who would want him dead. The shooter, Safira? Or someone trying to protect her? I need someplace private, my kingdom for a bat cave! Oh well, home it is. Jonathan goes home knowing Callie won't be there. He should be uninterrupted for a while. Jagger greets him at the door, and they go to the back of the house. Jagger explores the yard while Miller makes himself comfortable. The glasses are eased from his pocket with hesitation. Confrontation with another person like Daeva Keket makes him nervous. He places them slowly onto his face and lets the images appear.

It's dark, and Miller stands over two individuals dressed in fatigues, combat boots, and caps, belly down in the grass with a clear view of the cabin windows. The lights inside are dim, and the glow of the fireplace is visible. Miller can see Renee approaching from a back room. The figures patiently wait for her to enter the space of an open window and one calmly pulls the trigger. But Miller hears no sound. The second shot is made in the blink of an eye. Atkins makes a move towards Renee. The second open window provides the next vantage point for the shooters. Two more shots, no noise. In the darkness, he can't tell if both rifles fired. Miller gets a closer look at the rifles. Oh!

Miller is standing in front of an empty black limo. No driver, no passenger. He steps to one side and sees the trunk is raised; a gloved hand disappears from the top. Moving toward the rear of the vehicle, Miller can see Safira making space for the plastic bag and after dismantling the stand and scope she places the weapon inside, but he is surprised to see the little figure in the corner of the trunk dressed in a doll-sized hospital gown, a casted arm, and a small patch of hair. The nasty little thing looks like it's been through a war zone and

> *the head is turned backward. She closes the trunk and Safira turns to go inside. Her driver is standing in the doorway observing, but when he catches her eye, he turns to go back inside. Safira quickens her pace to catch him.*

Thankful that the second dark spirit did not make his or her appearance, Miller knows he has to get to the limo before everything is disposed of. Safira can't get away with killing Officer Atkins and Renee or Clayton. Even if he was one of the "bad guys", he didn't deserve to be killed that way. Miller pictures the young nurse in the corner. Poor thing is going to be traumatized for a while.

"Branson, we need a search warrant for Safira Waterman's limo. Get a rush on it and meet me there. Tell them we have to search it before it is cleaned out."

"What are we looking for?"

"Evidence from the Atkins shooting. Hurry, I'm on my way over there now."

Miller suddenly realizes he only noticed one rifle in the car. Who is the other shooter? Where is the other rifle? Clayton didn't mention the second person. Maybe it was him. Maybe he's protecting whoever hired him. Miller arrives at the home of Safira Waterman, doing a visual search of the grounds; he wants to make sure the limo is still there.

Branson arrives fifteen minutes later, warrant in hand; Miller is at the door and motions for Branson to go to the back of the house.

"Hello again, Ms. Waterman."

"Detective. What can I do for you?"

"I have the warrant to search your car."

"Why do you need to search my car, Detective?"

"We still have an ongoing homicide case involving Officer Atkins and his girlfriend. Ms. Waterman, where is your limousine?"

"Well, I'm not sure, my driver is usually in charge of that car. I just ride in it."

"Ms. Waterman, where is your driver?"

"I don't know, if I don't need him to drive me somewhere, he is free to go his way."

"And how do you reach him if you need to go somewhere?"

Miller's cell phone buzzes. "Detective, I have something in the garage you need to see."

"Ms. Waterman, show me to the garage, please."

She sigh's a heavy sigh, "Well if you insist."

"I do."

The two walk towards the back of the house and out of the door leading to the garage. Branson is standing there with the driver preparing to clean up after his employer. The look on Safira's face told him almost everything he needed to know.

"Branson, help finish wrapping up our Christmas gift and take it and him to headquarters. I'll follow you in with this one," he says, nodding at Safira.

He leaves the garage with Safira in tow, and once inside he flings her into a chair. "Why did you kill Atkins?"

Safira is silent. Her eyes fixed on Miller. "I know why you killed Clayton Woodstock, he knew too much. You couldn't risk a sworn confession about him being your driver that night. Clayton knew you shot the couple in their cabin. But why? Why did you shoot them?"

"I had to! Okay, I had to. He kept telling me about everything he's done for me. Now I had to show him how grateful I was. I remember what happens to disloyal people. I was there that night he and Elizabeth fought about my mom and me. She wanted him to get rid of me when I was very little. She never liked me and called me the child of his tramp. I heard the names he called her, the threats, but she tried to stand her ground. When she told him she would go to the police about the blue diamonds, Maurice went ballistic. He told her he had had enough of her, but he told me not to worry, he would never let *her* hurt me. Her, he said, not *him*. He never said he wouldn't hurt me. But he doesn't know, I saw what he did to my mom. So when he told me what I had to do, I did it; I knew he was testing my loyalty."

"You're talking about Maurice, aren't you? What did he do to your mom?" asks Miller.

"I can't tell you. If he finds out I know, or that I told someone else, he will kill me."

"He needs to go away for the murder of Elizabeth too, but I'm going to have trouble proving that one. Help me help you to get him for your mom." She hesitates then looks at Miller with the eyes of a scared child.

"I was only six. He didn't know I was there. My mom had a headache and laid down in her room, but she said if I was quiet I could play with my dolls on the floor in her closet. She let me play there a lot. But that day, my dad came in while she was sleeping. I almost came out to surprise him, but he looked angry. I watched him take a pillow and cover my mom's face. She kicked a lot and tried to get him off, but mom wasn't strong enough. She stopped kicking. She got very still. Daddy took the pillow and put it back on the bed and left. I remember sitting on the floor for what felt like hours. Crying. I could hear him calling my name, but I was too afraid to answer him. I didn't want him to know I was still in the room. When things got quiet, I came out of the closet. I stopped to look at my mom and kissed her face. Then I went back to my room. When the ambulance and police came, they tried to talk to me, but I wouldn't say anything. I didn't talk to anyone for a long time. After that, daddy brought me to the United States."

"Keep going, you're on a roll. Who is the other shooter with you at the cabin?"

"Clayton Woodstock."

"That's convenient since he's dead. And before he could confess to anyone else, you used the doll to kill him? Who did you get it from?"

"Yes, and I'm not going to tell you."

"Why not."

"Because she's scarier than Maurice, she can kill you without being in the same country," she says, with a look that worried Miller a little.

"You let me worry about that. I've got my own personal scary. What's her name?"

Safira turns away. "I don't know her name; she just goes by the name Bone Lady."

"Get up. Let's go."

He delivers Safira to the holding area of headquarters and fills out his paperwork for the last couple of days. Waterman, Woodstock, Atkins, the drama makes his head spin. He's ready to go home.

Callie should be there by the time he gets home. Miller spots the little yellow sports car in the yard; the light on the porch and the one in his heart are back on. He jumps from his car and runs up the front stairs. He hears the music upstairs, pats Jagger on the head, and makes a beeline for the bathroom. Rose scented bath oil; he stops long enough to breathe it in. "You're home!" he says, kicking off his shoes and unknotting his tie. Jonathan falls into the tub laughing.

Callie shakes her head, laughing. "I'm home; I've missed you, Jonathan."

"I've missed you too," he says, kissing her lips then leaning his head against her breast.

"You didn't tell me about Officer Atkins. I'm so sorry," she says, with soft strokes on his head.

"I didn't want my work in between us again. I don't want anything in between us, ever. Oh my, God, I'm so glad you're home!"

THE MORNING SUN brings Miller out of his best sleep in weeks. He opens his eyes to see the most beautiful woman next to him. He smiles as he uses the tip of a finger to move one of her wayward curls off of her face. Callie smiles in her awareness of her soon-to-be husband, and that makes him smile even more. He then strokes the bare shoulders and follows around and down her back. He notices her body rise to his touch. He kisses her in a way that makes her moan, and they bring in the new day wrapped in the love that brought them together.

Miller hates to leave her after being away from her for so long, but his clash with Maurice Waterman won't wait. He showers and dresses in a baby blue shirt and gray slacks, takes one more look at his fiancé, rakes his fingers through his curly cut, and leaves for work.

"Branson, Miller here, I'm headed over to talk to Maurice Waterman. Meet me there with a backup team."

"Watch out for the dogs, Branson warns."

"Dogs?"

"Yeah, he's got four massive Dobermans."

"Those would be the ones Atkins threatened to shoot?"

"Yeah, but how'd you know?"

"Clayton told me before he died."

Miller arrives at the wrought iron gate and is greeted by the beasts. He uses the intercom system to call the house. "Hello, this is Detective Jonathan Miller from Hammond Police. I need to speak with Mr. Waterman."

"May I tell him the reason for your visit?"

"It's about his daughter, Safira." The system got quiet, and the dogs turn towards the house and run. Moments later the gate swings open. Miller drives through and walks up to the front door. The same elderly man greets him and shows him to Waterman's office. "I have some other officers coming, please let them in when they arrive."

"Hello Detective, please have a seat." He points to a chair. What is this about Safira?"

"She's been arrested for the murder of Officer Atkins."

"There must be some…"

"Don't bother, she's already admitted to it and the rifle and clothes she used were found in her limousine. The question I have is why? Did she have a reason to kill them, or did you?"

"Well, I didn't like the man, he was rude and smug. He disrespected me in my home. He threatened to shoot my Championship Dobermans. In my circle, that's not acceptable behavior. But I had nothing to do with his death."

"In my circle, you don't kill people for being rude, or there would be a lot more dead people in Hammond. Did you teach Safira how to shoot?"

"Yes, she learned to shoot as a child. She's very good, too. We would go hunting together in the northern hills of Louisiana."

Miller hears the rest of the team coming in the door. "All I need now is to find the second rifle."

Maurice gets quiet.

Miller knows without a confession from him or the truck driver, Anderson, he will never get him for Elizabeth's death. *I wonder if I can spook him.* "It's only a matter of time before you are held responsible for the deaths of Elizabeth Waterman and Carlita Santos, you know." Waterman looks up, and the expression is one of surprise. "Yes, I know. I also know Elizabeth's ashes are scattered in the back yard, so I have you on insurance fraud as well." Maurice tries to maintain a calm front, but the small beads of sweat on his brow give him away.

"Detective, I don't know what you're talking about," he says, moving towards his bar. "My wife was killed in a car crash, and she's buried in Parklawn. Would you like to see the police report? I still have a copy of it."

"If I have her exhumed, am I going to find her in a casket?" Miller looks him in the eyes. "If I go through the paperwork and court orders to dig her up, and she's not in there, I'm going to smack so many charges on your arrest sheet, you will never see another day outside of a prison again. I also have a warrant out for the arrest of Anderson. So when I find him, he's gonna spill his guts to save his neck and I'm gonna add conspiracy to commit murder and murder for hire charges."

Waterman's eyes are clouded over now.

"How do you know about Anderson?" he asks.

"I have my sources," Miller responds.

"So how much do you want to go away, half a million, two million?" he sips at his drink.

Branson sticks his head in the door; two officers are standing behind him.

"Did you just offer me a bribe, Mr. Waterman?" Miller stands up and moves closer.

"I'm offering you a way out of this mess, without the hassles of trying to prove anything, no paperwork. Come on, you make what 30K a year. I can give you enough to retire. Three million and you get Safira out too?"

"So I turn my back on your murderous nature, your diamond smuggling business and you make me a millionaire?"

"Yep, that about sums it up."

"You both heard that offer, right?"

Branson and the officer nod.

"Officer, please introduce yourself and offer Mr. Waterman Hammond's newest fashion accessory. I'll finish this up back at headquarters." Miller says, irritated by Waterman's attitude.

Miller walks out as Branson and an officer handcuff Waterman and escorts him to a squad car while reciting the Miranda spiel.

Miller's phone buzzes in his pocket and he stops long enough to read the ID screen. It's the lab.

"Kevin, you've got something for me?"

"Yes sir, and you may not like it. We are just getting the bullets in the Atkins case. I don't know where they've been. But we've got two sets of bullets. The .223 mm is definitely from the 700 Remington, but we have two 270 caliber that could be from an Ruger Predator. You're looking for two different rifles."

"I knew I had two shooters but didn't know if both fired. I have to get back to Safira. She's got to tell me the truth. Thanks, Kevin."

"Branson, Get back to Maurice Waterman's residence and search for a rifle. He taught her to shoot, so what did he use? I'm going to talk to Safira."

"Got it, on my way."

~~**~~

Miller makes it to the jail and waits in a small room. An officer delivers Safira to him dressed in her new gray jumpsuit. She enters the room and looks at Miller with a new sense of hatred.

"How long do I have to be here?"

"You're kidding me, right? You shoot two people, and you want to know how long you are going to be in jail? When I add in selling the blue diamonds, well, let's say, you shouldn't make any vacation plans."

"I haven't seen my lawyer yet. He'll get me out."

"If your lawyer is your father's lawyer, he's a little busy right now. Your father is a few doors down facing a list of charges. Now if you give me a written statement about your mother, Elizabeth, and anything you know about his deals with the blue diamonds, then you could cut a deal."

"You're trying to get me killed. Maurice won't stand for that."

"I just told you, Maurice is already in custody. He can't do anything else to you."

"You're cute, but you're stupid. Do you think he can't hurt somebody in here? How do you think I met the Bone Lady? He and Elizabeth knew her in Brazil. I've told you; she can get to you from another country. I don't believe for one minute that Elizabeth was his first murder."

Miller looks at her in disbelief. "Do you believe the Bone Lady helped him commit the other murders? Would the Bone Lady know?"

"I don't know, maybe some of them. I heard stories. Some were horrible, some were just bizarre, but a lot of them had the ugly dolls left at the scene."

"Is the doll we found yours or Maurice's?"

"Maurice had that Priestess make it just in case."

"Making it isn't a crime, who used it, Safira? Who is responsible for Clayton Woodstock's death?"

"Maurice, he slammed the doll around and twisted its head. He had fun and laughed. I tell you, the man is unstable."

"You've been working with him a long time, what can you tell me about his diamond business?"

"He's making millions on the blue diamonds. His clients stateside and internationally can't get enough of them. He's found just enough people in the local governments who he can pay to turn a blind eye. He pays people to issue false certificates, and others get them over the borders. Everyone is making a lot of money respectively. But once they get into the hands of people like Maurice, the money is limitless. Have you seen them? They're exquisite!"

"I've seen them, they are beautiful, but they're not worth the lives of children. I would trade them all if it changed the quality of life for the people of that country. I would sell them all if it would educate the children and feed the families. A stone, rock, gem, or whatever you want to call them is not as valuable as human life."

"You're naïve if you believe anyone thinks like that. These diamonds are worth more than any other diamond in the world. People are eating them up like Beluga caviar."

"And that's worth killing people?"

"Yes."

"Well then, I guess I will continue to be stupid and naïve, but I'm going to do whatever it takes to make it a little less palatable for all of you." He stands and knocks on the door for the officer outside and watches as he escorts her back to her cell. These people make me tired, but as long as I'm here, I might as well see Maurice. Miller gets the officer to bring Maurice to the room. He arrives with the same look, "What, no one is happy to see me today?"

"I prefer the rat that ate my dinner last night, but since you're here, what do you want?"

"I thought maybe we'd finish the conversation we started at your home."

"I don't have anything to say to you without my lawyer present."

"We've got Preston, Ilysa, Safira, and my father in a cell. Jack Chandler and Clayton Woodstock are both dead and there is still a hunt for Anderson. He's going to turn the key to your cell so that it never opens again. All the players are now accounted for. So do you want to tell your side of the story, or just settle for life in prison?"

"My legal representative should be on his way. Maybe, just maybe, I'll talk to you then."

"If he walks through that door, whatever leniency I might have been willing to give you, and there wasn't much, is out the window. I have you for two, no four homicides, trafficking, and selling of illegal blue diamonds, involvement in a kidnapping and attempted murder of a police officer. After your attorney heard the charges against you, he may have decided to hand you over to a public defender. Either way, at your age, you're likely to take your last breath in a prison cell. So let's start with, why did you kill your wives?"

"One was an adulteress, and when I caught her she threatened to take Safira away from me, the other was an annoyance and threatened to turn me in to the police if I didn't stop my billion-dollar business and get rid of my daughter. I had Safira very late in my life, and she's precious to me."

"Just like Anthony Atkins and Renee Vacherie were precious to their parents? Why did you make Safira shoot them?"

"That officer came to my home and threatened my champion dogs! Rude, arrogant, disrespectful, unprofessional! No one treats Maurice Waterman like that. No one!"

"The last time I checked, rudeness nor arrogance are a crime punishable by death. But shooting a twenty-four-year-old to make her death an example to someone is. I can almost guarantee that where you're going no one will give a rat's butt who you are or how much money you have. That attitude of yours will make you somebody's favorite punching bag." Miller pounds on the door and the officer arrives to remove Maurice.

MILLER'S PHONE BUZZES in his pocket as he leaves the holding area

Gonna be one of those days. "Miller here," he answers.

"You won't believe what I just found."

"Please tell me it's the second rifle?"

"I searched Maurice's home and found nothing."

Branson, you told me you found something!"

"You didn't let me finish. I am feeling the butler's eyes on me everywhere I move, and he's getting antsy. I decided to expand my search to his quarters and tucked way back on the top shelf was the rifle. Miller, the rifle is his."

"That old man can't be my second shooter. Bring him in for questioning. I have a stop to make." Miller goes to the area where prisoners are processed. He flashes his shield and ID. "I need to see the personal belongings that came in with Safira Waterman."

The officer in the cage leaves and returns with a small box. "Sign here first."

Miller first looks at the log-in inventory sheet and then opens the box. There is a sealed envelope, plus the clothing she came in with. Miller dumps the content of the envelope and finds the one thing that will put Safira away for life. He takes a picture and secures the bag with fresh tape and initials the tape. Miller leaves to go back to his office.

Branson loads the old man into his squad car and tosses the Ruger Predator rifle into the trunk. The lab will determine if it's the same weapon. Branson drops the Butler in the holding area and takes the rifle to the lab.

"Detective, special deliveries have been made. The Butler is in holding whenever you get there, and Kevin has the rifle."

"Great, good work Branson. I will see the Butler in a moment." He lingers in his office, then decides to call Callie.

"Hello," her voice, soft and comforting comes over the wires.

"Hi there," he says.

"Hi there."

"I'm having a weird day and just needed to hear what normal, sane, and calm sounded like again." She is back to the unruffled, tranquil woman he has come to love. Even the planning of a wedding didn't send her over the edge like other women.

"Don't let the craziness of Hammond get to you. They won't care if you end up in a psych ward," she laughs. Even the sound of her laughter eases his tension.

"I knew that calling you would help. Thanks."

"You can always call me. If you need me to move mountains, I will."

They both laugh. "See you later."

"Absolutely."

Miller is emotionally empowered to finish his day and heads for the holding area. His phone buzzes in his pocket.

"Miller here."

"Detective Miller, this is unit 728. We were patrolling the area near the shipyards, and we think we found the waste management guy you were looking for."

"Anderson?" asks Miller. "That's great!"

"Well, yes and no."

"What are you telling me?"

"Well we found him, but he's kinda in bad shape. We're waiting for a wagon to show now. He's gonna have to go to North Oaks Medical."

"But he's alive, right?"

"Yes sir, he's alive. Just beaten up pretty bad."

"Can he speak?"

"He's babbling incoherently," says the EMT.

"Okay, keep me informed." Jonathan wonders who is responsible for this one. Everyone connected with this case is locked down. Except for The Bone Lady, but would she just randomly hurt someone, or was she instructed by Maurice.

He continues to the holding area and settles into a room awaiting the Waterman's butler. The elderly man arrives looking rather tired and upset. Miller assumes it's his first night in a jail cell.

"Have a seat Mr. Menendez. Is this right, you are sixty years old?"

"Yes, that's right." The slight South American accent came through in his nervousness.

"How long have you worked for Mr. Waterman?"

"My wife and I have worked for the Waterman family since Safira was a baby. My wife helped Ms. Carlita when the baby was born and stayed with Mr. Waterman after Ms. Carlita died."

"The tiny brunette at Safira Waterman's home is your wife?"

"Yes, that's my beautiful Rosa," he says with a smile.

"Mr. Menendez, do you ever go hunting?" The old face turns away, silent.

"Mr. Menendez? Sir, do you hunt? The Ruger Predator rifle we found in your living quarters, is yours, correct?"

"The rifle is mine, but I haven't used it in a very long time."

"Sir, my crime lab has the rifle now, and they are testing for evidence that it was used in a recent homicide."

"I haven't used it. I'm not as steady as I used to be, my sight is not so good."

"Does anyone else have access to your weapon?"

"I don't know. I don't think so, but there isn't anybody else except Mr. Waterman."

Miller goes to his office and calls Kevin in the lab. "Detective Miller here, anything on the rifle that was brought in today?"

"Yes, sir, I just finished running ballistics. The bullets and markings match the second bullet that was pulled from Renee Vacherie. I also have a partial print on the casings in the rifle. It is a match to Maurice Waterman."

"I can't believe he was mad enough to do his own dirty work. He made Safira kill Atkins, but he killed Renee himself. I don't have enough ink in my pen to write all of the charges he is facing. Thanks, Kevin."

I don't even need Anderson to finish him off. But I'm going to get him for participating in Waterman's scheme.

JONATHAN HAS BEEN putting off this phone call for weeks. His feelings towards Ilysa are strained and trying to do her another favor is difficult at best. Remember this is for Callie, not Ilysa. He makes a call to Alan Smith in the DA's office.

"Hello, Alan, Miller here, how are the criminals treating you these days?"

"Probably a little better than they treat you," he laughs. "How are you and that pretty lady of yours?"

"We are doing great, and she's the reason for this phone call. She and I are getting married this May. As you know, her mom is still being held for her part in the illegal diamonds deal, but Callie wants her mom at her wedding."

"Man, I may have to cash in on every favor owed to me. Let me make some calls and see what I can do. And Congratulations!

With that out of the way, Jonathan has two more people to tell but wonders if Branson will accept being his best man. He nervously calls him into the office.

"Ted, we've been working together for about almost four years now, and you are like a kid brother. You also know things between Victor and me are a little stressed, and I'm not talking to my dad. Ted, what I'm trying to say is, Callie and I have set a date, and I'm asking if you will be my best man at our wedding."

"I would be honored, Detective. If you change your mind and ask Victor, I will understand. Kid brother, huh?" They laugh.

"I appreciate your outlook, but I've known and trusted you longer."

"Thanks, Detective. That means a lot to me. But I'm there for you no matter who you choose. Just tell me we're not wearing pink!"

"Believe me, I've had that conversation with Callie. We are not wearing pink."

"Thanks," says Branson. "But you are going to at least ask him, right? I mean, he is kinda the only family you have here in Hammond."

"I know. I'm still so pissed off at that guy. You don't treat family like that. Preston, poor stupid Preston, kidnapped his daughter and didn't know it. Callie could have killed him."

"Wait, what? You're telling me Matt Preston is Callie's father and not Paul? When did she find out?"

"She hasn't. Ilysa never told either of them. Paul suspected, but never mentioned it to Callie."

"How did you find out?"

"Ilysa. I knew something was up. If you were being sought by the police, would you stay in town? No, but not only did she stay, but she also made a couple of visits to Preston in the hospital. I walked in on them holding hands at his bedside. And he and Cora have the same birthmark."

"Well, if she doesn't know now before the wedding would probably not be a good time to mention it."

"I told Ilysa she would have to tell them, but I don't want Callie to be mad at me because I knew and didn't say anything to her."

"I think Callie is level-headed enough that even if she gets mad, it's not kinda mad that will last."

"I hope you're right. So I guess that means Paul is escorting her down the aisle?"

"Unless the cat scratches its way out of the bag, yeah, I guess so. I mean she does still believe that Paul St. Claire is her father."

"I just want to be a fly on the wall when she finds out. Branson stands to go back to his desk, but at the door, he turns back to Miller with a huge grin.

"What's the grin for?" Miller asks.

"I just thought of something. I get to plan the Bachelor party!!" he laughs and spins on his heels.

"Boy, don't make me shoot you before my wedding," Miller laughs a warning. "And while you're at it, help me think of some great places to take her for a honeymoon. I think we both could use some time away. Oh Branson, one more thing. Take a look at this." Miller pulls up the picture he took with his phone at the processing office. "Does this look familiar?"

"Damn! That's it."

"I was hoping you were going to say that. She took Renee's engagement ring from the scene and was wearing it when she was processed. It locks Safira's cell door for a very long time."

~⁓**⁓~

Friends and family of Jonathan and Callie gather on the front lawn of Blythewood Plantations and others finalize the preparations inside. The sun is partially behind fluffy clouds easing the Louisiana heat on the guests. The sound of a nearby church bell rings out the eleventh hour, and the minister appears from the front door. A few minutes pass and Jonathan, Ted, and Victor appear from the front door and stand in line to the left of the official; then Jagger makes his debut as part of the family holding his basket in his mouth. An officer, in his dress blues, escorts Ilysa down the stairs and to a seat; since Jonathan is in the police department, they agreed it wouldn't look so awkward. A limo arrives at the far end of the long brick path and Callie's co-worker, dressed in Lily yellow, is the first to get out. She is followed by Cora dressed in Hydrangea blue.

The limo leaves and takes its place beside the church. Once Cora is in place, a horse-drawn carriage arrives at the path and Paul St. Claire, dressed in a shimmery silver tuxedo, arises from the back seat. He steps down and offers a hand as he assists Callie down. He takes just a moment to spread her bridal train out behind her, and the Bridal March begins. Everyone stands as the father and bride make their way down the covered path. The gem-studded bodice curves around her breasts making a small heart shape. The satin waistband hugs her tiny frame allowing the bottom to flow around her. The bazillion ringlets are pulled high on her head and encircled with a jeweled crown. A delicate pearl teardrop falls inches below her collar and two more dangle from her ears. As she gets closer to the steps Jonathan relives his first breathless encounter with the most beautiful woman he's ever seen. Ted pokes him in the back to release the hold, and he begins to breathe again. Miller looks at him with *thank you* in his eyes and runs his fingers through his curly hair, only he's forgotten that he cut them off for today. He laughs at himself, and Ted just smiles. But when Miller turns back to Callie, he is blown away again by her beauty, and it shows on his face. *Wow! She's mine*!

Callie sees her mom at the front of the seating area and tears fill her eyes. She stops to kiss her on the cheek as she passes. Jonathan said he would try, and he did. She notices the officer seated beside her and puts two and two together. Callie smiles at her two men waiting for her and mouths the words *thank you* to her soon-to-be husband. Jonathan is tall and handsome in his tux and Jagger is looking fresh in his bow tie, sitting tall next to him.

The minister begins, "Please join hands. Detective Jonathan Miller, you have something you wish to say to Callie?"

"Callie St. Claire, you have taken my breath away from the very first moment I laid eyes on you and every day since. I knew I would have to find a way to make you a part of my life. I've waited a long time for someone with beauty, brains, and boldness of spirit. You are everything I could ever hope to find, and I promise my love and fidelity, my honesty and trustworthiness; I promise to provide and protect, and I promise you all that I have and all that I am for the rest of my life."

"Callie St. Claire, you have something you wish to say to Jonathan?"

"Jonathan Miller, you came into my life at a time when I thought everything was about to fall apart. But piece by piece you have connected them and you have become the glue that holds it all together. I have come to know that you are true to your word; that you have had this same expression on your face since we first met. Now I know what it means. I am the luckiest girl in the world to have found someone like you to love someone like me. You are everything a girl could ever dream of, and before all of our friends and family, I promise my love and fidelity, my honesty and trustworthiness. I promise to care and build a home for us and I promise you all that I have and all that I am for the rest of my life."

"Do you have the rings?"

Ted gives Jagger a little nudge. Jagger carries a special delivery in his basket and the couple exchange rings.

"By the authority given me by the church and state, before God and everyone here, I now pronounce you husband and wife."

~~**~~

The ceremony flows without incident, and the two are in seventh heaven. They celebrate and dance into the evening. Jonathan has married the love of his dreams.

Daeva Keket watches from the shadows, and she is not the only one. The Bone Lady also watches, but she doesn't watch with blessings for the newlyweds. Daeva feels the presence of another and knows that the two will have a very long relationship with…the spirits of darkness.

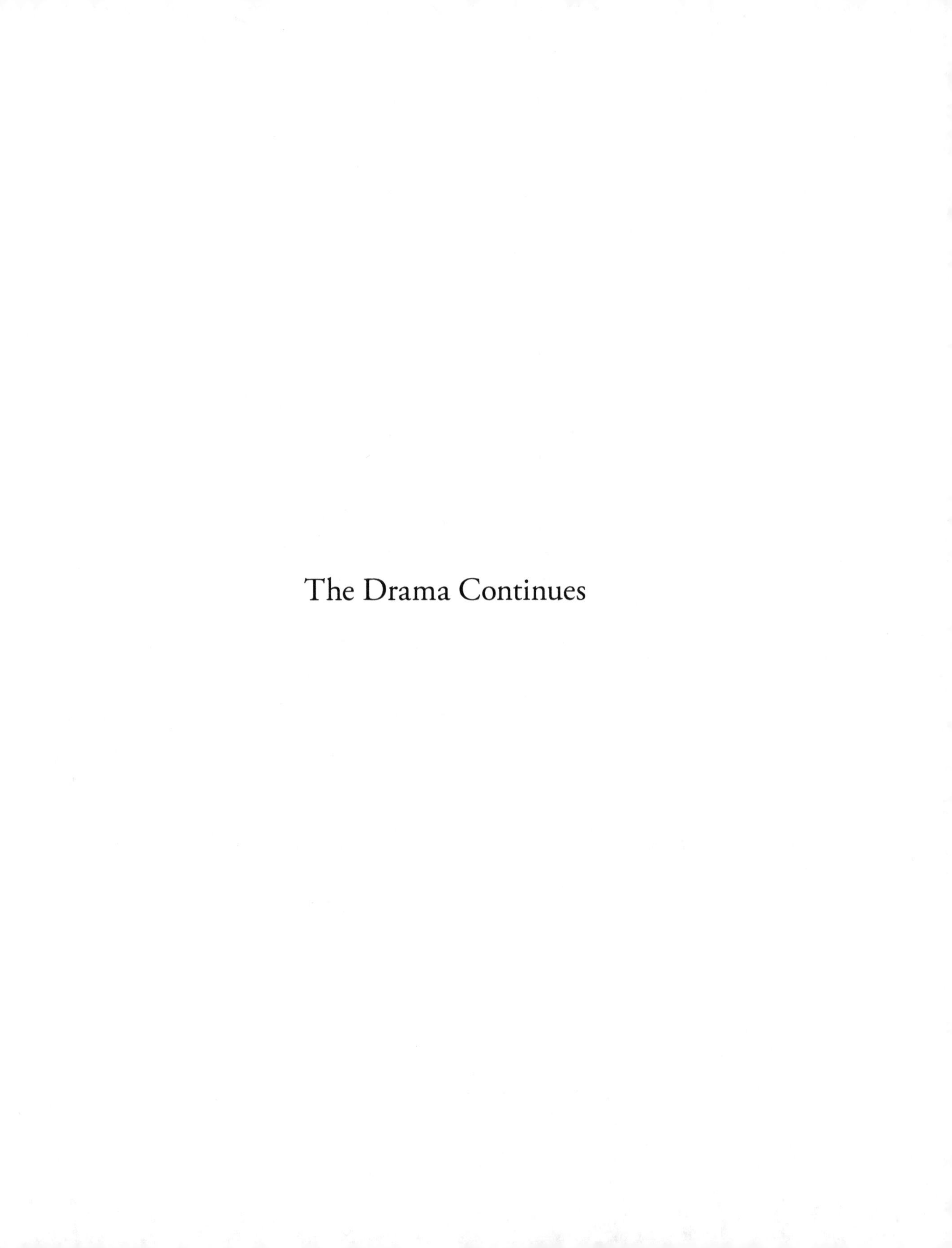

The Drama Continues